Mountain Blood

Patricia Knutson

This book is a work of fiction.
All names, places, characters, and circumstances
are imaginary, and any resemblance to
actual events, or to persons living or dead,
is entirely coincidental.

ISBN - 13:978-1478374008
ISBN – 1478374004

Jacket illustration and typography by Linda Knutson Designs
Photography by Nan Hatzes

I dedicate this book to my colleagues and friends Tondalaya and Glenn,
and to all the students who taught me so much.

*Loneliness and the feeling of being unwanted
is the most terrible poverty.*

Mother Teresa

Chapter 1

The sleepy-eyed attendant at the last Exxon station where she had filled up her parched white Mazda had told her she should watch out for deer, and even bear (he had pronounced it to rhyme with *far)*, on the so-called highway that curled upward into the dusky purple haze of the Blue Ridge Mountains toward the college and the town. But he hadn't told her about the steady, smoking string of heavily-stacked logging trucks that would be barreling down from West Virginia in the opposite lane. It was just another of the inconsequential circumstances that had made the whole trip move slower and take longer. Three days from metropolitan New York to that far northern point in rural Virginia was what she had planned, allowing for a random stop here and there, maybe a gingham-and-lace bed and breakfast or a rustic log cabin on a dark crystal lake, all of which she hoped would help with the healing process along the way.

The interval of the rhythmic, sluggish pull up the steep incline gave Chris an opportunity to gather her thoughts and look at herself in a way that she hadn't been able to do for a very long time, ever since the accident . . . and Jack's death. She gazed at the densely timbered hills and the awakening valleys of spring-green mountains, dappled softly by the brush of the April sun, and she felt an unfamiliar twinge of hope, a shiver of raw possibility. She was closer to thirty-nine than forty. Maybe there was still time.

She knew she had a strong inner core, that staunch, gut-level determination that had sifted down to her from resolute New England ancestors who had plowed the coastal waters before they battered and slashed their way west through these same granite canyons. After all, she had practically raised herself, since there had been no one but her and the alcohol-soaked roommate she called "mother." She had grown up alone, trailing behind other pubescent girls after school as they giggled and ambled their way home to small, crowded apartments in Brooklyn, never joining them when they stopped at the drugstore to get a Coke or sample the lipstick at the cosmetic counter. Chris couldn't remember ever being a part of the pack, or a member of a clique.

She thought about how this agonizing *alone and lonely* business was relatively recent in her life. It had come after Jack. He had been the first person to name her "beautiful," to tell her she was "a knockout," the first one to really love her. Jack would slowly comb his fingers through her long auburn hair and tell her that she had a sexy blonde's blue eyes, but a sensuous redhead's erotic appeal. She remembered how he would touch her and sway with her to the sometimes gentle, sometimes unrestrained lovemaking that would follow. And then there was the baby.

Chris slowed the car and coasted onto a rutted gravel road that led to a scenic overlook, a misty, grassy shelf on the mountainside, a place almost cathedral-like, where one could take stock of earthly things amidst the formidable magnificence of the rugged, seemingly endless expanse that surrounded her. For reasons she couldn't understand, it was just then that she knew her decision had been the right one, this decision to come here to these mountains, to this unfamiliar place and school and people. She realized that she had thought about Jack and the baby, and when she had wiped fatigue and weariness from her eyes, there were no tears. Seventeen tortured, fearful months, that time of raging nightmares and disconnected thoughts. Such a short time ago, so long ago.   For the first time in what seemed like forever, Chris thought she might get a reprieve. She just might have another chance.

Chapter 2

"Y'all ever been to Clayton Forge before?" The round, gray-haired woman behind the motel's streaked Formica-topped counter didn't look up when she asked the question.

"No, it's my first time." Chris tried to sound conversational. "I'm going to teach English at Jackson Clayton College - I'll be living here."

With this new piece of information, the deeply wrinkled, bronzed face snapped into viewing position, and she squinted as she surveyed Chris from head to toe. Her thin, wiry hair was frizzed in a short, tight perm, and Chris couldn't help comparing her to one of the dried apple dolls she had seen when she stopped at a general store halfway up the mountain. A plus size, mostly white tee shirt stuck out in front of her, supported by her large sagging breasts, and its faded sunflower pattern followed the shape of her protruding belly.

"Ya' don't say. Didn't know the college was hiring. Usually hear it 'round here . . . when they're hiring. Most of the teachers live 'round here . . . come from round here." She went back to swiping Chris's credit card on her antiquated machine.

"Yes, well I heard about the job from a friend of mine who teaches over at the state university, over at Tech, and here I am." She thought she sounded like a complete ass, but she couldn't shut up. "I have an appointment with James

4

Cantrell and some of the professors in the morning. I'm sure I'll hear all about the college then."

"I doubt that," seemed to come from the shifting sunflower on the other side of the counter.

Chris felt like a babbling schoolgirl reporting to the adult in charge. For God's sake, she was a college professor from New York, and this was some old broad in a rundown motel in Appalachia. What in the hell was going on? She took a deep breath.

"Where ya' from?" The apple-head bobbled up again.

"New York. Well, I most recently lived in New Jersey, but I'm from New York."

"Y'all from New York, and you wantin' to come live in Clayton Forge?" The ruts on her forehead deepened as she lowered her head slightly and looked appraisingly at Chris. A row of nicotine-stained little teeth barely showed themselves through a slit of a grin.

"Yes, I'm really looking forward to it. I've rented one of the new townhouses over on River Road. Do you know where that is?" Chris was trying hard to relax with her inquisitor.

"Guess I do . . . born here," she stated flatly. "Y'all don't know nothin' 'bout that school, that college, do ya'?" The drawling voice didn't stop for an answer. "Things been happenin' over there. Don't think we even heard the half of it. Some woman disappeared about six months ago. Just up and gone one night, so they say. Think they said she was a teacher." Steely blue eyes now looked directly at Chris. "Most folks round here thinks it wasn't no case of her goin', if ya know what I mean. Most of 'em thinks she's dead." She made a throaty sound that could have been a laugh. "Guess they had to get a teacher from somewheres else. Won't be no one round here goin' over there. Alls I know is I sure wouldn't want to work over there, particularly if I was from down yonder," she said and nodded toward the direction Chris had recently traveled.

5

"Here's your card – room's third one on your right." She flipped the credit card toward Chris and pointed out the smudged window. "Don't allow no smokin' in the room, no loud music, and no TV after eleven. Anything else?" Class was dismissed.

"No, thank you. Oh, by the way, I'll be staying until my furniture arrives, which should be early next week, maybe Monday."

"If you made the reservation, we got it." She had already disappeared behind the brown curtain that separated the desk area from the next room.

The metal storm door banged behind her as Chris left her welcoming committee. "Down yonder," she muttered as she opened the bright turquoise green door to room number three at the only lodging in town, The Starlight Motel.

Chapter 3

Chris's four undergraduate years at City College had been more liberation than education, a life-saving gift from Anne Parsons, the high school guidance counselor who said she was "bright" and helped her find the right campus and the financial means to access it. A grant and some student loans, supplemented by four years of wiping up tomato sauce at Giambelli's Pizzeria, and a yearly holiday job at Macy's, paid for her degree and teaching certificate, which she considered nothing short of a miracle. Looking back, Chris couldn't understand what had motivated her, what had driven her to be a good student, an A student, because she and Mother Winnie never talked about it. They talked about *Jeopardy* and *The Price Is Right*, or *As the World Turns*, but they never discussed Chris's world outside their three-room apartment. Winnie stuck a few crayoned papers on the refrigerator door, back in the early elementary years when Chris asked her to, but she never asked about school or events or friends. There weren't many of the latter two, and life for the mother and child existed almost exclusively behind their closed door. It was as if both of them expected Chris to manage life on the outside.

Long before her sixteenth birthday, Chris realized that "poor Winnie Alford," as the random social workers and priests and derelict neighbors who drifted in and out of their lives referred to her, had only one agenda, and that was drinking. The welfare checks and the silent, undefined "sickness" that they supported were not part of mother and child's conversations, either. It was just understood that they were always there. Winnie's unnamed, mysterious illness appeared at unfortunate times, like Chris's graduation from high school, and again for college commencement, marking Chris as the only member of the class who attended ceremonies alone. She had walked across the stage with her class at Brooklyn High School, and she had come home after to find Winnie passed out on the old brown living room couch, an empty vodka bottle nestled securely beside her. Graduation was never mentioned again. Chris ignored the college ceremony and picked up her diploma in the registrar's office.

She couldn't remember a time in her life when her mother didn't have a clinking glass in her hand, or on her nightstand, or beside her in the kitchen as she peeled the foil from the gelatinous TV dinner or stirred the overcooked Kraft macaroni and cheese that most often made up their main meal. Winnie Alford was a devout, committed worshipper at the altar of the bottled gods who anesthetized and sympathized as they controlled and defined her shallow, lackluster life.

"Mama, I'm twelve now. I think I'm old enough to know about my father, about who he was, or is," Chris offered in a quiet, reasonable tone on a crisp December Saturday. She didn't want to stir up the hornet's nest that last summer's approach had provoked, but all the bells and brightness of the holidays made her wonder about this man who might have made them into a family.

"It hurts me to talk about it, Chrissy . . . I told you that before."

And then the routine would begin again. Winnie would reach up and hold her forehead, like she was shading her dull, gray eyes from a bright and blinding light. She would sit silently for a moment or two and then begin to shake her head slowly from side to side, as if she just couldn't believe what was happening, just couldn't come to grips with what Chris was doing to her.

"It upsets my whole body when you mention it, when you talk like that, and I'll wind up in bed for a week if I'm not careful. I know you wouldn't want to make me have a setback with my sickness that plagues me all the time, would you." Then another headshake, a deep sigh, and soft, soft words: "My own daughter, the one I have given all I have to make happy."

"Mama, I'm sorry. I don't want to make you sick. I just thought . . . "

She always interrupted, as if she had not heard Chris's apology. "Maybe I'll be stronger in a few months or so, if the Lord lets me live that long. Then I'll tell you what I know. Now be a good girl and get me a glass and some ice. I need to take some medicine to calm me down."

The periodic attempts to bring up the identity of her unknown father were always rebuffed by an un-well Winnie and regretted by a guilt-ridden child. There were no photographs, and there were no stories, only deep, dark silence for the first twenty years of Chris's life.

During her third year of college, Chris came home one frigid February afternoon to change into her uniform before going to Giambelli's, and the apartment was empty. Winnie never went anywhere: Chris did the grocery shopping, bought her mother's booze, carried the dirty clothes down to the washing machine in the basement, and brought the dry ones back up to the third floor. She opened the door into the dim hallway as people will do when they don't know where to look, as if the missing one might be concealed in some hidden nook in the small, barren space.

"Hello, Chris." Vera Whetstein had obviously been

waiting for her. "Your Ma took sick, Honey, and me and Harry had to call the ambulance.   I'm so sorry, Chris." The old lady folded her boney arms across her flat chest, pulling the bright multicolored flowered housecoat closer around her.

"Yeah, me and Vera heard her fall, or heard somethin' fall, and we right quick called William to come up with a key. We just knew somethin' wasn't right in there." Harry's big eyes seemed to cover his thin, pale hawk-like face, as he shuffled closer to his wife.

"Where is she? Where did they take her?" Chris felt the panic rising in her throat.

"Queens Hospital. Here's a card the EMT gave me . . . said you could call this number and find out about your Ma. We're real sorry, Chris. Can we do anythin' for you?" Harry awkwardly patted her arm. "You call us if we can. We'll be right here."

Chris had not made it to the hospital before Winnie died of a massive cerebral hemorrhage in the emergency room. She didn't cry at the hospital, and she didn't cry when she got home. A sense of nothingness seemed to enshroud her as she moved robotically through the next week that ended when she sprinkled her mother's ashes on the grave of the only family member she had ever heard of, Winnie's brother Arthur who had died before Chris was born.

Chapter 4

The pink-hued neon sign in the window of The Starlight Motel flickered eerily through the heavy, wet morning fog that blanketed the seemingly lifeless mountain town. Chris's plans for a walk before whatever breakfast she could find had been thwarted by the drifting banks of gray, rolling mist that spread across everything in sight. Instead she flipped on *Good Morning America*, more for the companionship than the information, as she began to piece together her schedule for the day.

The meeting with the powers that be at Jackson Clayton College was scheduled for ten o'clock. As she looked through her journal and notes, Chris remembered the January interview in New York with the college president, Dr. Cantrell, and the dean of the Department of Arts and Sciences, Dr. Shelton. Both men had been in New York for a conference of small colleges, which coincidentally occurred just at the time when she was to be interviewed for their advertised faculty position. She recalled the correspondence, emails, and telephone calls that had preceded their meeting, and she momentarily relived the gut-wrenching anxiety and apprehension that had ping-ponged back and forth with the certainty that this was a change and a move she needed to make. God, how she had wanted that job. Both men had impressed her, not only with their obvious professionalism, but with their openness and expressions of support for the kind of education she believed in, the kind where instructors were self-directed and independent and encouraged to be innovative. Dr. James Cantrell was close to sixty, but there was nothing old about him. His heavy gray hair, angular face, and striking blue eyes put his six foot stature in the movie-star-handsome category. He had a deep, clear voice, modulated by a soft Virginia accent, and he seemed to laugh easily. Richard Shelton was in his late forties, soft spoken, with no hint of the old South in his conversation. He, too, was tall and had the same chiseled good looks that his boss possessed, just a younger version. Gray was obvious at his temples, but the rest of his hair was dark brown, almost black, a striking contrast to his deep blue-green eyes. Chris had been immediately aware that she was attracted to him, in an uncomfortable sort of sensuous way. She hadn't felt anything like that for a man for a long time, not since Jack, and it somehow made her feel guilty and strangely angry that he had affected her that way. When they shook hands after the interview, Chris was conscious of his strong hands and slim fingers that seemed to linger on hers for a little longer than one would expect in a routine business handshake.

Shelton had written the letter offering her the job, and he would be the one she reported to, her boss. After she accepted formally and returned the signed contract, he had called her and told her how happy he was that she would be coming to the college and Clayton Forge. There was a certain sense of contagious excitement in his call, and Chris found herself responding in a familiar and personal way that she later felt may have been inappropriate. She thought she had giggled too much and had been too girly. It was not the image she wanted. He offered assistance in any area that would help her with the move; he told her he looked forward to working with her, getting to know her better, introducing her to Clayton Forge.

After the call, she went over and over the conversation, recalling every word and each inflection.

Now, sitting here in this run-down motel, Chris didn't feel any of the arousal or eagerness of that first meeting and the subsequent phone call. "You're a romantic idiot," she mumbled, as she sorted through the four thin white bath towels that made up the supplied linens in the dimly lit rose pink bathroom.

After all the frustration and grief she had experienced over the past year and a half, it was no wonder she would look for some good luck, some positive sign that had to be waiting just around the corner. She believed in luck, good and bad, and God only knows she was ready for some of the former.

"But, Chris Baby," she said aloud, as if talking to the smiling Katie Couric on the eighteen inch screen in front of her, "grab some reality. So far there are no signs of the good stuff. Cousin Daisy Mae out there is most likely the norm around here, not the handsome Mr. Shelton and the glib Dr. Cantrell."

The little showerhead spurted sharp streams of water that stung her skin as she tried to keep the cheap plastic shower curtain from wrapping around her legs, and water poured onto the bathroom floor, a result of the slow drain and the shallow lip on the much-painted metal shower stall. By the time Chris had struggled through the water episode, mopped up the floor, and tried to apply make-up with the help of the one light bulb over the bathroom sink, she was convinced that this was the motel from hell and that she was in the process of making one colossal mistake.

She frowned as she surveyed herself in the only mirror in the room, a frame hanging over the cheap veneer dresser. In her navy blue linen sheath dress and matching sweater, she thought she looked more like she was going shopping at Saks Fifth Avenue than going to a get-acquainted meeting at a remote mountain college in the heart of Appalachia. She threw

13

aside a pair of navy pumps and grabbed a pair of low-heeled sandals to take the New York edge off of her sophisticated outfit.

"This is who I am, Boys. This is the best I can do," she mumbled.

When she opened the door of Room #3, the swirl of the dense cloudy mist rolled against her face and into her nostrils, seeming to engulf her, ratcheting up her already high level of doubt and a major case of the jitters. Nothing seemed right.

"How am I supposed to find my way to anywhere in this mess," she muttered, as she slowly worked her way to the only car parked in front of The Starlight Motel.

Chapter 5

Chris had poured over the southwestern side of the Virginia map a half-dozen times during the past month, each time tracing her finger over the snaking red line of County Road 230 that ran straight north out of Clayton Forge and seemed to end at the little asterisk marked Jackson Clayton College. She had all but memorized the territory between the town and the college, and she knew there was nothing between the two but state forest, in what should have been a twenty-minute drive. She gripped the leather-covered steering wheel as she guided the compact sedan around the sharp turns and up the steep grade, aware of her constant braking and accelerating pattern that marked her as a novice at this kind of driving. The yellow line in the center of the shiny wet asphalt was her only guide through the dense, smoke-like blur that held the peaks and valleys in its sodden grasp. Chris was encouraged by a hint of amber light, reflecting the sun's relentless assault that would soon open up the vistas that must lie just beyond the winding roadway.

Suddenly, as if an enormous gray curtain had been lifted, a sunlit sign and multi-storied, steepled buildings appeared ahead on her right – "Jackson Clayton College" – and beneath the name, "Knowledge Is Opportunity." Chris stopped her car just inside the ornamental black wrought iron gates that marked the entrance to the college grounds and got out to appraise the tangible part of the choice she had made. Her first impression of the multiple clusters of light-colored graystone buildings, classically trimmed in black and white colonial architectural design, sent her spirits soaring. It looked like a beautifully familiar New England college campus set amidst the splendor of a glorious Appalachian spring. Neatly manicured bright green swaths of lawn bordered the maze of sidewalks and paths that meandered through the campus and connected the entrances, brick and stone terraces, and outdoor living areas surrounded by well-tended gardens. Masses of bright yellow daffodils, apricot and white jonquils, and early red, purple, and white tulips were naturalized on the rolling banks and small hills that naturally made up the mountain landscape. Carefully planned circles and squares of the same flowers were scattered across the view as far as Chris could see, interspersed with blooming red bud trees and large banks of lavender and white rhododendron and pale pink mountain laurel.

"This is gorgeous," Chris said aloud as she turned toward the sound of the river that bordered the east side of the campus. She couldn't see the flowing water, but she had seen its serpentine gray line on the map, and she knew she heard the rush of the New River.

Chris noticed that thick black forests of mountain pine and glistening hardwood trees covered the slowly rising foothills that ran upward to mountain peaks, surrounding the pristine campus on all sides, appearing to grow to the very edge of its well-defined boundaries. The only apparent road in or out was the one where she stood.

"Welcome," a familiar voice shouted from behind her.

As Chris turned around, she saw Richard Shelton jogging down the road she had just covered.

"Hello," she called back. "I hope you didn't get lost in

16

that muck I just drove through. I must have passed you, and I didn't even see you."

He stopped a few feet away from her and wiped his face on a towel he had pulled from the belt of his red jersey jogging shorts. His sleeveless white tee shirt clung to his sweat-soaked body and outlined muscles that had been defined by what was obviously a regular routine.

"No, I'm used to it. I'd shake your hand, but . . ." he looked down and gestured at his wet body. "You got a real mountain welcome with this pea soup that's been hanging over us. It's worse than usual. How was your trip?"

"Good," she laughed. "Well, this morning was a challenge, but here I am. What a beautiful campus."

"Yes, it's pretty impressive, and spring is my favorite time in the mountains. Every season has its own character, but this one is hard to beat, particularly up here. Dr. Cantrell is a real nut about flowers and landscaping, so we're never without the best of the season." He laughed as he turned around and looked at the scenic view that spread out before them. "He spends a hell of a lot of college money on growing things other than students."

"This is a little paradise surrounded by wilderness. I've traveled some and lived up and down the northeast coast, but I don't believe I've ever seen anything that surprised me quite as much as this campus did . . . the beauty . . . and the contrast." Chris was aware of how happy she was to see him.

"Contrast it is," he said. "I hope you're as enamored in six months as you are now. Well, I guess I'd better get on with my clean up, or you and James will be meeting without me. Glad you're here, Chris," he said as he moved off toward one of the buildings to their right.

"See you in awhile," she called after him.

Bryant Hall was the first building everyone passed after entering the Jackson Clayton campus. A well-placed sign labeled it "Administration" and listed the departments and offices inside the high double doors across from the parking lot where Chris had parked. The president's office was first on the list – Room 111.

Vivid oil paintings, soft, vibrant watercolors, and sharp photographs of what appeared to be local scenery and parts of the college campus lined the wide terra cotta tiled hall that led past several closed doors on the way to the president's suite. As Chris turned to enter Dr. James Cantrell's office, a uniformed state trooper with his hat in his hand met her in the doorway on his way out.

"Excuse me, Ma'am," he said, as he stepped back into the room to make way for Chris to pass. He hesitated and then turned toward a middle-aged woman sitting at the desk that faced the door. "As I said, I don't think you need to worry, Mattie. I think that guy's just getting his laughs in a way that isn't funny, but y'all let me know. For sure let me know if anything else like this comes up."

"I will, Buster. I know you're right, but it's just real unsettling. I work with these kids all the time, and I never seem to be able to pick out the normal ones from the bad apples. They all look okay to me. But he's been one I've felt funny about for a long time. You know what I mean? Anyway, thanks for coming by. Seems like you've been here too much of late. We sure appreciate it."

"I'm sorry to keep you waiting," she said as she acknowledged Chris, who had stood quietly on the edge of the conversation between Mattie and Buster. "May I help you?" The woman smiled warmly as Chris moved further into the well-decorated, light mocha colored room.

"Yes, thank you. I'm Chris Alford. I'm here to see Dr. Cantrell at ten."

"Oh, Miss Alford, I'm so happy to meet you. I'm

Mattie Marcum. Dr. Cantrell and Dr. Shelton have said such such nice things about you. We're really glad you're here."

As she spoke, she smiled warmly and moved around her desk to shake Chris's hand. Mattie was a slim, attractive blonde in her fifties, who had the same soft southern accent that Chris had heard when she first met James Cantrell. She wore just enough makeup to highlight her deep blue eyes and high cheekbones, and her fashionably tailored dark blue dress was very much like the one Chris was wearing.

"It's quiet right now," she laughed, "with the students on spring break and most of the faculty hiding out somewhere. You picked a good time to get to know the college. By the end of this week things will be crazy again, and final exams will add to that a few weeks from now. Make yourself comfortable," she said as she pointed to the sofa and the chairs on either side of it. "I'll tell Dr. Cantrell you're here."

Chris looked around admiringly at the burgundy, beige, and gold stripes and patterns that adorned the upholstery. The overstuffed sofa and armchairs were intermingled with elegant mahogany tables and side chairs that appeared to be antique. A large painting of Monticello hung over the long colonial settee that anchored a seating group at the end of the rectangular room, and portraits of two distinguished men in formal attire from the early 1800's dominated a side wall. Chris studied the two austere-looking, bearded individuals whose painted eyes seemed to stare boldly back at her from within their ornate gold frames, and she knew their names must be Jackson and Clayton.

"I'm glad I don't have to work for you two," she mused.

"Chris," James Cantrell greeted her from the doorway to his office. "How wonderful to see you again. We've all been so excited about your arrival." He crossed the room and took Chris's hand.

I'm so glad to be here." She smiled and shook his hand. "What a beautiful campus you have. I can't wait to see the rest

19

of it. The spring gardens are magnificent."

"Glad you like it. Please come in – Richard's on his way. I hear you two ran into each other a little while ago. He's out there on those trails every morning and most evenings except in the worst of weather. It has to be a real ice storm before it keeps him in. He's amazing, particularly for a Florida boy. Tougher than some of us mountain folks," he laughed

"He's from Florida? For some reason he struck me as being a New Englander." Chris thought about what she had said, but decided it was an acceptable comment since they were having a light conversation.

"No, South Florida, if I remember right. Chris, if you'll excuse me just a moment, I need to fill Mattie in on a couple of things before you and Richard and I get started. Please, sit down . I'll just be a minute."

He stepped out of the room and began a quiet conversation with Mattie on the other side of the open door. Chris looked around at the floor to ceiling mahogany bookcases on two walls, lined with books interspersed with mementos and photographs. James Cantrell's desk was massive, the kind one might expect to find in the office of a senior partner in a very large New York or Washington D.C. law firm. Stacks of papers, magazines, and a few portfolios covered most of its surface, with framed snapshots and black onyx desk accessories crowding the edges. Sofas, footstools and easy chairs in leather and tasteful paisleys and stripes in the reception room colors were expertly scattered around the large room, giving the impression of casual, relaxed living. Chris suspected that there was more formality and discipline here than a firsthand impression revealed.

From where she sat, Chris couldn't help but hear the sing-song cadence of the voices resonating from Mattie's office, spoken in low, confidential tones.

" . . . important to keep it quiet, Mattie . . . after Allison . . enough problems . . . try . . . no danger . . ." The conversation rose and fell, revealing only fragmented statements.

" . . . can't sleep . . . and now this . . . should have told them . . . where is he . . . Tabor . . . dangerous." Chris heard fear in Mattie's broken speech.

" . . . later . . . Richard." His voice rose as he said, "Hey, Rich. Chris is in my office."

As the two men walked into the room together, James leading the way, Chris observed them as they interacted and spoke to each other. Were they friends? Was there respect between them? What persona did they assume that separated and identified each of them in this academic community, in their positions of leadership and integrity, doctoral education and responsibility? A nagging sense of anxiety that she felt in the middle of her chest told Chris that she knew very little about either of them, or of this place.

Chapter 6

"You have one of the prime offices in Cantrell Hall," Richard said. "I think you'll like it."

He walked with his hands casually stuffed in his pockets as he and Chris strolled along a gently inclining path. The walkway led toward another picture-perfect, colonial-style building set atop a small hill surrounded by towering shade trees. Each brick in the herringbone-patterned path was outlined with closely cropped, creeping thyme that obviously had been planted long ago to create the effect Chris now observed.

"It's one of three faculty offices in Cantrell that has its own private little patio. All of the Arts and Sciences people have views of mountains, but not everyone can come and go through a private entrance and a landscaped garden."

"How did I get so lucky? There must be a hitch," Chris laughed.

"Actually, James suggested that you take that office; he thought it might be a little welcoming bonus. I agreed it was a good idea."

"Cantrell Hall? Sounds like Dr. Cantrell's family has been around here for a long time." Chris looked admiringly at the soft patina of the large, antique brass hinges that secured the eight-foot, black double doors in front of them.

"That's an understatement. He's related to both Jackson and Clayton. I've heard it said that he'd have to go out of the county if he wanted to get married, or he'd break the law." Richard smiled as he opened the door and waited for Chris to enter.

A large terracotta tiled rotunda encompassed the center of the stately building's contemporary interior. Its generous cut-out squares, rectangles, and raised boxes of dark, loamy earth were thickly planted with lush tropical plants, lacy ferns, and specimen trees. The dome of the three-story arboretum was formed of small glass panels artistically woven together with narrow bands of burnished gray lead. Fifteen foot walls of glass and redwood made up the back and sides of the building. Delicate orchids in bright shades of citrus green and soft mauves and pinks climbed the mottled, rough trunks of trees that lifted their exotic branches toward the beckoning light above. Splashes of yellow and white calla lilies mingled with the vibrant purples and oranges of birds of paradise, and bright red amaryllis stood staunchly above the crawling emerald-hued vines.

Chris had never seen anything like this, other than the botanical garden she had visited with her fifth grade class in New York.

"Richard, I feel like I'm dreaming," she said quietly. "What a place." She turned slowly, looking at the sunlight streaming down on the garden that surrounded them.

"It's something, alright," he said as his gaze followed hers. "Thanks to an army of gardeners who work directly for James, I've never seen it look any different than it does right now. It's still a mystery to me. I've been here six years, and I still don't know much about how it came to be, or how much it must cost. I told you, Cantrell's a master at horticulture, and he's obsessed with the landscaping. He spends a lot of his time here, right in this area. I believe he could tell you exactly what's

23

planted where – every tree and flower. Last year there was some kind of breakdown in the mechanical side of all this . . . electric or water system . . . I'm not sure. He was a wreck over it. His garden crew had to dig up some of the beds . . . pulled up a lot of the tile floor, I guess. James was here overseeing the whole thing. They had to close the building for a couple of months . . . moved some classrooms and some offices. It was a total mess. I didn't see any of it. Most of us didn't. We were given a day to pack up and move out what we could.   No one was allowed back in the building until all the work was completed."

"It's extraordinary, Richard," Chris said. "Such a surprise from what I expected. The students must love going to class in such a beautiful setting."

"Yes, I think some of them do appreciate it. Others don't. Many of them won't notice at all. You'll find we have an unusual mix of students here, Chris – mostly local mountain people, whose attitudes tend to be different. We'll talk about all of that when you get settled."

Chris sensed a change in Richard's voice as he moved away from the topic.

"Come on, I'll show you around. Maybe we can find some live bodies I can introduce you to."

She followed Richard through the garden toward one of the four halls that led like spokes to and from the central rotunda.

"Hey, Glen," Richard called out. When did you get back from Paradise?" Richard guided Chris toward a slight man with a salt and pepper mustache and a thin fringe of gray hair around his well-tanned, bald head. Wrinkled khaki pants and a blue oxford cloth shirt with rolled-up sleeves seemed too big for his thin body and looked as if he had worn them far longer than for a regular workday. Pewter wire-rimmed glasses perched precariously on his small pointed nose and completed the stereotype of the typical college professor.

"I came in on the 5:00 a.m. Red Eye Express early this morning. The flight was nothing compared to the drive from Charleston in all the fog. Had a great time in St. Thomas – hard to come back."

"Glen, I'd like you to meet Chris Alford. She's just joined the English department. Chris, this is Glen Cooper, one of the world's best math teachers."

"Hi, Chris. Welcome to our Garden of Eden," he smiled as he shook her hand. "I don't know about 'world's best math,' but I can tell you there are a lot of creative writing topics around here for you English teacher types. Unfortunately, though, I haven't figured out how to work any of this ambience into algebra or calculus."

"Good to meet you, Glen. I'm speechless. What a workplace."

"Pretty amazing, but it's nice to get a perk now and then, isn't it," he laughed. "There aren't many. Our boss here runs a pretty tight ship," he chided. "Where's your office? Maybe we'll be neighbors."

"I haven't shown Chris her office yet. We were just on our way." Richard hesitated. "She's going to be in 305," he said.

"Allison's office?" Glen's words were just above a whisper and sounded as if they were riding on a deep breath after someone had belly-punched him.

"Yes. Well, her old office." Richard stared at Glen.

Neither of the men spoke for a few seconds, and Chris sensed a shift in their demeanors.

Glen turned to Chris and said, "Well, I guess I'd better get back to the mess on my desk . . . lots to do . . . glad to have you here . . . let me know if I can help with anything." He looked at Richard as if he wanted to say something more, but instead gave a little half salute and muttered, "See you around," as he walked off down the hall behind him.

Richard gestured to their right and said, "We're going to the back of the building. Your office is down there."

"Who is Allison?" Chris asked.

"Someone who used to work here." Chris felt Richard's touch on her arm as he pointed to the two shallow lighted steps leading from the walkway into the interior of the resplendent botanical display. "Your hallway is the only one with steps into the garden. It's always good to have a landmark in case the lights go out," he said with a smile. "Power failures in these mountain areas aren't uncommon."

As they turned down the hall, Chris was drawn to a life-sized, wooden figure of a mountain woman standing in front of the floor to ceiling window at the end of the long corridor. The details of the woman's face were intricately and sharply carved, the eyes, the mouth, and the lines of her forehead revealing the weariness and pain of her impoverished life. She wore a simple, long dress that folded and wrinkled over her hunched shoulders, and in the curve of her arms she carried a baby. The soft drape and smooth surfaces of the expertly chiseled and polished wood beckoned to be touched.

"How beautiful," Chris said softly. "She looks so alive – so real."

"The artist is an old man who lives in Baileytown, about an hour's drive over on Heather Mountain. I suspect he knew her at one time in his life. Maybe she was his mother or possibly his wife. You can still see way too much of that same look on some of the faces in and around Clayton Forge."

"Is there a committee in charge of acquisitions or gifts? There's so much exquisite art everywhere I look."

"You might say so. The committee consists of one man - James Cantrell."

Once again, Chris was aware of the soft-toned but bold hues of pastoral watercolors, expertly hung on off-white walls between the closed office doors. She was certain there were no reproductions among them. Photographs of majestic blue Appalachian mountains and shadowy valleys represented the changing seasons. These were similar to those she had seen in James Cantrell's office and, similarly, they were tastefully scattered among the vivid colors. Several quilted, hand-stitched wall hangings appeared to be made of old, rough-woven fabrics in earthen colors. They quietly merged the traditional artistry of the mountain people with the contemporary talent that surrounded them. Soft lights set in the white plaster ceiling were expertly focused and highlighted the gallery walls leading toward the end of the hall and room 305.

Chapter 7

A dark, menacing storm of anguish and guilt raged through Chris's dreams on a regular basis, accompanied by a wide-screen, Technicolor replay of the horror. Dr. Tharringer and the other two psychiatrists who had preceded him had tried to lead her to believe she wasn't to blame. However, she had examined it and analyzed it hundreds of times, and, clearly, she was responsible for everything.

"Chris, things happen in life that aren't anyone's fault," Dr. Tharringer had said. "We can never know what will result from the simplest routine decisions or inconsequential actions. We can make assumptions, and history and logic can play a big part, but we can never really know for sure what the ultimate outcome will be."

But Chris knew cause and effect were blatantly obvious in her case. When she considered again and again how she might not be guilty, the answer always came up the same, in spite of Dr. Tharringer's platitudes. She had insisted that they make the trip to Pennsylvania. Jack had been against it from the beginning, cataloging all the negatives each time they talked about it. Something inside of her wouldn't give up, and she had badgered and pecked at him relentlessly until that evening in September when she had won her ill-starred victory.

"It's a bad idea, Chris. This isn't a good time for the show . . . lots of reasons. You know that."

"Jack, you're not being rational. How often are you going to have the opportunity to have such a prestigious showing of your work? You've been waiting a long time for this. Don't miss it for some contrived inconvenience."

"I'll have the chance again. My paintings are in a gallery in Washington, and Alan Sloan himself told me after the big May show that he feels I have some important New Yorkers who are buying. Spring is a hot time in the Philadelphia market, Chris. Even Larry wasn't upset when I told him I couldn't do the Philly show on such short notice. You know he's a good agent. He's not going to accept my doing something that will be a bad move. It's money out of his pocket, too."

"But you can do the Philly show. You have all the paintings ready – you're ready – and the Clare Gallery is ready for you. They're offering you a pre-holiday opening at one of the top galleries in an art capitol of this country, and you want to turn it down? That's just plain stupid."

How well she could remember every word. She could see his face, his eyes.

"Chris, you can't fly. Dr. Borassa told you that you have to take it easy these last two months, and you would be just weeks away from your due date in November. Even if I would decide to do this, which I probably won't, you need to stay home, and that seems to be a problem for you, too."

She remembered that she knew he was angry at this point. His face was flushed and his arms were tightly entwined across his chest.

"So we drive. We're talking about a two-hour car trip at the most. For God's sake, Jack, I'm not sick – I feel great. You seem to think I'm an invalid. I'm going to feel just as well then as I do now. Look, I'm seven months pregnant with a healthy baby boy, and he needs to go to Philadelphia in November to share in the glory of his famous father's burgeoning art career."

That had made him laugh. Then they were in each other's arms and both laughing as he held her head against his chest and said, "Okay, Baby, you win. I'll do it. As long as you're sure it'll be okay."

She remembered most of all that she had felt exhilarated by the "win."

* * *

As Chris slid her feet into the pale blue terry cloth slippers that waited to carry her into the reality of another day, she felt exhausted and wrung out from the relentless haunting that had invaded her night once again. Filtered sunlight permeated the closed blinds and cast a soft morning glow on the cozy, butter-colored bedroom that she had almost finished decorating. The thirteen hundred foot townhouse on River Road, advertised in the Clayton Forge weekly newspaper as "close to town" and "new," had turned out to be a remote, five year old green vinyl-sided duplex that needed repainting and much cleaning. However, the views from each of the five main rooms more than made up for the deceptive advertising. The soaring peaks of Bear Mountain rose majestically, as if framed by the white enameled woodwork of her living room windows, and the other ranges, ridges, and escarpments of the Blue Ridge Mountains were breathtakingly visible in their ever changing moods from all living areas of the house.

Chris had spent May and June moving in and adjusting to the isolation of her new River Road home, while attempting to settle in at Jackson Clayton College. She had met numerous other faculty and staff members, but the few weeks left in the semester after she arrived in April had not resulted in even casual relationships. At best, she remembered a few names, and a few remembered hers. Mattie Marcum invited her for a cookout, and she met Mattie's husband Jason, who worked at the local grain and feed store. Glen Cooper brought her a bouquet of flowers as a housewarming gesture before he left for his summer in Maine. The college librarian Laurel Buchanan took her on a get-acquainted tour of Clayton Forge and bought her lunch at the Timber Ridge Cafe, the day before Laurel left for two months of missionary work in Honduras. Everyone was friendly, but no one was familiar.

Richard was mostly absent. He sent Chris a few email memos regarding her fall teaching assignments and college protocol, and he stopped her on campus a couple of times to give her new information, but he didn't call her at home nor did he invite her to dinner. Richard's lack of follow-through on his earlier suggestion that he "wanted to get to know her better" was no mystery, however, when Chris recalled the day that he had shown her around the college and taken her to her new office. She knew why he had put a chasm between them.

Chapter 8

The white paneled door to Room 305 opened with a soft rustle as it skimmed the top of the pebbly beige carpet that covered the floor wall to wall. The spacious room smelled of fresh paint and turpentine, and Chris knew immediately as she looked around at the ivory colored walls and satin patina of the white colonial moldings that the entire space was new, as new as if it had been recently built and decorated for the first time. Chris had noticed that the door to Room 305 was the only one on the corridor that was solid wood. The neighboring offices had three small panes of glass set into the top panels, making the interiors visually accessible to any who chose to look in. She smiled as she recalled her former colleagues at NYU and their elaborate attempts to protect their windowed sanctuaries from ever-present students. Some simply put posters on the inside of the glass-topped doors. Others covered the opening with collages made up of photographs of trips or families and posted them facing in or out, depending on the professor's degree of need to maintain the fine professional line that separated teacher and student.

Chris posted student poetry on her window. If a student wanted to write poetry, she wanted the world to read it, and she had provided a forum. It had been amazing how this "poetry wall" became a positive and popular part of her English classes, encouraging the most reluctant and unlikely poets to contribute. It even motivated a few other faculty members to incorporate student work in their efforts to protect their privacy from the very ones who contributed to the screen as well as the need for it. Chris was never entirely comfortable with the whole concept of avoiding the students. She was aware that there were times when reluctant professors sat behind their veiled, locked doors and ignored the tentative knocks from the other side. She had done it, too, when she needed to cry, when the agony of her searing loss overwhelmed her, but even then she felt deceitful and guilty. Somehow the poetry wall made her feel better.

Now there was no need for camouflage. Neither was there the forum of the poetry wall. She had planned to establish an even bigger display here at Jackson Clayton College, maybe even include some creative writing, but the faculty handbook clearly stated that nothing was to be posted on the outsides of doors nor on the walls of corridors. Anything that was to be exhibited in the few locked glass cases that hung on walls in some campus buildings required administrative preapproval, which further reading translated specifically as Dr. James Cantrell's agreement.

When Chris first reviewed the rules in the manual, including those for any kind of displays on college property, she felt a rush of anger, a sense of stifling control.

"Heavy handed," she had told herself. "Interference with academic freedom," she judged.

But after she cooled off, she rationalized. This was a new job, a good job she needed for lots of reasons. She hadn't even talked to a student at this point in the summer, let alone conducted a class or persuaded anyone to write anything. Considering the quality and quantity of the professional art lining the halls, Chris told herself this was an understandable rule.

As Chris walked into the room, she faced a dramatic floor to ceiling wall of glass ahead of her. A six foot width of plaster on the far right side of the expanse held a wood trimmed glass door that opened onto a beautifully landscaped, walled courtyard. Chris gazed at the diminutive private garden, a fifteen foot square which lushly showcased a dwarf flowering pink dogwood, a heavily blossomed, miniature Japanese cherry tree, and numerous brightly blooming magenta and pale pink azaleas. Multicolored tulips and pale yellow-white jonquils zigzagged in colorful rows and bunches around the trees and bushes, pushing their multiplying leaves and fragile heads ever closer to the patio bricks and cement planter walls. A small, round, honey-colored teak table and two matching wooden chairs sat off-center on the left side of the red brick and cement square that made up the patio. A slatted bench crafted in the same pattern as the other furniture was cemented in place on the right. The six foot wooden wall that surrounded this astounding tiny park had a wide, un-gated opening on its back side and fronted onto a narrow strip of lawn that ran the width of the building. Chris stared at the heavily forested dark mountains that bordered the college grounds. Cantrell Hall was the last building on this far, somewhat remote side of the Jackson Clayton campus, and she could see that no more than fifty yards of feathery, soft spring-green grass vulnerably separated it from the looming, ever-moving Appalachian wilderness.

"Richard, I find it hard to believe that this space, this place, is my office," Chris said, as she stood mesmerized.

"Yes, well, I have to say it is pretty spectacular. Not your routine academic digs, for sure. James was really impressed when he met you in NYC, really wanted you to come on board He had planned to put the new teacher over in Laurel Hall, one of the older buildings close to the college entrance. It's okay, actually nice, but it's nothing like this. After you accepted the job, he told me he wanted to do a little better for you than the other office."

Richard smiled slightly as he continued to look at Chris, and she once again recalled her uncomfortable, sexual attraction to him upon their first meeting.

"I don't know what I did or said," she laughed, "but whatever it was I'm glad I did it. This looks more like a dean's office, or some administrator's place."

"Actually, before my time here, this office belonged to the Dean of Arts and Sciences. As I understand from James, she had been here for ten plus years and was getting close to retirement when she was diagnosed with cancer and couldn't finish the school year. I guess it happened quickly, in the middle of the fall semester. James was in a hurry to find someone, I was in the right place and time in my life, and I got the job. That was when James decided it would be good to reorganize offices. He put all of the deans over in Bryant Hall, and he opened up this office to faculty the following semester."

A grin spread across his angular face after he finished the bit of history. "Now in your case, Chris, we thought this office was necessary. You know, big city college sophisticate comes to Podunk U in the woods. We had to do something to keep you."

She liked the contagious laughter in his voice. "Hardly a sophisticate," she replied with a smile. "But thanks anyway."

"Seriously, we do have above average offices and facilities here, Chris. Across the board, it's the best I've ever had in my twenty years of academia. Anything you want is here for the asking – books, teaching aids, electronic equipment. James Cantrell is not a penny pincher." He hesitated a minute before continuing. "But then this college has to offer more. They have to compensate and offset the isolation and remoteness that can get to a person after awhile. We are way the hell up here, not easy to find or be found."

They were comfortably silent as Chris slowly roamed the office, opening and shutting the drawers of the new mahogany desk and exploring the newly painted shelved closet. She gently swiveled the bright blue upholstered chair, which was oddly feminine. It, too, was unused. How did they know a woman would be hired to occupy it? Had they purchased it just for her?

"Who was the woman who had this office before me, the one you and Glen mentioned?"

She was looking at the width of the bookcases that partially lined one wall when she asked the question.

"Allison Montgomery," he said matter-of-factly. "She taught English here for three years. Come on, let's go take a look at your private garden."

Richard had moved as he talked and unlocked the door in front of them.

"Why did she leave?" Chris asked as she walked toward the door.

"Chris, Allison was a woman with an abundance of problems, and my observation was that she had little common sense. I'm not free to discuss Allison Montgomery. I've already said too much about former employees." He pushed hard and the door opened with the crack of freshly painted wood.

Chris was caught off guard by Richard's unexpected reaction to her question, and his words stung her, but she needed to know. "I didn't ask you to discuss her. I only asked why she left." Chris knew the minute she spoke that she had stepped over the line.

"Look," he said in a tone she had not heard from him before. "I have tried to be polite about this, but I was Allison Montgomery's supervisor, her boss, while she worked here, and that relationship and confidentiality does not disappear with the termination of her employment. I will say it again. I am not free to discuss with you any aspect of Allison Montgomery's life or employment history."

Chris was simultaneously sorry for her seeming indiscretion and alarmed at his angry, chameleon-like response. Richard stood with his back to the patio door he had just opened, his feet slightly parted, his hands on his hips. His somber face was flushed. Somehow, Richard Shelton seemed taller and bigger, physically superior. If he intended to intimidate her, he had succeeded.

"I'm sorry, Richard. Please accept my apologies for being unprofessional. I understand what you're saying, and I truly regret any misunderstanding or problems I've caused." Chris felt that he had stopped just short of directly reminding her that he was also her supervisor and her boss.

Again they were silent, but this time it was different – precarious and uncertain. They stood facing each other, and Chris felt Richard's physical closeness, his command of the space that surrounded them. He dropped his arms to his sides and shifted his weight from leg to leg, looking down at the newly carpeted floor before he spoke.

"Chris, let's set it aside . . . it's okay. Do you want to take a look out here on the patio? I have to get back to my office in a few minutes," he said quietly as he held the door for her.

"Thanks," she said awkwardly. "It really is beautiful. I sincerely appreciate all you and Dr. Cantrell have done for me."

"Glad you like it . . . it's yours now, Chris. Move in and put your stamp on it."

Richard reached into his pocket and pulled out a short silver chain with several keys swinging from it. "Here are two keys to your office and one for the front door of this building. Anything I can do for you, just let me know. Phone works – I'm only an extension number away."

He was gone within ten minutes of the encounter and its

perfunctory aftermath, and they had not exchanged a paragraph of conversation since.

Chapter 9

The rumble of distant thunder echoed from the lower valleys, and the mountain breeze stiffened as it ran through the black green pines and leafing maples that surrounded the carefully disguised shelter. He hoped it would rain and blow, because it always made him feel good, to be here on his mountain, in his hidden sanctuary, when it stormed. The carefully crafted mud and stick walls barely pushed above the ground, and the velvety green moss and multicolored lichen had spread themselves like frosting across the shadowed spaces on his concealed earthen roof. Summer blooming briars and the creeping curl of wild vegetation had quickly covered any vestige of a man-made structure. It always pleased him when the odd climber or ranging hunter came close to his hideout when he was there, because they never saw it. They never sensed another's presence. Maybe eyes sensitive to the mountain landscape might see an odd rising in the ground where he had rounded out air holes, or might notice the flattened places in the damp leaves that he had been unable to brush away, but no one coming here had such a sensibility . . . except him.

He wondered if someday, when he was old and he died,

if someone might discover the elaborate subterranean room he had painstakingly hacked out beneath the rocky mountain earth when he was just a boy. Would anyone guess who had built it, or even know who he was, or what he did here? Or would his mountain world protect him one last time, filling and covering the camouflaged refuge, so it would remain a clever secret, the only place where he had ever really been worthy. Sometimes when the feelings, the raging, urgent hunger and longing ran rampant like a rising heat throughout him, he came here because he knew what he needed to do, and he would lie hour after hour on his belly or sit cross-legged on the damp earth, his aching arms pressing the binoculars to his squinted eyes. In the morning, the early sun would dance off the shiny metal barrel of the rifle propped beside him, and with the progression of the waning day, it would cast the rifle's long, thin shadow across the trampled grass.

His Mawmaw had said, "Y'all are a smart young un', smarter than me and yer Pap," and she had signed him up for school in Clayton Falls. Pap said he was dumb as an ass and should go down to a valley town and work when he was old enough. In the beginning, school had excited him, before the other kids had made him see there was something bad and wrong about him. In first grade he had been proud to be a blue bird, one of those whose group had mastered reading before the robins or the cardinals, and he remembered the teacher had acted like she liked him. He had learned to add and subtract sooner and faster than some of the others in his class, and numbers were fun for him, until he realized no one ever wanted to be his partner in the arithmetic games the teachers planned. The classroom and the lunchroom and the playground became more painful with each new school year he began, not because the work was too hard, but because his focus had necessarily become survival in an unfriendly world of desperate loneliness.

He never had a friend, and no one got to know him. To the other students, he was only what they saw and heard. As the childhood years advanced, he was often the center of attention, the butt of the joke or the object of a bully's torment. Through middle school, he regularly got off the school bus with a bruised and swollen lip or a torn shirt, just because of who he was, and teachers or bus drivers never seemed to notice.

At the beginning of seventh grade, he decided he couldn't stomach the meanness that arrived every school day with the noisy, bright yellow bus. He began getting out of bed in the cold darkness of the mountain morning and trudging through the barely-lit woods and along the empty road to the old brick school in Clayton Falls.   By the time he finished his freshman year, he was heading up the mountain to his special place almost as many days as he was taking up a seat in a classroom. He failed his sophomore year because he hadn't gone to class and he'd ignored most of the work when he was there, and he wanted to drop out of high school.

"Y'all ain't gonna do it, Boy. I ain't lettin' ya do it," Mawmaw had shouted and ranted when he told her. "Don't be a damn fool. Y'all wanna end up like Pap – no place to get a decent job? Mines ain't hiring no more."

She had pushed him and prodded him relentlessly, looking almost sick with the fear and worry he was heaping on her. Because he never wanted to disappoint her, and because he had average ability and intelligence, he had been able to turn his failure into a meager success. He suffered through enough days and weeks and months to get his diploma. He went to his sanctuary and slept on the ground for four nights to escape senior week and the caps and gowns, and Mawmaw didn't try to stop him.

He had been born with everything wrong. No one living, not even Mawmaw, knew who his father was, and his ma had died birthing him, so Mawmaw and Pap ended up with him.

People still talked about Pap's drinking binge that had lasted weeks and weeks, after he found out his daughter Amber Jean was pregnant, and how nothing he threatened or did could make her identify the father of her unborn child. Her wild, hillbilly Pap had waved his loaded rifle over his head Comanche style, as he abused and cursed and threatened over half of the men in Clayton Forge and the surrounding shacks and cabins, accusing teenagers and grandfathers alike of implanting their venomous seed in his virgin daughter's womb, but he never learned the truth. For awhile after Amber Jean was buried in the cold mountain earth, Pap continued his inquisition, accusations clouding most conversations he had with another man. However, as he lost interest in life itself, he let the search for the boy's father slip away, along with every other thing that once had meaning for him.

Although she never went to church, Mawmaw had some religion, and she had named her grandson Tabor. She told him that Mount Tabor was a special place Jesus had gone, and that it was a "high and proud mountain by the Sea of Galilee." He had decided some time ago that God and Mawmaw's Jesus had no interest in his life or the likes of him. Tabor, like his name, was an oddity, "a freak" his classmates had called him. He was big – not just tall or muscled or fat, but of giant proportions overall, particularly when compared to the lanky and often underfed strain of Scotch/Irish folks who populated his small, ingrown part of the world. Thick, coarse, curly black hair hung to his shoulders into puberty, a stark and startling contrast to his pale, colorless white skin. His beard at fourteen years was heavier than Pap's at fifty, and the boy reached six feet five inches and weighed two hundred fifty pounds by the time he was fifteen.

Mawmaw had to go to the Baptist church in Clayton Falls, where they had clothes in the basement for people like them, to find a couple of cheap shirts and a pair of jeans that would fit him. She also chopped at his hair, and later she tried to teach him how to shave around the tender patches of acne-stained skin on his ashen face, but they both soon accepted that an occasional trim with her dull scissors was all that could be expected from either of them. And so he grew.

Tabor's voice had no modulation, and his flat, toneless speech signaled to the hearer that serious problems inside his head were probable. His voice had changed with the seasons one year, to a deep bass, but the flatness never left him. The agony of his appearance betrayed the reality of the lonely soul who lived within, and it became who he was.

Pap came from the coalmine over on Hogback Mountain that had run out ten years ago, so he spent some of his time trying to scratch enough for them to eat and a few dollars from the rocky Appalachian dirt, and more of his time coughing while he drank the rock-gut whiskey that he bought at the state store every Friday night. Ever since Tabor could remember, Mawmaw had worked on the clean-up crew at Jackson Clayton College, often walking the steep mountain paths after dark when she finished late. She proudly told him that she was related to Mr. Clayton way, way back, and she boasted that she and James Cantrell were fourth or fifth cousins. She said the two of them never spoke of it, but she knew he felt the kinship by the way he said hello to her when they happened to meet, when she was cleaning around his office or pushing the dust of the day down the hall with her mop.

When Mawmaw repeated her story to the boy, Pap would look at her with his rheumy, half-drunk eyes and call her a "damn lyin' fool."

"The only way y'all ever had any goddamn relationship "way back" with any highfalutin sons-a-bitches like them," he would drawl, "was that one of yer goddamn ugly relatives might 'a laid on her back and opened her skinny, bowed legs for some big shot over there."

Mawmaw ignored his toothless abuse and pushed on with her one goal in life, which had been to get the boy into the college, and she did it. Because she worked there, and she said because of Mr. James Cantrell, he had been able to go "free," as she called it. But for Tabor, it had been by no means "free."

Only Mawmaw believed she knew him. No one else wanted to. There had been one precious other who had reached out to him, one who had wanted to help him and who had tried to save him. But now she was gone from the college and from his life. The tragedy of her going had driven Tabor further into his desperate, troubled isolation, and he found solace only in the place where he became part of his mountain, and in the binoculars and the gun that gave him a sense of covert power.

Tabor would go to the college again in the fall, for Mawmaw, and because of the pretty girls. He liked the red-haired ones, the ones whose long, silky hair rippled down their creamy backs, and in front, fell on each side of their unblemished faces to rest on ample chests. Their eyes were always bright blue or a sparkling green, and their skin was pale and, he believed, soft as mountain moss. Some of them wore tight, white shirts, and he liked those girls best of all. He looked at them every chance that presented itself, at their big joggling breasts with pointed nipples that outlined the stretched thin cloth that barely covered them. If he could, he would look for the faint little crease between the legs of their skin tight jeans, or he would watch the up and down of their backsides, outlined by straining denim that ran up the crack of their rounded cheeks. Then he would get the feelings, and the heat between his legs would bring an aching, raging need to possess one of them, to have one of them love him. He would let his mind roam and imagine that she would want to come to the mountain with him, that she would want him to do things to her. But it never happened, and he always went to his place alone.

44

The college had made it easy for him to watch. Halfway through his first year as a student, Tabor had taken a pair of expensive field glasses from a biology lab after hours, when Mawmaw had been cleaning the room and he had waited for her. The German-made binoculars had been lying on the teacher's desk, and when Mawmaw went out to get water for the mopping, it had been simple for him to put them under his big hooded sweatshirt that was his winter jacket. The college had also cut down a dozen thick, feathery pine trees on the edge of the campus, thus greatly improving his viewing range. From his lookout, Tabor could now see many of the walkways and also the big brick patio outside the activity center where students gathered to eat or smoke or socialize. He never went to the popular student center when he was at the school, but he came to know it so well from afar.

The tree cutting had also opened up two buildings where faculty members had their offices, and he delighted in his new secret window on their unapproachable, mysterious world.

Before the binoculars, he had dared to look in their office windows or watch, from the cover of shrubbery, the comings and goings of a select group of young women he had singled out. Now he could watch them for long, uninterrupted hours, and scrutinize them more closely, hoping to catch one at an indiscreet, private moment.

Tabor's obsessive devotion to the chosen girls and women he so carefully watched had interfered with the two developmental classes in which he was enrolled for his first year at the college, and he had failed English and squeezed through math. He recognized that it was in his best interest to do better in the new fall semester, because the college provided him an abundance of opportunities to fulfill his fantasies. Without access to the campus, he would lose touch with those he sought. He needed to be close to them, to feel and know their nearness in flesh, before he could watch and before he could successfully plan.

Chapter 10

Chris set the frosted glass vase filled with bright yellow daisies on the bedside table and rearranged the red and green plaid pillows on the white quilted sofa bed one more time. She then stood back to survey the small, pale-green library guest room. The color of the paint she had bought at Kennedy's Hardware in Clayton Forge was "Homestead Green." She liked its effect in the limited space, which she had trimmed with white woodwork. Chris had spent little time decorating the room, using it as a catch-all for things she didn't know what to do with as she unpacked, until she received the call from Rachael Lackner.

She had been happy to hear from her old college friend, but she was also apprehensive about the painful link with earlier days and lost times. They had both been English majors who didn't know anyone when they came to City College as freshmen, and they had easily developed that limited commonality into a comfortable, lasting friendship. Rachael had been Chris's only bridal attendant when she married Jack, at the small "family" wedding where Chris had no family. Later she had held Chris in her arms and cried with her at Jack's and the baby's gravesides. It was Rachael who had urged Chris to change her life and leave her job in New York City, as they talked into the early morning hours of so many marathon telephone calls, and it was Rachael who discovered the teaching position at Jackson Clayton College that provided the impetus for the dramatic change she advocated.

"I want to come and see for myself what kind of luxury you're living and working in over there in Clayton Forge, Chrissy," she had teased when she called and invited herself for the Fourth of July weekend. "I'm so excited to see you," she bubbled. "We have so much to catch up on – we'll have to stay up all night just to get it all in."

"Oh, Rachael, I'm thrilled you're coming. I've heard and read that the town has a big barbecue and fair on the Fourth, with booths of handcrafts and art, and then fireworks at the local high school athletic field. Real local color. I'm not much of a tour guide yet, but there's a lot to show you right here on the campus and close by. Bring your walking shoes or some boots, and we'll do some hiking around the mountains."

"Sounds great," she said. "Chris, you sound good. I'm so glad." Her voice was suddenly serious and caring.

"I'm better, Rachael, a lot better. We'll talk about everything when you get here. The next two weeks will drag waiting for your visit, but it will give me time to get the paint buckets out of the guest room."

"Don't go to any trouble. All I want to do is see you and enjoy having fun together. Sounds like a novel, doesn't it – two New York City broads cut loose among the moonshiners!"

Chris laughed as she once again was caught up in her friend's familiar sense of humor.

"I think you'll be surprised, Rachael. Jackson Clayton is not your typical example of rural academia. It's not what I expected up here. But, I can introduce you to a few classic examples of Appalachian ethnocentricity, like a real charmer I know at the Starlight Motel."

"Can't wait . . . see you soon."

The anticipation of a house guest had motivated Chris to complete the last details of decorating her house, which mostly involved the guest room, and to set aside the unpacking and organizing of her new office in Cantrell Hall. Over the past month, she had spent some quiet, pleasant afternoons and evenings placing books on the fresh, white shelves of the newly painted bookcases in Room 305 and putting supplies in the drawers of the sleek mahogany desk and matching credenza. Sometimes she would take a sandwich and a bottle of water and sit at the little table on her beautiful patio, while she ate a late lunch or an early dinner. On those occasions, she was often the only one in Cantrell Hall, which added to her increasing peace and serenity. She would gaze almost reverently at the magnificence of the astounding mountain world that surrounded her. Chris had come here with hope, and she had begun to feel the healing.

She had not begun to organize the file cabinets nor to work on her syllabi and lesson plans for the fall semester. She determined that after the gala reunion with Rachael, she would jump into the heavy-duty planning and creating that would carry her into her new position as Associate Professor of English, and introduce her to the college in a way no brochure or administrator could ever do.

By mid June, Chris's undisturbed afternoons and tranquil evenings on her office patio became productive times, when her mind regularly wandered to thoughts of students and classes. A sense of real excitement, an eager anticipation, began to rise in her once again, and the emotion of being herself, as she once had known it, brought her to tears. Richard had assigned her three sections of freshman English and an upper level American Literature course. Chris had taught similar courses before at NYU, but she knew she would make changes and add new things this time around. She always did. That was part of her creative process. She would think of different ways to grab the students, to coax them to learn, so they didn't know they were giving in. It was a challenge, an unspoken contest of wills. It always started out as "you" and "us," but slowly some would trust her, let her in. Others would come more slowly, but she had great patience. Chris set her goals high, and her rewards were heady. She also knew she would silently grieve for those she could not touch, the lost ones. She once told an old veteran professor that she "had lost" a few students during a particularly trying semester, and he told her, "Chris, they were lost long before you ever met them." She had always remembered that, because it helped her a little in the process.

Chris was pleased with the final touches she had put on the guest room, and she thought happily how much Rachael would like it when she arrived that evening. She had bought a couple of steaks at Blount's Market, which was the only grocery store in town, and a couple of bottles of Jacob's Creek cabernet from the store's limited selection of wine, for the reunion that she knew would extend into a night of talk and laughter, and some tears.

During the decorating frenzy of the past two weeks, Chris had not spent any time in her office or on the campus. She had not even picked up the mail from her box in the faculty mail room in Bryant Hall. Since Rachael had estimated that she would arrive in Clayton Forge about seven on Friday evening, and all was ready and waiting, Chris had at least three free hours before Rachael's arrival for continuing her task at Cantrell Hall, for getting back in touch with what she was creating there. Before she left the house, she stacked the CD player with Sinatra and Streisand, set the table on her screened porch with a red and white checked cloth, and poured the charcoal into the barbecue that stood just outside the porch door.

Chris's experience had been that Friday afternoons were notoriously devoid of faculty and staff on most college campuses, and summer Fridays were doubly so. That insured that she wouldn't get caught up in any conversations or other diversions and would be able to move ahead quickly with her work. It felt good to be filled with positive feelings – her best friend's visit and a job and school year she was eagerly anticipating.

As she drove through the imposing gates of the campus, Chris smiled at the solitary car in the front parking lot and the absence of any visible person on the grounds.

"I wanted peace and solitude, and this is solitude, for sure," she mused, as she drove slowly around the roadway and pulled her car into a parking space outside Cantrell Hall.

As Chris automatically activated the car lock, she laughed at her routine. "Once a city girl, always a city girl," she thought as she walked toward the building. Once again she was in awe of the mountains, aware of their mystery and splendor. The silence engulfed her.

"Well, I don't expect I was missed by anyone around here," she reflected as she walked down the hall toward Room 305.

She could not have been more mistaken.

Chapter 11

Tabor carefully set the rusted miner's lantern down into the dugout, leaving just enough light radiating onto the trampled ground above it to allow him to see for a few feet around him. He was always aware that the beam from even a simple flashlight could be seen as a bright point in the blackness of the forest, an unfriendly beacon threatening to reveal his hidden place. The humid June air hung around him, glistening on the black coils of his heavy beard and running with the sweat on his grimy face. He rubbed his stinging eyes with beefy hands and moaned softly as he drained the last drops from the plastic milk jug he had filled with water two days earlier. Tabor hadn't been able to leave the hidden compound for the last four days, and he had slept little. Overwhelming excitement upon his discovery had now turned to oppressive, unbearable anxiety, as he watched and waited for her return. As the days passed, and his vigil proved fruitless, his anger grew.

The first time Tabor had seen her was way back in the early spring. He had gone to the college one morning to look for Miss Allison's grade book, before anyone else could see it. He had hoped that Dr. Shelton and Dr. Cantrell wouldn't know where it was and wouldn't have had time to find it, with all the commotion and excitement going on with Miss Allison being gone. Tabor knew where the book was, because she had taken it out of her cabinet one day when he was in her office. If he could take it and hide it, then maybe he wouldn't fail English. Mattie had been taking a walk around the back of the campus, and she had seen him on the patio outside Cantrell Hall trying to open the door to Miss Allison's office.

She had come running toward him, shouting "What are you doing? You can't go in there! Get away from that door!"

Tabor had panicked as Mattie got closer to him and he had tried to run around her, but she wouldn't stop.

"Stop!" she called. "I saw what you were doing . . . I'm calling the police on you this time!"

"Leave me alone, or you'll be sorry," he rumbled. "I'll get you . . . you better get away from me. I'll get you."

His low monotone threat stopped Mattie's approach. She had always felt he was kind of crazy, but until now, she had not really been afraid. They stood with less than fifteen feet separating them. Tabor loomed above her, his long, ape-like arms slightly raised from his sides.

"Don't you come near me," she said resolutely. "Buster is just over there at the office, and he knows I'm here," she lied. "And he knows you're over here, too. He'll put you in jail if you don't get out of here. I saw you trying to break into that office."

"Leave me alone," he growled. "Y'all will be sorry if you don't . . . real sorry."

Tabor had run toward the woods behind Cantrell Hall, and Mattie had not tried to stop him this time. She turned and ran toward the administration building, and she did not see him alter his course and run parallel with her toward a small grove of cedars planted at the edge of the Bryant Hall landscaping. From his close proximity to the building, Tabor had watched Buster's patrol car drive up and park in front of the main door, and he had smiled as he recognized Mattie had been lying to him. She had been afraid of him, just like others had been.

53

As he waited for Buster to leave, Tabor watched another car as it approached the administration building, and he watched as its driver parked between the white stripes of the parking lot and stepped onto the pavement. His heart raced as he saw the golden glisten of Chris's auburn hair in the morning sun and the soft, angular beauty of her face. A low, guttural sound escaped from his throat as he strained to see more of her. She turned slowly in a circle as she looked all around her and up at the mountains surrounding them. It was then that Tabor knew she was the most beautiful woman he had ever seen, so much more than all the others.

Later he had watched Chris come out of Bryant Hall with Dr. Shelton, and he saw them follow the winding brick walkway across the campus to Cantrell Hall. Tabor noticed the way they strolled together and the way they gestured and laughed, as they walked side by side and close to each other. Clearly, Dr. Shelton thought she was beautiful, too. Tabor felt the angry flush of heat in his face and a tightness in his heaving chest as he determined, "Dr. Shelton ain't goin' to have her, not this one. She's goin' to be with me . . . be mine."

All through May he watched from his mountain lookout, sometimes for hours before he saw her. Not until June did she start coming everyday to Cantrell Hall. Once Tabor had taken a great chance, and he had watched her up close, from the thick laurel grove that was only about twenty-five yards from her office patio. With every day, she grew more fascinating and desirable, and with each day he spent with her, Tabor became happier.

"Where y'all goin' everyday, Boy?" Mawmaw had asked him the second week in June.

"Up the mountain . . . goin' to camp some 'afore summer's over," he replied.

"How long y'all be up there? Ain't no use worryin' over ya like I been," she said.

"Maybe four or five days. No use worryin', Mawmaw. I'm jest glad to be in the high woods . . . like I always been. I like the critters up there better'n the ones down here."

She had looked at him with sad eyes and had reached over and gently patted his arm.

"I know, Son. Folks ain't treated ya' right, has they. Go and find your peace on the mountain."

Pap never knew he was gone and wouldn't have cared if he did.

Now, Tabor's beautiful one had gone away. At first he wasn't worried. Frustrated maybe, but not worried. Then when a few days became a week, and he watched carefully all day without seeing her, he began to think maybe she wouldn't come back. Then it was two weeks. Tabor needed to go home to get water and some more food, but he was afraid he would miss her. So he didn't eat. Sometimes terrible thirst overcame him. But he couldn't leave. He tried licking drops of water from rocks in the early morning, like he had seen the deer and the possums do, but weakness soon overcame him, and he had to leave his torturous post and go down from the mountain.

"Son, y'all are lookin' bad. Campin' up there with this hot weather gives a person the summer sickness. Don't be stayin' out there too long, or y'all be gettin' sick. School starts afore long, and ya' gotta be ready. Y'all hear me?"

"Yes'm, Mawmaw. I'm all right. Jest want some water and some bread and peanut butter. I'm havin' me a good time up there."

That was two days ago, and now the water was gone again. Tabor slumped forward in the dull light of Pap's old lantern, rocking back and forth as he held his head between his massive forearms. Great sobs came from deep within him as he felt an overwhelming disappointment and loss. He lay down on the rocky ground and cried himself into a deep sleep.

* * * *

55

The sun was high in the cloudless sky as Tabor was awakened by the heat on his face. He knew he had slept late into the day, and he had to go home. His mouth was cottony with thirst and his stomach knotted from hunger. He listlessly picked up the binoculars and ranged over the Jackson Clayton campus, knowing he would not find anyone there. It was coming up the Fourth of July, and no one would be at work. As he moved left, a chill ran through him and he could feel the tingle of the hairs rising on his arms. Her car was there. Her car was in the parking place. She had come back to him. Tabor stood up and lowered his head as he peered through the opening in her patio fence, trembling with anticipation as he looked for her.

Chris opened the glass door and stepped out into the bright, warming sun. The mountains were glorious today, and she was exhilarated by thoughts of showing it all to Rachael. She loved the silence, the peace. The loneliness she had felt in the teeming city was gone, replaced by the quiescence of solitude. Stretching her arms toward the sky, she swayed slowly and rhythmically from side to side, feeling the breeze as it caressed her lean body and blew her hair around her face. Slowly, Chris ran her hands down her sides, feeling buoyed by a regained sense of wellbeing and happiness. Twisting her thick, shoulder-length hair into a tight knot, and then letting it go, she shook her head and finger-combed her hair loosely back into place. She took a deep breath and exhaled through her mouth before turning back toward the office door.

Tabor breathed heavily as he watched his beautiful angel, his goddess of love. He should have known she wouldn't leave him. She wasn't like the others. The feelings warmed his legs and his thighs as he saw her lithe body move in a flowing wave from side to side. As she ran her long fingers through her coppery hair, he moved his hands on himself, pretending it was her. She would want to do that he knew. She would want to come to the mountain with him. When he asked her, she would smile and tell him she wanted to go with him. She wouldn't do what the others had done. He knew it. Tabor gasped as his body shuddered, and he loved her even more.

Chris busied herself with the final organization of her office and made a list of things she would do after Rachael left. She felt satisfied and positive, almost high with her soaring spirits.

Before turning off her desk light about six o'clock, she looked out onto her patio and at the darkening landscape beyond. The slowly setting sun cast a pink glow in the lavender hued sky, turning the mountains a deep smoky blue.

"Until this summer, I didn't believe the Blue Ridge Mountains were really blue," Chris said softly to herself. "Now I know."

She closed her office door and walked down the corridor toward the exit, excited by the thought that Rachael would be with her in an hour.

Tabor watched until her car was out of sight beyond the college gates. He was disappointed that she had not come out on the patio again, but he knew she would be back with him soon. Neither of them could stay away. Now he would go home and stay the night there. Mawmaw would fix him a good supper, and he could get supplies for the coming week. It was all going to be okay. Tabor had so many plans now, and this time they would work. His beautiful lady could never imagine what wondrous things he had in store for her.

Chapter 12

Rachael wasn't half way up the walk that led from the driveway to the front door before Chris was embracing her in an all-encompassing bear hug. She dropped the canvas duffle bag she was carrying and wrapped her arms tightly around Chris, returning her dear friend's warm, sincere feelings.

"I can't believe you're here!" Chris laughed, as each of them pushed back, holding each other arm to arm, before hugging again. "Oh my God, I have missed you so much."

"Me, too, Chrissy . . . you look wonderful . . . so radiant," she said as she surveyed her friend closely. "I think this mountain air really agrees with you."

"You look pretty amazing yourself, Girl. How about that long, streaked hair. I love it!

Come on in. I have been so excited about your visit."

Rachael stopped before they reached the small front porch and looked around her.

"Look at those mountains! My gosh, Chris, the views are magnificent. You really lucked out. What a beautiful spot – a vacation house you live in all the time. You're not far from the town, but it seems like you're out here in the untouched country . . . wildflowers and everything."

"Well, it wasn't exactly as advertised, but after a couple of months here, I've decided I like it. The house and I have kind of settled into each other. At first I thought it was too remote, but I'm okay with that now. The mountains really are something, aren't they . . . almost like a living, breathing being. I'm beginning to feel it more and more. I never cease to be moved by their grandeur. I've decided they have a definite spiritual presence that grows on a person."

"I can see what you mean. We have mountains we can see in the distance from the Tech campus, but they're more like background . . . nothing like this. These are right up in your face . . . really."

"Welcome," Chris said as she opened the door for her visitor.

"Oh, I love your house. You always were a decorator. If you hadn't become an academic slave, you definitely could have had a big-time decorating career in New York."

Rachael and Chris stood inside the front door, facing the brick fireplace that Chris had painted white. It was a dramatic change from the nicked and soot-stained hole in the wall that confronted Chris on her first visit to the house.

"You should have seen this place, Rachael. It was really grim and grimy . . . almost sent me back to NYC the day after I arrived."

"Well, you certainly changed it, because it's a *House and Garden* picture now."

"Here's your room . . . small, but, hopefully, comfortable. There's a bathroom and shower, and that door leads out to the screened porch."

"I'm never leaving – can you get me a job?" Rachael laughed.

The two women again became college girls, as they sipped wine and talked nonstop of the nineteen months they had been apart. They laughed over recalled college memories, and speculated about acquaintances they had not seen since graduating. Rachael had accepted her teaching position in

Virginia six months before Jack died, and she had left New York when Chris was two months pregnant. The plan had been that she would come back for a baby shower and the birth of Chris and Jack's son. She was to be the baby's godmother.

In the early dark hours of an October morning that still haunted her, the telephone call came from Jack's only brother, who had found Rachael's telephone number in Chris's handbag. He was the next of kin, the bereaved one who had to take charge of finding some semblance of sanity in the midst of total, abject tragedy.

"Hello . . . is this Rachael Lackner? My name is Jason Alford . . . I'm Jack Alford's brother . . . Chris's brother–in–law." His unfamiliar voice was shaky, tired.

"Yes, I remember we met at their Christmas party a couple of years ago." Rachael knew it was going to be bad.

"Yes . . . Rachael . . . I know you're Chris's best friend . . . she had your name . . . as the person to call." He stopped and she heard his sharp intake of breath.

"Is Chris okay?" she asked softly, fear numbing her, making it hard to breathe.

"Rachael . . . there's been a terrible accident . . . Chris is alive." The grief that came from him in halting, slurred words was palpable, sucking life from Rachael as he spoke. "Jack . . . Jack didn't make it."

"Oh, dear God . . . oh, no . . . oh, God . . . no."

She could not feel her body, as she tried to grasp the meaning of what the caller had said. Was she dreaming? It was four in the morning . . . was she still asleep? She heard the sobbing of a man on the other end of the telephone line, and, for a moment, she tried to remember who he was.

"Chris is in critical condition . . . she has internal injuries. The doctors don't know . . ."

"Jason . . . the baby . . . their baby?" she asked.

"They . . . couldn't save him . . . Chris's injuries . . . died in the hospital."

The two casual acquaintances held on to each other over the four hundred miles that separated them, connected by what would never be again. They were silent for a minute.

"Jason, I'll come as soon as I can get a flight. Where is Chris?"

"She's at Good Samaritan Hospital, north of Philadelphia . . . close to Levittown . . . they were on their way to Jack's art show . . . in Philadelphia."

Rachael had flown out of Roanoke on that foggy, rain-soaked morning, spending most of the flight with her forehead pressed against the cold, viewless window next to her seat. The plane had been half empty, and, mercifully, she had no one sitting next to her. Although she did not feel as if she was crying, tears ran ceaselessly from her swollen eyes and lay in tiny puddles on the window ledge. Flight attendants brought her cups of tea she could not drink, and plastic glasses of water that went untouched. Just as she did not remember the drive to Roanoke, she didn't remember the cab ride from the airport to the rambling, gray hospital.

In the twilight of the intensive care room, Chris lay quietly under the mass of monitors and tubes that hung over the bed, her chest rising and falling rhythmically with the beep of artificial breath. Rachael stared at the flatness of her midsection, emptied too soon of the life it had nurtured. She saw no sign of injury to Chris's face, nor to the limp hand she held between both of hers. Jason sat beside her, and the doctors talked to them . . . about Chris having been unconscious since the head-on collision that killed five people . . . Chris's husband and her child, and the three teenaged boys whose car was on the wrong side of the highway. Only Chris had survived the horror. The doctors were kind, but matter-of-fact, as they

61

solemnly spoke of Chris's precarious condition and summarized her catastrophic injuries in recited medical terms. Internal bleeding. Six broken ribs. A severely compromised liver. They had removed part of her pancreas and had repaired other organs. She could not breathe on her own. Her heart rate was poor. She might not live through the day.

Rachael could still hear the staccato of their quiet revelation.

Chris refilled their wine glasses and they clinked them together once again.

"Here's to my best buddy," she toasted.

"And here's to the sister I always wanted and finally found," Rachael returned. She waited for a moment, and then she looked directly at her friend. "Chris, how are you feeling – physically , I mean."

"Remarkably well. I sometimes can't quite believe that my body was able to recover the way it did . . . really speaks well of those great doctors who glued me back together."

"And how is everything else? Are you okay emotionally?" Rachael had thought so often about this moment, this time when they would be able to talk about what had happened. This was the first time she had seen Chris since she took her home from the hospital . . . and since the memorial service that followed.

"I think so, Rachael. I wasn't okay when I first got here, but I know I'm getting better." She sat quietly for a moment before she continued. "I don't suppose I'll ever really be over it. I mean . . . it will always be a wound . . . but it will heal . . . and sometimes, it will probably tear open again."

"I have thought so much about when we would talk about it . . . whether you would ever be able to . . . whether I would be brave enough to bring it up. I hope it's okay, Chris. Just tell me if it isn't. I don't want to be the one who tears it open."

"You aren't . . . you won't be," Chris assured her. "Things are happening to me that confuse me, but I'm feeling more positive. It's like I know I will have a life . . . I mean after Jack . . . but I don't know what it will be. Does that make any sense?"

"Yes . . . it's the first time in two years I've heard you say that, Chris. And, yes, it makes perfect sense because it's true. You are getting better." Rachael leaned to the other end of the sofa and put her arms around Chris. "Yes, you are definitely getting better."

"Rachael, I've never really thanked you for all you did for me. You gave me six months of your life and helped me live. It had to be so hard for you . . . and Jason . . . to tell me about Jack . . . and about the baby." Her eyes filled with tears. "It's still hard for me to say it, but I think it helps me every time I do."

"Neither Jason nor I knew what "hard" was, Chris, when we saw what you had to do, what great mountains you had to climb. You're the one who showed us. How is Jason? Do you hear from him?"

"Yes, occasionally. He's in San Francisco and still trying to make it in the art world. It has been tough for him. Jack was his hero, his big brother, and Jack was the artist Jason always wanted to be. He has little money and isn't able to travel much. I don't know if we'll see each other very often . . . now."

"Tell me about the school . . . the job . . . the people . . . all the details. From what I can see, it's wonderful."

Chris reviewed what she had already told Rachael in emails and on the telephone.

"I have to say, there are some odd things around here, but I guess it's the cultural differences I'm having to adjust to. Also, I made a real mistake with Richard Shelton early on in our relationship. I feel like he is supersensitive when it comes to the teacher who was in my position before me. He seems adamant about not talking about why she left, which seems like a reasonable question for me to ask . . . but he didn't think so. Anyway, I have to repair a few bridges before the semester starts, or it could be quite a frigid winter."

"You said he's single. Is he someone you could get interested in?"

"Oh, Rachael, I'm not ready for that. I mean, how could I be?"

"Well, you are single . . . and Jack has been gone two years. You don't have to get involved, but it's okay if you do."

"I'm quite sure Richard Shelton has no interest in me other than as an English professor on his faculty. As long as I do the job, we'll be fine. If I don't, I'll go the way of the mysterious Allison Montgomery. She's the one I replaced. Maybe he was involved with her. Maybe that's why he got prickly when I asked questions."

"You didn't answer my question. Could you be interested in him?"

"I don't know . . . yes . . . maybe. But . . . there's something unsettling about him, a gut level kind of feeling. I can't quite figure it out, but I don't feel quite comfortable when I'm around him. It's like he isn't who he seems to be."

The friends talked during dinner and into the night, as they knew they would, and they shared more stories and drank more wine than they had in many years. They went to bed full of plans for the next day, unaware that they would become part of another's plans also.

Chapter 13

Clayton Forge on the Fourth of July had taken on the aura of a Norman Rockwell painting. Mountain breezes ruffled the red, white, and blue bunting and fluttered through the assortment of American flags that decorated storefronts, banks, and professional offices along the main street. The little town had been cordoned off for three blocks around its center, and tabletop merchants, artisans, and food vendors had set up their booths where dusty pickup trucks were normally curbed. Rough wooden picnic tables with attached benches dotted the court house lawn and the two church yards, providing a place for locals and tourists to eat their deviled egg and fried chicken lunches they had packed, or the hotdogs and spicy vinegar barbecue they had bought from the ladies at the Baptist church. The sweet-smelling fragrance of cotton candy floated on the popcorn-scented air, and clusters of noisy children formed around the stalls that sold these once-a-year treats.

No one living could remember a time without the Clayton Forge street fair on the Fourth of July, although there seemed to be no history of its beginning. Not much in the village had changed over the years, least of all this time-honored tradition that always brought together remote mountain dwellers and the folks who inhabited the town. Some could recall when the streets were unpaved, and others remembered a particularly wet spring and early summer when the dusty roadways turned to thick, molasses-colored mud. The columned old brick and stucco court house still stood one block east of the town square, and it still housed the police station, two six by six jail cells, and the lone courtroom that processed whatever was dumped on it by the three lawyers in the area. Clayton Forge had grown haphazardly, much like other little American towns whose time had quickly come and as quickly gone with the advent and demise of cotton mills and coal mines. A sprawl of ramshackle, rambling buildings on the south edge of the town was a dismal monument to the best of days that had long since passed.

Mawmaw smoothed a tiny yellow crocheted baby's sweater as she laid it on the rickety card table in front of her. Every year since she could remember, her family had set up shop in the same place across the street from the courthouse, within a block of the center of town. The same was true of the other resident merchants surrounding her. Everyone had his or her regular place. Last year she had made almost two hundred dollars selling her embroidered pillow cases and dainty crocheted baby clothes at the fair. She couldn't remember a time in her life when she had not come to town for the big celebration. When she was a little girl, she used to help Granny or her ma set up the rows of shiny glass jars with pickled peaches or spicy tomato relish they made every year for sale. She could still remember hauling the heavy plank table and the fragile mountain specialties down the steep, winding path to the little town in two old slatted pine wagons. Back then, just local folks came and bought or traded wares, but now tourists came to ogle the mountain folks as much as the merchandise they offered.

"Tabor, go get that other box over yonder," she said as

66

she pointed toward the spot in front of the courthouse where they had piled the three containers earlier in the morning. "I need to have it all close by when it comes time to put out more pieces."

He dutifully trudged across the empty section of the asphalt street and picked up the sagging cardboard box from a patch of damp grass. "This one, Mawmaw?" he called in his booming monotone.

"Well, what other'n could it be, Boy? Do y'all see any other'n there? Bring it on over here."

Tabor hugged the big, soggy box to his wide chest as he shuffled along the grassy strip that ran behind the uneven line of display tables. He did not see the two round metal tent stakes that lay half on the grass and half on the graveled edge of the street, and he stepped on the smooth end of one of them. His big boot rolled forward as if on greased wheels, and the bulging box flew from his arms, hit the ground, and seemed to explode. Tabor sprawled headfirst onto the loose gravel at the road's edge, unable to save himself or the precious cargo he was delivering.

"Lord 'a mercy, Tabor, look what y'all done . . . can't ya' do anythin' right?" Mawmaw shouted. "All my work is covered with gravel and dirt! Get up, damn ya', and help me get this cleaned up."

"I'm sorry, Mawmaw . . . I didn't mean to . . . ."

The pain of embarrassment overwhelmed the discomfort of his gravel-scraped hands, as he attempted to hoist himself up off the ground in front of the few locals who stared, chuckling at his cloddish misfortune. He grasped a pink ribboned infant's cap in his dirty hand and held it out to her.

"Don't go gettin' blood on my crochet," Mawmaw scoffed as she grabbed it from him. "Y'all has to be the clumsiest one I ever seen . . . tries a body's patience," she grumbled. "Jest go on . . . yer help's more trouble than it's worth."

The old woman began shaking the bits of grass and twigs from each of the little garments, muttering to herself as she carefully laid them on one of the two card tables she had covered with clean butcher paper. Tabor seemed rooted to the spot where he had first righted himself.

"I'll get y'all some lemonade, Mawmaw," he offered sheepishly.

"I said jest go on. I don't need nothin' but to get my things on these tables . . . and somebody to buy them. Go get yourself somethin' to eat. I give ya four dollars . . . that's enough for whatever y'all want. Walk around and see what people has brought. Don't be botherin' me for awhile."

Tabor wandered aimlessly down the roped-off street, his line of vision on the pavement in front of him. He wanted desperately to go back up the mountain, but he had promised Mawmaw he would stay the day and help her carry home the things she didn't sell. He would go back tomorrow . . . that would make two days he had been away. Anxiety plagued him as he thought of his beautiful lady being at their meeting place without him. He would definitely go back first thing in the morning.

"Have you ever had a funnel cake?" Chris asked as she and Rachael approached the crowded town center.

"No, I don't believe I have. It sounds like something a spider would make," Rachael laughed.

"I can smell them . . . they make great ones around here," Chris said. "I had one at a little bazaar I went to at one of the local churches a couple of weeks ago. The college librarian introduced me to the arts and crafts of the region and to funnel cakes . . . and to her Baptist church."

"I'm game . . . for the funnel cake," Rachael replied as

they entered the buzz of activity. "Chris, I can't believe we're actually here. It really is a slice of American life, isn't it . . . Fourth of July in Appalachian wonderland."

"Yes, it sure is. Let's just wander around and see all the arts and crafts. Other than the bazaar, I haven't really been to anything like this since I've lived here. The people from this area are talented. Wait until you see some of the art over at the college. We'll go over there tomorrow."

"I smell something good," Rachael said as she raised her nose to the scent. "It has to be barbecue. Let's go in that direction. That mountain climbing marathon you took me on this morning made me ravenous."

"I'm hungry, too. Have you ever seen such an array of quilts and handwork?" Chris said, as she stopped in front of one of the make-shift booths on the street. She picked up a beautifully smocked and embroidered toddler-sized dress. "What a dear little thing," she said softly.

"Look at this . . . look at this beautiful crochet work." Rachael gently turned over a yellow infant's sweater.

"Can I get y'all something?" Mawmaw smiled at the two women she had never seen before.

"No, thank you. We were just admiring your beautiful handwork. I wish I did have someone to buy it for," Rachael said with a smile. "Did you make all of these things yourself?"

"Yes, Ma'am, I did. My family's always done embroidery and crochet, and some quilting, ever since I can remember."

"This is truly special," Chris said. "There aren't many people who have the artistic ability you do. Look at the little rosebuds on this sweater, Rachael." Chris turned to Mawmaw. "Unfortunately, we don't have any children, or friends who have little ones," she said as she gently put the delicate crocheted sweater back on the table.

"Lots a' folks 'round here do some kind of handiwork. I ain't a knitter, but my neighbor makes beautiful things. She raises her own sheep and sheers 'em herself . . . spins her yarn and everything. Her booth is right down there . . . just past the courthouse, on the same side of the street as this."

"Thank you . . . we'll stop and see her."

"Y'all tell her Suelean sent ya'. Have a good day now," Mawmaw called as Chris and Rachael walked away from her table.

"What a sweet lady," Rachael said quietly. "What did she say her name was? Suelean? How old do you think she is?"

"I think you have the name right . . . hard to tell how old she is. My guess is she's younger than she looks. She probably has had a tough life. Richard said there is a lot of poverty back in the mountains and hills. People work themselves to death, I guess, and never get anywhere."

"I'm not used to seeing people with missing teeth, like that poor lady," Rachael said. "Let's face it, Chris . . . you and I came from pretty poor families, but dental care was always available through the school clinic or the free clinic run by social services."

"I don't think a lot of these people in the mountains and hills know anything about free clinics, even if the care is available. I'm too new around here to know much about it, but I am good at observing, and I'm seeing things I haven't seen before."

Chris and Rachael bought their barbecue and coleslaw lunch at the Baptist church and sat on the cool ground in the churchyard, shaded by the leafy umbrella of a massive old oak tree. They enjoyed the peaceful ambiance of the moment – the savory country food, the clear warm mountain air, and the comfort of their friendship.

Tabor sat on the flat, worn side of a boulder at the edge of the church cemetery, facing across the bleached white markers and stone crosses to the mountains beyond. He ate his second barbecue sandwich in two big bites and wiped the grease from his bearded mouth on the back of his hand, before crumpling the thin sandwich paper into a tight ball that dropped to the ground. He reached deep into his overall pocket and pulled out a large pocket knife and a six inch block of pale pine.

His heart wasn't into the festivities of the fair this year. If it hadn't been for Mawmaw, he wouldn't even have come. The last two years, he had brought some wooden toys he had whittled and carved, and he had made twenty-five dollars selling them off of Mawmaw's table. People he didn't know had said they were real good, and he had sold all of them. But he had been too busy to make anything this year . . . too busy with more important things. There had been Miss Montgomery . . . and Dr. Cantrell . . . and all the hullabaloo at the college. It didn't leave him any time for his carving. And now, all he could think about was getting back to his lady, no matter where he was, no matter what he was doing.

Now that he knew she was moving into Cantrell Hall, he couldn't contain his excitement. He could see her up close every day . . . and then he would talk to her . . . and she would want to see him. It was as if all the rest of the world had been blocked out and replaced by his overwhelming love and devotion to his beautiful lady. How happy he felt – how lucky. Tabor smiled when he thought about how the Twining brothers would be surprised when they saw she was with him . . . and then they would be jealous. He would show all of them, all those people who had called him "freak" and laughed when he walked by. Even Pap would have to change his ways.

Tabor sat with his back to the town as he began to slowly peel away thin curls of wood from the block, rotating it slowly between his big hands. He hadn't carved for a long time, but he wanted to do it now. He wanted to become really good at it, so

71

he could give her a present she would like. He pushed and pulled with the sharp blade, slowly cutting and scraping the soft pine into the shape of a delicate sleeping cat. It was effortless for him . . . when he wanted to do it. Now he had a reason, unlike any reason he had ever known.

"Come on, Rachael, let's go see what all the other booths have to offer," Chris said as she packed the remnants of their picnic into an empty paper bag. "I'll take this over to the trash can, if you'll buy me another lemonade," she bargained.

"I'll do it," Rachael called as she walked toward the door to the church basement where the food was being sold. "I'll meet you at the front of the church."

Chris walked slowly toward the little cemetery that sloped gently down from the churchyard toward the valley below. Straight ahead of her, silhouetted against the spectacular beauty of the Blue Ridge, she noticed the slumped back of a large man who appeared to be concentrating on something he held in his hands. As she got closer, she could see that he was carving. Chris tossed the bag in the green can that stood outside the cemetery fence, but she did not turn back toward the church and Rachael and the fair.

Chapter 14

"Are you staying around here for the Fourth of July, Richard?" James Cantrell asked as he clasped his sun-tanned hands behind his head and leaned back casually in the oversized leather desk chair.

"That's my plan," Richard answered from across the massive desk that separated them. "There's an outside chance I'll go backpacking with a couple of friends from Florida, but I think it's a pretty slim chance. The two of them can't seem to pin down a block of time when they can both come up here, so I don't think the trip will take place until fall. How about you?"

"Oh, I'll be here for sure. I don't think I've missed one of the street fairs in twenty years. An old college friend of mine from Richmond will be here. I think you met her last year at my Christmas party . . . Sharon Edwards. She's also my lawyer, so we'll spend some time on a few business matters as well as taking in the festivities."

"Sure, I remember meeting her."

"She's actually arriving Friday morning – flying to Martinsville and then driving over." James leaned forward in his chair and rested his arms on the dark mahogany desk. "Mattie told me you needed to see me today . . . said it couldn't wait until after the holiday weekend."

"That's right, James. I should've brought this up a long time ago. We should've talked about it a long time ago." Richard sat upright and looked directly at the man behind the formidable president's desk. "Now a situation has come up I need to address, and I can't do that without a candid conversation with you . . . about Allison."

James lowered his head slightly, returning the intensity of Richard's stare. "Some things are best unsaid, Richard. It's advice that has taken me a long way in life. It's like writing a letter . . . once the words are in print, they're on record."

"James, we've left too much unsaid, and there's way too much unanswered. I can't continue to operate efficiently in my job without some new guidelines for dealing with faculty questions. The rumors are eating us up in the town. Have you noticed the way people look at us when we walk down the street or go into a store?"

"No, frankly, I haven't noticed. Who is this 'us' you're talking about? I think you're letting a lot of small town gossip get to you, Richard. There's nothing here to answer or talk about . . . nothing to hide. I'm going to be candid with you. I think you've blown an unpleasant incident with a mentally unstable woman completely out of proportion."

"James, you're my boss, and you know I've respected you and your position for six years. We've worked closely and we've worked well together, but I've come to a point where I need you to answer some of my questions. I have a gut level feeling that you're not sharing with me all you know about Allison Montgomery's disappearance . . . or "departure," as we've been calling it. I've stuck to the limited details and the story you instructed me to follow with everyone, including the state police, but I can't do that anymore."

James sat motionless as he listened to the man he had hired as dean six years earlier, his mind racing to figure out where the conversation was headed.

"Richard, maybe we should start with your telling me what happened, or what you think happened." James could feel anger rising in him as he determined that Richard Shelton wasn't going to make a fool out of him.

"I think Allison is dead," Richard said deliberately. "And I think you know she's dead. What about the blood in her office, James? Blood on the carpet . . . on the door? We've never talked about it . . . haven't even mentioned it."

"My God, Richard . . . what an allegation. How would I know if she's dead or alive? The police looked at the blood, tested it all. Of course it was Allison's blood, but there was no evidence of violence of any kind." James glared at Richard, his eyes narrowed and unflinching. "You seem to have a short memory, Richard. You were there when all the investigation was going on. You talked to the FBI agents just like I did. We commented on how thorough they were and how closely they worked with the state police in checking out every possible detail. Remember, Richard? The Feds were around here for over four months talking to everyone . . . crawling all over us . . . and they never came up with anything suspicious."

Richard sat silently through James's recap of the history they both knew was accurate.

"Look . . . I told you long before Allison left that she had attempted suicide before she ever came to this college. When I shared that bit of information with the police, they're the ones who said she might have cut herself, intentionally or unintentionally. There wasn't much blood . . . a cut finger . . . a sliced wrist . . . who knows. All I know is that she's gone from here, and I have to say I don't feel any regret. I don't wish her any bad luck, but you know as well as I do that she had become useless in the classroom and had turned into one major pain in the ass, to put it bluntly. Frankly, I don't know where you're coming from, Richard, or what point you're trying to make."

James's face was flushed and his eyes flashed with outrage as he continued. "You're the one who told me she was gone. I saw her one morning, and she seemed normal for her, and then you burst into my office the next morning and told me she had left – that she was gone. Where is all this new suspicion coming from? How in the hell can you tell me that you think I know what happened to her . . . or that I know she's dead? "

"People are asking questions, and no one around here has heard a word from her. I think Glen may know something, or maybe he just thinks he does. Haven't you heard anything about her, James? Don't you wonder where she went? I can't believe you're so cool about this."

"'No' is the answer to both questions. I haven't heard anything about her or from her . . . and I have absolutely no interest in where she went. Allison and I were professional friends, employee and employer, nothing more. In the beginning, she was good at working with troubled students. I think she could identify with them. But she was a disorganized instructor and an unstable person. She was absent from the classroom more than any other faculty member on our staff. Students complained, papers went ungraded. You said so, Richard, and I agreed with you. I don't know what triggered her sudden departure, but I think it was just that – a sudden departure. Allison lived in a furnished rented house, and she took most of her personal belongings with her. There's nothing suspicious about this . . . unless you know more than you're telling me."

"Chris Alford asked me why Allison left. I gave her the standard answer you and I had discussed, but she couldn't understand why I wouldn't tell her more."

"You're the dean, Richard. It shouldn't matter whether one of your faculty members is satisfied with your answer or not. It has nothing to do with her job. You need to make that

76

clear to Miss Alford and anyone else who wants to probe something that isn't any of their business."

"James, why do you think Allison left in the middle of the night in the middle of a semester?" Richard's voice had an unpleasant edge of misplaced authority and accusation.

"For the reasons I gave you originally, which I have just repeated in great detail in this conversation that is becoming tedious," he said, without trying to cover his resentment and offense.

"With all due respect, James, I don't think you're telling me the complete truth."

"You're bordering on calling me a liar, Richard, and I don't accept that from anyone. I will repeat my earlier question to you: why do *you* think Allison left as she did? And since we're casting stones, are you sure you're telling me the whole truth? Perhaps you haven't even leveled with yourself. I know something of your relationship with Allison when she was here. It was no secret."

"I never had a personal relationship with Allison, James. She wanted one . . . but we never had one beyond dean and faculty member." Richard stood up. "Well, I guess this was a waste of time, wasn't it, yours and mine. I had hoped we could clear up some of the questions and misconceptions here, but I guess it can't happen. I hope you have a good Fourth of July, James," he said as he walked out the door.

James Cantrell didn't change his position in the chair after Richard left. He stared out the window and thought of the last six years and the events and changes that had taken place around him. Richard Shelton had been hired in the middle of a school year, at a crisis point for Jackson Clayton College. He was a skillful administrator, a bright guy who had a good career ahead of him. He had proven to be everything James had hoped he would be when he hired him, and having him as second in command had unquestionably had a positive impact on the school.

Now it seemed that James was up against another brick wall. He had hoped Richard would handle Allison Montgomery's departure as they had discussed, like a true professional administrator should, by shoving it aside or burying it inside of himself and moving beyond it. James knew it happened all the time in academia as well as in government and in private business. People in their positions didn't need to like it, but they accepted it. Now it seemed unlikely that Richard would do that. James leaned forward and rested his forehead on his upraised clasped hands, contemplating the few weeks before classes were to begin. He was aware that there were things he would have to do in the near future, issues he would have to settle by acting on them. Allison had proven to be a colossal, disheartening disappointment, and he couldn't afford another mistake.

Chapter 15

"Hello," Chris called as she approached the outcropping of rocks and the single boulder where Tabor sat. "I hope you don't mind . . . I'm interested in the carving I've seen around here . . . and I noticed you're carving something." She spoke haltingly as she climbed up toward him.

He continued to flick tiny chips of wood from the face of his tranquil cat and did not look up when he heard an unfamiliar voice. As Chris waded softly through the ankle-high grass toward the front of the silent artist, she was startled by his size and appearance. Even as he sat slumped forward in his trance-like concentration, she could tell that he was closer to seven feet tall than anyone she had ever seen firsthand. His long, curly black hair appeared matted in places, as it spiraled downward and joined his equally unkempt bushy beard. Bits of bread clung to the tight, wiry twists below his mouth, and the far right side of the wooly mass appeared to have recently been soaked with a quantity of water or other liquid. His enormous rough hands gently cradled a delicate carved cat that looked to be almost complete.

"How beautiful," Chris said softly, admiring his work from the place where she had stopped. She briefly thought she might have violated his space, tourist style, when he had not responded to her first casual greeting.

Tabor glanced in the direction of the voice, expecting the stranger to beat a hasty retreat when she got a good look at him. Instead, his heart stopped beating, his lungs stopped sucking in air, and he felt what it must feel like to die. He could not will himself to breathe or speak or move. He was as an old movie reel that had been stopped halfway through the show, his carving hand suspended in midair, his face frozen in unmistakable shock. Perhaps this was the cruelest of all the pranks and jokes that had been played on him over his twenty-three years, a trick that could only come from Mawmaw's God or his opposite. Tabor was seeing her, his beautiful lady, when it was really someone else . . . and the moving, talking illusion of her would disappear. It floated in front of his rigid, motionless body, words that he could not hear moving her smiling, pink lips.

"I'm so sorry," Chris said as she took a couple of steps backward. "I didn't mean to startle you or disturb you," she apologized. "Your carving is wonderful."

Chris had turned toward the cemetery entrance and was about to leave, embarrassed by her insensitivity toward the silent artist who only stared at her.

"No," he shouted, "don't go away." The strange, toneless rumble of his deep voice compelled her to stop. "I'm Tabor."

Chris turned around and looked at his hulking form standing ten feet in front of her.

"You can have it," he said as he held out the small carved figure.

Chris walked slowly toward him as she spoke. "Oh, no, I couldn't take it," she said. "It's so nicely carved, really quite beautiful. You must have someone else you want to give it to."

"No . . . no," he seemed to stammer. "It's fer you . . . fer you." Tabor continued to hold the cat out in front of him.

80

"Well, I'd love to buy it from you," she said. "Please let me buy it. How much would you sell it for?" she smiled, as she stopped less than three feet in front of him.

"No money," he said. "I made it . . . fer you . . . it's fer you . . . a present."

Chris felt a sudden sadness for him. "Poor fellow," she thought. For a strange moment, she thought of herself, walking home from school behind all the other girls.

"How very kind of you," she said. "I'd be honored to have it. What did you say your name is?"

"Tabor," he said. "Like in the Bible." He continued to hold the cat away from his body.

"Tabor . . . that's a nice name. I'm Chris," she said as she smiled at him. "I'm so happy to have this beautifully carved cat. I'll put it on the desk in my office, so I can see it every day I'm there." She reached out and took his offering, her fingers lightly brushing his as she grasped the wooden form.

"Here you are," Rachael said as she walked up to where Chris and Tabor stood facing each other. "What are you up to?"

"Rachael, this is Tabor. He's a carver," she said as she showed the little figure to Rachael. "He's been so kind, and he's given this beautiful cat to me."

"Hi," Rachael said as she held out her hand toward the motionless man.

Tabor stood and looked at her, not knowing what he was to do with her extended hand. He said, "Hey . . . I'm Tabor."

"You're really good at this," Rachael said as she looked closely at the smooth carved piece Chris had handed her. "Do you make these and sell them?"

"No . . . I ain't sold none since last year . . . at the fair."

"They really are nice. I'm sure you wouldn't have any trouble selling them," she replied.

"Well, I guess Rachael and I had better go and see the rest of the fair, so we don't miss anything," Chris said. "It's been nice meeting you, Tabor. Thanks so much again. The cat really is lovely."

Tabor's breath came in rough, short bursts and his pulse beat a staccato rhythm in his head as he watched the two women walk down the incline toward the churchyard and the street beyond.

"I'll see y'all again," he shouted after them, but the noise of the crowd obscured his words.

"That little cat is so delicate," Rachael said as they walked toward the display tables ahead of them. "It's amazing that a guy like that could carve something so fine. What do you think is wrong with him?"

"I'm not quite sure," Chris said quietly. "Whatever it is, I'll bet he's a real tragedy. I wouldn't think there's much help up here for anyone who has any kind of problem. Public money seems to go to the more populated areas, the areas that vote for the representatives."

"He's so big, physically, and so . . . unattractive," Rachael replied. "And then that voice. I mean, even if his mind is normal, looking and sounding the way he does probably frightens away anyone who might otherwise be nice to him. He's huge, isn't he? Just his size is intimidating."

"He has everything we can see working against him," Chris replied, "and we don't even know anything about his background . . . or his life. I still say he's probably a real tragedy. I feel so sorry for him. Imagine what it would be like," she said pensively.

"Maybe he comes from a whole happy family that looks just like him," Rachael laughed, as she felt the change in Chris's mood. "Maybe the guy is as happy as can be. With our imaginations, you and I should write a novel. It would be a best-selling tear-jerker for sure."

"I think I'm right about this fellow," Chris said, still feeling the loneliness that Tabor's presence had brought back to her. "He may be a novel waiting to happen," she continued, "but I don't think there are any happy endings associated with him. I just have that feeling."

"How about one of those funnel cakes you wanted me to try?" Rachael said as she looped her arm through Chris's and pulled her in the direction of the sweet smell of frying dough. "Grease and sugar are my two favorite food groups," she laughed. "I invented yo-yo dieting, but I'm not going to think about that this weekend."

Rachael's light-hearted mood was catching, and Chris joined her in laughing their way through the rest of the day. The small, carved cat rested securely in the bottom of Chris's large satchel handbag, wrapped in a piece of tissue to protect it. Thoughts of its creator had no part in the remainder of the two friends' day. In the evening, they ate thick-wrapped corn dogs and paper cartons of French fries as they watched the red, gold, silver, and blue bursts of fireworks exploding over the town's community park. Children's screams and adult's "oohs" and "aahs" surrounded them as they joined in the happy celebration that drew them all together.

Tabor sat above them on the side of a small hill, never taking his eyes from the two women he had followed for most of the afternoon. Her name was Chris . . . she had told him herself. He would never hear another name that meant so much to his aching heart. His Chris . . . who had a present from him now. She had a piece of him close to her, and he had watched as she had touched it and had softly run her fingers over its smooth, round body. He had stared at her long, shiny hair and watched as the breeze played with it, hair that was like a summer sunset over his mountain, changing from rust to gold as she turned her head and talked to him.

It was dark now, and he could no longer see Chris or Rachael among the crowd of people who mingled on the park grounds. He pulled himself to his feet and lumbered down the backside of the hill toward Mawmaw's booth on the main street. She would need him to help her carry everything back to the house. She might even be looking for him now. Tabor hoped she had had a good day selling her handiwork. It would go easier for him if she had.

He thought about the miracle of their meeting today, how he and Chris and he had stood face to face, and how he had felt the seductive brush of her soft fingers on his hand when she accepted her present. Tabor began to believe that the touch of her hand had not been by chance. Her talk to him had all been so nice, so gentle and sweet from her lips. She liked him. He could tell. Now that they knew each other, he might change his plans. He reveled in the thought that things could be easier now, and he wouldn't have to move along so slowly. Joy and excitement coursed through him as he imagined all that the future held for him . . . for them.

"Well, Rachael, how did you like the Clayton Forge Fourth of July and street fair?" Chris laughed as they hiked back to the car they had left outside of town early in the day.

"Oh, Chrissy, I loved every minute of it. It truly was a special day, in lots of ways. I hope I get invited back next year," she replied with mock seriousness.

"Only if you come often in between holidays," Chris joked. "I loved it, too, Rachael. It's the first time I've had a really good time in so long. One more thank you I owe you," she said quietly.

"It goes both ways, Chris. I'm so thankful you're here. I have good feelings about you and the college, and even this funny little town. I think this is really a good match . . . for you and them. I've been so worried about you, Chris, about all the problems of living in the city, on top of everything else you've had. But now, you're here, and I believe you're . . . safe and secure." She hesitated for a moment. "Sounds strange, but those are the words that come to my mind. I think you're in a perfect place to establish a new life. They're so lucky to have you, Chris. Never forget that."

"I feel good about it too, Rachael, and I suppose you're right about 'safe and secure.' I guess I would say I have begun to find some peace again. It's the first time I've had that feeling for a very long time."

Chapter 16

The college faculty began to drift back into their offices in late July, just in time for the hot, dry, almost windless days which mark the end of a Blue Ridge Mountain summer. The bright greens of early summer, brought on by frequent morning showers, took on a yellow hue, and mountain trails crackled underfoot, where once their beds of moss and pine needles had been resilient. Underground sprinklers and watering hoses that ran throughout the Jackson Clayton campus drew daily supplies of water from vast unseen wells and springs, and the college grounds were sprinkled daily, just as the sun rose over the mountain, sparing them the parching and withering of everything that grew beyond their boundaries.

Chris spent most days in her office, quietly writing and editing her course materials, readying herself for freshman orientation the second week in August. Occasionally colleagues would stop by and introduce themselves, frequently commenting on how nice the office looked, sometimes expressing surprise that so much had been changed "since Allison." No one said, "since Allison left," or "since Allison died," or "since Allison dropped off the face of the earth." Just "since Allison." Chris stopped short of asking, "Since Allison *what*?" She could still too vividly remember the scalding remarks from Richard that her questions had provoked.

86

"How's it going, Chris?" Glen asked as he stopped outside her open door one morning.

"Hi, Glen. Welcome back. How was your Maine summer?" She was glad to see someone she knew.

"Good . . . as good as it gets in a kid's camp for the rich and famous. Really, it's a pretty great place to work for six weeks. This was my third year. Makes me happy to come back to the college crazies, though. I can't believe I actually taught in a high school before I regained my sanity. So, are you rewriting Freshman Comp, or are you plotting nasty surprises for the little critters when they get here?"

Chris liked Glen's humorous banter and his easy, relaxed manner. She was confident that it was a cover-up for an intellectual mind that could successfully challenge any Mensa or MIT professor.

"I just have new teacher jitters," she laughed. "New York University is a long way from Jackson Clayton and Clayton Forge."

"You'll wow them, Chris. They'll be bowing and scraping before we leave the month of August. Just wait and see. Seriously, everything going okay for you?"

He came into her office slowly, looking carefully all around him as he entered.

"I think so, Glen . . . thanks for asking. Sit down. How ow about some iced tea . . . iced green tea, to be exact. I brought it in this morning."

"I don't want to interrupt your train of thought," he said. "I need to get on the same track myself, but I'll sit for a few minutes. Sure . . . thanks . . . I'll have some tea. Now I can say I went for tea in the new teacher's office," he said with a smile.

"Just walking in here every morning is an experience for me," Chris said. "I've never seen orchids blooming the way those in the atrium are blooming . Who in the world spends the time caring for all the plants? I've only seen one of the grounds crew in here on one occasion, and I've been in my office on and off all summer."

"Most of the time Cantrell himself does it, at least the fertilizing and fine-tuned care. You can be sure he's around, even when you don't know he's around," he said.

"I haven't seen him much. Once or twice on campus, and I saw him from a distance at the Clayton Forge street fair on the Fourth."

"I've never been," Glen mused. "I'm always onto my summer job before that. What did you think of it?"

"Fun . . . real local color, as my friend said."

"The local color isn't always fun, Chris. You need to be aware around here. No one wants us to feel that way. Quite the contrary, but just be cautious in everything and everywhere."

"Can you elaborate? I mean, give me some specifics?" Chris had found Glen's tone to be uncomfortably serious.

"Not names and dates, Chris . . . not that specific . . . but you need to know who you're dealing with, on and off campus. There are some real loose cannons . . . odd, ignorant people who will never like us college types. It's not a bias or a prejudice I have, it's just a fact. Cantrell and Shelton will tell you this is a paradise, witness the beauty of the horticulture. But that's all surface. Underneath, there is much, much more, and some of it's ugly."

"Do you mean the students, or the townspeople?"

"Both . . . and others. A lot of the students are local people, mountain people. They're here on all sorts of scholarships and grants, some of which I've never even heard of. Cantrell is committed to educating them, because he's one of them . . . or he was. He's got deep roots here, Chris, and he has deep pockets . . . real deep pockets. His great-grandfather laid claim to a couple of mountains that were the site of the biggest coal finds in this part of the Appalachian Mountains. The money just kept coming out of the ground, and the Cantrells are still capitalizing on those mines. I don't know any more of the details, but I know this part is true."

"I think it's admirable that James Cantrell uses his money to help students who might never see the inside of a college otherwise," Chris replied. "What's the negative?"

"I agree with the help part . . . don't get me wrong. But he carries it to the point of not accepting the reality of some of them and their ways. There are some students who have been here on and off, Chris, who shouldn't be outside of institutions, as far as I'm concerned. One of my former colleagues said she thought it might be inbreeding, but we don't dare say that. That smacks of prejudice and all the wrong kinds of messages. There are some great people who come through this college, and some of them are among the best I've ever had the pleasure of working with, mountain people with the highest intellect and a strong will to learn. That's why I'm here – the rewards in that are obvious. But there are some others who scare the hell out of me. It seems to be a kind of pattern that keeps repeating itself. Cantrell won't hear of it, and if there's a side to take, his is always on the other side of the faculty. Just be careful of what you say and who you say it to."

"Glen, it sounds ominous," Chris said to him. "I've been teaching in a school inside a major metropolis. We had everything and everyone there, too, just a bit different background, but real trouble at times. I can't imagine this situation could be worse than that."

"Chris, I want you to know that you can ask me for help anytime you need to, even if you aren't sure you really need it. Don't hesitate. We're in this building, and that puts us on the other side of the campus from a lot of other people. Just know that you have a friend you can call on at anytime. Okay?" Glen had leaned forward in the chair and rested his elbows on the tops of his knees.

"Thanks, Glen. I appreciate your offer, and I will call on you if ever I need to." Chris thought carefully before she continued. "Glen, I hesitate to ask you this, so please stop me if you don't want to answer. What happened with or to the teacher who was in this office before me . . . Allison Montgomery? Why did she leave?"

Glen stared at Chris without moving. He seemed not to have heard what she said.

"Glen, I'm sorry . . ."

"It's okay, Chris," he interrupted her. "I figured you'd ask me that at some point, and I can understand why you would. I don't know what to tell you, really. What I've been told by Cantrell and Shelton? What I knew about Allison? What I saw? What I believe? I don't know if all of it's true, or none of it. I don't know if it's fair to you or to any of the others to tell you anything."

Glen sat silently for a minute and then he stood up.

"Chris, let me think about this for awhile. I won't tell anyone you asked, so don't worry about that. I just need to think it through. I promise I'll tell you something. It's not right to keep you in the dark about something that hangs over all of us and is bound to affect you, too. Is that okay?" His manner was almost apologetic.

"Of course it is, Glen. I'm totally ignorant of anything other than the fact that Allison left overnight . . . or suddenly. At least that's what I heard she did. I'm sorry if I upset you. I didn't mean to do that."

"It doesn't take you to upset me about this, Chris. Believe me, it's never far from my conscious thought. Well, I guess I'd better go and try to do some work. I haven't even thought of the classes looming just ahead. Let's get together again sometime later this week or early next. I'm really glad you're here. I mean that."

"Thanks, Glen. I'm glad I'm here, too," she said as he walked out the door.

"I think I'm glad to be here," Chris thought as she attempted to get back to her lesson plans and outline of assignments.

Confusion and doubt swirled around her and crowded out the tentative peace that she had so recently welcomed. Why was everyone so secretive about the mysterious Allison Montgomery, seeming almost frightened to talk about her or the circumstances of her departure from the college? Who or what was Glen talking about when he said, "Just be cautious in everything and everywhere"? Would Glen now literally disappear from her life as Richard had done after she asked about Allison?

As Chris lay in her bed that night, she kept thinking of a similar time when she couldn't let something go, when she kept pressing her point until she had won it. Would she now find that she would once again win her point by getting the elusive information she was seeking . . . and ultimately discover that she was the real loser in the end? For the first time in two months, Chris's dreams raged with a graphic replay of the accident and Jack's and the baby's deaths.

Chapter 17

Tabor wedged himself uncomfortably into the soft-seated gray chair in the lobby of the Student Services office, dreading the impending meeting with Clara Staunton. Mawmaw had given him the money this morning, a stack of wrinkled fives, tens, and twenties that she had crammed into a previously used yellow envelope on which she had scribbled out the original name.

"Don't y'all lose this, Tabor," she had warned him. "There's near to four hundred dollars here for ya' to sign up at your school. Ain't gonna be no more 'til December, so y'all take care . . . ya' hear me, Boy?"

"Yes, Ma'am," he had said.

Mawmaw had been so happy when Tabor had volunteered that he wanted to go back to his classes at the college. She had meant for him to go whether he was happy about it or not, but she felt good because he finally seemed to understand the importance of what she had planned for him. She had told him he would do better in life than she and Pap had done, and better than his ma had done, too.

"Your ma worked at the college just like me, from the time she was a girl of sixteen," she had told him so many times. "She didn't have no schoolin', so alls she could do was clean up after the folks who did. But y'all gonna be different, Tabor. Y'all got a good brain, and yer gonna learn to work with them computers and fancy machines they have over there . . . gonna get respectable work."

He had thought he could pay the gray-haired lady at the desk for the two classes he had signed up for and move on, just like last year. But it hadn't worked out that way. The gray-haired lady looked like one of the unfriendly skinny hens that pecked around Pap's dusty chicken yard. She had looked at him over the top of her little round glasses when he stood in front of the long counter that separated her from the rest of the people waiting in the room. When he had pushed his enrollment sheet and Mawmaw's money toward her, she had left it lying on the counter, and she had picked up her telephone without saying a word to him.

"Tabor Maclean is here, with an enrollment form and money," he heard her say in her scratchy chicken voice. "Yes," she continued. "I thought so, too, but apparently not. Okay. I'll send him in." Then she had smiled as she listened, and she finished the one-sided conversation with "Good luck."

She had loudly cleared her sinuses before she said, "You need to talk to Ms. Staunton about this. She's a guidance counselor."

As if Tabor didn't know Clara Staunton was a guidance counselor. He didn't really understand what her fancy title meant. All he knew was that she didn't like him. Last year he had been sent to talk to her several times, and each time she ended her little speech with, "Tabor, you know that this is unacceptable. You know you're going to have to do better if you want to continue at Jackson Clayton College."

Funny thing was, he hadn't wanted to go back to the college after some of the miserable times he spent in Miss Staunton's office. But now it was different, and, for sure, he really wanted to be here. No one else knew, but being at

Jackson Clayton now was the most important thing in his whole sorry life.

"Hi, Tabor. Come on back to my office."

Clara Staunton's brittle smile could not hide her disdain for the detestable, oversized young man she had to confront once again. She had worked hard to pull herself out of the ugly pit of her ancestry, and she had succeeded. At sixteen, Clara had left the hillbilly home buried deep in a high Appalachian pass, where she had been born, and she hadn't been back. She had worked two waitressing jobs in order to pay for two years at the community college in Irondale, and she had been awarded academic scholarships that took her through two more challenging years at Tech. Clara Staunton was a smart, well-educated guidance professional who didn't want to be reminded of what had spawned her. Unfortunately for both of them, Tabor reminded her.

"Well, how have you been, Tabor?" she asked as she struggled to focus on her role in their testy relationship. "Here, sit down."

"Okay, I reckon," he said while he looked down at the floor in front of him.

Clara always felt overwhelmed when she and Tabor were in the same room. She was five feet and a few inches tall, and painfully thin. They both knew he could stomp on her at will, like an unwelcome wood roach that he might find under his bed. One advantage that Clara knew she had was that her hair was mousy brown. God only knows she had had too many conversations with this disgusting boy, as well as with students, faculty, and administrators, about him and red-haired girls.

"Tabor . . . we need to talk." She tried to relax and appear friendly, the "I'm here to help you" approach. "I understand you want to register again for the developmental English Composition I course and an Internet Technology course." She looked at the registration form in front of her.

"Yes, Ma'am," Tabor said in the loud voice he couldn't moderate. "I'm gonna do better this time."

"That's what we need to talk about . . . you failed the English class last year, Tabor. You only have one more chance to pass it. If you fail a course twice, the college rules say you can't take it again."

"I ain't gonna fail it again," he rumbled flatly.

"Well, I think we need to talk about it. Are you sure you want to take two classes this semester? Maybe you should just take English, and give all of your time to it."

"I can't," he said. "Mawmaw pays, and she said I need to get on with it."

Clara couldn't help but stare at the peculiar giant who sat across from her. He shouldn't be here, and they shouldn't be having this conversation. Tabor would be more at home in a circus sideshow than in a four year academic institution. Damn Cantrell! Damn the others who demanded that she find a place and make it work for misfits like him. She knew he wouldn't make it, and then what would happen? Who would he come hunting with his rifle?

"If you take those two courses, Tabor, you'll have to be here five days a week. English Composition meets on Monday, Wednesday, and Friday, and Internet Technology meets on Tuesday and Thursday. Maybe we should find another class that meets on Tuesday and Thursday. Then you could take English Composition next semester."

"No. I want English Composition," he said. "I told y'all I'm gonna do okay this time." Tabor's flat staccato sounded firm.

"There's something else, Tabor . . . something else I need to talk to you about." She had hoped the conversation wouldn't get this far. "The problems last year, between you and Professor Montgomery . . ."

"There weren't no problems between her and me," he

95

interrupted as he looked directly at Clara. "We was good friends."

"Tabor, your teachers are just that . . . your teachers. Of course, they're friendly to you, and that's a good thing, but you have to respect their privacy."

Observable patches of pale skin that shone through Tabor's heavy beard growth turned a deepening pink. "What them people said about me botherin' Miss Montgomery was lies," he said. "Ain't no truth in it . . . her and me was good friends."

"Well, just remember what I'm telling you . . . for this year."

"Miss Montgomery ain't comin' back this year," he replied sullenly.

"I know, Tabor. I mean remember to respect the privacy of your new teachers this year."

Clara wanted to get him out of her office as quickly as possible. She felt nauseous from the acrid stench of his sweat and the disarming guttural growl of his voice.

"Tabor, Dr. Cantrell asked me to talk to you about one more thing, also. We weren't sure whether you would be coming back to the college or not, but he asked me to discuss this with you if you did."

She picked up a file that had been lying next to his registration form, and she removed a small sheaf of handwritten papers that had been clipped together.

"These are complaints filed by other students last year, and a few reports from faculty and staff about the complaints. Tabor . . . you have frightened some of the girls . . . some of the students who were in your classes. They felt you were behaving inappropriately around them. Two of the girls said you had touched them . . . their hair."

"Y'all already told me that," he rasped. "Last year.

Them girls made that up. I never touched no one that didn't want me to. I told ya' that already."

"Tabor, I need to tell you that if we have any more complaints like these, from students or employees of the college, Dr. Cantrell might have to ask you to leave the school and not come back."

Tabor glowered silently at Clara. Why did folks always believe what the liars said and never believe him? He knew how Miss Montgomery felt, before she changed and all the trouble. And those girls had all but asked for it. That was always the way. They wanted him and the other boys to look at their big breasts and their bee butts . . . like they were offering them up for grabs. Then when it came right down to it, they ran the other way. Even Mawmaw had said those girls weren't dressed fit to be out of their bedrooms. Now, they could be the reason he would have to stay away from the college, when his whole life depended on his being here. He wouldn't pay any attention to those ninny-bitch girls. He didn't need to anymore. He had a real woman who knew him . . . and she liked him. Everything was going to be different now.

"Okay," he said. "I don't want to mess with any of them girls . . . they're all liars . . . I won't pay them any attention . . . for sure."

"It's important for everyone, Tabor. I'm glad you understand."

Clara closed the file with a snap that ended the conversation, and she stood up behind her desk.

"Okay, Tabor, I'll okay your registration for Developmental English Composition I and Internet Technology. As it was last year, you'll have the benefit of the Leland Cantrell Scholarship money to help pay your tuition. Let's see here," she said as she looked down the list of class information, "I suggest we put you in Professor Christine Alford's class at ten o'clock

97

on Monday, Wednesday, and Friday. Professor Alford is new at Jackson Clayton this semester. I think you'll like her."

Tabor sat as if paralyzed. He felt weak, as if he couldn't stand. His Chris . . . his beautiful lady . . . she was going to be his teacher . . . just like Allison Montgomery. He could for sure promise Clara Staunton that he wouldn't be interested in any of the red-haired girls.

"Yes, M'am," Tabor said as he stood up. "I reckon that class for English would be fine."

Clara watched the dark lumbering figure take his signed registration form back to the front desk. She was relieved that she didn't have to explain to any of the other English faculty that they had to take on Tabor Maclean. She suspected some of them would have resigned before accepting that. The new teacher had come from the streets of New York, and Clara guessed she had faced worse than Tabor. Besides, new people had to pay their dues, just like Clara had when she first came to the college. Hopefully, Christine Alford wouldn't end up like Allison Montgomery.

Chapter 18

Chris had slept less than five hours when National Public Radio's Steve Inskeep awakened her with his broadcast of the 6:00 a.m. news. Her legs had cramped painfully and her stomach had churned as she spent the night mentally reciting her bit part for Freshman Orientation. First impressions were so important. They could make or break a teacher . . . just like that. Nineteen and twenty-year-olds could spot a fool in the blink of an eye. Would she say the right things to at least get their attention? Would she say too much? Would they accept her, with her New York accent and her city ways? She had looked at the clock multiple times . . . one . . . three . . . five. Would the alarm go off on time? Orientation started at nine. Would she sleep right through it? And so her night had crept along.

She and two other English teachers were to share the chore of teaching writing and research to three hundred first year students, all of whom, students and teachers alike, were required to attend this first introductory gathering and presentation.

"There's nothing new in this," Chris thought as she fished for her slippers beside the bed.

"Why am I such a wreck?"

The planning part of this initial briefing for these

freshmen had left Chris with an uncomfortable awareness that she knew little of what was expected of her or others. Mary Ella Sensabaugh and Hal Southern had stopped by her office last spring and introduced themselves as "the other two English teachers." Immediately thereafter, each had joined the mass faculty exodus to "anyplace but Clayton Forge for the summer," and Hal had not returned as of last Friday afternoon. Chris had left messages for Mary Ella several times last week, but this Monday morning found her calls and her questions unanswered. Richard's email directive to all faculty had been short and general:

The orientation for first year students will be held in Lancaster Hall auditorium on Monday, August 17. The attached schedule includes all departments and faculty. Each department will make a brief presentation of introductory information specifically focused on that department's involvement with freshmen and requirements. All faculty are required to participate. Please contact me for more information.

An outline schedule was attached and listed times for each department's performance. Mercifully, the English Department followed math and science. If all else failed, Chris could follow her old orientation notes from NYU and conform them to what she observed coming from the math and science departments.

Chris had waited until Thursday to call Richard for some guidance, hopeful that her colleagues would make contact before desperation sent her to the dean.

"I have a few questions about orientation," she said, making every effort to sound light and cheery.

"Hasn't Hal contacted you?" he asked.

How could she answer that question without ruining her relationship with Hal Southern, the department head, before she even had a relationship with him?

"Well, he did stop by my office before he left for the

summer," she hedged. I just haven't had a chance to talk to him this past week." Chris knew her response sounded feeble, as if this was a last minute effort and she was unprepared.

"I'm assuming he's back, since the orientation is Monday." Richard seemed to hesitate before he continued. "The presentations need to be short and focused on your class, a very brief overview of what your goals are and how they will be achieved. I'm sure this is similar to what you did at other colleges." He sounded reserved, formal.

"Okay, that's fine. Thank you. I just wanted to confirm that this was what you wanted." She felt awkward.

"You might call Mary Ella Sensabaugh," he said. "Just in case Hal . . . hasn't been able to get to his messages. She's one of our old timers. Mary Ella would be a good one for you to talk to." There was a moment of silence before he said, "Everything else going okay, Chris?"

"Yes, I feel right at home," she lied. "I've enjoyed the summer here, and I'm all settled into my office. Everything is great."

"Have you been over to Lancaster Hall?" Richard's voice was more relaxed. "The orientation will actually be in the Caleb Mountain Center, which is part of Lancaster Hall. The place can be a maze if you aren't familiar with it."

Chris was encouraged by his conversational tone. "Yes. Actually I've had a tour of Lancaster Hall and the center. Laurel Buchanan showed me all around the college and the town before she left for Honduras."

"Laurel's a good guide," he said. "She knows almost as much about this area as James does. Glad you two got together."

"Yes, I really appreciate all she did for me. I think I can find my way on Monday." Chris hesitated before she said, "It's nice to talk to you, Richard. Thank you."

"It's nice to talk to you, too," he said. "I'll see you

Monday."

Chris sat for some minutes as she reviewed their conversation. Hopefully, Richard had set aside their unfortunate encounter in her office last spring, and they could develop a positive professional relationship. She would have to watch herself and avoid controversy. Chris hated walking on eggs, particularly at this early stage of their interaction, but she knew she had no choice.

The warm water coursed over her upturned face, washing away the fatigue as she stood under the shower's gentle rain. Chris could feel the anxiety subside as she walked herself through her workable plan of action and talked herself out of serious first-day stage fright. How many times had she stood for the first time in front of a group of young adults and gone through her routine? It was like typing or riding a bicycle – you might need some practice, but you never forgot the basic skill. The fleeting thought of riding a bicycle made her smile. Chris had never had a bicycle as a child, and she had never known anyone who had any interest in teaching her how to ride one. Her only experience had been looking at pictures of dads running beside six year old girls as they zigzagged their way down picturesque country roads on shiny new Schwinns. Early in their relationship, Jack had suggested they take an autumn bike trip to Connecticut, along safe and quiet paths he had traveled. When she had told him she couldn't ride a bicycle, had never learned how, he was incredulous. Within minutes of her confession, Jack had committed himself to teaching her what he considered to be a necessary life skill. Chris laughed softly as she thought of the mishaps and the laughs, the fun and the love that had colored that special weekend . . . such a long time ago.

Chris dressed quickly in a simple beige A-line skirt and a short-sleeved apricot colored silk shirt that complimented her lightly suntanned skin. She secured her shoulder-length auburn hair in a loose but well-wrapped knot at the nape of her neck, and hung a multi-strand necklace of ivory, gold, and amethyst colored beads over her shirt. She secured the small gold hoops to her ears before stepping into low heeled beige sandals.

She took one last look at herself in the full length mirror on the back of her bathroom door before she left the house a few minutes before seven. Her plan was to spend at least an hour walking around the grounds and Lancaster Hall to familiarize herself with the new atmosphere. What had been a serene, abandoned campus from mid-May to early August, would now be a broiling mass of high octane youth, covering their nervousness and insecurity with loud posturing and attention-grabbing screams. Many would seek a group to fit into, the luckiest being those who knew at least a few other people. The lonely singles would be those who had come in from outside the area, and their defense would be an uninterrupted stare straight ahead and a controlled effort to avoid smiling or making eye contact.

A clutch of excitement grabbed at her, the adrenaline rush just before the curtain rose on act one. The mystery of the unknown mixed seductively with a sense of dangerous challenge, creating a euphoric high. This was what it was all about, this teaching, student, academic world that had infected her at the same time it had enabled her. This was what it had always been about. She could make more money elsewhere, lots more. She was smart enough and she could write well enough to go to law school. Jack had told her so, and she was tough enough and she had learned to speak eloquently enough to go into politics, but she knew, more than she knew anything else, that she would never leave the classroom.

As Chris pulled into one of the ten faculty parking spaces next to Cantrell Hall, she noticed that eight of them were unoccupied. "No one gets up as early as I do for freshman orientation," she thought as she pulled her briefcase from the back seat of the Mazda. She would drop off her briefcase in her office and then begin her rounds of familiarization.

At 7:00 a.m., the campus was awake but not buzzing like it would be by 8:30. Chris strolled from Cantrell Hall toward the center of the colorful quadrant that held Lancaster Hall. Flower beds were ablaze with bright yellow and orange marigolds and purple asters, backed by giant zebra striped purple and green leaves of ruffled yellow cannas. Tight budding heads of fat, round chrysanthemums signaled that autumn was only a few weeks away. Chris breathed deeply as she marveled at the beauty of James Cantrell's landscaping. She had heard enough to know that he was the designer behind this astounding palette. As she approached Lancaster Hall and its neighbor, the college library, she recalled Laurel Buchanan's humorous but proud commentary on her part of the Jackson Clayton campus.

"Chris, you and I learned what we know from a multitude of libraries we visited over our education years. Libraries – a place where books and films and audio materials were housed. It was so pure and so simple . . . an easy to understand Dewey Decimal System and an available card catalog. Those were the good old days. Now, we don't have libraries. We have "learning resource centers" that house the books and films and audio materials, and we don't have the old Dewey Decimal System anymore, nor do we have the comfort of a card catalog. We have the Library of Congress system of cataloging the materials, and we have computer searches. All has changed. If you're over fifty and not a librarian or an English professor, or if you don't know how to use a computer, you're confused as hell. All I can say is this: the Jackson Clayton College Learning Resource Center has the most impressive collection of confusion for a college its size in continental America."

Chris stopped in front of the library and looked at the

two large complexes. The Student Union and dining facilities were housed in Lancaster Hall, a rambling two-story brick building that had been expanded regularly as Jackson Clayton College enlarged its programs and its student body. The appealing brick and clapboard colonial architecture that prevailed throughout the picturesque rolling campus was evident in Lancaster Hall as well, but its many renovations and expansions had challenged architectural teams as they struggled to add multi-paned windows, paneled doors, and decorative dentil moldings to an otherwise contemporary, sprawling building. A spacious and luxurious burgundy, beige, and gold auditorium and theater was the most recent addition on the first floor, having been built with financial gifts from anonymous donors and a substantial contribution from the Cantrell Family Arts Trust. The magnificent state-of-the-art facility had been christened the Caleb Mountain Center for the Arts, having taken the name of the highest and most prominent mountain peak that rose close behind the college grounds. Rumor had it that James Cantrell's family owned most of Caleb Mountain, and that many of his kin still resided there. Classrooms, laboratories, conference rooms, and a bookstore filled out Lancaster Hall, the largest building on campus, making it the social center for students as well as a gathering place for faculty and staff. The stately columned library shared the south side of Jackson Clayton's magnificently landscaped campus with Lancaster Hall, making the location the busiest and most populated during the school year.

Chris went into Lancaster Hall through the double doors marked *Caleb Mountain Center.* Minimal lighting in the large auditorium gave it an eerie air of emptiness and emphasized her awareness that she was alone in the cavernous space. A door just below the stairs and to the right of the stage had a hand-lettered sign taped to it that read "Internet Technology Classroom." Chris guessed that learning about the computerized workings of the state of the art equipment in this large public space must be part of the first year technology course. She was once again aware that the color scheme in the auditorium was identical to that she had seen in Bryant Hall and James Cantrell's office. Perhaps he had a hand in everything that concerned this college.

Chris observed the chairs set in several semi-circle rows on the stage, and she noticed the lectern and microphone that stood in the center.

"I guess we sit on the stage and speak at the lectern," she mused. "It would have been nice to hear this from someone else, but at least I know it beforehand."

Chris did not hear the main door open in the back of the auditorium, nor did she see the lone figure that quietly sat down in the darkened back row. He watched her closely as she wandered about the dim, cavernous space, observing her every movement. He felt the power of knowing that they would be together, here and other places he knew so well on campus. This time it would all be different. He would make sure of it.

Chris looked at the stage one last time and walked out the side door of Caleb Mountain Auditorium. She felt confident that everything would work out just fine today and in the future as well.

So did he.

Chapter 19

"Chris, I wanted to congratulate you on that fine presentation you made this morning. You and Mary Ella carried the ball all the way," James Cantrell said as he stood in the doorway to Room 305. "Hal Southern apparently got hung up in fog coming over the mountain from Taylorville. When he called this morning, he said he couldn't see a foot in front of him."

"Thank you. Mary Ella was really the one who presented most of the English Department's information. I just added a few details, but I'm glad you're pleased with the result," she said.

"Great job," he said as he looked around at Chris's office. "This looks wonderful. I like the way you've arranged and organized everything. It looks as if you've been here ten years."

"It's such a beautiful space, Dr. Cantrell, and the patio is so special."

"Please call me James," he said with a smile. "We're all in this on an equal basis, shoulder to shoulder. Are you finding everything you need, Chris, here on campus and in the town?" he asked.

"Yes, I'm happy I was here for the summer. It helped me get acclimated before classes began. I had plenty of time to look around. A friend of mine visited over the Fourth of July, and we even did some exploring around the mountains together," Chris said, as she realized how easy he was to talk to.

"That's good. There's so much to see around here . . . more than meets the eye on first glance," he said. "I've lived in these mountains my whole life. They're a part of me . . . and I of them, I guess I would say. There are some remote but breathtaking overlooks, waterfalls, high flower-covered meadows, not far away, but not easy to find either. Some years back, we had a group of faculty members who were interested in hiking and camping, kind of a loosely organized club, and I led some of the treks. It was a lot of fun. We had some good times. It fell apart when a couple of our members left and another got married to a non-hiker. Maybe I'll see if we have enough interest to get a group together again."

"That sounds like it would be fun," Chris responded. "I'm a real amateur when it comes to trekking, and I've never climbed a steep mountain, but I really enjoy being outdoors . . . and I do like trail hiking, particularly with all this around us," she said as she gestured toward the mountains beyond her patio.

"I'm glad you're enjoying your view," he said quietly. "I had a feeling that you would like this space."

"I really was overwhelmed when I saw it," she said. "When Richard brought me over here, I couldn't believe it was going to be my office. I have to tell you, James, the arboretum in the center of this building is breathtaking. I've never seen anything like it . . . the orchids . . . the tropical trees and plants. I never get tired of looking at it . . . there's always something new to see when I come in the door."

James smiled broadly. "I truly love to grow things," he said. "The tropicals, and particularly the orchids, are really my hobby. I've tried to learn as much as I possibly can about them, and yet, in so many ways, they remain mysterious to me. I don't feel I'll ever really know them." He laughed as he leaned back against the doorframe. "That will teach you to get me started on plants."

"Really, I think it's fascinating," Chris said sincerely.

"I'd better get back to the office and do a few things before this evening's freshman walk. Did anyone tell you about the walk?" he asked.

"Not really. I heard a couple of students talking about it, but I wasn't really tuned in. What is it?"

"It's a tradition at Jackson Clayton College. Other colleges in the USA do the same thing, so it's not exclusive with us, but it's been going on here for a long time. All the freshmen gather at the college gate at 4:00 p.m. on the day of orientation, and the president and each department's dean lead a procession down the road to Clayton Forge. We walk down the main street of the town, all the way out to the community park, and the townspeople always turn out to watch and cheer us on. It's kind of a welcome and an introduction for the students, but it also gives the townspeople some sense of being a part of what we do here at the college. It takes us about three hours from start to our arrival back on campus. When we get back, we have a big barbecue and social get-together for the students. I've never heard anyone say they didn't like it or didn't have a good time. The students from outside the area get to know people other than those in their dormitories, and the locals who are day students get to know those who board. Whoever thought of this a hundred or so years ago, really had a good idea."

"They sure did . . . what a great plan," Chris replied.

"I've enjoyed visiting with you, Chris, . . . welcome aboard. I knew from the first time I met you in New York that you were going to be a great addition. We're fortunate to have you with us."

"Thank you so much for everything," Chris said as she stood up, "and thanks for coming by."

Chris watched as James straightened a painting that hung in the hall outside her office. She suspected that he would also stop and remove a few dead leaves from his thriving plants before he left the building.

She went back to her desk to continue looking over her class rosters, which she had printed after orientation this morning. Chris thought about James's comments about Hal and Mary Ella, and about her participation in orientation. She knew that she had saved the day for the English Department, and she suspected that James Cantrell knew that also. Mary Ella had stopped her earlier in the day, before orientation, as Chris was on her way back to her office.

"Hey, Chris," she had said breathlessly, as she jogged to catch up. "I'm so glad I found you. I've been sick with some stomach bug all weekend, and I just couldn't do a thing to get ready for today. And now, I got a message from Hal, and he's stuck over in Taylorville. I'll tell you about all that when we have more time, but now we need to get ready for our part of the program."

Mary Ella seemed to have trouble catching her breath, even though she and Chris had been standing still for a few minutes. She was no more than five feet tall, and twenty-five or thirty extra pounds obviously made it difficult for her to navigate the gradual mountain grades with any speed.

"Okay . . . I wasn't sure what to do exactly, so I've made some notes, and I've followed some of the format from a previous orientation. Do you want to come back to my office and take a look at what I have?" Chris asked.

"Yes. We have about an hour. I've been teaching here forever, and I can tell you that orientation at JC never changes. Thanks, Chris."

The two teachers had divided Chris's tentative presentation, and Mary Ella had added a few small items from previous years. The two had loosely rehearsed their part of the program and had succeeded in looking professional and prepared when they shared the podium and the mike. James had been right when he said Chris and Mary Ella had "carried the ball all the way." What he didn't say and may not have known was that there wouldn't have been any ball to carry if Chris hadn't prepared as she did. As for Hal Southern, he was just another unknown entity to Chris.

She looked at the computer printouts of her four classes and thought how these unknown names would soon be flesh and blood people she would never forget. Chris's goal always was to know all their first names within three weeks. Looking at a student in class and calling him or her by a name was one of the more dramatic and important things that a teacher did within the first weeks of a class. However, she wouldn't write any names in her grade book for the first two weeks, because students added and dropped classes as they added and dropped acquaintances. What one started out with in college was not necessarily what he or she would end up with. Jack had teased her about her grade book, because she hated to use Whiteout to erase a name. She had grumbled when she had to do so in the third week, blaming the errant student for not knowing what he wanted to study. "Wishy-washy" she had called them.

"Playing school," she would mutter. Jack had laughed and told her she was a "neat freak."

"Poor kids," he had mocked. "They don't know how lucky they are to have dropped your class. Miss Obsessively Neat, except in the bathroom and in her closet, of course." And then she would pretend anger and jump on him wherever he sat, pounding and pummeling him as they both rolled around with laughter . . . and it always ended in hugging and kissing.

Jack was with her in every part of her life . . . at home when she cooked his favorite food . . . at school in the numerous ways he had entered in . . . when she walked a mountain path which he would have liked. She never wanted to be without him, but she wondered if the gnawing, lonely ache would ever leave her. Would the tears ever cease to gather when she remembered what had been so precious to her?

Chris got up and walked out onto the patio. Her view behind Cantrell Hall had not changed with the influx of the first year students. After the upperclassmen returned, she guessed that she would see an occasional student walking or running around the college perimeter, but chances were good that the quiet and the serenity of her office location would remain intact. She looked out to the mountains beyond, feeling the closeness of their stark, imposing grandeur. Even after her short time here, she could understand James's feeling that he and the mountains were part of each other. It was as if the towering masses were alive, watching her, changing her as she watched them.

As Chris turned to go back into her office, she noticed a large spot of what looked to be dried, trampled moss or compost, and the faint streak of cleat marks running through it. For a moment she felt uncomfortable at the thought that some unknown person had been on her patio, outside her office door. Immediately, she mentally scolded herself for her ridiculous anxiety. It was obvious that one of the gardeners had carried it on his boot when he was tending the beds.

Chapter 20

Tabor stood back against the wall at the far end of the long hall, watching the steady stream of students disappear through the door into Room 330. He was too far away to clearly see faces or to hear more than a droning buzz of voices, but he already knew there were no friends among them for him. It didn't matter. The thrilling sense of excitement he felt at this moment had nothing to do with any of those meaningless strangers. His focus was on his plan, and his plan was perfect. He would wait until the numbers dwindled down to one or two, and then he would walk through the door alone and surprise her. She wouldn't be expecting to see someone she knew, least of all him. Tabor leaned his head back, and his eyes closed as he savored a heightened awareness of her. He was overcome with a greedy passion as he anticipated the physical closeness he would know in the next few minutes. He was keenly aware of the difficulties ahead of him, the need to be calm when the others provoked him, the necessity of quieting his raging jealousy, and the struggle to control the feelings that overcame him.

On the day of orientation, Tabor had watched from his mountain sanctuary. He had almost made up his mind to join the other freshmen in Lancaster Hall, until his chilling remembrance of last year's orientation had extinguished any possibility of attendance. How quickly the class bullies had spotted him last August. How cleverly the attention-grabbing freshmen clowns had found him to be a perfect spotlight for them. Nothing could make him go through that again.

His first thoughts this year had been of nothing but seeing and hearing and being near Chris, but as he remembered, he convinced himself that his time with her was just beginning. There would be many classes, and countless other reasons for being together. With every passing day, they would know each other better, and then . . . .

At this point in Tabor's thoughts and plans, the enormity of his relationship and his future with his beautiful lady would often overwhelm him, and the vivid, detailed fantasy would catapult him into a wild frenzy of unbridled mental and physical arousal. At the same time, he would be filled with the ugly perception of who he really was. The need for sexual gratification would crush him and drag him into a dark cavern of semi-consciousness, where he would violently tear and cut and abuse his own hated body. Tabor never remembered when these episodes started, nor did he remember what he did when he was transported into this hell. Hours later, when he escaped back into his reality, he would awaken and see the drying blood on the blade of his knife and feel the throbbing, self-inflicted pain. He was deathly afraid of the times he couldn't remember.

By the time Tabor was able to pick up his binoculars again on orientation day, Chris was back in her office, working at her desk. As he adjusted his focus, he had seen her switch her attention toward the door, and he could see she was talking to someone. Tabor was unable to see her visitor, but he could see a man's figure standing in the doorway. Tabor scrambled over the dry, dusty grass as he frantically tried to bring the man's face into view, but the scope of his viewing field would not allow it. Who was he? What was he saying to her? Tabor saw her smile and then lean back in her chair . . . she liked this man. That was when he decided he had to spend more time on campus with her. It was time to move into the next phase of their relationship, time to speed up his plan. He had to be braver and take some chances. He couldn't afford to let anyone else get in the way.

Chris smiled as the covey of students flitted and sauntered into the room.

"Welcome," she said as she made eye contact with a tall, lanky boy wearing a railroader's cap. He tipped two fingers off the striped bill in response.

"Sit anywhere you like," Chris announced to a group of girls pausing at the side of the classroom. Each was a clone of the other . . . micro-mini jean skirts barely covering little, round bottoms, pastel tank tops stretched tightly across budding, nubile breasts, and the soft flip and flop of the sandals secured between two toes.

"Hey, is this English Comp I?" a boy with a distinct southern accent asked.

"This is it," Chris called to him over the rising din of voices.

"Thank you, Ma'am," he shouted with a wave in her direction.

Slowly the room took on new life, and only a few desks remained unoccupied. Chris listened to the tumult of youthful voices and felt a familiar excitement as she laid the class roster on the lectern.

"Okay, everyone," she said loudly, as she raised her hand to quiet them. "Welcome to English Composition I. I'm Professor Christine Alford."

"I'm here," the deep, flat voice shouted from the doorway at the back of the room.

All heads turned as if synchronized and looked toward the announcement. A low murmur, mixed with some distinct laughter, rolled across the classroom.

"Come in . . . there are a couple of seats up toward the front over there," Chris said as she looked at the familiar figure that lumbered across the back of the classroom. "We were just getting started. Welcome."

Tabor looked at the two available desks and sat down behind a small blond girl wearing shorts and a Virginia Tech tee shirt. Chris saw the girl roll her eyes as Tabor bumped her desk in his efforts to squeeze himself into the cramped space.

"Hey," he said as Chris looked at him and smiled. "Do y'all remember me?"

His loud, cartoon-like voice brought guffaws from the back of the room.

"Yes, indeed," Chris said with a smile. "I do."

She turned her attention to the rest of the class. "Okay, I'm going to call roll. Put up your hand when I call your name, please. I want to put a name and a face together."

The remainder of the fifty minute class period flew by, filled with Chris's usual "expectations and requirements" speech and distribution of the syllabus, and it ended with questions and a writing assignment for Wednesday. The jovial, wise-cracking students who had entered Room 330 in Cantrell Hall, exited it with low-level conversation and considerably more solemn faces, having suddenly recognized that college and work had begun. Chris gathered her scant sheaf of papers and the two bulky textbooks into her navy and green canvass bag before she noticed the student standing in front of her desk.

"I thought y'all would be surprised when you seen me here . . . in yer class," he said in his odd, toneless voice. "Remember, I give ya the cat I made?" Tabor smiled down at her.

"Yes, of course. I remember you very well . . . and I have the cat back in my office. I also remembered your name is

Tabor," she said to him.

"I knew y'all wouldn't ferget," he said happily. "I'm gonna do good in English. I ain't gonna fail it again."

Chris was touched by his honesty. "I don't care what you did last year, Tabor. What is important to me, and to you, is what you do this year. If you work hard and come to class regularly, you can do well." She smiled at him again as she subtly moved the two of them toward the back of the classroom and the door.

"Can I see the cat?" he asked. "Can I come to yer office and see where y'all put it?"

"Well . . . yes . . . of course. I gave everyone a copy of my schedule when I passed out the syllabus. Come by anytime when I have office hours."

"I mean now," he said intently.

"Oh . . . well, sure. My office is in Room 305 in this building," she said as she walked along the hall beside him. "It's around the corner and down the long hall, all the way to the end."

"I know," he said. "I know where it's at. That's where Miss Montgomery used to be . . . before everything happened. I used to visit her sometimes. We was friends." Tabor was silent for a moment and then he added, "She ain't comin' back no more."

Chris suddenly felt cold. He knew Allison . . . and he probably knew what had happened to her, or why she left. The perversity of the situation slammed into her full force. Here was the one person who could undoubtedly answer her questions. The damnable truth was that it didn't matter, because she couldn't ask him anything.

Chapter 21

"Come on in," Hal Southern beckoned to Chris as she hesitated inside the door to the Bryant Hall conference room. "Do you know everyone in the English Department, Chris?" he asked as she made her way toward one of the burgundy and gold upholstered chairs scattered around the rectangular mahogany table.

"We know each other," Mary Ella winked as she looked at Chris.

"I'm Ron Dowd," a tall, graying man in his sixties stood and offered his hand to Chris. "I've been in Alaska all summer, and I haven't had the pleasure of meeting you," he said with a smile. "Welcome to Jackson Clayton College."

"Thank you. It's nice to meet you," Chris said as she shook his hand.

"Hi, I'm Ben Evart. I'm the drama part of the English Department."

Chris reached across the table toward the stocky, red-bearded man who had identified himself. "Hello, Ben . . . happy to meet you."

"Yes . . . he really is the drama part alright," Ron Dowd quipped, with a theatrical roll of his eyes.

"He's just jealous because I know more about

Shakespeare than he does," Ben shot back.

"As you can see, Chris, we're a pretty serious group. I hope you can help us lighten up a little," Hal laughed. "Well, I guess that's the lot of us," he said, as he opened a new spiral notebook lying on the table in front of him and signaled the beginning of their departmental meeting.

"We're most fortunate to have increased our number to five, once again, with the addition of our new colleague Christine Alford. Welcome, Chris," he said formally. "It's our great pleasure to have you in the department."

"Thank you.   I'm very happy to be here," she acknowledged.

"We have the first day of class under our belts, and traditionally, at the end of that critical first day, we gather to informally discuss the year ahead. Let's just take our usual approach . . ." Hal paused and looked at Chris. "Sorry, Chris, I forgot that nothing about us is "usual" to you yet. Here's how it goes. We spend as much time as needed this afternoon talking about anything anyone wants to talk about . . . policy, schedules, students, the administration . . . anything that comes to mind . . . no formality . . . no set time. If it isn't close to midnight when the meeting is over, and if we're all still speaking, we usually go down to the Timber Ridge Café for some food and beverages."

"Sounds good," Chris said.

"Okay, guys, how was your fabulous first day?" Hal put his hands behind his head and leaned back in his chair.

Chris mentally scanned the circle, curious about the politics and unspoken hierarchy that linked her four colleagues. Ron Dowd could be James Cantrell's cousin. There was an uncanny physical similarity between them, from their angular high-boned faces to their crystalline blue eyes and heavy thatch of silvery white hair. Handsome, long-limbed men who were enhanced by the fine wrinkles that fanned out from the corners of their eyes, they were the kind who never lost their appeal to women.   Ron's self-introduction had been delivered in the prolonged soft syllables that Chris had first heard coming from James Cantrell, and his well chosen words had rung with the same gentlemanly tone that she recalled from her first meeting with James in New York.

Ben Evart didn't lend himself to easy assessment or categorization.   He clearly had no southern accent, nor any accent Chris could pick up.   His shaved, shiny head and muscular shoulders and arms indicated a possible athletic bent, maybe a regular gym routine.   His yellow polo shirt was two buttons open, exposing wisps of copper-colored hair rising from his well-muscled chest.   The only hint at drama teacher and theater buff was his striking thick, but tight clipped, carrot red beard.   It was almost flamboyant in its natural color.   In a way, Ben looked like some of the stereotypical pictures of Shakespeare she had seen in literature textbooks, or actors who had portrayed the bard in New York City's Theater in the Park. Chris stifled her humor as she chided herself for her wild, judgmental character sketch.

Hal Southern was still an enigma.   When she had walked into the room some minutes ago, he had hailed her as if they were old friends, or at least acquaintances who had spoken at length on numerous occasions.   Reality was that they had exchanged no more than three minutes of conversation when he had dropped in for a cursory introduction last spring, and she had not set eyes on him nor heard a word from him until this moment.

Mary Ella had told her, "Hal knows more about William Faulkner than anyone I've ever read.   He was actually at the University of Virginia when Faulkner was there as writer in residence . . . he tells everyone he sat in on some of the lectures

Faulkner gave. Hal has written two books considered to be the categorical authority on Faulkner. That's why none of the rest of us will ever get a chance to teach American Literature, no matter how much we might know about all the thousands of others who wrote books and poems." Mary Ella was obviously not in agreement with the position Faulkner had earned for Hal, but she seemed accepting of the futility of changing it.

Chris admired this bit of history she had heard about Hal Southern, but she knew there must be much more than that to this odd man. He looked like an old hippy, who had modestly conformed to a traditional college professor's dress code. His mousy brown and mostly gray hair was neatly pulled back into a five-inch pony tail, secured by a simple brown wrapped elastic. His light blue polyester and cotton no-iron shirt needed ironing, and the khaki slacks were frayed at the use spots. He topped it all off with brown leather Bjorn sandals over wrinkled tan socks. Chris marveled that this man could have been named department head by Richard Shelton or James Cantrell, considering the obvious disparity between him and the two of them.

One thing was clear to Chris after her group examination Mary Ella Sensabaugh was the only choice for female pal in the English Department. Chris knew that, with time, she would get to know math gurus and science types, but that was never quite like having someone to share your own discipline. Problems and frustrations were course and class specific. Chris liked having men as good friends and discussion partners, but men and women approached and interacted with students differently. There were advantages and disadvantages for both sexes. There were some innate characteristics that the opposite sex couldn't identify with, some primal issues that only another of one's own could understand. It was on those few rare occasions that Chris would want another woman's input, and

Mary Ella would be the one. Rachael would always be there, but Rachael didn't know this college.

Ben was talking when Chris pulled herself back to full attention. "Have any of you ever had Crystal Dalton or Abby McKendry in your classes?"

Hal considered the question momentarily and then said, "No, I don't know them."

"Mary Ella, did you have them in your Comp I or Comp II classes?" Ben asked.

"No, I know who they are, but I've never had them in a class."

"Then Allison must have taught them both semesters their first year," Ben said. "I correct myself. I should have said both of them sat in Allison's classroom . . . when she was there. I gave all of my Drama I students an in-class writing assignment this morning, which I always do, just to see if they're up to the theater reviews I assign every week. I'll swear, those two don't have a clue as to how to write an essay. It's as if they just arrived from a second rate high school. I read through the samples before coming over here, and there are eight or ten others who clearly were out of their league. I don't have time to teach drama *and* Comp I," he said emphatically, looking directly at Hal. Ben's face and exposed neck had turned a shade darker. He crossed his arms in front of his chest and said, "I don't intend to teach Comp I."

"Okay, let's not get into a wrangle about what Allison did and didn't do," Hal said somewhat defensively. "She's not here . . . and we don't know . . . so let's move on. If we need to establish some special tutoring for a handful of people, or for a classroom of people, I'm confident Richard will go along with it. Put together a list of students from your classes who might be candidates. Let's see how many there are. Get back to me next week and we'll talk about it. We'll work on offering a free

Comp I brush up."

"Thanks," Ben said sullenly. "I'm afraid it will have to be more than a brush up, folks."

"Since we're onto it, anyone else have any questions or concerns about students or class numbers? We'll know later this week and next if we have any bigger problems." Hal waited for the group's response.

"Could you share with me what your policy is about office hours and students after hours?" Chris asked. "Do you have an open door policy, or are you pretty strict with maintaining posted office hours?"

There was a moment of silence as the others seemed to weigh Chris's question.

Ron Dowd spoke in his rolling sing-song drawl. "I've always been pretty casual about seeing students when they drop in. If I'm in my office and the door is open, I'll usually talk to them. In all my years of teaching here, I've never had a problem with that. I've never had anyone hanging around in an annoying way, so it has worked for me. If I can't see someone, I'll tell him so, and it usually works out. We make an appointment or he comes back another time." He paused before carefully proceeding. "But I know there were some problems last year, some pretty serious problems, as I understand it. Hal or Mary Ella, you probably know more about that than I do."

Mary Ella's face flushed when Ron mentioned her name. "I wasn't involved," she said breathlessly. "Not at all. I don't know anything other than what you told me, Hal. I never turned in anyone's name or reported that I had a problem personally."

"I don't think this is answering Chris's question," Hal said. "Chris, you've been teaching a long time. You know how students and classes differ year to year . . . and what works for some teachers doesn't work for others. You're free to establish your own open or closed door policy. The only thing we're required to do is to have regular office hours three times a week. We have to maintain those. If I were new on this campus, I would stick to those office hours and close my door most of the other time. Get to know the students . . . then make a decision."

"Thanks. That's probably good advice. I asked the question because I had a student who came back to my office today. He asked if he could come with me after class, and I said 'yes.' He's a nice enough young man, but I was afraid he was going to camp out for the night."

Chris's humorous suggestion brought laughs from her colleagues, all of whom were familiar with the student who stayed too long.

"Probably his first time away from home," Ben offered wisely. "I think sometimes they stay on and on when they're lonely, but I ain't their papa," he added with a smile.

"Could be," she replied. "I can see why he would be lonely . . . he's an odd one."

"Most all of the Comp I English students are new on campus," Mary Ella said. "I think most of them are scared to death, but they don't dare show it. Don't all of you remember your first semester at college? I remember mine. I was so naïve . . . about everything."

"Mary Ella, Sweetheart, you still are," Ben chortled, as he patted her arm.

"Not everyone in Comp I is new on campus," Hal said. "We have five students who are repeating it this semester."

"I believe this fellow is a repeat," Chris said. "He told me he wasn't going to fail again, and I assume he took English I at this college. I don't know that for sure, but I did see him this summer at the street fair in Clayton Forge."

"Who is he?" Hal asked. "Or maybe it's better if you don't tell us. One of us had him in class last year, if he went to this school, and we probably have a jaded opinion, based on his lack of success. I think it's better to form your own opinion of a student, rather than taking on another teacher's opinion . . . at least that's my philosophy."

"I agree with you, Hal," Chris said. "He seems as if he wants to do a good job this year, and I'm hoping that he does. He deserves an unbiased second chance."

"It could be he was in Allison's class," Ben said sourly.

"I believe he was. He knew where my office was and he told me she had been in that office. If he brings his sleeping bag, I'll call on the rest of you for some help," she laughed. "In the meantime, I think I can handle it."

"You know, Chris, you do have access to any student's records that you request. You can get them from Student Services and most of the time you can get a report from the disciplinary committee and any of the review committees. Don't hesitate if you think it might help you," Ron said. "I've done it on a few occasions."

"Thanks, I'll remember that," she said with a smile. Chris hesitated, then took a deep breath. "May I ask what kinds of problems you were referring to, Ron . . . last year?"

"I think Hal is better able to answer that question than I am, Chris."

The four teachers sat silently, eyes on Hal. He cleared his throat and fumbled with the top pages in his spiral notebook. The hum of the air conditioning became apparent for the first time since they had entered the room.

"I'm not really privy to much information," Hal said as he looked down at the table. "As far as I know, Richard Shelton and James Cantrell . . . ." He cleared his throat again and looked up at the four who waited. "I'm only called a department head. It's not much different, if any different, than being a professor. The guys in this building don't share much

125

with us. I think all of you, possibly with the exception of Chris, know about as much as I do concerning last year's problems."

"Well, we want to hear what you know," Ben said. "I'm glad you asked the question, Chris, because, frankly, I don't think we ever really knew what was going on. Was it true? Was it fantasy? Tell us what you know, Hal."

Hal turned slightly toward Chris. "Last year, a former English teacher, Allison Montgomery, had a few incidents she reported to Student Services, about a student who was harassing her . . . frightening her, she said. A week before Allison left her job here, she sent a letter to Marsha Tilley, one of the guidance counselors, and it upset Marsha terribly. I don't really know what the letter said . . . never saw it . . . don't know who did, other than Marsha. Rumors were flying all over the place. Someone who supposedly saw the letter said that Allison believed a man on campus was going to kill her. All of you heard that rumor. Within a week of that letter, Allison packed up and left campus overnight, and Marsha resigned a week later and left. All of you have heard what I'm repeating to you. You know the mess we were in when Allison left. Four teachers had to pick up a five-teacher load. With Richard's help, we did it. Was there a student harassing Allison? Was there a letter? Even if there was a letter, was there a real threat, or was it Allison's mental condition? None of us will ever know. The local police, state police, even the FBI were around here for a long time, and looked into all sorts of things. We all remember. But there was nothing found, as far as I know."

Hal's face was pale and the dark circles under his somber eyes seemed to deepen. He looked down again before continuing.

"We might as well get it all out on the table. All of us but Chris worked with Allison. We observed her wild mood swings, we saw the papers piling up on her desk, and we fielded questions from confused or angry students. She missed more class time than any teacher I've ever worked with. I believe Allison was a deeply troubled woman, and I think it is best that she left this job in this college. I wish her well, wherever she may be. I've had no communication from her, and I have not been asked for a recommendation as her immediate supervisor. The rumors are still floating around everywhere . . . on the campus . . . in the town. We need to forget them and move on with our lives. Chris, that's the best and most complete answer I can give you." Hal looked directly across the table and said, "Ben, please don't ask me to repeat this again."

"Did Allison ever tell anyone in this room who the 'student' or 'man' was that was frightening her, or threatening to kill her?" Ben examined his fingernails as he asked the question.

"It doesn't matter, Ben . . . let it go," Hal said quietly. "It wouldn't be fair to that person or those people, would it, even if she had told someone? No one did any harm to anyone. That's what I believe."

"It would be 'fair' if the creep had killed Allison, wouldn't it?" he said in a soft, sarcastic voice. Then identifying him or them would be 'fair.'"

"No one told me anything," Mary Ella said, her eyes widening as she spoke, "but I think maybe it was that big, ugly boy with the long black hair who was hanging around Allison all the time. She was giving him cupcakes and loaning him books and trying hard to be nice to him. But then I think she got scared. She never talked to me much about anything, but I saw her slam her door one day when he was coming down the hall, and I heard her lock it from the inside."

Hal stood up and said, "This conversation has gone too far, and it's over, as far as I'm concerned. All those faces, names, and accusations are gone with last semester. This is a new year. Let's do our job for the people who are here, and forget about the rumors of years past." He sounded eloquent as he ended the meeting.

"Anyone for Timber Ridge Café?" Ben asked. "We always end on a happy note . . . remember?"

„"Sure, I'll be there," Ron said, "as soon as I take this stuff back to my office."

"I'm in," Hal replied. "Why don't we meet there in thirty minutes."

"Chris, you want to ride with me?" Mary Ella asked. "Just leave your car here, and I'll bring you back on my way home. We never stay late . . . school tomorrow."

"Thanks, Mary Ella. I'll meet you in the parking lot . . . fifteen minutes," Chris called to her as she picked up her bag and briefcase and headed toward the door.

As she walked back to Cantrell Hall, Chris felt the light breeze that rolled lazily off of the mountain, and she listened to the rising calls of the cicadas and tree frogs as they revved up for the coming August evening. It all seemed so peaceful, so right for her. Yet, as she reviewed the afternoon's conversation, the thought that kept floating menacingly to the top of all others was that of Mary Ella's description of "the big, ugly boy with the long black hair." Chris fought desperately against the realization that she did not want to accept, but she knew Mary Ella had been describing Tabor Maclean.

Chapter 22

Tabor was close to running by the time he got to the rutted, dusty path that served as the Maclean's driveway. Mawmaw sat on the splintered edge of the rickety back porch, shelling fat green field peas into a black cast iron pot, intending to cook them with a piece of fatback pork for their evening meal. She swiped at the lazy autumn flies that occasionally tangled and buzzed in the thin wisps of her dull gray hair, as she was lost in the thoughts she shared with no one. Mawmaw often sat with her legs hanging over the front edge of the uneven, rotting floor, sometimes swinging them, childlike, back and forth over the sharp precipice, as she looked down the long hill toward the chiseled banks of the stream below that changed with the seasons. Its rocky bed was dry now, as it waited for spring, when the melting winter's snow would bring it to wild, rushing life once again. This was a place of peace for her.

"Hey, Mawmaw . . . I been to class today . . . got me some books with the money the school give me, like ya said . . . and me an' Miss Christine Alford talked at her office."

"Slow down, Boy. Y'all are sweatin' and breathin' like a stuck pig." She smiled up at him as he crowded in next to her on the teetering old boards that had once supported posts and a railing that protected the precarious edge. "I'm glad yer happy about goin' to college this year. I knew it would get better fer ya. Some things jest take time, Tabor . . . like I told ya."

Mamaw looked at him and remembered the seven year old who had run up the same ruts in the driveway on his first day of school, sweat glistening on his smooth, round face, calling to her and holding out flapping pieces of paper covered with a child's bright red and green Crayola dreams. That was before he knew what she had always known, before he had seen the ugliness and felt the viciousness that was heaped on misfits like him. In later years, her heart had broken when he had told her, "There ain't no one to be my friend, Mawmaw. There don't seem to be no right place for me anywhere."

She knew that she alone loved him, this strange and oversized giant of a gentle boy in a seething and angry man's body. Sometimes when she couldn't sleep, she would sit on this back porch with the little portable radio Dr. Cantrell and Mattie had given her for Christmas some years back, and she would listen to the mournful country ballads about love gone wrong and sweethearts who died young. With the music tuned down low, she would watch the fireflies darting among the moonlit squash vines in Pap's disheveled garden, and she would cry over the boy. . . her Amber's boy. It was the only time tears fell from her soulful eyes . . . never when Pap hit her in a drunken fit of meanness . . . never when her thin, blue-veined legs throbbed and ached so much she could hardly stand . . . not even when Amber Jean had left them. Those tears were down deep inside her soul, buried with so much else. But she couldn't keep all the tears for Tabor inside her. She remembered thinking that it would have been easier if he had died with his mama, harder then, maybe, but easier for him later. Pap had said so more than once, that the boy should have died with Amber Jean. And he had wished it to be so.

It had pained her to watch him grow, to see him slowly withdraw from the treacherous world into the only safe place he knew, inside himself. Perhaps her sinfulness with Pap when they were just children, and Amber Jean's after her, had brought God's terrible punishment down on the boy. She didn't know. She heard what the preacher man said when she went to the summer tent meetings in Clayton Forge, but she wasn't sure how God really worked. Did he strike out at those who broke his rules by hurting their little children, or did God weep with her when she wept over Amber Jean's son?

Mawmaw remembered that Lucas Maclean had come to help her pa with building the new chicken house when she was fifteen. He was tall and swarthy, but blue eyed . . . the dark Irish mixed with the fair Scott. His square, white teeth glistened as he smiled at her, and his tanned teenage body was hard and lean. "Y'all sure are a pretty thing," he said to her one day, while she was piling hay in the barn, and then he reached over and pulled her down to where he sat. Surrounded by the clover-laced fragrance of the first cut hay, he gently put his mouth on hers, and, for the first time, she felt the soft brush of his unshaven young face and the urging of his tongue into her slightly open mouth.

Every day after that, she wrapped soft pink ribbons in her long golden hair and laughed and twirled about him while he worked. Soon he told her he loved her, and she knew she loved him too. Then their summer had become one long, seductive secret in the cool dark caves up by Walker's Gap, with Lucas holding and kissing her breasts and setting her on fire with what he did between her legs, things she had never imagined and couldn't let herself think about even now. When her Ma had said to her one day when she was late for supper, "Suelean, don't y'all go lettin' any boy put a baby in ya, or y'all be sorry the rest a yer life," she really didn't know what Ma had meant. By the time she had realized that she was just like their brown and white cow in the pasture when her pa borrowed the Tate's bull for the week, it was too late. Sulean McDannell was fifteen and with child when she married Lucas Maclean in the little Baptist church in Clayton Forge . . . and he still said he loved her.

"Yeah, Mawmaw, me an Miss Chris is gonna get along fine. She likes me, and I ain't gonna miss no more classes."

"That's good . . . that's real good," she said quietly. "Tabor, y'all got to remember that this Miss Christine is yer teacher. Y'all got mixed up about that before. She ain't yer best friend, Tabor, and she ain't like you and me. She ain't gonna know ya that well."

"Y'all don't need to talk like that, Mawmaw. This is gonna be different." He toed the gathered dust with his big cleated boot while Mawmaw talked to him.

She didn't want to spoil his good feelings, yet she had seen and heard too much to let it go easily.

"Tabor, when we went to talk to Dr. Cantrell last year . . . remember that?"

"Yes, Ma'am," he replied.

"Well, he said you was a special student to him and he knew you was smart, and he wanted to see you finish at the college so you could get one of them jobs he has over in the computer rooms. Remember all that, Tabor?" she asked quietly.

"Course I remember. Why do y'all think I can't remember things?" he asked with obvious irritation.

She had to walk softly, but it had to be said. "Tabor, y'all need to remember that Dr. Cantrell can't help ya if ya get in any more trouble with them trampy girls over there. They jest try to upset you young boys, and then they go and make a whole lot a trouble when ya pay them any attention. Y'all gotta leave them alone."

He stood up and turned to look down at his grandmother. "Mawmaw, I don't want them scrawny girls no more. I got me someone better. I tried to tell ya. ." He clenched his fists in frustration.

Mawmaw's high, moaning cry shattered the air around them. "No, Tabor, that's what I'm tryin' to tell ya. Y'all gotta accept that ya got no one . . . no one like y'all think ya' do. Ya got no one."

Tabor was momentarily startled by Mawmaw's tears. He had never seen her cry. But his malignant anger overcame all else.

"I ain't stayin' with ya' no more," he roared. Y'all are jest like all the rest . . . tryin' to tell me I don't know. It's you that don't know," he shouted as he punched his fists at the empty air.

"You that don't know," he repeated, swinging his big hand over his head, as if to propel it downward in a crushing blow that would destroy whatever loathsome thing he found beneath it. "Damn y'all to hell!" His loud, flat bellow thundered and echoed menacingly around them. "Ya ain't nothin' but an ugly old woman who don't know nothin'," he boomed at her, his shaggy beard outlined with the crimson of his fury. "I hate ya . . . I ain't never comin' back here . . . y'all jest go to hell."

Blind rage consumed him as Tabor jumped from the porch to the dusty gravel path and lumbered like a wounded bear toward the escape of the road beyond. As Mawmaw tried to scramble to her feet to bring her beloved Tabor back, the awkward, heavy black pot of field peas tipped forward. As she grabbed at it, she lost her balance, and she fell headfirst over the edge of the porch floor, its precarious drop-off no longer protected by posts and a railing that had long ago rotted away. She somersaulted heavily to the ground, banging her arm on the edge of a cracked cement block that lay abandoned on the steep hill. Tumbling and rolling a third of the way down the trash strewn slope, Mawmaw landed face first on the bare, rocky mountain ground.

She felt the warm trickle that started above her left eye and moved down her wrinkled cheek, but she couldn't raise her arm to it. Her crumpled body lay quietly, as if in a distorted, peaceful sleep. The last thing she remembered was Tabor's anguished shouting, and her lucid realization that they had already been damned to an earthly hell.

Chapter 23

Blue-white forks of neon lightning flashed in the dusky sky next to him, seeming to have bolted straight up from the yellowing green of the dry valley below. James Cantrell wondered how many times he had driven this snaking band of narrow asphalt that wound erratically around and around Caleb Mountain, rising up to end at 3,200 feet above sea level at the mountain crossroads of Tuggles Gap. This was Cantrell country. There was scant history of this area and his people before the coal rush, but stories and some evidence existed to connect the family name to credible Revolutionary War patriots and courageous champions of the Confederacy who fought to the end in the American Civil War. Tuggles Gap was no more than a five mile notch that nature's cataclysmic upheavals had carved out of the topside of Caleb Mountain. It existed by default, settled by early pioneers who lost heart when they lost their way trying to cross its hellish, craggy peaks, futilely searching for the legendary New River Valley.

James had never been without the great wealth and financial extravagance that his grandfather and his father had created from the mountain's black gold that they claimed as theirs. With every hole they blasted, with every shaft they ran, the awesome power of what lay underground in the unrestrained excessiveness of the shiny, black layers became the Cantrells's single focus and driving obsession. As a boy, James had watched the ashen, weeping women who kept vigils outside the collapse of poorly reinforced mines. Some clasped pale, silent babies to their heaving chests, while others clung to the tiny hands of spindly-legged children . . . waiting . . . always waiting . . . for those they knew would never again breathe the piney mountain air. As he grew, James had lost count of the gaunt mountain men with flickering lanterns still attached to their bowed heads, who had died far below the earth's surface, sacrificed to the insatiable monster of Cantrell profit and big business.

"They can't make money like I pay them anywhere else. It's their choice," James's father would say arrogantly as he shrugged off the twelve-year-old's questions about the reoccurring sequences of death.

Exasperated, he would run his big hands through his silver glazed black hair and look down at his only son with open contempt.

"No one's gonna respect you, Boy, if you don't toughen up . . . you have to be the boss around here someday. You can't mince around because some few hillbilly miners died down there. Look at all those we feed every day . . . look at the houses we give them. Nobody all the way down to Martinsville has jobs like these boys do. They'd starve if it wasn't for us. Y'all just got to toughen up. A man needs to go after what it is that he wants, and then he needs to grab it and hold on . . . anyway he can. Respect is the key, Boy. Without respect a man has nothing."

As the miners died inside the earth, James watched as his father and his grandfather before him died from within, infected by their voracious greed and incurable addiction to more and more. By the time he was sixteen, James knew he could not . . . would not . . . stay. At eighteen, he was a wealthy man, his trusts and accounts having been swelled to overflowing with his incontestable share of the black magic that continued to flow out of the rich, bottomless mountain. The last time he saw his father alive, he had watched his father's lip curl in disgust when James told him he was going to go to college.

"I'm following your advice," James had said. "I know what I want, and I'm going after it . . . anyway I can." He had found some grim, visceral pleasure in repeating his father's words. "I'll get my own kind of respect," he had said boldly. "There's no real respect from widows and orphans. You get someone else to wallow in that shit pile of respect."

His father's heavy-boned face had become a dark, malicious mask, as he bitterly eyed this flesh of his flesh with revulsion.

"I'm ashamed of you, Boy. No Cantrell has ever been ashamed like I am. You won't find respect, James . . . shame and grief will rot your bones . . . and you'll never know respect. You're nothing to me . . . you're nothing."

James's chest felt tight as the dull, empty ache gnawed at his soul. It was always the same when he came up the mountain. "The ghosts of ages past," he thought bitterly.

Few people at the college knew he went to Tuggles Gap, or would have cared if they had known. Only Mattie and Richard knew he had the big rambling Victorian house his grandfather had pretentiously built, but neither of them had ever seen it. Grandad Cantrell had wanted to give loud notice to the world that he was now separate and apart from the hillbilly mountain men whose ancestors had come side by side with his to settle Caleb Mountain . . . the same hillbilly mountain men who breathed the sooty dust in his mines and died bringing his money to the top. After his father's death, James had sold the mining business as soon as he legally could. Formidable hired-guns . . . tough men, by James's father's standard . . . ran the mines now, but the royalties and much of the profit still belonged to Cantrell. The big house and all the land was still Cantrell, and it would be as long as there was a Cantrell to receive it. The gray stone mansion sat imperiously on a small bluff, its mansard roofs, high arched windows, and iron roof pinnacles overlooking the small town. It was a haughty observatory with a 180 degree view of the black open maws of the endless mine entrances.

James had been born in the big master bedroom on the second floor, in the high-backed, dark oak bed last slept in by his dying father. On the rare occasions when he had to return to the old house, James slept in the pale yellow room down the hall, the room he thought of as his mother's room. It was here that she had died when he was seven, along with the unborn son she had never been able to release into life.

James cranked the wheel of the silver BMW sharply to the right, feeling the slight bump as the big sedan climbed over the raised driveway entrance. Audrey or Lester had turned on the massive black lanterns that sat atop the expertly crafted granite stone posts, as well as the perfectly placed smaller lantern replicas that lined the graceful, curving drive that led to the front door. The Abernathys were simple mountain folks, never having traveled beyond Clayton Forge in their lifetime. The elderly couple had moved into the two tacked-on rooms at the back of the rambling structure when James's father had died. They had worked for James for thirty-five years, maintaining every detail of the house and gardens in perfect order, never asking questions, always appearing happy to welcome him "home."

The imposing estate with its well-manicured grounds and extensive gardens had been much more important to him over the past decade than it had been in earlier days, although that would not have been his choice. Without it, he recognized that he might not have been able to continue his passionate mission at the college, he might not have been able to complete the visionary task that would guarantee the survival of the Cantrell name and all that was attached to it. Now, maybe the madness, the absurdity, the unreasonableness were at an end. This time he had researched and investigated thoroughly, and this time he felt confident that it could be as he had always meant it to be. As James stood in the last lingering light of the fading day, he surveyed this other world of which he was a part, and he painfully, but meticulously, cataloged the disastrous mistakes he had made. They had shaken him to his core. His stupidity, his frailty, could have been fatal . . . but he had prevailed. This time he would proceed with an aging man's caution. He had risked all, and this very well could be his last chance.

James pressed down on the polished brass handle and pushed the heavy, carved door into the high-ceilinged, softly-lit entrance hall. The familiar fragrance of roasting meat and fresh baked bread wafted from the kitchen, strangely comforting him. He had only tomorrow to make sure all of his instructions had been carried out to his satisfaction. It was at times such as these that his perfectionism and his obsession with detail paid off. He reluctantly accepted that one more autumn trip would be necessary, before the first snow and before a heavy freeze had overtaken the mountain landscape. As he resigned himself to it, his heart suddenly soared with thoughts of the changes that would come with the new birth of the Appalachian spring. That was the next trip he dreamed of, the one that would begin a new, long-awaited life.

Chapter 24

"Rumor has it that the English Department partied big-time down at the Timber Ridge last night," Glen said with a mischievous grin. He leaned casually on one hand against the door casing in Chris's office, peering at her over the top of his wire-rimmed glasses.

"You must have a direct line to the rumor mill," Chris laughed as she looked up at the slightly disheveled math teacher. "Come on in."

Chris couldn't help but smile at her colleague's startling island attire, an obvious attempt on his part to hang on to his Caribbean dream vacation. The big, bright red, green, and yellow hibiscus flowers on Glen's oversized cream-colored shirt seemed to overwhelm his small frame, giving the appearance that a big shirt was walking around with a bespectacled pin head and stick figure arms. LL Bean chino pants completed the incongruous outfit. Chris liked this character who was becoming her friend.

"Honest to God, I think the only good thing that comes out of these ridiculous first week meetings is the booze at the end of the day. I would say the food, too, but we're talking about the Timber Ridge," he said as he ballooned out his cheeks.

"Well, I know it was hard for me to drag myself out of a warm bed this morning, and I only shared a bottle of wine with two other people. Some folks, who shall go unnamed," she said with a giggle, "might have had difficulty making it to their second day of classes."

"Ben's a buddy of mine," Glen laughed. "I saw him crawling up the hall this morning on his way to his office. He said it was a rousing good time."

"It was fun," Chris said. "It was good for all of us . . . really good for me to get to know them."

Glen had pulled a small green plaid upholstered side chair closer to where Chris sat behind her desk. He stared over her shoulder for a moment at the cloud shadows that floated gracefully in dark patches across the illumined sides of the timbered mountains. The views never ceased to humble him.

"Look at that, Chris . . . those shadows on the mountains. I never get over it . . . as long as I've been here. It's damn mystical," he said softly. "That's why I stay."

"It is mesmerizing," she agreed. "Almost . . . compelling. You know what I mean?"

"Yes," he said. "It takes over."

They sat in comfortable silence for some seconds, both captivated by the changing hues of the blue-violet Appalachian range. Suddenly, a glinting prism of icy brightness flared off of an unseen sunlit ledge, vanishing as quickly as it had appeared.

"Did you see that?" Glen asked. "It looked like there was a giant reflective crystal over there. Amazing what a light show the sun can create on those escarpments."

"I did see it," Chris replied. "There . . . I saw it again. It's like the mountain is sending us a message," she laughed. "It's a reflection of some kind. We could sit here and be entertained all day."

"You have a ring side seat," Glen mused. "I've always felt this office is the best in the building. I'm happy for you . . . really happy you have it."

"Thanks, Glen. You can come and share the view

anytime you like."

"I told you I'd get back to you, Chris . . . about the questions you asked." Glen didn't look at Chris when he spoke to her, but continued to look past her out the window. "I've thought about it a good deal . . . and I'm willing . . . not really sure it's the right thing . . . but willing to give you my take on all the crap from last year . . . and Allison."

"Glen, I don't want you to feel pressured. I don't have any right to expect anything from you, and you don't have any responsibility to tell me anything. I'm beginning to get the message that this is a much bigger issue than I comprehended when I asked my initial questions. If you want to talk about it, of course I want to know answers, but I don't expect it."

"Chris, I don't want to start rumors, or fan the flames that are already burning. For now, I'd like this conversation to stay inside this room, between the two of us." He had leaned forward with his elbows on his knees and was staring between his legs at the floor.

"You have my word, Glen." Chris quietly got up and went over to close the office door.

He straightened and stretched his back and began talking, almost as if his words were being recorded.

"I think I knew Allison Montgomery as well as any of the rest of the faculty knew her, which I've decided was not well at all. She was a real enigma . . . sweet, kind . . . scattered, jittery. She came here three years ago, and I never really knew where she came from . . . where she'd been." He looked intently at Chris. "I met you about three months ago, and I know more about you than I ever knew about her."

"I tend to be kind of an open book," Chris replied with a slight smile.

"She and I used to hang out together sometimes . . . coffee at the union or in our offices . . . occasionally a beer or two at Timber Ridge. We talked about school, shared classroom stories, the usual. I enjoyed her company. Nothing romantic, just friends. As far as I could tell, she appealed to the students, she had a following. Allison was a pretty, freckle-faced redhead with a sense of humor, and in the beginning, an easy laugh. I think the kids found her approachable.

"About half-way through her second year here, I noticed a change. She started missing lots of classes, calling in sick, or worse. Mattie or Richard would come looking for her because she just hadn't shown up. Students would wander around asking if anyone knew where Professor Montgomery was. About the same time, Allison and I stopped getting together. She was never available to have a coffee . . . never said why . . . just said she couldn't do it. When I did see her she looked shaky, like she was on the edge of being sick. I asked her one day if she was okay, and she said she had a lot on her mind . . . said she would sit down and tell me about it one day."

Glen leaned his head back against the soft, rounded top of the chair and closed his eyes. "I should have pursued that," he said. "I should have pursued that . . . but I didn't."

"Glen, are you sure you want to continue this?" Chris asked gently.

"Yeah . . . I do. As all this bizarre behavior became more apparent to me, I began to notice that this big bruiser of a kid, a student of hers, was hanging around her office a lot, sometimes sitting in the arboretum waiting for her to come in, sometimes sitting on the floor outside her locked office. I don't usually pay much attention to what students look like, but this guy was an attention-getter . . . rough looking . . . wild black hair and a *Deliverance* kind of beard. A couple of times I asked him if I could help him, and he always said he was waiting for Allison, 'Miss Allison,' as he called her. One time I came up behind him. His back was to me and he had his ear pressed against Allison's closed door . . . listening at her door, for God's sake."

Chris felt her throat constrict as she stared at the door in Glen's story . . . her door.

"I yelled at him and said, 'What the hell do you think you're doing?' and he whirled around like he was going to hit me. He said the same old thing . . . 'waiting for Miss Allison,' and I told him to get the hell out of Cantrell Hall. I could tell he was mad. I decided I had to talk to Allison about him, so I called and left a message on her telephone . . . just said I needed to talk to her. She called me from home two days later . . . said she'd had the flu, and we could get together the next day. We planned to meet in the parking lot about 6:00 p.m. and go to Timber Ridge for something to eat . . . her idea. The next day I waited until after 7:00 and decided she wasn't coming. As I was driving by Bryant Hall on my way off campus, I saw Allison's car parked outside the building. It really ticked me off. I thought the least she could have done was call me, so I parked and went into Bryant to find her. The place was pretty deserted by this time . . . some cleaning people around, one old woman mopping the floor . . . but no one else. Then I saw lights reflecting from Cantrell's suite, so I strolled down that way. There was only one lamp lit in the reception room, and Mattie's desk was all closed up for the day, but a light was on in Cantrell's inner sanctum, and I heard voices. I had no right to do it, but I stood outside in the hall and listened . . . and I heard Allison's voice . . . and Cantrell's."

"I'm not sure you should say anymore, Glen," Chris said. "Don't compromise yourself. I don't have any right to hear any of this." She found herself pleading with him.

"I should have told someone a long time ago," he said quietly.

"Allison was crying. I could hear her repeating over and over again, 'Please don't tell me anymore . . . I can't hear it . . . please don't.' Cantrell was talking softly, like he was trying to soothe her. He kept saying, 'It's okay, Allison . . . it's okay. You need to listen to me. I wanted you to know.' I couldn't see them at all, but I heard her say, 'Don't, James . . . not now . . . I have to go . . . please.'

"I left at that point because I didn't want to get caught outside the door. I used the far end corridor exit because I didn't want to be obvious when I went back to my car. I decided to cruise back around Cantrell Hall, in case Allison did come back here before leaving. I sat outside in my car, maybe twenty minutes, and when she didn't come back to her office, I decided to go home. It was after 8:30 p.m. by this time, dark and cold outside, and Allison's car was still in the parking lot when I passed Bryant Hall. But Cantrell's office lights were out, and I didn't see his car. As I was driving around the first curve in the highway toward Clayton Forge, I saw the big, hulky kid who had been hanging around Allison. He was running along the side of the road with a big bag slung over his shoulder. It looked like an oversized gym bag. When he saw the car lights, he took off into the woods, dragging the bag behind him."

A spasm gripped Chris's stomach as she looked at Glen's tight, pinched face. She sat silently, wishing he would stop, hoping he wouldn't.

"I'm not sure why I did it, but the next morning I came to campus real early, a little before 7:00 a.m. Allison's car was still in the same place in the parking lot. I am absolutely sure of that. She wasn't in her office, and she didn't meet her classes. I never saw her again. When I walked over to Bryant Hall after my eight o'clock class, her car was gone. The next day, the story spread by Cantrell and Shelton was that she had left in the middle of the night . . . for personal reasons."

"Glen, have you told all this to anyone else?"

"Some details. The state police and the FBI know I was on campus that evening, waiting for Allison in the parking lot, but I didn't tell them I heard her crying in Cantrell's office. I think that would have cost me my job. They questioned me

because I had been waiting for her. Cantrell said he had talked
to her later in the evening, so the police took his word as fact,
which was in my favor, of course. I did tell the officers, and
Shelton and Cantrell, about the big dark-haired kid who was
hanging around her, and that I had seen him that evening, but
no one seemed to take much notice. When one of the FBI guys
said he wanted to check that out, Cantrell said he knew him . . .
said he didn't believe he would harm anyone. Right in front of
Richard and me, Cantrell told the police that he would
personally vouch for the guy and keep an eye on him. That
seemed to be enough for everyone else. I don't know whether
the FBI took it any further or not."

Glen sat in exhausted silence, staring at nothing. Chris
listened to his shallow breathing and the soft tick-tick of the
little banjo clock she had hung on her office wall. Words had left
her.

Glen raised his head and looked directly into Chris's
eyes. "Chris, I don't think Allison left in the middle of the
night, at least not by herself. I don't believe we know what
happened to her . . . I'm afraid to know," he said, struggling to
control the quavering in his voice, ". . . but I think Allison is
dead."

Chapter 25

As soon as Chris opened her office door and stepped out into the hall, she could hear the low droning echo of voices coming from the other end of the building. As she turned the corner and headed down the long corridor that was anchored by Room 330, she saw the milling, leaning crowd that clustered outside the classroom. All eyes were on her as soon as they spotted her. She stepped out confidently, long, striding steps and a smile and eye contact leading the way.

"Door's locked," called out a tall, lanky tow-headed boy from the midst of three others who looked just like him. Knitted athletic shorts, white tee shirts, and rubber flip-flops uniformed them, along with half a dozen others hanging in their own observant clusters. "Guess we gotta go home . . . no place for class," he quipped, eyeing his grinning followers as he spoke.

"You wouldn't get your money's worth then, would you," Chris laughed. "I certainly wouldn't want to be responsible for that."

"Try us," came a terse reply from the far side of the crowd.

Chris slid the key into the lock and pushed in the door with one graceful sweep. She flipped on all the overhead lights

147

and stood casually inside the door as the throng filed in and spread out over the room. As she might have predicted, it appeared that everyone had shown up for this second class of the semester. Resolution and commitment were still high . . . first year students on their way to a college education . . . the lure of fame and fortune and the American Dream. They would give her a few days, this week, and then she would have to do more than smile and be friendly to keep them coming. They would quickly abdicate their attendance responsibility in favor of her ongoing dog and pony show. After all, they were the generation brought up to be entertained. Wasn't she part of that entertainment? What did she have to offer that would keep them interested? What new and exciting games did she have to pop onto X-Box?   For most of her teaching years, these disparate, slightly cynical thoughts had taken up fitful residence in Chris's first few weeks of a semester. She accepted that part of it was her unhealthy obsession with being super teacher, wanting to be all things to each of them, and another portion was her own insecurity at the prospect that she might not make the grade this time.

"Hang in there, Kiddo," she had told herself this morning on the foggy drive over to campus. "Today is the day it starts to get interesting."

Her chilling reflection on yesterday's conversation with Glen had caused multiple reactions in Chris. The seductive possibility that something horrific had happened, the overt suggestion that Allison had been murdered, frightened her. She had stepped clone-like into the proverbial shoes of this other person, her office, her classes, her colleagues . . . even her unfortunate misfit student. If Chris let it take over, if she allowed it to immobilize her, there was no hope that she could succeed in this place, in this college. More upsetting was the way she had soaked up everyone else's suspicions and judgments about Tabor. She no longer seemed to be able to look at him as the odd, shy, giant of a guy who had touched her with his gift. Now he was a force to be reckoned with, an intruder into her space and her privacy . . . a big, dark, unkempt shadow that might appear ominously at any time. The din of silent recrimination had kept her awake last night, and it clanged away inside her head this morning. Chris told herself that this was not how she interacted with her students, these were not problems that Tabor had presented to her, and she was not the disorganized, unstable, elusive Allison. Yet, as she stood at the lectern, waiting for the quiet, she noticed first of all that he was not there. When she called the names and acknowledged the faces, his was the only one unanswered.

"You have a writing assignment due today. I told you it was a kind of journal assignment. How did everyone do?" Chris asked and waited.

"I thought it was hard," came a soft reply from a slight, big-eyed girl in the front row. "When you said the topic was, 'Why Am I Here Today?' I thought it would be a piece of cake, but it wasn't. I mean . . . like . . . it made me really think of just why I am in college . . . like . . . I didn't really know."

"Good comments," Chris said with a nod. "It isn't as easy as it sounds on first hearing the topic, is it. Good. Someone else?"

After a few seconds of silence, "Yeah . . . well . . . my paper got all caught up in being mad at my dad . . . when I really thought about it. I mean . . . he's really the only reason I'm here . . . I mean at Jackson Clayton." The second speaker looked as if he could be an Olympic swimmer, with his closely shaved suntanned head, large, muscled arms, and the requisite jersey shorts and formfitting undershirt.

One by one the class began to cautiously share a piece of themselves. Alert listeners stared intently as they became entrusted with something almost sacred. Chris slowly

149

encouraged the hesitant ones with questions she hoped they couldn't resist, nodding her acceptance of whatever they said. The atmosphere in the room became heady as they were all pulled gently into the vortex of their common human need. Chris reveled in the adrenalin surge of an early win.

Suddenly, the classroom door banged open as it was shoved forcefully against the wall, shattering the quiet that had enveloped them. Startled students pivoted in unison as they looked over their shoulders toward the intruding noise. Tabor clumped silently into the room, his eyes darting around in search of the haven of an empty chair. A new kind of intoxication infected the group, as the air hummed with a low-grade laughing whisper.

"Here, Tabor," Chris said to him, as she pointed to a desk by the row of windows. There's a seat over there behind Lilly."

The thick rubbery cleats of his big boots squeaked obscenely against the vinyl floor tiles, adding to his obvious discomfort before he could reach safety. The disrespectful noise added to the rising tide of glee that seemed to overtake the classroom.

"Okay, everyone . . . let's get back to what we were talking about . . . Jason, you were interrupted in the middle of your sentence." Chris tried to grab control.

"I don't remember," the boy replied, barely able to hold back the laughter that was about to erupt from his deeply flushed face. "I mean . . . I forgot . . . when he started . . . making that noise."

The class exploded into loud, uproarious shrieks and guffaws, spurred on by the common ground they had positively established earlier.

"Quiet!" Chris shouted. "Get yourselves under control. You sound like a high school English class . . . and I don't teach high school."

Slowly the wave subsided and students began looking at

their watches. Five minutes. Might as well pack up their backpacks. Nothing else would happen today.

"From here on out, check your syllabus and study guide for assignments. I gave those documents to you on Monday. Please leave today's writing assignments on the back desk by the door on your way out. See you on Friday."

Tabor continued to sit at the desk he had only occupied ten minutes earlier, staring unflinchingly straight ahead. Chris looked closely at him for the first time since he had entered the room and knew something about him was different, disturbingly different. She recognized that he wore the same yellow shirt he had worn in her office on Monday, but it was now stained and smeared with oily, dark reds and deep, nauseating browns that looked as if they might have bubbled up from some unknown evil place. His matted hair and beard were flecked with dried white matter that could have come from within as well as from without, and his huge hands were caked with the same red muck that stuck to his heavy black boots.

"Tabor, are you all right?" she asked as she walked toward his side of the large room.

"Yes, Ma'am," he said flatly.

"Are you sick?"

"No . . . I ain't sick."

"I have to go, Tabor, so you need to pick up your bag and move on also," she said. "Are you finished with your classes for the day?" She tried to establish some normalcy.

"I don't have no more classes. I'll come with y'all," he said in his loud monotone.

"I have someplace I have to go right after this class," she lied," so I won't be going to my office."

"I ain't goin' back to my Mawmaw's . . . my house . . . no more," he boomed. "I ain't goin' back there ever again."

Chris still stood in front of the empty classroom, and

151

Tabor remained in his seat. She was overcome with confusion and doubt . . . the second day of class, and she didn't know what to do. An ugly, familiar tightness banded her chest.

"Tabor, I don't know what's going on, but maybe you need to talk to someone over in Student Services . . . one of the guidance counselors, perhaps."

"No!" he said loudly. "None of them people wants to talk to me . . . they don't like me. I ain't got nobody to talk to ceptin' y'all." He looked up at her and she saw his heavy-lidded brown eyes were glazed with tears. "Even Mawmaw says I don't have no one."

"Why don't I walk with you over to the guidance office," she offered. "There are some nice people over there you probably haven't even met."

"No . . . not over there!" he shouted. "I ain't gonna go to them anymore . . . I done said that already."

"I have to go, Tabor . . . I have another class in awhile . . . let's both leave now." Chris blanched as she haltingly explained herself to him, aware of her rising anxiety.

Slowly he stood up. He reached down and grasped the frayed straps of the small, worn backpack that lay beside the desk, hoisting it over his shoulder with a flip.

"I'm gonna go to my mountain place," he said flatly. "I got me a house up on the mountain. That's where I'll be livin' now . . . it's nice up there."

"Good . . . I'm glad you have a nice place you want to go to. Everybody needs that, Tabor . . . we all do."

"I want ya to see my mountain place sometime," he stated in his flat staccato. "Y'all would like it."

Chris didn't respond to him. Tabor loped along beside her as she walked slowly down the empty hall. She had to go somewhere other than her office, since she had told him she wouldn't be going back there, but she was uncertain as to where

152

that might be. As they neared the main doors to Cantrell Hall, Chris turned to leave the building.

"I'll see you on Friday, Tabor." She hesitated for a moment. "Do you understand the syllabus I gave you on Monday? Are you clear about your assignments?"

"I guess," he said. "Where y'all goin' to now?" he asked.

"I have an appointment," she said. "I'm going to an appointment."

"Where is it?" he questioned. "I'll walk with ya. I can walk with y'all to where it is."

"No, Tabor. We both need to go our own way. I'll see you on Friday."

"But Miss Chris," he hollered loudly after her.

She kept walking, aware that he was standing and watching her every step. Would he follow her? This was Wednesday. Week number one had one more class day to come. God . . . what was happening? Where was all this leading? Chris tried hard to fill her heaving lungs, aware that the oxygen was thin. Her hands were icy, her fingers numb. She knew what she had to do, what she must do. Again she heard him call her name . . . 'Miss Chris.' Just like 'Miss Allison.'

Chapter 26

"Suelean," she heard him say. "Suelean . . . y'all finally waked up."

Pap hadn't called her by her baptized name for such a long time, not since the boy had come to them. She felt the soft flannel underside of the multicolored patchwork quilt against her left hand as she rubbed her rough, stiff fingers against it. Mama's quilt . . . the one she had given to them after their wedding. She looked at him as he leaned forward from the big maple rocking chair he had pulled close to the bed. A faint, familiar smell of stale whiskey floated between them.

"I reckon y'all took a hell of a fall offen the back porch, Woman," he said as he shook his head slowly back and forth. "I come back yesterday evenin' from carryin' a truck of wood down to Miss Meyers, and I found y'all lyin' out thar in the dirt, half-way down the damn hill. Scared the hell out'a me, Suelean . . . thought y'all was dead. Y'all looked like ya was dead." His heavy-lidded, red-rimmed eyes were wide with expression.

Her head throbbed and ached when she tried to turn toward him, so she lay staring straight up at the rough, unpainted pine of the old ceiling. She began to mentally explore her body's parts, slightly moving each foot, flexing and minimally raising each hand and arm. A hot, jagged shard of pain shot through her right arm as she tested it.

"Pap . . . did I break my arm?" she whispered in a barely audible voice. "It hurts terrible . . . I can't move it."

"I reckon we needs to be goin' to Clayton Forge to see Doc Reilly, or one a' them nurse-doctors he has over there. Yer arm looks crooked to me. Ya might could have broke it," he said matter-of-factly.

"Where's Tabor?" she asked.

"How in the hell do I know?" he muttered angrily. "That damn fool ain't ever around when he needs to be. I ain't seen nothin' of him since I come home last night and found you. Hell . . . if y'all had waited for him to find ya', y'all would'a been dead." Pap stood up and walked over to the door, coughed deeply, and spit outside.

Ain't ya seen him . . . or talked to him?" she asked tentatively.

"Damn it, Mawmaw, stop worryin' about that asshole kid. He's goin' on twenty-three . . . if'n he ain't able to take care of hisself now, he ain't never gonna be able to."

"I feel like I can't breathe very good," she whispered, "like there ain't enough breath comin' into my body."

"I'll go get the truck. It's only about ten in the morning, so we can go down and find someone at Doc Reilly's now." She sensed an unfamiliar urgency in his voice.

Mawmaw was too tired to speak anymore. She nodded her head in agreement, knowing she had to get to a doctor, wishing, instead, that she could sink deep within the soothing comfort of the familiar quilt and gently float into a long, peaceful sleep. She heard her husband's shuffling steps on the dirt path outside the old house, and she heard him pause and cough again. It was a deep, rattling, rasping hack that tore up from his wheezing lungs, and more and more frequently invaded his conversation and interrupted the simplest parts of his daily life. Her Papa had had the cough, too. 'Coalminer's cough' the old folks had called it . . . 'caught it from the damp air way down under the ground,' they said. Once you had it, it never went away. And then she remembered the blood that she had seen when her Papa coughed most of the time. She suspected that Pap. . . her Lucas . . . had the blood now, too.

She waited for the broken staccato of the old Chevy truck's motor, wondering how she would be able to stand the agony of moving her shattered arm. No one must ever know about her argument with Tabor just before she fell. Even though the boy had nothing to do with her accident, Pap blamed him for everything. If Pap ever got any notion that Tabor might have had something to do with her injuries, what she feared most might happen. Killing your own flesh and blood must surely be the biggest sin, the unforgivable sin, in the eyes of God, but she didn't have any doubt that Pap had it in him to kill his only grandson.

"Mawmaw, we gotta get y'all out 'a the bed. Y'all was sleepin' when I put ya' in it, so ya' didn't feel no pain."

She had trouble focusing as she looked up at him. Until this moment, Mawmaw hadn't noticed how colorless Lucas's face had become, almost gray, like the foggy mountain air that wrapped itself around them on an early March morning. She closed her eyes, not wanting to see how he was, what he had become. What would happen to Tabor if she died . . . and if Pap died?

"Come on, Mawmaw . . . gotta get y'all down to Clayton Forge . . . y'all gonna have to help." He leaned closer to her and asked fearfully, "Are ya hearin' me, Suelean? Can y'all answer me?"

"Yes," she said. "I'm so tired, Lucas. I don't know if I can go."

"Here," he said gently. "I'll put my arm under ya' and y'all grab hold around my neck with yer good arm."

She did as he told her. The last sound she heard was the deep, agonizing wail that rose out of the very center of her, before it carried her off into a merciful, dreamless sleep.

When she awoke, she was lying on a paper-covered examining table in Buzz Reilly's office, the bright light from a goose-necked lamp shining into her eyes.

"Here she comes. How ya' doing, Miss Maclean?" The lean, smiling young doctor patted her hand as it lay across her stomach. "Glad to see you're back with us again," he said cheerfully.

"I don't remember . . ." Her voice trailed off to silence. She was still so very tired.

"I don't expect you do," he said softly. "You have a broken arm, and I suspect a couple of cracked ribs. That's a lot of pain that your body decided it wasn't going to put you through, when Mr. Maclean had to get you to the truck to bring you down here. Our bodies take care of us better than we think they do," he said as he tapped his stethoscope gently against her chest.

Buzz Reilly was almost a pretty man, with his dark chestnut hair and blue-green eyes set atop the sharp angles of his high cheekbones. He was Amber Jean's age. They had been in school together, before Amber Jean stopped going. Folks used to say he was a smart hillbilly boy who made good. Funny thing was, he got away, went to a big state college, then to the medical school, and then he came back to his mountain home. Here he was in this shabby storefront he had made into a doctor's office . . . two narrow examining rooms, a clattering old X-ray machine, and a little lab, just beyond the waiting room lined with cheap green plastic chairs. Surely he could make more money in a city. At least there, most of the people he saw on a daily basis could pay. Mawmaw liked him, and she felt good every time she saw him and he called her "Miss Maclean." She could count on one hand the local folks who used her last name . . . those who respected her. He was one of them. He might have grown up poor, but he was raised proper. The other thing he had going for him, as far as she was concerned, was that he was one of the very few people in the world who Pap regarded with any favor.

"I'm going to examine you, Miss Maclean, just to make sure you don't have anything else going on because of your fall. You just lie still . . . I'll try not to hurt you."

"Where's Pap . . . Lucas?" she asked weakly.

"He's out in the waiting room. He was here with you until a few minute s ago, when you began to wake up. Vicky was going to give him a cup of coffee and see if he would eat something. She had some good looking donuts out there."

He continued to carefully scan her body, listening, touching as he talked to her.

"Miss Maclean, tell me what happened, how you had that fall."

"Did Lucas tell you?" She looked at the doctor's gently-graying hair and wondered if Amber Jean would have gray hair now.

"Yes, he told me he found you lying in the yard, half way down a steep hill. What do you remember?"

"I was sitting on the back porch shelling peas. I fell off. That's all I remember."

Buzz Reilly looked down at the frail, worn woman. How many more like her would he be able to see today? Would her life change because he properly set a fractured arm and patched her back together? Not likely. Not even a chance. Could he stop the violence because he discovered it? He knew the dismal answer was always the same.

"Was Mr. Maclean at home when you fell?" He tried to sound calm when he began the questioning. He mustn't alarm her.

"No, he wasn't home."

She guessed that the doctor thought Pap had gone on another of his drunken rampages, like the time she had gone to another of his drunken rampages, like the time she had gone to work with two black eyes and she had fainted in the hall right outside Dr. Cantrell's office. Mattie had rushed her to Doc Reilly's office, fearful that Mawmaw had suffered life-threatening injury at the hands of her raging husband. That time, Mawmaw had told the doctor what had happened, how she had stood between Pap and Tabor, protecting the cringing boy from the heavy blows delivered by his grandfather's alcohol-fueled fists.

"Where was Tabor when you fell?" he asked.

She hesitated. She was so tired . . . she couldn't think fast.

"He wasn't home, either." Mawmaw pushed hard to get the words out of her throat.

"So you were all alone, when you were shelling peas?"

"Yes . . . all alone."

Buzz Reilly wondered if a tumble off of a porch would cause the kinds of injuries he saw here, or if there had been some impetus, some propelling force. Was she lying to him, protecting someone? Did it matter? Would it matter?

"So, where is Tabor right now?   Is he still living at home?"

"Yes, he's goin' to college over at Jackson Clayton." Mawmaw wanted the young doctor to stop asking questions about Tabor. Better he should ask more about Pap.

"Good for him. Have you seen him since your fall?"

"Yes . . . well, no . . . I don't think since the accident."

"You don't remember? When was the last time you saw him . . . Tabor?"

"Umm . . . the morning . . . when he went off to his school."

A knock at the door was followed by Vicky Suddeth's pretty face. "Here are the x-rays, Dr. Reilly, for Mrs. Maclean."

"Thanks," he said as he reached over and took the large rectangular films.

"Okay, let's see what we have here."

Buzz Reilly propped the dark films in front of the lighted viewer that hung on the office wall. He stared at the images for a few seconds.

"It's as I suspected," he said. "You have two cracked ribs, and you have a break in one of your lower arm bones . . . the bone we call the radius. There isn't much we can do about the ribs. I'll give you some pills for the pain, but they generally heal themselves pretty quickly."

He stopped before he talked about her arm. What he needed was a hospital closer than an hour away, and better equipment than he had been able to muster so far. He knew most of the local people would never go to a hospital, no matter how close it was, and he also knew many who needed a hospital would never even get to his office.

"Miss Maclean, I'll need to set your arm and put it in a brace and sling for awhile. I'll put you to sleep for a short time, maybe thirty minutes, so you won't feel anything. It's what we need to do to get you healing."

"All right, go ahead," she said. She trusted him, this thin, young doctor who was getting gray hair, who once knew Amber Jean.

"Are you sure you've told me the whole story of your fall?" he asked.

"I reckon so."

"If you think of anything new, something you maybe forgot, you can call me," he said. "I'll write down my home number. You can call me there if you think of something."

"Okay," she said quietly.

But she knew she would not need the number.

.

Chapter 27

"There's the whole murky story, Rachael. I feel as if someone slammed into me with a loaded logging truck," Chris said with a deep sigh, "the first week of classes."

"My God, Chrissy, you have to tell the dean, maybe even Dr. Cantrell. Forget all the protocol crap . . . pecking order and all that stuff. You have to get some help right away. You can't pretend this guy isn't dangerous."

"I'm not sure there is any danger here, at least not to me. Really . . . what has he done that's threatening?"

Chris could feel the heaviness that hung low in her aching forehead and pressed against the backs of her burning eyes. She had called Rachael Wednesday night about nine o'clock, and they were still on the phone at ten. As close as they were in so many ways, Chris was aware of her friend's tendency to magnify problems and to over-react in a less-than-crisis situation. But Chris also knew that she had called Rachael because she was afraid.

"What has he *done* . . . what has he *done*? Are you serious? He's stalking you, Chris! You can't ignore that. I don't want to scare you, but it sounds to me like you may have a deranged killer here. What I want is for you to get in your car and drive down here. Play sick for a few days, until you can get your head together. There's no way you would find me hanging around up there, not for another ten minutes," Rachael said emphatically.

"I can't leave, Rachael, not the first week of classes. I just wanted to talk it through with you, to see if I could hear myself coming to conclusions, or maybe verbalizing a good plan of action. I don't want to bury this poor guy. Everyone else has written him off as some kind of a freaky loser, but he's enrolled in college, Rachael. He failed last year, but he's dusted himself off and he's trying again. If I report him to Richard or Dr. Cantrell, the kid is gone from here. He'll never get back in."

"With what he's done . . ."

"But that's just it . . . what has he done?" Chris interrupted. "That's what I'm hearing around here, a lot of conjecture, a lot of suspicion, but no real facts. For all anyone seems to know, the mysterious Allison could be working in a fish cannery in Alaska, hiding out from the world. And there's no evidence at all that Tabor did anything to her. You've reacted just like the others, I think, because you know what this kid looks like, how he presents himself. Remember what you said when you saw him at the street fair, about him being so unattractive looking and intimidating because he's so big? Would any of us be feeling what we're feeling if he was a good-looking, well-spoken athlete with an "A" average?" Chris's voice had risen an octave and her face felt flushed. She shouldn't have dragged Rachael into this.

Rachael didn't reply for a few seconds. She knew her next words needed to be carefully chosen.

"Chris, you have such a good and generous spirit. That's why you'll always be twice the teacher I am. But you can't successfully use your wonderful gifts when dealing with a seriously disturbed student. You've lost your ability to be objective about this guy Tabor. That's what I think has happened. You can't change his head . . . maybe his mental illness, for all we know . . . with gifted teaching. For heaven's sake, Chris, a good and loving mother can't heal a schizophrenic child. She can help him, she can, perhaps, influence him in positive ways, but she can't cure him. You can't afford to be wrong about this, Chris. I feel very strongly about this . . . you can't afford to be wrong." Rachael's voice caught in her throat as she finished her sentence.

"I know, but it goes both ways. I can't afford to be wrong if he's an innocent victim, either. I think he's probably been a victim most of his life," she said, blinking back the annoying sting of tears. "Maybe I should try to talk to him, quietly and unemotionally."

"And what if you do, and you're wrong about him, Chris? What then?"

"Maybe I could get Richard to sit down with us . . . Tabor and me . . . and see if we could work it out. Maybe that's a possibility."

"Then Richard is out of the picture after the talk, and you and Tabor are right back to where you are now. I think he's got a sick love crush on you, Chris. I don't think talking is what he's after. Think about it." Maybe she needed to scare Chris into being sensible.

"He's never even come close to any physical contact," Chris said defensively. "I can't believe that's any part of it. I think he's lonely. I know he is, and I'd guess I'm more of a mother figure, someone who might care about him. At thirty-nine, I'm certainly not a sex object to him."

"You're assuming he's a normal, rational thinker, a regular type of guy. Chris, that clearly is not who he is. I can't understand why you refuse to see what's going on here."

The conversation dragged to an unsatisfactory close at

ten-thirty, leaving Chris as isolated in her indecision as she was before she called her best friend. Panic and frustration were evident in Rachael's lingering goodbyes, as if hanging on the telephone would keep Chris safe awhile longer.

"Chris, please promise me you'll talk to someone at the college, someone you can trust, so you won't be hanging out there all alone. This is serious," she said. "I'm so worried about you. You have to accept that this is a bad thing that's happening. You have to accept that."

"I'll talk to someone," Chris said. "Don't worry . . . I'll take care of myself. Thanks, Rachael, for listening and being there. I'll be okay."

"He could be crazy . . . he is crazy . . . and that Allison character might be a murder victim. I know . . . she could be in Alaska, but you cannot rule out other possibilities."

"I'll talk to you soon, Rachael."

Chris hung up the telephone and leaned her head back against the bright plaid of her favorite easy chair. The conversation with Rachael had exhausted and confused her, and she was no closer to making a decision as to what she should do. Who should she talk to? Rachael said, ". . . someone you trust." And who was that? Chris ran down a mental list of her recently acquired colleagues, new acquaintances that she was just beginning to label as 'friends.' She couldn't possibly know who was trustworthy and who wasn't. Maybe her idea to talk to Richard was the best option. What was she to say to Richard? "Richard . . . I have some uncomfortable feelings about a student . . . he came to my office and stayed too long . . . and he's being exceptionally nice to me . . . unfortunately he has poor social skills and a disarming voice . . . and . . . oh, yes . . . he's so big and ugly that he's intimidating. No, he's never touched me . . . no, he doesn't curse or act wild in class . . . no, he's never threatened anything. It's just that I have these feelings about him . . . based mostly on what others have told me . . . about their opinion of him . . . and about what they suspect was his relationship with Allison . . . you know Allison, Richard . . . the one you don't want to talk about? All this doesn't make any sense to you, Richard? I can't imagine why."

Chris got up and belted the big red velour robe tighter around her middle. The hot, golden days of late August were routinely ending with night time temperatures in the low fifties, a sure sign that the spectacular palette of an Appalachian autumn was just ahead.

Chris fixed a cup of lemon grass tea and carried the chunky NYC mug out onto the dark screened porch. She sat down in the slat-seated rocker that she had painted barn red just before Rachael's visit, wondering if she was truly not in touch with the reality of a dangerous situation. How could she know? Had the teachers at Columbine High School or the professors at Virginia Tech wrestled with the same puzzling uncertainty that now obsessed her? Had they been right, or had they been wrong, or would they never know? Had they tried to help the hopeless, or save the floundering, only to lose their lives in a battle that was lost before it had even begun? Chris's thoughts swirled and spiraled in tortured disarray, as she attempted to find some semblance of order and reason in her increasingly troubled situation. Just after her grandfather's clock struck eleven, she locked the door leading to the porch and picked up her telephone.

"Hello, Richard, this is Christine Alford. I would like to come by your office tomorrow, Thursday, August 27, to discuss one of my students. Please leave a message as to what time would be convenient for you. Thanks."

"It's your job, Richard. We all have to do our jobs," she thought as she turned off the last light in her bedroom.

Chapter 28

"She's feelin' right poorly. I don't reckon she'll be up to workin' next week . . . maybe not next after that, neither."

Lucas Maclean stood nervously in front of Mattie's desk, wishing he was anywhere but in this hostile foreign territory. He felt the sharp focus of the haughty woman's slightly narrowed blue eyes as she stared at him, fixing her gaze as if he was a dangerous wild animal that had just wandered into a heavily populated urban neighborhood. He knew she didn't like anything about him, which she had told him one time in no uncertain terms. What was it she had called him that day in Doc Reilly's office, when he had come down to pick up Suelean? "A vicious drunk hillbilly." The idea that he had to stand here and be civil to this high-handed bitch, who had conveniently forgotten where she came from, was almost more than he could bear, but he would do it this time for Suelean. He had promised her.

"My word . . . that's terrible . . . poor Suelean." Mattie glared at him a little longer in that mean, unnerving way before she said anything else.

"How did it happen . . . this time?" He sensed the contempt in her question.

"I don't rightly know. I wasn't even home 'til past dark. I found her layin' out yonder of our back porch, half way down

166

the hill. She was barely breathin' when I got to her. Doc Reilly says she has a broken arm and two busted ribs. She's hurtin' now a powerful amount."

"Let me get Dr. Cantrell . . . just a minute."

Mattie got up from her desk and rapped a couple of times on the door at the side of her office. She opened the door, stepped inside, and closed it behind her.

Lucas wished she hadn't gone to talk to that high mucky-muck Cantrell. That's all he needed was that tight-assed son-of-a-bitch gettin' involved . . . probably gettin' the law involved, too. This time Lucas hadn't done a damn thing, except probably save Mawmaw's life . . . but that didn't mean they would believe him.

"Hello, Lucas. What's going on?" James Cantrell greeted his shabby visitor with reserved politeness.

"Well, I been tellin' Mattie here, Suelean had herself a bad fall on Monday offen our back porch . . . broke her arm and two of her ribs. Doc Reilly says she's gonna be fine, but he says she ain't gonna be able to work for a couple a' weeks . . . till she mends some."

"Where is she now?"

"Home, in the bed restin'. The doc give her some tablets, said they was to take away some a' the pain and help her sleep."

"Do you need some help taking care of her?" James asked.

"No, I reckon I can take care of her . . . bought some meat at Blount's . . . already cooked up a mess a' stew."

James and Mattie stood side by side, a few feet away from Lucas, their eyes seeming to penetrate his as they looked directly at him.

"How did she fall, Lucas?" James asked pointedly, his question seemingly answered before he asked it.

"I told y'all I don't know. I was gone to nearly eight o'clock at night. I done carried two loads a' wood over to

Miss Myers up on Tabler Mountain, and that's a damn long drive in my old loaded truck . . . took me most a' the day. Suelean was fine when I left. Said she was fixin' to clean up the vegetable garden and do some work around the place. She says she jest fell offen the porch . . . don't seem to remember what made her fall."

Lucas's last two words caught in his throat as a hacking, rasping cough launched itself mercilessly from deep within him. He gasped helplessly for breath as he pulled a dark, stained gray rag from the pocket of his frayed jeans and put it in front of his mouth. Spasm after spasm overcame him, draining any remaining color from his already ashen face.

"Here," James said, as he took hold of Lucas's elbow and guided him toward a leather chair, "sit down. You don't sound like you're in much better shape than Suelean is."

"Jest a damn cough," he wheezed, as he wiped at the dark wetness that stained the corners of his mouth.

"Sit here for awhile until you feel better. Mattie, would you get Lucas that package of cough lozenges you bought for me last spring. They're in my upper right desk drawer."

James turned his attention back to the thin figure slumped in the oversized chair.

"Lucas, seems to me you need to see Doc Reilly yourself. That's a bad cough you have there."

"I don't take to doctors . . . ain't never been to one that helped me none." Lucas struggled to catch the oxygen from the shallow breaths his lungs sucked in. His boney hands trembled as they lay immobilized on the arms of the big chair that seemed to swallow him in its sumptuous depths. "It's quietin' now . . . I can feel it settlin'," he said.

"Are you up to talking a little more?" James asked him.

"Guess so . . . can't stay long. Suelean's home by herself." Lucas sounded as if he had just completed a long, arduous foot race.

"Where is Tabor now?" James asked quietly.

"Don't know. Truth is, I don't give a damn," Lucas said bitterly. "He jest ain't no good . . . never will be."

"Could he have been at home when Suelean fell?"

"Reckon he could a' been, but then he's taken to stayin' away lots a' nights . . . goes up and camps in the woods. Reckon he wasn't home."

"Maybe we need to find Tabor and ask him," James said calmly. "I agree with you, he probably wasn't around when she fell. I know he's close to his grandmother. If she was in any trouble, as she was with her fall, he would have helped her if he was around."

"I wisht he would stay gone," Lucas growled. "Wisht he would jest go somewhere else and leave us be. Nothin' good is ever gonna come of him. I knowed it when he was a little kid. Killed his mama . . . her bein' so small and all. You knew her, Mr. Cantrell, our pretty little Amber Jean, when she worked with her mama here at yer school. I told Mawmaw . . . Suelean, when we learned what had happened . . . when Amber Jean tried to birth him . . . that the boy was the spawn of the devil. I ain't never changed my mind."

Pap's bloodshot eyes glowed with the hatred he felt for his grandson, the one he blamed for all the ills that had befallen the Maclean family for the past twenty-three years.

James Cantrell did not move as he listened to the bitterness that poured out of the sick old man. Yes, he had known Amber Jean, and now he knew her son. Was he wrong in what he was doing for this boy Tabor? Had he made yet another error in judgment?

"Lucas, I don't think Tabor is bad, and I know he's smart enough to get through this school. The problem is that he doesn't feel good about himself, and he has a hard time fitting in. I believe he can lead a good, productive life, with some help. That's why I've encouraged him to learn something about

169

Internet technology. There are good jobs in that field. And I sure don't think he would do anything to hurt his grandmother. I've seen the way he is when he's around her."

James seemed to be talking to himself. Lucas stared at him, as if he had heard none of the words James had spoken.

"You know, Lucas, I'd like to see you and Suelean and me working together to try and help Tabor put together some kind of a life for himself. I'm confident that it can happen, with all of us working to help him."

Lucas continued to look blankly at James and then suddenly scooted toward the front of the chair. "I gotta go," he said. "Gotta get home to Suelean. I don't need them cough drops."

As James watched Lucas push himself up from the soft patina of the chocolate leather, he realized that the grizzled old hillbilly had not heard or understood anything he had said to him about Tabor. It was as if James had spoken in a foreign language, one that had no familiarity to Lucas, one that was far beyond the realm of his experience or comprehension. Lucas had nothing within him emotionally that would allow him to reach out and help Tabor, even though the boy was of his flesh and blood.

"Lucas, tell Suelean that we want her to rest and get better. Tell her not to worry about her job . . . it'll be here whenever she's able to get back to it." James thought carefully about what he was about to say. "I want to make sure she has everything she needs to help her get well. Here . . . I want you to take this money and buy whatever it is she needs . . . her medicine . . . or maybe something special she likes to eat . . . anything at all she might want. All of us here love Suelean. She's an important part of the college, and she does a lot for us. It's just a little 'thank you' from all of us."

Lucas took the bills from James's extended hand. He could see several fifties and he spotted some twenties in the stack.

"Well, if things was normal and all, I wouldn't take it, but seein' as work is slow right now, and Suelean's gonna have some bills from the doc, I'll take it . . . for her. I'll go down to Blount's and stock up on some food for her. Much obliged, Mr. Cantrell. I reckon y'all can expect to see her around here in a couple a' weeks. She ain't gonna want ta' lay out for too long."

"Lucas, when you see Tabor, would you tell him to stop by and see me? Tell him, if you would, please, that I want to talk to him about doing some work for me."

"If I see him, but I don't reckon he's gonna be back if he has to face up to me without his Mawmaw. She spoils him . . . takes up fer him like he was a little sissy boy. But if I see him, I'll tell him y'all wants to talk to him."

Mattie had quietly brought the cough lozenges to the reception room where Lucas had first approached her, but she had withdrawn quickly to the copy room after handing the bag to Dr. Cantrell. Shortly after hearing Lucas Maclean's version of the story about Suelean's accident, she had made up her mind that he was responsible for whatever it was that had happened. She couldn't stand to stay in the same room with the disgusting man whose violent, drunken temper had more than once wreaked havoc on the gentle Suelean. There had been painful, serious injuries which Mattie had seen firsthand . . . two black eyes and a concussion one time, broken and missing teeth another. Suelean claimed she had lost the teeth in another mysterious fall, but Mattie knew the truth. The poor woman's badly bruised and battered face that accompanied the missing teeth was evidence enough that the hillbilly drunk she had married was the perpetrator. Mattie believed Suelean led a tragic, cursed life, sharing her bed with the nasty, foul-mouthed Lucas, and her home with her frightening monster of a grandson Tabor.

Mattie had encountered both of these stinking, obnoxious

characters too many times, and she feared both of them. Why Dr. Cantrell allowed either of them to set foot on the college grounds she couldn't understand, considering all the problems each of them caused on a regular basis. Deep within, Mattie had strong feelings that Tabor was more than frightening and physically repulsive. She believed he was responsible for hideous crimes no one had yet discovered. It was a feeling she had carried ever since that day when Allison had disappeared. Dr. Cantrell always talked about when Allison "left," but Mattie didn't believe for a minute that any voluntary leaving had taken place. Being in the president's office had its responsibilities, and one of those Dr. Cantrell had stressed was keeping her mouth shut. He hadn't said it in so many words, but he had said it in his nice, kind way. She did maintain the confidentiality the office required, but that didn't mean she wasn't privy to a lot of information. Most of all, she heard a lot and she saw a lot, and there was no one she could talk to about it. Her husband Joe wasn't interested. On the few occasions she had tried to share her concerns with him, he had told her she was watching too many soap operas.

When Mattie was sure Lucas had gone, she went back to her desk. Dr. Cantrell had retreated to the privacy behind his closed door, and she was thankful for that. Sometimes there were things about her boss that puzzled her, too . . . odd happenings that caused her more than a little concern. She didn't think for a minute that she knew him well, but she had few reasons to believe that any of the unknown should trouble her. The only exception to that were the shadowy, perplexing events involving Allison Montgomery.

Chapter 29

Tabor threw the split pieces of dry pine on the growing pile of firewood he had gathered and cut over the summer months. He had rounded out enough air vents at the top of his dugout to allow him to burn a small fire for a few hours, long enough to heat up the six foot high interior on a cold winter's night and hot enough to cook whatever he had managed to kill and clean for his one meal. A couple of experiments with bigger fires over longer spans of time had resulted in his underground shelter being clogged with acrid, blinding smoke that cut off his ability to breathe. Tabor remembered the panic that had consumed him when he had crawled across the narrow dirt floor, gagging and retching, as the evil, pungent black clouds seemed to reach out with long tentacles and attempt to drag him back into an underground tomb. He wouldn't make that mistake again.

His head ached and the blood pounded in his temples as he tried to figure out what he should do, what he could do, about the way everything seemed to have gone wrong. For awhile, ever since he had first seen Chris, Tabor had been able to project himself into the future. With each prophetic encounter with his beautiful lady, he had known that his life had been changed forever. She liked him. She even told him

173

she liked his name. She had taken him back to her private office after the first day of class, and he had seen the special place she had made for his gift to her. He could tell that she was happy to see he was in her class because now they could see each other every day. But then something had changed. Within minutes, the whole world seemed to have been turned upside down, and he had no idea as to why.

And then there had been the problems with Mawmaw. She had always been the one he knew he could count on to understand, the one who believed in him. Now he had turned her against him, too.

Pap was right when he said Tabor was worthless. He couldn't make anything turn out right. Frustration and rage transformed him, and he hurled his wood-chopping axe at the five inch trunk of a golden-green maple that stood at the edge of the camouflaged clearing, burying the sharply honed blade deep in the bark and pith of the young tree.

"Damn them all . . . I hate them all!" he shouted. "I hate all of you!" he bellowed as he raised his arms and shook his fists at the darkening, silent forest. A guttural, moaning cry rose and fell from his half-open mouth as he paced back and forth, back and forth, across the dry, mossy ground, his broad shoulders slumping forward over his large, lumbering body.

What was he going to do? He had no money . . . soon he would have no food. During his more rational moments, Tabor accepted that he could not live through the Appalachian winter in his mountain place. He struggled to understand what had happened . . . why Chris had walked away from him . . . why Mawmaw had refused to believe him. At the thought of his Mawmaw, Tabor's eyes filled with tears. He knew she must be very angry with him. She might not even want him to come home. He had told her he wouldn't ever come back, but now he needed to go back to Mawmaw, just for awhile, until he could get things right with Chris.

As the last arch of the red-rimmed sun fell behind the horizon, Tabor found himself hugging his knees as he sat beside the crude, hand-dug stairs that led down into his shrouded den. The hush of the mountain darkness seemed to settle him. It was strange how time in his wooded sanctuary was not the same as time in the other world. Sometimes it just slipped quietly away, and he didn't even feel it go. He could easily manage his life in the forest, ably completing all that he had to do, never running out of time. Out there . . . down there . . . it was different. Tabor tried to live in the AM/PM world, but most of the time he was late, or he forgot the unimportant things altogether. While other people finished their chores, or their assignments, or their tests within a time limit, he struggled with deadlines. He had decided he would talk to Chris about this time problem, ask her to give him some of that help she had talked about. Allison had worked with him and encouraged him, and she had said he was doing better. That was before she had changed everything, before she had turned her attention toward another.

Maybe he should wait one more night before he went home, let Mawmaw cool off some before he went back and told her he was sorry. Should he go to his class tomorrow . . . Chris's class? He had told her he wouldn't miss any, and he didn't want to disappoint her.

Maybe they could talk tomorrow after class, and he could tell her about some of his plans.

Thoughts of his heckling, teasing classmates threatened to undermine Tabor's resolve, but he overcame their ugliness with images of his smiling, beautiful Chris.

Tonight, he would eat the last piece of the squirrel he had shot and roasted, and he had enough water left to drink some and to wash his face. He couldn't do any of his assignments, but he would explain that to Chris tomorrow. Tabor reached for his rifle and ran his hand down the cold, steel barrel. He would clean it and take it with him in the morning, just like he always did. He never left it in the woods. Pap hadn't taught him much when he was a boy . . . he hadn't even talked to him most of the time . . . but he did tell Tabor that you could tell a lot about a man by the way he kept his gun. Tabor took better care of his gun than he did of himself. One of his few happy childhood memories was of his fifteenth birthday and this gun. Mawmaw had come home from her job at the college, and she had brought him the gun. She said someone over there had bought a new one, and he had given her his old one for Tabor, along with a few boxes of ammunition. That was also the only time in his life that he remembered Pap paying him any attention. Pap had taken him out into the back field, and he had taught Tabor how to shoot. The rest of the learning Tabor did on his own. The one thing in his life that he knew he could do well was aim his rifle and hit his target.

Tabor carefully cleaned the barrel and rubbed the shiny walnut stock with the oiled cloth that had been wrapped around the rifle when he received it. He carefully wrapped the gun in a piece of an old blanket before putting it back in his big gym bag. The only thing Pap had ever said about Tabor's precious gift was that he couldn't believe that anyone would be so goddamn dumb as to give away free such an expensive rifle. Pap had asked Mawmaw who it was who had given it to her, and she had said it was someone Pap didn't know.

Tabor's spirits were higher now, much improved over what they had been in the earlier part of the day. He felt better since he had worked out his plans for tomorrow, how he and Chris would set things right, and how he would go home and be forgiven by Mawmaw. As he pulled the ragged edge of his dirty blanket around him and prepared to sleep, Tabor hoped Mawmaw would have a piece of beef on hand so she could make him a steak and gravy supper, with lots of fried potatoes and onions and some of her good biscuits to mop up the thick, brown sauce that covered it all. He sighed deeply, happy for the peace that so often escaped him. What was it Mawmaw always said? "Tomorrow is another day." Tomorrow was going to be a real good day, his and his beautiful lady's day. He would make sure of it.

Chapter 30

Richard Shelton glanced at his watch before he wrapped his sweat-soaked tee shirt and running shorts in the damp towel and stuffed them into his tattered black gym bag. Before placing his worn Nikes in the small bathroom closet, he examined the fraying edges of the worn soles, judging that he had a dozen more runs before they would need replacement. It was 8:00 a.m. His daily work-week routine hadn't changed much in the six years he had been at Jackson Clayton, and his arrival time in Bryant Hall was generally predictable. He was an early riser and a committed runner and jogger, no matter the mountain weather. At least five days a week, Richard was sprinting along a gravel road or rhythmically trotting a woodland trail by six, frequently as the sun was rising, and he almost always hit the shower in his luxurious office bathroom by half past seven. One of the things that had attracted him to this remote campus was the expanse of unfamiliar rolling landscape, backed and framed by the towering, looming peaks of the dark forested mountains. The opportunities for exploring on foot were limitless, and he relished the challenge that the Appalachian and Blue Ridge Mountains presented.

The other quirky element of the job opportunity that had appealed to him was the elegant comfort and accommodation of the executive suite, the offices of the President and the Dean of

Arts and Sciences. The standard supply of desks and chairs included in most academic jobs was anything but ordinary at Jackson Clayton College. Expensive leather chairs the color of toasted French bread and bold dark green and gold decorator fabrics mixed tastefully with the solid, dark mahogany desk and side pieces that made up the office he had been shown during his interview on campus. He and Cantrell each had their own separate bathrooms, complete with bisque marble sinks and ebony granite counters and showers. They shared a well-appointed stainless steel kitchen, which was far more opulent than any Richard had ever been privileged to have in the homes he had rented or owned over the years. Surrounding and enhancing this overwhelming display was a collection of art which far exceeded anything Richard had ever seen outside of a museum. For some odd reason, which he never quite understood, the office suite had been the scale-tipper in his job decision. The competitive salary and generous benefits package at Jackson Clayton had been comparable to those offered by Goucher College in Baltimore, which had been his second choice of the three schools he had interviewed, but there were no dramatic mountains and there was no executive suite in Maryland. His primary goal had been to get away from Florida and all the memories, as far away as he could. Jackson Clayton College had come up with the winning combination for him.

During the first five years of living and working in the mountains of rural Virginia, Richard never questioned nor regretted his decision. However, this past year, his sixth year, was clearly in a category all by itself. It had all been going so well, until Allison Montgomery had entered the placid picture, and then he had watched helplessly as his life, once again, seemed to blow up around him.

After tossing his gym bag at one of the camel leather chairs that flanked his dark green pillowed sofa, Richard touched the message button on the flashing telephone.

179

"Hello, Richard. This is Christine Alford. I would like to come by your office tomorrow . . . ."

He drew a deep breath as he listened to the rest of her short message. ". . . to talk about a student," she had said.

"And your 'tomorrow' is now our today," he said softly.

He sat down at his computer and quickly worked through the privileged, classified information that flashed onto his administrative site. He enlarged *Class Rosters* when the category appeared on the screen and scrolled down to Chris's name. Halfway through the list of her Comp I students, Richard stopped and stared at *Maclean, Tabor*. That's who it was . . . he needn't go any further. That's who she wanted to talk about.

Damn whoever had put him in her class. It was a real cop-out, to say the least, to unload on the new teacher and avoid confrontation with the veterans. On the other hand, whose class was any better, or any worse, for dealing with Tabor Maclean? It was Cantrell who deserved the curses. He was the one calling the shots and making the final decisions; he was the one who refused to get rid of the festering sore that had infected so many others on this campus. God only knows he and others had tried to reason with James, had tried to present a strong argument for eliminating the problem. This mentally ill kid belonged in an institution . . . at the least in a special educational environment. He was clearly misplaced in a college classroom with average nineteen and twenty-year-olds. James insisted he was "a smart kid," "just needed a chance," and he always pulled out entrance exam results that had been minimal but nevertheless within the normal range. James had to be aware of the great risks they were taking, allowing this strange, skulking giant to roam the campus, particularly after all the complaints from female students and unsettling reports from faculty about his bizarre behavior. As far as Richard was concerned, it was just a matter of time before another loaded and deadly time bomb went off on another college campus, and this time he feared it would be their own.

He pushed the four buttons on the telephone and waited.

"Hi, Chris. Richard Shelton."

"How are you, Richard?"

"Fine . . . how about you?"

"Good, thanks."

"I just got your message, and I'm free to get together anytime this morning, anytime before noon. How does that work for you?" His hands felt clammy as he gripped the telephone.

"It's a little after eight now . . . how about nine o'clock?"

"Sounds good. You want me to come over to your office?" he offered.

"No, that's okay . . . I'll come to yours."

"Look forward to seeing you at nine."

He stared out the big double paned windows toward the intersecting brick walkways that connected Bryant Hall with other campus buildings. The early autumn sun seemed to illuminate the few students who hurried along the paths toward their nine o'clock classes. In another twenty minutes, the sidewalks would be crowded with their classmates who hustled to avoid closed doors or "Late" speeches. Richard was glad he was going to see her again, even though he had done little to make the meeting happen. The discussion would be difficult, but he had to avoid another disaster. He knew he hadn't handled her questions about Allison very well. The truth was that after that communication fiasco, he hadn't been sure they would ever sit down and talk again. Chris's telephone call had reinforced his feelings about her. She was a strong, capable woman who would do her job, even when her boss acted like an ass hole. Whatever nine o'clock held for either of them, he had to make sure their meeting ended at least fifty percent better than it had the last time.

Richard wasn't sure how he could deal with a discussion about Tabor without bringing in some of his prior knowledge about last year's events, and all of that involved information about Allison. The hell with Cantrell . . . he was going to do what he had to do. Chris deserved much better than he or anyone else had given her so far. If it exploded into an out-of-control major conflagration, so be it. He didn't really feel that he had anything to hide, not about Allison's problems with Tabor. Richard wouldn't just throw Chris to the wolves . . . another sacrifice on the Cantrell pile. There was no doubt in his mind that the secrets and lies eventually would come to the surface. The unknown factor was *when* that would happen. If now was the time, he was ready.

When Richard first arrived on campus, James had inspired him with his sincere and humble attitude about the workings of the college and his spoken objective to include the faculty and administrative people in decisions that would enhance and further its altruistic goals. "This isn't my college," James had said emphatically. "It belongs to the people of these mountains, the people whose lives can be changed by what we do here. Our mission is to serve them and give them opportunities they would never know if it weren't for Jackson Clayton College. This is our goal, Richard. I'm only the facilitator. It's you and the faculty who will bring the dreams to life."

Richard could remember being emotionally charged with the desire to jump on board and become a part of this "mission." For the first few years, it had seemed real and possible, even though it also became apparent that James Cantrell's hand was the only one on the tiller. At that point in time, Richard had never heard the name Tabor Maclean, and no one knew anything about Allison Montgomery.

The telephone buzzed, jolting Richard out of his journey back in time.

"Richard Shelton," he said reflexively.

"Richard . . . this is James. I need to talk to you right away. Are you free?"

"Actually, Chris Alford is coming for a meeting in about five minutes. She asked to see me today, so I don't think I should cancel."

"Okay . . . right. When you're finished with Chris, can you come by? How about lunch in my office?"

"That's fine . . . sure. Everything else on my calendar I can juggle. I'll see you around twelve."

James seldom called meetings, and he almost never expressed or even intimated urgency about anything. Richard remembered the last time he had been summoned in this fashion . . . to discuss Allison Montgomery's departure.

"Hi, Richard," Chris said as she stood smiling in the doorway.

He felt the same attraction he had felt when she walked into the lobby of the Grand Hyatt Hotel in New York a year ago, when he and James had met her for the first time. Although he had seen her countless times since then, Richard was aware each time of Chris's magnetism, that indefinable, seductive element that mysteriously draws people together. He stared at her long, coppery-colored hair as it rested softly on suntanned shoulders, the thickness of the left side fastened above her ear with a tortoise shell comb. Her emerald green, sleeveless silk shirt seemed to be one shade darker than her startling blue-green eyes. He couldn't help but follow the soft folds as they skimmed her breasts and ended at the black calfskin belt that was threaded through the loops of her ecru slacks.

"Hi, Chris . . . come in," he said as he stood to welcome her. "It's good to see you . . . please . . . sit down." Richard closed the door as Chris moved toward one of the chairs that flanked the sofa in a casual seating group.

"It's good to see you, too," she said with a smile as she looked up at him. "I won't keep you long. I know this first week is a busy one for you."

"I didn't have anything on my schedule for this morning," he said as he smiled back at her. "I'd rather sit and talk with you than do the other things on my list for today. The first couple of weeks are tougher for the faculty than they are for the administrators. I remember those days," he laughed. "And I still miss them sometimes. How are things going so far?"

He purposely gave her an entry.

"By and large, everything is wonderful . . . really . . . I couldn't ask for more. Richard, I hesitated to call you because it's only the first week of class. I've been in the academic trenches long enough to know that things ebb and flow the first couple of weeks of school. That's not a problem for me." She hesitated as she gathered her thoughts.

"Chris, did you come to talk about Tabor Maclean?"

She was caught off guard by Richard's question, startled momentarily into silence.

"Yes . . . yes, that's the student I want to talk about. How did you know?"

"I took the liberty of looking up your class rosters. When you said you wanted to talk about a student, I thought it might be helpful. I don't recognize or know most of the freshmen," he said, "but I do know a few, and I know Tabor. I thought he might be the one."

"I don't know whether I feel better or worse," she said honestly, "about your knowing him. I don't want to bury this boy, Richard. I don't want to create any more problems for a student who obviously has a load of them. I really think I can get along with Tabor, and help him, but I decided I might need a little guidance."

"Tabor's a problem, Chris.   This isn't the first conversation I've had like this. Tell me what's going on."

"I'm aware that I don't know much about the local people . . . customs of the area . . . that kind of thing. I'm from New York, a city girl.   I have a lot to learn about rural Appalachian Virginia. That's why I decided to seek your help right away."

"You did the right thing, Chris. I'm grateful you didn't wait to call me."

"Tabor hasn't done anything threatening, and he hasn't been rude or disruptive in class.   Actually, he's been pretty passive, considering the attitude the other students have toward him. I sound like I'm beating around the bush . . . I just need to say it. Tabor seems to have become overly interested in me. He acts as if we have a special relationship, separate and apart from the other students. He seems to have developed a little crush on me. I don't want to hinder his learning or classroom experience, but I can't handle the personal attention he seems to need. I can't let this interfere with the other students' needs and their class time." Chris took a deep breath and shifted in her chair.

"Richard, I believe he's terribly lonely. I don't know anything about his personal life, at home or outside of school, but I think he's crying out for a friend, or someone to care about him. I'm embarrassed to be saying this, but I don't know how to keep him on the right side of the student-teacher professional line, to gently communicate to him that his behavior isn't acceptable . . . professionally."

"I'm not sure anyone can successfully communicate "gently" with Tabor," Richard replied.   "I appreciate your sensitivity and genuine concern about your students. That's an attribute reserved for the very best teachers," he said sincerely. "But Tabor is in a separate category, Chris. I'm going to be honest with you, more honest than I was in our last real conversation."

185

Richard stopped speaking and looked directly into Chris's eyes. She smiled at him, acknowledging the veiled apology for his part in the Allison Montgomery question and answer mess.

"I appreciate that, Richard. I'll be honest with you, too."

"Other teachers have had problems with Tabor, and more than a handful of students have filed complaints about him. You may not know this, yet, but Tabor likes girls with red hair, and more than once he's acted inappropriately around them. I've never seen any of this first hand, but I know some of the girls whose hair he has stroked or touched, and the few I know aren't the type to make up stories like this. He's been too free with his hands, according to other complaints . . . touching girls when they aren't looking . . . sneaking up behind them and touching them . . . bumping into girls in the hall, and seeming to inadvertently touch their breasts or their buttocks. It doesn't appear that he has the ability to understand personal space."

Chris was stunned by Richard's statement . . . "girls with red hair." Was that why she was suddenly involved with Tabor and why she now found herself in the dean's office?

Richard continued. "Last year, Allison Montgomery went far out of her way to try and help Tabor. She tutored him, she opened her office to him outside of her regular office hours, and she encouraged him every opportunity she had. In my opinion, she went overboard. Tabor soaked up the attention, and the end result was his obsessive, deranged preoccupation with Allison's every move. He waited for her in the parking lot beside her car. He sat outside her office door, watching and waiting for her when she was off campus. I don't know this for a fact, but a faculty member told me Tabor had shown up at Allison's home after nine o'clock one night, wanting to come in and talk to her. I think he slowly drove her crazy.

"Allison waited too long to tell me. She told James long before I knew any of this, but he didn't act on it. By the time

Allison approached me about Tabor, it was too late. That brief conversation was the last one I had with her . . . and the last time I saw her." His voice had trailed off with his last two sentences.

Before Chris could respond to Richard's revelations, he said, "Chris, we have to make sure that Tabor doesn't turn your days and nights into a series of terrifying, destructive events, as he did with Allison's. I have to enlist James Cantrell's help. I don't have the authority to do this on my own, or I would."

"Richard, I'm not Allison, and Tabor hasn't done anything to me, certainly nothing I consider threatening or dangerous. I don't want him to be thrown out of school. I'm asking for your help in keeping him here on an acceptable basis. I'm hoping we can get the message across to him as to what appropriate behavior is, between teacher and student. I don't want to shame him or accuse him . . . I want him to feel okay about what happens."

"I believe it's way too late for that, Chris. I'm afraid it was too late last year." He wondered if he should stop here and just tell her the way it was going to be. "There are some things that you don't know, some things that I have come to know, after sifting through opinions, and facts, and gossip. I need to talk to James, and we need to make some big decisions that we implement now."

"I'm not happy with that. If I had known that this would be the result of my meeting with you, I wouldn't have come to ask for your help." Chris struggled to sound reasonable and not belligerent.

"Chris, please don't take this on yourself. What you're experiencing here started a long time ago, probably before any of us were involved with Tabor. Intellectually, he's on a par with a number of other students here who do well in our developmental classes, but he's a sick boy. I should say 'a sick man' since he's twenty-three years old. He isn't able to help himself, and we aren't able to help him, either. Maybe some professionals can . . . we can hope for that. But we need to take care of what we can, here at this college, with you, with the students and other faculty who may be affected if we don't."

Chris sat silently, hearing his rationale, feeling regret for what might have been her impulsive action based on a conversation with Rachael. What if Richard was right, and Tabor was dangerous? She already knew the consequences to Tabor if she was correct and Richard had his way. It would be the end of a boy who didn't have other options. Was there any intermediary step she had overlooked?

"Richard, would it be possible for me to sit down with you and Dr. Cantrell to talk about this?" She took the chance of offending her superior, with her unspoken challenge to his opinion and authority.

Richard hesitated, wondering if her suggestion was one step in a logical sequence, or a disastrous, deadly mistake. He knew the decision was his. He didn't believe Chris would go to Cantrell without his, her boss's, agreement.

"Okay," he said calmly. "I have a meeting with James at noon today. I'll see if I can arrange a time within the next twenty-four hours when all three of us can talk about this."

"Thank you. I really appreciate all you're doing to help me, Richard. I really do."

"I'm sorry you had to be thrown into this pit, Chris. You should've had at least a semester to settle in before you had to deal with a Tabor kind of problem. We'll work this out together."

Chris stood and reached out her hand to him. "Thanks," she repeated.

She started toward the door and then turned around to face him.

"I never saw a picture of Allison, Richard. What color was her hair?"

Chris's words echoed hollowly in her ears, as she immediately regretted her absurd question. It was tactless and unsuitable for a meeting with the dean. He would think she was an idiot, an incompetent new teacher on his faculty who was looking for an excuse for her inability to handle a difficult student.

He stared silently at Chris, as if carefully preparing for his next move in a masterful chess game. "Allison's hair was red, Chris, subtle, coppery red . . . almost like yours."

Chapter 31

Pap felt the rhythmic vibration of the old truck's noisy, idling engine as he counted the crisp bills a second time. Two-hundred dollars . . . two-hundred red-hot, for-real dollars in his shaky old hands.

"Damn," he said aloud. "Cantrell musta' thought Mawmaw needed some kind a' special food, givin' me all this goddamn money."

He lit a Camel and sucked deeply, feeling the momentary pleasure as the pungent smoke hit his lungs. Coaxing the reluctant stick shift back and forth a few times, he chuckled as the grinding gears clanked into place, and the smoking Chevy lurched slowly out of the college parking lot. The cigarette hung limply from the left side of his slight smile, as he turned right toward Clayton Forge. A left turn would have led him up the mountain and home.

He would buy Mawmaw some food. She already had her medicine. He figured fifty dollars would more than feed the two of them for awhile. No need to get fancy with their eating, just because someone had handed him a wad of money. Pap mumbled to himself as the truck jostled and bounced him into the little town.

"I'll buy her a couple a' them big Hersey bars she likes so well . . . bring her somethin' special. Ain't no harm in doin'

M o u n t a i n   B l o o d

somethin' nice," he said. "Get me some Redman, too. Hell, I ain't bought me a chew fer a couple a' months. Get a carton a' Camels this time . . . stop the damn runnin' up and down the mountain fer a pack."

Pap pulled into the gravel parking lot beside Blount's Store. The town was quiet. Only two other cars sat in the space that had been bulldozed and carved out to hold twenty-five.

He had been on the crew that had expanded the store's parking lot, back when there was still some piece work in construction, back when Amber Jean was a little tyke. Between the work he had at the mine and the odd jobs, they'd had some better days back then, he and Suelean and Amber Jean. She was such a pretty little girl, their Amber Jean, with that soft, blonde, angel kind of hair and those big, round blue eyes. And she was a sweet child, too. As it turned out, she was too pretty . . . and too nice. He and Suelean had never had any more babies . . . just didn't happen. He never knew why. For awhile they made love, just like before, but they never made another baby. Then when they had to take on the boy, everything changed.

"Hey, Lucas. Haven't seen you for awhile," Hazel Blount greeted him as he pushed his way through the old double glass door. "Everything okay with you folks?"

"No, it really ain't," he replied. "Suelean took a fall. Broke her arm real bad and busted a couple a' ribs. She's layin' home in the bed."

"Oh, I'm so sorry. Can I do anything to help her?" Hazel's face registered genuine concern as she moved around the counter and closer to Lucas.

"I come to buy her a few things, food and such. I don't reckon there's anything y'all can do, or anyone can do. Them bones jest need to mend."

"Well, y'all tell her I'm thinking about her, and I'll put her on my prayer list. Make sure you tell her, now."

Hazel Blount and her husband Lloyd had owned

the store for as long as Lucas could remember. Before them, Lloyd's father had operated a general store and a grist mill that had served the mountain people as well as folks in the little town. Lucas could remember going to Blount's when he was a boy, with his father in their old wagon that the big grey horse had pulled. They would buy a heavy sack of flour and a bag of sugar a few times a year. Everything else they ate, they grew or made for themselves. Lloyd Blount had died four years ago. He'd taken sick and Hazel took him down to Martinsville to the hospital . . . and that was the last anyone saw of him until he was laid out in his coffin. Lucas had taken that as an omen, and he vowed he'd never go and die in a hospital. No doctors were going to kill him with their experiments.

Hazel continued to run the store, with the help of her two sons who had built their houses next to the old farmhouse where she still lived, the one that Lloyd's grandfather had built at the turn of the century. By Clayton Forge standards, the Blounts were a well-to-do family. Hazel was into her sixties. She and Lucas had been in school together, up to the sixth grade when he quit. She was portly now, with her gray hair pulled back into a bun at the nape of her neck and thick-rimmed glasses hugging her wide pug nose. She had been a looker in high school, one of the girls who graduated along with twice the number of boys. By that time, Lucas was a father and a pretty good provider for his young family. Even though he was a poor mountain boy and Hazel and Lloyd were town kids, they had always been nice to him , even when they were in high school and he only should have been there.

Lucas wandered up and down the narrow aisles of the store, picking up a few cans in one place and some packaged goods in another. He bought several loaves of white bread, since Mawmaw wouldn't be baking for awhile, and a five pound bag of potatoes to add to the one they had at home. Stopping in front of the display of chewing tobacco, Lucas studied the wide range of choices. There were old brands he didn't like and new ones he'd never heard of. After a minute or two of looking, he picked up a tin of Redman and put it in the basket next to four Hersey bars. As he neared the end of the last aisle in the store, he pulled a twenty-four bottle case of Budweiser off the bottom shelf and shoved it onto the lower rack of the cart. With the beer and cigarettes, he wouldn't have to come down the mountain for awhile. No need to waste gas.

"Guess I'm ready," he said to Hazel as he pushed the half-empty cart up to the cash register. "I need to get me a carton of Camels, too."

"Y'all still smoking I see," Hazel said. "I heard you coughing back there . . . sounded just like Lloyd did. I wish he had stopped . . . but he never would. He nearly went crazy when they wouldn't let him smoke in the hospital."

Lucas bristled at her busybody chatter. Women just didn't know enough to keep their damned mouths shut. What business was it of hers if he smoked . . . or if he died, for that matter. Suelean knew better than to bring up the cigarettes, or the few drinks he might take. It was a man's right to do what he wanted.

"I'll tell Suelean y'all asked after her," he said as he put the plastic bags into the cart.

"How's your grandson?" she asked. "I haven't seen him in here for a long time."

"Don't know," he said gruffly. "He's pretty much gone off on his own. We're glad to be free of him."

"Lucas, you know there's a school over in Martinsville that teaches people like him how to do things. You know, things like fixing trucks or cars, and then they can go out and make a living for themselves. We know some folks whose boy is over there, and they think it's really wonderful. Y'all ever think about sending him someplace like that, so he could get himself a job?"

"Don't know nothin' about it," he mumbled. "He's a lazy son-of-a-bitch . . . he don't wanna' learn how to do nothin'. See y'all later."

By the time Pap got out of the store, his mood had taken a nose dive, with Hazel's yammering about smoking and telling him he should send his no-good grandson to some school. On top of that, the groceries cost seventy-four dollars. She was near to scalping people with her high prices. If there was any other place to buy food, he wouldn't go back to Blount's. He loaded the bags into the back of the pickup and slammed the door hard when he got in. Mawmaw was probably still sleeping off the pain pills she had taken before he left, so he had no need to run right home. It was about four in the afternoon, which was a good time to stop for a beer or two over at Millie's Bar. Maybe he'd see someone he knew at the bar. No harm in having a little conversation after the kind of day he'd endured.

Several pickup trucks were parked in front of the neon Budweiser sign, and the faint twang of country music floated out the open front door of Millie's. A loaded logging truck cast its giant shadow over the smaller vehicles, as it sat unoccupied at the edge of the dirt lot. Lucas didn't recognize either of the two men who perched on the stools at the old wooden bar, both of whom were engaged in a quiet conversation with the flaxen-haired Millie.

"Hey, Lucas, where y'all been?" she called as she walked toward him where he had sat down at the far end of the bar. Millie catered to the truck drivers who ferried logs and supplies up and down the winding mountain highway, but her favorite customers were the locals who passed through her establishment on a somewhat regular basis. She had celebrated her fiftieth birthday some years ago, but she dressed like a teenager . . . short little jean skirts and tight, stretchy tee shirts. Multiple silver earrings lined the shells of her ears, and others dangled from the piercings that covered her lobes. When she reached across to squeeze his hand, Lucas could see that every finger and even her thumbs were ringed with turquoise and silver. Millie had been pretty once, but backbreaking work and an abusive husband who was now in prison had taken its toll. She had a bad scar that ran from the right side of her mouth up toward her ear, the result of a harsh lesson her deadbeat spouse had tried to teach her. Millie's only child lived with her grandmother in Hillsville. Most folks around here had never even seen the girl.

"Y'all don't come see me much anymore, Honey," she said with a theatrical pout.

"Well, I'm here now," Lucas said gruffly. "I've had a damned bad day, Millie. Give me a glass of whiskey. . . a double. Beer ain't gonna' help me none today."

She reached for the bottle of amber liquid that stood with a dozen others of varying color on the shelf that ran along the mirrored wall.

"Hard stuff, huh?" she laughed. "Must a' been a doozy."

"Jest pour it," he said, with the edge of impatience creeping into his voice.

"Well, pardon me," she said with a haughty toss of her head. "Mr. Grouch." Then she reached over and patted his hand. "Y'all know I'm just pickin' at ya' . . . that's just me," she said quietly, with a little smile. "I'm sorry ya' had such a bad day."

"I'm jest gonna enjoy myself a little now," he said. "No harm done if a man enjoys hisself now and then. God knows, I don't have many times like that."

Lucas picked up the short, clear water glass and poured half of the contents down his throat. He gasped as it burned its way down his esophagus. Deep, convulsive coughs overcame him, causing the two men at the bar and Millie to turn toward him.

"Honey, are you okay? she asked. "Here, I'll get y'all

some water," she said as she hurried toward the faucet.

"I'm okay," he choked. "Don't need no water . . . jest got stuck in my throat," he wheezed, as he lifted the glass and downed the rest of the whiskey.

Millie and the two men stared at him. Lucas was determined not to cough again, as he breathed shallowly in an effort to pacify his rebellious lungs. He looked solemnly at his two gawking bar mates and turned back toward the silent Millie.

"Gimme another glass a' whiskey," he rasped.

"Lucas," she began.

He rose to his feet and shouted, "I said gimme another goddamn glass a' whiskey!"

"Okay . . . okay," she said timidly. "Y'all are a big boy . . . whatever ya' say."

He repeated his demand a third time, and she complied silently. One of the strangers at the bar looked aside at his partner and inconspicuously shook his head. The other pointed an index finger at his temple.

Pap successfully walked out of Millie's Bar by touching and holding every solid surface along his whirling, gyrating way. He missed the single, cement block step from the shallow porch and prevented a sprawling, head-first fall by grabbing one of the two by fours that held up the corrugated metal roof. The three in the bar heard the grate of the old Chevy's struggling gears and the squeal of the spinning tires as he shot onto the damp, dew-covered asphalt. One of them speculated that he would be lucky if he made it home alive.

When Buster and the other state trooper found the two mangled, overturned trucks a little after midnight, they agreed Lucas probably hadn't known what hit him . . . or more accurately, what he had hit. The twenty-six year old driver of the logging truck had not even had time to swerve, as the vehicles hit head-on and plunged together over the steep rocky incline, carrying their drivers to instant deaths. Hersey bars, cigarettes, and broken beer bottles marked the path of Pap's fall, the only mementos of a shattered life.

Chapter 32

The hot, muggy August afternoon reminded Richard a little of Florida, just before the hurricane season started. As he walked toward Bryant Hall, he felt the stiffening breeze that stirred the dusty branches of the tall Scotch pines and the bronzing maples. Clumps of rolling gray clouds preceded the low, distant rumble of thunder, signaling relief might be coming for the parched, dry mountains and the scorched valley below.

"Change is on its way," he thought as the wind ruffled his hair and flapped at the short sleeves of his navy blue shirt.

His curiosity about the meeting he was about to have with James vied equally for his attention with the perplexing situation he had just discussed with Chris. Richard wasn't convinced that a meeting between Cantrell, Chris, and himself would solve anything. It might even make things worse. Last year, he had come close to angering James with recurrent demands that Tabor Maclean be dismissed from the college. At the least, he had pleaded with him to get the kid out of Allison's class, strongly suggesting that something tragic would happen if James didn't act. For some bizarre, unexplainable reason, the president consistently defended Tabor and refused to take any action that would separate him from Jackson Clayton College. James repeated his mantra . . . that he knew the boy . . . that he was confident he wasn't dangerous or violent . . . that he was capable of getting a two year degree to qualify for a job in Internet technology, which could change his life. "I've known Tabor's family for many, many years, and I'll get personally involved to help him get through. That's what we do here."

Richard knew for a fact that Cantrell had met with Tabor, one on one, and had counseled the boy. He had gone so far as to review his homework and help him with writing assignments. James had told Allison about his involvement with her student, and he had asked her to report back to him with any problems or progress. After Allison had gone, James had revealed all of this to Richard. She had never mentioned it.

"Hi, Mattie," Richard said cheerfully as he walked into her office. "I think it might rain . . . sure feels like it. I just made a quick trip to the library, and the weather changed in the fifteen minutes I was over there."

"Hi, Dr. Shelton. I sure hope so . . . we're going to dry up and blow away if we don't get some water up here soon," she said. "Dr. Cantrell asked that you go into his office as soon as you got here. He said no need to wait until lunch time. I ordered from the cafeteria for you, and they're going to deliver about twelve or a little after."

"Thanks, Mattie." Richard walked around her desk and knocked on the president's door before opening it.

"Hi, James."

"Richard, good to see you. Thanks for coming on such short notice."

The same firm handshake, the usual manly pat on the shoulder, and the broad, friendly smile indicated business as usual. Cantrell didn't appear to be a man in distress, but he was hard to read. Richard never felt he really knew him.

"I sensed there was some urgency in your call," Richard said as he sat down in one of the oversized chairs facing the front of James's desk.

"Yes, there are some things we need to talk about . . . problems, I'm afraid, in the Jackson Clayton family."

James had not suggested that they sit over in the informal area of his office that resembled a comfortable men's club, but, instead, he had put the barrier of his executive desk between them. There was something slightly intimidating to those who sat on the opposite side of the boss's desk.

Richard disliked the term James enjoyed using and had thrown into the conversation once again . . . "the Jackson Clayton family." It sounded overly sentimental and sappy, certainly inappropriate for the head of the college to use. What did the term mean to James . . . that he was the big benevolent father of them all?

"I'll get right to it," he continued. "First thing this morning, Lucas Maclean came in to see me. He talked to Mattie first and then to me. You know who he is, don't you Richard? Suelean Maclean's husband, Tabor's grandfather?"

Richard nodded. "Yes, I'm aware of the whole family."

"He says he came because Suelean had asked him to. Seems she's home in bed because she has a broken arm and a couple of broken ribs. Apparently . . . or so he says . . .he found her lying unconscious in their backyard when he came home from being gone all day. He put her in bed and took her to see Doctor Reilly the next morning. From what he says, she's pretty badly banged up."

"That's terrible . . ., how did it happen?" Richard asked, as he recalled the pleasant, quiet mountain woman who cleaned his office and brought him fresh rhubarb from her garden in the spring.

"Lucas says he doesn't know, says Suelean told him she had been sitting on the edge of the back porch shelling peas, and she fell off. He claims that she doesn't know how it happened . . . or doesn't remember."

"What about Tabor?" Richard asked. "Where was Tabor when this happened?"

"I asked," James replied. "Lucas says that Tabor hasn't been home for awhile . . . I believe he said a few days. He says he doesn't believe Tabor was there when his grandmother got hurt."

"Do you believe that, James?" Richard sat on the front half of the chair's large cushion, leaning forward toward the grandiose desk front. "Do you believe any of this?"

"Well, yes, I believe most of what Lucas told us." James seemed surprised at Richard's question. "Suelean was injured . . . she has broken bones . . ."

Richard interrupted him. "Of course, I believe that, too. I think you know what I mean, James. Do you believe that no one else had anything to do with Suelean's injuries?"

James hesitated for a few moments, slowly tapping his finger tips hand on hand, as he rested his arms on the desktop. "No, I don't believe that Lucas is telling us the whole story. That's why I wanted to talk to you about this. I think someone other than Suelean may be responsible for her injuries."

"I do, too, James, and I know who I would put at the top of that 'responsible' list," he said emphatically. "The strange thing is that I was going to ask to talk to you about some serious problems that have arisen in Chris Alford's Comp I class, problems caused by this same 'responsible' person."

"Richard, you and I have to come to some agreement before we go any further. We may not be able to agree on all the elements here, maybe who the key players are, but we have to take some steps to protect people."

"I couldn't agree with you more. You and I have a big responsibility here, James, a hell of a big responsibility. As you know, I've had grave concerns about Tabor Maclean . . ."

James jumped into the middle of Richard's sentence.

"Tabor . . . this isn't about Tabor," he replied vehemently. "This is about Lucas Maclean. He's an admitted, convicted wife beater. I've seen firsthand what he did to Suelean on a couple of previous occasions. This guy is a drunken, abusive good-for-nothing. If it wasn't for Suelean, the family wouldn't eat half the time. He hates Tabor, absolutely hates him. Suelean has shared with Mattie her great fear that he'll kill his grandson someday."

"How do you know it wasn't Tabor who hurt his grandmother? What if Lucas is telling you the truth . . . what if he was gone all day? He'll probably have some proof of that if he was working. Then what? Are you still going to blindly defend a twenty-three year old man we still refer to as a 'kid,' a man who has probably killed someone in the past . . . and may be on the verge of doing it again?"

Both men had switched into fighting mode, as their voices rose and words sharpened. James's face was flushed and beads of sweat stood out on Richard's forehead.

"Richard, you decided last year that Tabor was responsible for a lot of trouble that I don't believe he had anything to do with. It's all because of Allison's whining about a situation she created and then decided she couldn't handle. She treated that kid like he was a member of her family, and then one day cut him off . . . no warning, no reason, just refused to be a part of his life anymore. No rational person does that sort of thing, but, then, you and I know, if we're honest about it, that Allison was not a rational person. She was making decisions, or not making them at that point, that defied understanding. You can't be objective about Tabor anymore because of all the trash Allison told you about him." James had stood up and was now pacing back and forth beside his desk as he spoke.

"You can fire me if you want to, James, but that's bull shit. Allison had every reason for being afraid of Tabor. He was stalking her, for God's sake. She couldn't get away from him. I can bring a half dozen people in here who will tell you some hair raising stories of what Allison went through with Tabor, some of which they observed firsthand. For some reason that only you know, you've decided that Tabor is innocent of any wrong doing, no matter how blatant the facts to the contrary.

"And now he's stalking Chris . . . Christine Alford. She's a veteran, James, a product of the big city and a teacher of city kids. She can handle difficult situations. I know it and so do you. Yet she came to my office earlier this morning and talked to me about problems she's having with Tabor in the first week of class. He won't leave her alone. He's glommed onto her just like he did Allison, and he's watching her every move. It's frightening as hell, James, and she's asked to talk to you and to me together about it. She actually wants to help him, but she doesn't know how to do that as he tightens his noose around her neck."

Richard's breath came in short, gasping spurts as he finished his emotional monologue. Somehow he had to get Cantrell to listen to him, to understand they were dealing with far more that a strange, mixed-up kid. More than ever before, Richard was convinced they were dealing with a psychotic killer who created his own insane fantasies and then went berserk when his chosen objects refused to conform. When it didn't work out, he worked it out his own way.

"You're drowning in your emotions, Richard. I know you had special feelings for Allison, no matter what you say. I could see it . . . and I can understand why you would believe what she told you. But I'm telling you, I got to know her very well, and I saw her chameleon-like behavior and the way she manipulated and used people. Tabor was just one of those unfortunate souls, and he didn't have the emotional capacity to understand or figure her out. Think back on some of the problems you and I had with her, above and beyond anything involving Tabor. She was undependable, missing classes without letting anyone know why; leaving papers and tests ungraded for weeks; sitting inside her locked office, refusing to answer her door or see students, even though they knew she was there; lying to you and to me about things she said she had done, which we later discovered she had never done. Richard, does that sound like a rational, reasonable person whose word you can count on? I'll admit, she fooled me on more than one occasion."

James sat down again and Richard leaned back in his chair. Neither man spoke or looked at the other, as each of them wrestled with issues he didn't want to accept or even acknowledge.

"What are we going to do here, James?" Richard asked, as he leaned back and closed his eyes. "The only thing we both know is that we have to do something to stop the freight train that's bearing down on us and a lot of other people."

James pursed his lips and looked out the window at the gathering storm. "I wish I had answers I was sure of, Richard. I really do. It's like looking out this window at those gray and black mountains and the sky around us. A storm is coming. I think it's going to be a big one, but there's not a damn thing either of us can do about it. I can't see how we can stop this storm that's overtaking us, either."

"May I call Chris right now?" Richard asked. "Let's get her over here so she can tell you what's been happening the past few days here on campus. In the meantime, why don't we send Kenny and Al, both good reliable campus security people, over to 'help out' at the Maclean's . . . and keep an eye on Lucas and Tabor without making it obvious. That way we can both feel better about Suelean lying there helpless."

"Yes, call Chris. Good idea about Kenny and Al . . . maybe send Mattie along to make Suelean feel better about having people there . . . another woman. It makes it look better, I think. Of course, Mattie may not want to go, but we can ask her. At least it's a step toward providing some kind of protection in a place where it's obviously needed. It doesn't seem logical that Suelean would get the kinds of injuries she has by falling unassisted off of her porch. Lucas did say that the porch hung over the side of a hill, but even so, I wouldn't think she would have multiple broken bones unless some force other than losing her balance had given her a shove."

Richard was punching the buttons on the telephone as he listened to James.

"Hi, Chris . . . this is Richard. I'm here in Dr. Cantrell's office and we wondered if you could come over and talk about the problem you and I discussed earlier. Yes . . . okay. Good. We'll see you in a few minutes. Thanks."

"Better make it lunch for three," he said. "She's on her way."

"I know we can work this out, Richard. We have to. There isn't any choice."

"I would agree with that. James, I think you and I need to share what we know about incidents that have occurred on and off campus that are pertinent to this situation with the Maclean's, any and all of them. I don't know if you're even aware of the experiences other faculty members have had involving Tabor, for example. And I certainly didn't know that Suelean's husband beat her up. I only met the guy a couple of times, but he may figure into Tabor's problems too."

"I have no doubt about it," James said pensively.

"Hello, James, Richard," Chris said as she came through the open door. "It's starting to rain . . . big drops . . . looks like there might be a storm coming."

"Welcome, Chris. Thanks for coming over. I think you're right, a major storm is brewing," James said as he stood up to greet her. "Why don't we go and sit in more comfortable

205

chairs. It's easier to talk over there," he said as he gestured toward the sofa and chairs gathered around a large glass and brass coffee table. "I hope you haven't had lunch, Chris. Mattie's ordered some for us."

"No, I haven't. Thanks for including me," she said with a smile.

"I hope you're still happy to be included after we're finished talking, Chris," Richard said as he sat down in another of the luxurious leather chairs that were casually grouped around James Cantrell's office. "I'm afraid we're about to drag you into another storm, and it may be a big one, too."

Chapter 33

Mawmaw was awakened by the short, sharp yip yipping of a coyote, sounding as if it had prowled close enough to raid her poorly fortified chicken house. Mountain folks knew from experience that it was bad news to hear those dreaded barks and howls at night, and they knew that a prowling coyote during the day pointed to nothing but disaster. It meant this mangy, ranging killer was hungry, real hungry, and he was going against his instinct to hunt only at night. He was risking all, and he wouldn't be particular about his meal. A scrawny chicken, a barnyard cat, or an unwary baby left to play in the sun would do. It could be that he was thirsty enough to know that death had him by the tail if he didn't get to water. Drought brought crazed wild animals from higher ground to drink at cattle troughs or rain barrels, and nothing would stop them but a bullet. Mawmaw remembered when she was barely six years old seeing a rabid coyote that had backed her little toddling brother up against their old barn, the animal's big, yellowed teeth bared and the white foaming saliva drooling from its snarling jowls. Her pa had shot the scraggly creature as it crouched in front of the hysterical, screaming boy. She would never forget that time, that image, and she feared a daytime prowler for that reason most of all.

She could tell that it was late in the afternoon because of the streaks of sunlight that lay across the bottom of her quilt. It was a gray day that smelled like rain was coming, but the persistent sun broke through the gathering, rolling clouds and left its mark where its light fell.

Mawmaw didn't have a clock that she could see, other than the big wind-up alarm that sat on top of the wooden crate beside her bed, and it had run down and stopped at eleven. Pap never wound it. He always said he didn't give a damn what time it was, and if she was fool enough to care, she could wind her own damn clock. Mawmaw set it every day for 6:00 a.m., but she was always up long before the loud clanging bell announced the time.

"Where is that ornery man?" she mumbled, as she tried to swing her legs over the side of the sagging mattress. Pain immobilized her as it shot red-hot through her chest and arm, causing her to fall back onto the flattened pillow. Her whole bruised body ached, and multiple cuts and scrapes burned along her thin arms and legs.

"Dear God in heaven," she moaned. "What am I gonna do?"

The ceiling circled above her, making her dizzy and nauseous. Her mouth was dry, her tongue thick and coated. Pap had left a Mason jar of water beside the bed, in case he was gone more than a couple of hours, but she had drained it long ago. She had asked him to leave the old porcelain chamber pot on a chair beside the bed, but she now knew she wouldn't be able to use it without someone to help her up.

"Where are you, Lucas?" she groaned. "Please come back and help me."

She drifted in and out of fretful sleep as she tried to remember what day it was and what had happened to her. Lucas had gone to the school . . . that's where he was. Where was Tabor? She dreamed that he had come home to help her, and he had brought Amber Jean with him. Did she hear Amber Jean calling to her?

Far in the distance she heard a voice say, "Suelean? Suelean? It's Mattie."

"I'm here," she heard herself say, but she couldn't make the noise of words. "I'm here."

"Mattie, y'all can't be goin' into the house by yourself. We don't know what we'll find," Kenny said as he warily pushed open the door. "Why don't y'all wait here until I look around." He stepped into the kitchen and stopped at the wide doorway to what he believed to be the living room. "Anybody here?" he called loudly.

"I'm here," Suelean heard herself say. "In the bed."

"I heard a voice," he said to Mattie as she waited in the middle of the kitchen. "I couldn't understand the words, but I believe it's Suelean."

"She must be alone," Mattie said. "Poor soul."

Kenny Watts was a burly, six-foot thirty year old who had come to Clayton Forge ten years earlier to marry Bonnie Hutchison. He had met her at a church camp when she was only seventeen, and he had vowed to follow her to the ends of the earth. At times, he felt he had done just that by coming to Clayton Forge. Kenny had grown up in Winston Salem, so he had lived around the mountains all his life, but he had never lived in a small, rural mountain town like this one. Jackson Clayton College had been his first and only job, and he intended to stay with it as long as he and Bonnie lived here, which he knew would be forever. She would never leave.

Dr. Cantrell had treated him well. Kenny was now head of the security force at the college, and he made more money than his brother who worked in the Ford plant in Winston. Dr. Cantrell knew he could trust him. Kenny had been asked to do some personal things for the president of the college that were "just between the two of them," as Cantrell had put it, and he was proud of that position of trust. Last year, he had driven Dr. Cantrell's big, silver BMW way up to Tuggles Gap, where he met up with Dr. Cantrell and drove him back down the mountain. Kenny didn't ask any questions . . . like "how did Dr. Cantrell get up to Tuggles Gap" or "who had driven him up to Tuggles Gap." For five hundred dollars, he could easily keep his mouth shut and his nose clean. This watch-dogging for Suelean was just one more of those special assignments, and he knew extra pay was part of the package.

"We're coming to see you, Suelean," Mattie called as cheerfully as she could muster.

The bleak, disheveled house smelled of musty wood ashes, the residue of a wood burning stove that had not been cleaned after last winter's use, and stale cigarette smoke. A worn brown sofa showing patches of white cotton stuffing, and two turquoise plastic covered chairs from the fifties or sixties completed the sparsely furnished eight by ten foot main room, its only light a single cheap glass fixture attached to the center point of the wood-planked ceiling. A narrow stairway with shallow, droopy stairs led up into darkness from one sidewall of the small room. The end of a bed was visible through the doorway on the opposite side .

"She's probably in there," Mattie said. "It's me, Suelean . . . Mattie." As she spoke, she moved ahead of Kenny and went through the door into the twilight of the small bedroom.

"Oh, Suelean . . . hello, Honey. Al and Kenny and I came to see how you are. Dr. Cantrell wanted us to come up and see you, and we wanted to come. We've all been worried to death about you."

Mattie spoke soothingly as she looked down at the pitiful, small figure that lay half under the patchwork quilt. The woman's right arm was wrapped in a rigid white band and seemed fastened to her upper chest in a sling, her hand extending toward her left shoulder. Under the sheath, a pale blue polyester shirt covered her upper body, and the elastic waistband of dark blue slacks was visible where the quilt lay crumpled beside her. Mattie had seen Suelean wear this same outfit as she worked in the hallways and restrooms and classrooms that she cleaned on a regular basis. Suelean's right cheek was bright red beneath a darkening circle that underlined her eye. Her upper lip was swollen, as if reacting to a blow from drunken rage.

"Mattie . . . I'm glad y'all come," Suelean whispered. "I'm in a bad way, Mattie."

"I know, Honey, I know." She looked at the empty jar beside the bed. "You need some water, don't you . . . let me get you some water. I'll be right back."

Mattie carried the Mason jar into the kitchen, where Kenny and Al stood talking softly.

"I looked all around outside," Al said as Mattie walked past him. "I didn't see no sign of anyone. Seems like Suelean must be here alone."

"She is alone, without water or anything to eat, as far as I can tell," Mattie replied angrily. "That SOB she's married to and her crazy grandson are nowhere around, typical of men like them. Since she can't cook and can't run and fetch for them, why bother with her."

Mattie let the water run until it was cold. The water pressure was low and the trickle clunked and spurted periodically as it ran slowly into the glass jar.

Kenny walked over to the sink. "Sounds like the pump is bad, or the well is running dry," he said as he looked at the meager stream that flowed from the old faucet. "Lots of folks around here have been losing their wells in this drought. I hope this one isn't running dry, too."

"Could be the filter," Al said wisely. He had lived in

these mountains all his life, and he could remember when folks began adding newfangled things like filters and pressure tanks to their households. "If ya' don't change the filter a couple of times a year, the sediment builds up to where the water near stops flowing. From the looks a' this place, seems like water filters wouldn't be changed if they did exist."

"Lucas Maclean is a pig," Mattie spat bitterly. "He would let his own wife lie here and die with no water at all." She walked briskly past the two men who gave her a clear path.

"Looks like someone cooked a pot of meat and potatoes, over there on the stove," Al said as he walked over and looked down into the lidless pot. "That's deer," he said. "Smells pretty good . . . it ain't old. I know good deer stew."

Mattie had set the glass jar on the vegetable crate that served as the bedside table, and she was slowly scooting her arm under Suelean's neck and shoulders. "I don't want to hurt you, Honey . . . you let me know if I do. I want you to be able to have a drink of this nice, cold water."

Suelean smiled weakly as she slowly raised her head while Mattie tipped the cold glass to her lips. "Thank you . . . it tastes so good."

"Where's Lucas?" she asked as gently as she could.

"I don't' remember. I think he went to talk to Dr. Cantrell, maybe this mornin'."

"Dr. Cantrell and I did see him this morning. He did come and tell us about your accident, but it's a little after four o'clock now. Did he say when he'd be back?"

"I don't remember. Seems like he was gonna' be later. Might could be he said somethin' about cookin' food." Suelean was exhausted by her first conversation since she fell, since the "accident," as Mattie had called it"

Where's Tabor? Do you know where Tabor is?" Mattie hated to keep questioning her, but plans had to be made for tonight. It was obvious Suelean couldn't stay alone, although the choice between Lucas or Tabor as caregiver was no choice at all.

"Don't know about Tabor . . . maybe he's still at school." Suelean didn't want to answer questions about the boy.

"Do you have a telephone, Suelean?"

"No, we had one fer awhile, but seems like we couldn't pay fer it regular, and the phone people come and took it out. Lucas said he wasn't gonna have nothin' to do with them anymore. If we need one, we go down to Blount's and use theirs. Hazel's nice about that."

"No need to try my cell phone," Mattie said. "It never works up here." She thought for a moment and then stood up. "Suelean, I need to go in the kitchen for a minute to talk to Kenny. Are you hungry, Honey? I'll see if I can find something for you to eat."

"I ain't hungry," Suelean said as she smiled up at Mattie. "Thank you, Mattie, fer comin' way up here to see me. Y'all are a fine friend . . . I appreciate it." Tears clouded her eyes and trickled down the sides of her cheeks.

"I'm so glad we came, and you don't need to thank me. I know you'd do the very same thing for me . . . or anyone else, for that matter. I've known you a long time, Suelean. I know what kind of a good person you are. Would you like to say hello to Al and Kenny, or do you just want to rest? You can say 'Hey' to them later . . . that's up to you."

"I'd like to see 'em," she whispered. "They're good boys. I knowed Al all his life, since way back when his mama used to work with me at the college. They're good people," she said.

Mattie hurried to the kitchen where Kenny stood leaning against the old metal sink. "Kenny, I need to get in touch with Dr. Cantrell. Do you have a radio or CB or anything in your truck that might get through to him? We need to make some plans for Suelean for tonight. God only knows where those sorry men are or when they'll get home."

"I have a radio phone, but I don't know if it'll work from back in here. It should, but these mountains are tricky when it comes to cells and radios. Dr. Cantrell told Al and me to stay up here until morning . . . said if Lucas or Tabor came back we should hang out somewhere close, but not to rile them."

"Rile them," Mattie huffed. "I'd like to shoot them. Would you see if you can get someone from the college on your phone. I'm going to stay up here with Suelean tonight. She can't do for herself."

"What if Lucas and Tabor come home? I don't think you should go up against them if they come home, particularly if Lucas has been drinking," he said. "I'll go out and see if I can raise anyone at the college. Al is out doing the rounds of the property again."

Mattie lowered her head and sniffed the pot of stew on the stove. "Whew, that's vile," she said with disgust. "It's hard to believe I was born in these mountains," she muttered.

A radio-phone conversation with Dr. Cantrell, broken up by static and moments of silence, resulted in his reluctant agreement that Mattie stay the night with Suelean. Mattie assured him that she would follow his wishes and tell Al and Kenny to stay close by for the night, never losing sight of both entrances to the Maclean's ramshackle house.

She fed Suelean a few spoonfuls of the brown gravy and venison, and gave her another of the Percocets Dr. Reilly had prescribed and given her free of charge. Mattie settled down on the sofa after raising each of the three cushions to make sure there were no surprises under them, covering herself with a tattered quilt she found on a closet shelf. She drifted off into a light and fitful sleep, waking every hour to check on the soundly sleeping Suelean.

Al and Kenny spelled each other on watch, finding they were both awake most of the time. It was Al who urgently shook Kennie awake as soon as he saw the headlights of the car

214

flashing on the road below them. Both men grabbed the rifles they had brought from home as they watched the car pull slowly into the driveway, not seeing the emblem of the Commonwealth of Virginia emblazoned on its side until it reached their lookout close to the house. They watched in silence as Buster Shewel and another state trooper got out and turned their flashlights on the trampled weeds of the dirt path that led to the back door.

Chapter 34

Tabor pushed the pile of dusty, soiled bedding into the corner of his dugout and climbed up into the misty quiet of a new day. He liked the way the mountain smelled in the early morning, like the fresh dug dirt in the early spring when Mawmaw planted her peas. The long, late summer grass lay against the ground, soft and wheat colored, turning amber toward its feathery ends. It reminded him of Chris's hair as it fell softly over her smooth shoulders. Everything beautiful reminded him of Chris, his beautiful lady.

His food supply was gone, last night's leftover charred squirrel having been the last of his meager store. He searched the pockets of his filthy stained jeans for anything edible he might have forgotten, but he found only the spent casing of a rifle shell and four wadded dollar bills Mawmaw had given him on the first day of class. It didn't matter. Excitement rose from Tabor's gut as he reviewed the tentative plans carefully cobbled together for the special day ahead. Maybe he and Chris would drink some coffee and eat a doughnut together after class. He could go without other food until later in the day. Having her with him after their class would make the wait worth it. He planned to buy the coffee and take it to her office. There was enough money for that. If he had enough money left after the coffee, he would buy doughnuts, maybe two of his favorite sugary brown twists that they sold at the student union. The thought made him chuckle aloud. He would buy all of it for the two of them, and Chris would be so happy. He remembered how she had smiled when she thanked him, and how she had looked at him when he had given her the whittled cat. Tabor desperately wanted to recapture that memory, to make it come alive again.

Overhead, the chittering of two lean gray squirrels caused him to look up. He watched as they leaped effortlessly from tree to tree, feverishly gathering the fat brown acorns that would feed them during the dark, snowy days of the months ahead. Their brown-flecked coats were thickening, as nature outfitted them for a hard Appalachian winter. Beyond the treetops, the sky was hazy, the sun overcast by the restless banks of clouds that grew larger as each rolling clump overtook the group in front of it. Rain was for sure on the way, and Tabor knew he had to get down the mountain in less than the twenty-five minutes it usually took him, if he didn't want to arrive at his class soaked and smelling like a wet hound dog. He drank the water that remained in his plastic jug, forgetting about his resolve to wash his face and hands before leaving his camp. As he always did, he took the time to restore the campsite to its natural look, dragging a wide pine bow across the dry, dusty ground and tossing any evidence of human presence into the dark hole of the underground hideaway. He would need to spend a day tidying up the inside before he showed his sanctuary to Chris, to make sure she felt comfortable there.

Tabor shouldered his rifle and entered the subdued light of the heavily wooded forest, walking directly ahead into the thicket, taking special care to avoid the same paths he had used before. He knew how to live and move in his beloved mountains, and he knew instinctively that a path twice traveled was a path that could be followed by others. He never risked discovery, no matter how urgent his trek. Today, he would walk faster, but he wouldn't be careless. The vining brambles grabbed mercilessly at his bare arms, leaving fine, red lines where they scraped away his toughened skin. Loops of Virginia Creeper snared his big boots as he pushed his way downward toward the college, tripping him and causing him to stumble to his knees several times. When he saw brighter light ahead, he stopped and looked for a good place to hide his rifle, a place he could remember but no one else could find. Tabor fitted the gun, butt first, into a long rotted-out hollow in the massive trunk of a dead oak tree, and then he carefully camouflaged it with a couple of armloads of dried leaves.

As he forced his way through the last snarled stand of fading wild rose bushes, he moved onto the highway a few hundred feet beyond the college grounds. Tabor almost always came this roundabout way, which avoided his leaving any sign of entry or exit onto the campus from the woods beyond. When he came straight down the mountain, it conveniently brought him out almost directly across from Chris's patio. On those rare occasions when he did use the shortest route, he would move swiftly to the protection of a thicket of laurel bushes and mottled white birch trees that lay to the right of Chris's private outdoor area, giving him up-close visual access to her office.

Five or six times he had sat hidden for most of a hot summer afternoon, as he watched his beautiful lady carry on her everyday life. How he longed to be part of that life, how he agonized over the times he had seen her with other men . . . Dr. Shelton . . . Dr. Cantrell . . . Professor Cooper. They all liked her, he could tell. Sometimes he was driven into an uncontrollable frenzy by their body language, as he watched one of them lean seductively toward Chris, or as he stared at the silent movie of their shared laughter. The faint heat of anger would overcome him, as he watched her lean back her head to laugh or toss her hair provocatively, a sure sign that she loved their attention. Would he lose, again? Would she choose one of them instead of him? He couldn't let that happen.

Tabor's worst times were the two times he had watched her with Dr. Cantrell. She seemed different with him, standing and moving toward the tall, gray-haired man when he arrived, laughing more when he leaned closer over her desk as they shared a piece of paper he handed her. On the second occasion, Tabor had seen Dr. Cantrell reach toward Chris, and it appeared that he had touched her arm. Tabor hadn't been sure of what he thought he saw, but the possibility soon became his reality. He stood up and wanted to shout and rush toward the heinous touching, but he was afraid he would never have Chris if he did. How could he tell her not to be with Dr. Cantrell? How could he warn her that this man was all wrong for her . . . that he, Tabor, loved her . . . and Dr. Cantrell never would love her like that?

When Tabor had helplessly watched Chris's encounter with Dr. Cantrell, he had sat despairingly in the shade of the fragrant bushes and silver-leaved trees that covered him, and he had cried. So much had happened that Chris didn't know about. He, alone, knew what had happened because Allison turned away from him and wouldn't listen to him. Toward the end, Allison wouldn't even talk to him, no matter how hard he tried to get to her. Sometimes he knew she was in her office, but she wouldn't answer his knocks or his calls. He had talked to her through her closed door, but she wouldn't respond, no matter what he said. For hours on end, he had sat outside her door, hoping to stop her as she returned from class. Then there was the trouble with Professor Cooper, and everything had come crashing down, as he knew it would. Tabor wasn't able to control it. Allison wouldn't let him. He was not given any choice.

All the way down the mountain, Tabor thought about Allison and Chris. This time, he would insist that Chris pay attention to him, listen to him. How could he get the message across to her that it was really a matter of life or death . . . her life or her death?

Chapter 35

"James, as I told Richard earlier today, I really want to help this young man, and I believe I can help him."

Somewhat regretfully, Chris sat in James Cantrell's office and repeated her unsettling experiences with Tabor, beginning with the chance encounter on the Fourth of July. As she recited the chronology for the second time, she was convinced that her decision to talk to the dean and the president of the college after less than a week of classes had been a mistake. Her telephone conversation with Rachael, coupled with the inflammatory gossip and personal interpretation from numerous colleagues, had definitely influenced her. This was not like Professor Chris Alford, champion of the underdog, teacher of the unteachable. She was sorely disappointed with herself.

"Tabor hasn't threatened me in any way . . . please understand that. At the worst, I would say he has attached himself to me in an inappropriate way. I believe he sees me as someone who cares about him, and he's correct. I do care about him, as I do about all my students. It's my impression that he's a very lonely, isolated, and confused boy. He's looking for a friend, a good friend. Rather than frightening, I find his situation terribly sad."

As Chris concluded her uncomfortable comments, she

watched James subtly nod his head in agreement before he spoke. "Chris, I can't tell you how much I agree with you, but more than that, I truly appreciate who you are and what you stand for. Your philosophy and attitude represent a solid gold teacher."

"Before you make Tabor into something that I don't believe he's capable of being, let's get all the facts straight. Just a review," Richard said sharply. "This is not a slaying of the innocent we're talking about here. Too many suspicions lead to Tabor . . . his behavior last year regarding classmates, multiple female classmates, and his overt stalking of Allison, to name a few."

"Richard, that's your opinion. You and I have talked about our differences on the "stalking" issue. A lot of that's conjecture and campus gossip. As far as I'm concerned, Allison was responsible for the attention she got from Tabor." James was clearly annoyed.

"James, neither you nor I know why Allison left, or, more importantly, how she left. I only know something major changed about her, and Tabor played a part in that change. That's not based on gossip. Ask some of your faculty."

James shook his head and frowned in open disgust. "Let's not drag Chris through the muck of the Allison situation. Let's get back on track as to why we're here." He stared intently at Chris, seeming to consume her with his eyes. "Chris, what would you like to see happen here, regarding Tabor?"

"What I'd like to do is re-channel his inappropriate attachment, use it to get him interested in his class and in bettering himself. I want him to feel accepted by me. It's important to me that all my students know that I accept and respect them. Tabor has just misread that acceptance, and he's taken it a few steps in the wrong direction. I think he and I can get it back on track. What I need is some input from the two of you as to how I might proceed at this point."

"Chris, Richard and I need to share with you some events that have just occurred that will impact on Tabor, or probably already have. I need you to keep what we're about to tell you confidential. Tabor's grandmother, Suelean Maclean, works here at the college in maintenance. She's been here for years. Within the past forty-eight hours, she was injured pretty severely . . . broken bones . . . maybe more. Her husband Lucas came by to tell me of the accident this morning. He's a drinker, and he's abused Suelean in the past. The circumstances of her injuries are suspicious . . . Richard and I agree on that point." James looked momentarily at Richard, who sat stoically listening to his boss's slant on the events.

"As to suspicions, yes," Richard said.

James continued, "Chris, I think Lucas Maclean very well could have pushed his wife, or worse, causing her to fall. I've seen what he's done to her in the past."

"And I think it's possible that Tabor hurt his grandmother. He has a volatile temper. Ask some of the counselor's in Student Services who have seen it erupt," Richard countered.

"Either way, responsible or not, this accident is going to impact Tabor in a negative way. I think you should be aware of this when you interact with him in or out of the class tomorrow and in the future. Suelean is really the only person the boy seems to trust. He has no relationship with Lucas, and his mother died when he was born." James waited for Chris's reaction.

Poor guy," she said softly. "Bad luck seems to follow him." Chris paused and gathered her thoughts. "I would like to meet with Tabor tomorrow and next week as I will with all the other students. Let me see if I can help him understand. If I can clear up some of the issues one on one, maybe I can clarify for him what our relationship should be."

"It's crazy, absolutely crazy," Richard fumed. "James,

how can we put Chris in that kind of a situation? The unknowns are overwhelming. It's irresponsible as administrators to ignore the facts and jeopardize her safety. I say we have to suspend Tabor for the semester. Call it anything you want to call it, but get him out of the classroom for a period of time. I believe we have to. We're exposing students and faculty to a really questionable unknown personality here."

"Richard, I don't want you to suspend Tabor. I don't think that's going to help anything. It just might be the proverbial last straw for him. Please let me see if I can work with him, at least tomorrow and next week." Chris leaned toward Richard as she spoke. "If his grandmother is unavailable to him because she's hurt, then he doesn't have anyone to turn to."

"Chris, there's a very good possibility that Tabor is the reason his grandmother is hurt." Richard fired the words at her. "You may have all the right attitude and philosophy, but that won't go very far if you're dealing with a psychotic personality. You'll be playing with fire, Chris . . . or worse."

Richard turned to James. "This is your call . . . you're the boss," he said, making no attempt to hide his anger.

James sighed deeply, as he gazed at the peaceful pastoral setting in the painting behind the sofa where Chris sat. After a long minute of silence, he turned toward Chris.

"Chris, it would be easy for me to suggest to Tabor that he should stay at home and care for his injured grandmother. There's a possibility that he would understand that, if I assured him that he could come back to his classes next semester. I do know he's very close to her, and she to him. I don't feel one hundred percent okay about your continuing to work with him as if nothing has happened. I don't think you can go it alone, so to speak."

"I'll keep you two informed on a daily basis, and I'll be alert. If anything appears to be going the wrong way, I can call on you at a moment's notice. I would like to try," she replied. "Everyone deserves a chance."

"And if I'm right in my 'conjecture?'" Richard asked sarcastically. "What then, James?"

"I think Chris has the right perspective about this boy," James said calmly. "I will only agree to it, however, if we know where he is at all times, while he's on this campus. When Kenny comes back here later tonight or tomorrow, I'll put him on it."

James explained to Chris the role Kenny was to play in the escalating drama. "Are you sure this is the way you want to proceed, Chris? We can remove Tabor from your class and enroll him in another class if necessary. Please don't feel pressured. No one is going to think less of you, considering all that's happened, if we move him."

"I'd like to try and work with him," Chris said. "What you've suggested sounds fine."

Richard stood up abruptly and looked down at James and then at Chris as he spoke. "I don't agree with any of this. I'm dead set against it, and I just want to go on record as telling you both that I think you're making a dangerous, wrong decision. I won't be a part of it."

He was gone before Chris or James could speak.

"I understand why he's upset," James said as Chris prepared to leave. "Why don't you stay and help me finish the pot of coffee?" he said. "We can talk about this situation a little more."

"Oh . . . okay," she said, laying her portfolio back on the sofa where she had been sitting. "Thank you. Here, I'll fill up the cups one more time. More than two cups of coffee, and I won't close my eyes all night," she laughed.

"Chris, when I said I appreciated you and your attitude, I really meant it. I knew when we met and talked in New York last year that you were exactly the person I had been searching for to fill the position in the English Department. You and I share a common philosophy about students and teaching. It's clear to me, after all the years I've been here, that we are a definite minority."

"I appreciate your comments, James. I can't imagine being a teacher without the caring feelings for the students. But I know what you mean . . . there are too many who have become jaded by the problems, discouraged by the failures. It's hard to maintain a positive attitude when you're overwhelmed by the negatives."

"Richard is a good man," he said emphatically. "I can understand why he has planted his feet on this one. It's hard to like Tabor under the best of circumstances, and the unfortunate episode last year with our former teacher didn't help any."

"I've gathered that you . . . the college . . . endured some difficult times last year."

"More than most people realize," he said quietly. "It was all so unnecessary." James sat up and changed the tone of the conversation. "Tell me about you," he said. "Do you have family in New York?"

"No. Actually, I don't have any family." Chris hesitated. "My husband was killed in an automobile accident on the Pennsylvania Turnpike twenty-one months ago. He was the only family I had."

"Chris . . . I'm so sorry. I had no idea."

"I didn't mention it when we met in New York. It wasn't relevant to the interview and, quite frankly, I wasn't able to talk about it then. It's easier now."

"I don't expect it ever gets easy to talk about it, but time does soften the painful things that seem to stream through our lives."

The silence between them felt awkward, but Chris had nowhere to go with the conversation.

226

"I was married once when I was twenty-two, . . . for two years. My wife drowned in a boating accident. All these years later, I still think of her, but it's different now."

"You know what I mean, having gone through it yourself," Chris said quietly. She was suddenly grateful that she had stayed to finish the coffee.

"Are you really okay with the decision about Tabor?" he asked.

"Yes, I am. If I doubted that I could make any difference in his life, I probably would say 'put him in someone else's class,' because I don't think the next two weeks are going to be easy. But I really believe I can help him, and I want to."

"Just remember . . . you can call on me anytime . . . anytime at all. Forget the sign on my office door, Chris. Think of me as any other colleague who's available to help."

"Thanks, James. I really appreciate that . . . and I will call if I need help."

"Let's make a deal," he said. "You call me within a few hours after each class with Tabor, and we'll talk about it, whether the news is good or bad. It helps to have a team mate. I'm afraid Richard won't be able to be objective about this because he has strong negative feelings about Tabor. We'll keep him in the loop, but we don't need to make him uncomfortable. Don't worry about the line of reporting. 'll let him know what's going on and that I asked you to let me know. Believe me, he'll be grateful."

James held out his hand to Chris. She shook his hand and said, "That's a deal. I'm happy to have a team mate. Thanks so much for your support."

"It's a good opportunity for me," he said with a smile, "to get to know you better. That's the best part of the bargain."

Chapter 36

"Hey, Buster . . . it's Al McGinnis and Kenny Watts," Al shouted to the two uniformed police officers who were halfway up the ragged dirt path that led to the Macleans' darkened house. Al had worked in security long enough to know you didn't want to startle an armed trooper by coming at him out of the black of night.

The two officers stopped and turned in the direction of the flashlight that accompanied the vaguely familiar voice.

"What're y'all doin' here?" Buster asked, as he waited for Al and Kenny, who were sprinting toward him. "Normally don't run into people way up here at three o'clock in the mornin'."

"Suelean Maclean had an accident yesterday, and she's laid up in bed. Neither Lucas or Tabor are here. Cantrell asked us to keep an eye on things and help her out. Mattie Marcum's inside tending to her . . . both probably sleeping now."

"Been another accident, too," Buster said softly. "Lucas got himself tanked up and he tangled with a loggin' truck over on Groundhog Mountain Road . . . head-on. He and the truck driver never knew what hit 'em. Both of 'em went over the side, and pretty far down the mountain."

"He's dead?" Kenny asked in a shocked whisper.

"Yeah . . . real bad accident. It was hard to identify Lucas. Took over an hour to get his body outta' the truck." Buster turned to the younger state trooper standing next to him. "Y'all know JT Simpson? Been with the force three months."

Al and Kenny stuck out their hands to Buster's broad-shouldered, powerfully-built partner.

"Don't believe I do," Kenny said.

"Good ta' meet ya," Al replied. "Y'all related to Jeffrey Simpson up Tuggle's Gap way?" he asked.

"He's my grandpa," JT answered. "Guess he knows just about everybody in these parts," he said with a chuckle.

"Glad to have ya' lookin' after us up here," Al said. "If y'all are anything like your granddaddy, y'er one hell of a good man."

"We came to tell Suelean," Buster said, as he turned and looked at the old house, barely visible in the light of the pale August moon. "It doesn't sound like she's in any shape to hear bad news like this, but I'm afraid I can't spare her. Come on, JT, let's get on with it. This is the bad part of an otherwise good job. See you fellas later."

"We came up here with Mattie. Y'all want me to go in and wake her up? Maybe that's better . . . to tell her first . . . before rousting Suelean. Mattie can help with Suelean when she hears about Lucas."

"Might be a good idea, Kenny. I don't wanna' scare Mattie," Buster said, grateful for some help in softening the blow he was about to deliver.

The four men straggled in an uneven line along the dark path, following the bobbing circles of light that played off the ends of Busters's and JT's flashlights. Each of them eased himself around a broken post that rose precariously from the wobbly front porch floor to support a phantom railing that had been gone for ten years. Kenny quietly opened the unlatched door and motioned his three companions into the living room

where Mattie lay sleeping on the old couch. He walked closer
to her, listening for a moment to her regular, rhythmic
breathing. He leaned over slightly and said in a low voice, just
above a whisper, "Mattie, it's Kenny. I need to talk to you."

She jumped immediately to a sitting position, asking
loudly, "What's wrong . . . is something wrong with Suelean?"
Her eyes widened in alarm, as she experienced that moment
between sleep and wakefulness where fear is strongest.

"No, Suelean's in there sleeping. I can hear her
breathing. Buster is here, Mattie. He needs to talk to you."

"Buster Shewell?" she asked hoarsely. "What in the
world has happened?"

Mattie sat clutching the ratty, torn quilt that had warmed
her minutes earlier, as she looked beyond Kenny and the silent
Al at Buster and an unknown trooper. The two policemen
stood holding their incongruous, big brimmed hats in their
hands. Even in familiar territory like this, in the poor, hard
scrabble farmyards and run-down houses of their own people
and kin, they wore their regulation uniforms on official
business.

Buster stepped in front of Kenny, a few steps short of
Mattie and the sofa. "Hey, Mattie. I'm sorry to have to wake
y'all up like this, but I have some bad news for Suelean. Since
you're lookin' after her, I'm hopin' you can give me a hand in
makin' it as easy as we can."

"What's happened, Buster?" Mattie was now fully
awake.

"I'm afraid Lucas has been killed in a bad wreck over on
Groundhog Mountain Road. Best as we can figure, it happened
about ten o'clock last night. It's now about three on Friday
morning. We got a call from some trucker who was headed
toward Martinsville and happened to be takin' a shortcut. He
saw the two trucks down the side of the mountain."

"Oh, dear God," Mattie said, as she wrapped her arms

around her chest. "Poor Suelean. She's so sick herself . . . I don't know what this will do to her. What about their grandson Tabor. Does he know?"

"No, Ma'am, not as far as I know. We haven't seen him. We thought he might be here, until we talked to Al and Kenny. I reckon we'll have to go lookin' for him, so he doesn't hear from someone else."

"Lucas might not have been much of a husband, by most people's standards, but he was hers, and she stuck with him all these years. She took care of him and the boy for most of those years. Do we have to tell her now?" Mattie looked up at Buster's kind, familiar face, now dimly illuminated by the flickering ceiling bulb that Al had turned on.

"I'm afraid so. There really isn't any good time to tell someone. I understand that poor Suelean is hurt pretty bad herself, but we have to inform the next of kin as soon as we can," Buster explained.

"Mattie?" Suelean's weak, wavering voice barely carried to the room beyond her bed. "Who's here? Is it Tabor or Lucas?"

Mattie's eyes filled with tears as she felt the next minutes closing in on her. "Poor, dear woman," she said softly. "I'll come with you, Buster . . . I'll do what I can." She wiped at her eyes as she stepped into her sandals.

"No, Suelean, it's just me," she called, as she looked up at Buster who was following her into the darkened room. "Suelean, Buster Shewell is with me. He's coming in with me."

"Buster? Buster's here?" she asked, confusion mixing with a rising fear. "Why's Buster here? Is it Tabor?" Panic edged her barely audible voice.

"Hey, Miss Sulean, sorry to wake you up like this," Buster said, as he leaned closer to her. "No, it isn't Tabor. How y'all feelin'? I hear ya had a fall a couple a days ago. Is it okay

231

if I pull up a chair here beside yer bed?" Buster pulled a spindly ladder back chair from the closest corner of the room as he asked the question. Mattie sat close beside him on a three legged stool.

"Y'all have bad news fer me, don't ya'?" Suelean said, her voice a soft whisper. "I knowed it the minute Mattie said ya was here." She turned her head away from both of them, as a wrenching sob broke painfully from behind her aching ribs. "If it ain't Tabor, it must be Lucas," she said.

"Yes, Ma'am, I'm here about Lucas. He's been in an accident, Suelean. I'm sorry to tell you he's dead." Buster knew he had to say the word. You always had to say the word so they could grasp the unbelievable reality. "He died instantly. We know he didn't suffer." Buster transferred the great weight of his painful responsibility to her aching heart.

"With his truck?" she asked stoically.

"Yes, Ma'am. He was drivin' up Groundhog Mountain Road, by himself, when it happened." There was no need to supply more details than she wanted to hear, not now. It was always better to let the first waves of shock settle down before stirring up the next ones.

"I knowed he wasn't gonna' be around fer much longer, with his cough gettin' worse every day . . ." her voice trailed off into silence.

"Suelean, I'm so sorry, Honey. Don't you worry, I'll stay here with you as long as you want me to," Mattie said, as she laid her hand gently on Suelean's frail arm, unable to hold back the tears of anguish she felt for this poor woman.

"Did y'all tell Tabor?" Suelean asked.

"No, Ma'am, we haven't seen him yet to tell him. If y'all want us to wait until he comes home today . . . I believe Mattie said he was goin' to the college . . . we can do that."

"If he comes home," she said wistfully. "He ain't been here for a spell. I reckon he'll be back soon, when he gets hungry. Don't make no difference who tells him. I don't expect it will make much difference in his life one way or t'other."

"Y'all want us to go over and find him at the college and bring him home?" Buster asked, unsure that he could carry out what he was offering.

"Reckon that'd be all right. Jest don't scare the boy. He's not like y'all think. He's got a tender heart. He don't even know I'm ailin'. That'll be what worries him. Please treat him nice," she said, sadness hanging on her slowly spoken words.

"Yes, Ma'am, you have my word," Buster said as he stood up. "I'm sure sorry for all your troubles, Suelean."

"Thank ya', Buster." She turned her head toward him as the tears ran from her eyes. "No one but me ever knowed Lucas, for who he really was . . . jest like the boy. Fer such a long time, Lucas was never able to show his real self, even to me. Pretty soon, he lost sight of Lucas. He jest plain lost hisself in all the troubles that got heaped on top a' him. But I always knowed who he was. I never forgot."

Deep, agonizing sobs poured out of Mawmaw's brittle, vulnerable body, overtaking the pain that had exhausted her, and devouring the last shreds of hope to which she had been precariously clinging. As she struggled to hang on to her sanity, she was able to form only one thought. She had to stay alive for Tabor.

Chapter 37

It was half past nine, but Chris tried not to focus on the magnified tick of the wall clock and the steady movement of its hands. She had unlocked her office door fifteen minutes before eight this morning, and more than an hour later, she was still struggling over the task that usually took her thirty minutes. She had sat numbly reading and rereading the names on the class roster, staring blindly at the grades from the first papers her Comp I students had submitted on Wednesday. On the first Friday of a semester, she always assigned students to a peer writing group, and this was D-Day. The overwhelming problem was the one blank space in the grade column, the one student who hadn't turned in a paper answering her provocative question, *Why are you here?* What was she to do with Tabor?

When it came to successfully teaching novices how to create sentences and paragraphs and how to build essays, step by step, peer review had proven to be one of the strongest and most useful tools in her teacher's bag of tricks. They would read each other's papers, and they would learn from each other. It always piqued their interest and aroused their curiosity when she told the students what was coming . . . questions . . . anticipation . . . even some anxiety. Few people in a class knew each other well at this point. Some knew no one. Who would they be matched with? Would there be boys and girls in a group? In a way, for them, it was a social thing, one more mixer in this college club they had just joined.

Chris always enjoyed the first Friday as much as the students did. She liked to form the groups before she knew much about the students, using the first essays as a guide of sorts. She tried to include a strong writer or creative person in each group, and she parceled the obviously weak and reluctant ones among the flock. They were a little like sheep at this age, really, which was the basic premise of her peer group success. In the years Chris had been teaching, many theories and catchy new twists on her craft had come and gone, and she had arbitrarily rejected some as bad ideas or contrary to her philosophy before even trying them. Peer writing groups had never failed her, nor had they failed a large majority of those who populated them.

She didn't need to read an essay to assess where Tabor was likely to fall on the ability spectrum. The class he was in was a developmental class, one where everyone was struggling to rise to "average college-level" work. Chris didn't doubt that Tabor could hold his own in this class, under normal circumstances. But the first week of class had clearly shown her that nothing involving Tabor was likely to be normal. She felt uncomfortable with how much she knew about him, more than she wanted to know so early in the school year. Would he fit anywhere, with anyone? Probably not. In two days, he had become the brunt of cruel jokes, the obvious freak to avoid. Should she scrap the writing groups to avoid problems? Was that fair to the others who needed the success a group would provide? Should she have taken James's suggestion and asked that the misfit be transferred to another class where he could fail without inconveniencing her? Or maybe Richard was right, and this time bomb needed to be off the campus and safely out of their way. And so her mind had rebelled and run off on wild, unproductive tangents that had created the twisting, acid-pumping knot in her stomach and the pounding, relentless ache between her temples.

Chris repeatedly pressed the silver button on the top of her pen, and it clicked as the clock ticked, and the tension mounted. Soon it would be too late to do what she had told the class she was going to do today. That was not the way to end the first week, with a cop-out on the teacher's part. What would change between Friday and Monday? Certainly not Tabor, nor the terms and conditions of his existence. Do it now, or don't do it at all.

"You said you wanted to work with him and help him," she berated herself silently, as she hated her indecisiveness. "Then work with him, damn it, and help him . . . or don't. Decide now." She picked up her pen and wrote names on the few remaining lines of the chart she had made entitled "Writing Groups." Class would begin in fifteen minutes, which allowed her enough time to gather remaining books and materials into her bag and get to Room 330 before most of the students arrived.

As she rounded the corner of her office corridor and started down the long hall, Chris saw the lone figure leaning against the wall across from the classroom. There was no mistaking the outline of the shaggy head nor the height and girth of the slouching body. She pulled in a deep breath and forced her shoulders back as she paced confidently ahead. As she approached him, she saw Tabor step slightly away from the wall and turn toward her.

"Hi, Miss Chris," he called. "I been here awhile. I didn't wanna be late."

"Good morning, Tabor. That's good that you made it on time. I'm glad you're working on making it to class on time every day." She smiled at him before opening the classroom door.

"I wanna talk to y'all about my papers and my work," he said as he followed her into the room. "Can I do that today?"

"It's better if you make an appointment, Tabor, on the days I have office hours. I can make one for you now if you'd like."

Anxiety grabbed hold of her. She had to calm down.

"I wanna make one fer today," he said. "I need one fer today. I want it ta be right after this class . . . today."

His flat, blunt speech pattern had the effect of making him sound insistent, demanding. She mustn't misread him. She needed to understand him if she was going to work with him. Chris felt her clammy hands trembling as she unpacked her materials and put them on the work table beside the lectern.

"I can't see you right after class today," she lied . . . again. Should she give in? What would she say to another student who asked the same from her? "It's easier for me, Tabor, if we have an appointment later today. That's what I ask all my students to do," she emphasized, "make an appointment." She tried to emphasize his sameness, his equal but not special membership in the group

"Why can't I come today after class?" he asked. "Where are y'all goin' today after class?"

"Tabor, it's not appropriate . . . it's not good," she corrected, "for you to ask your teacher where she's going after class. I wouldn't ask you that question, either, because where each of us goes after class is our own personal business."

She looked at him to see if he was understanding her words. For the first time this morning, Chris noticed his startling, almost shocking appearance. His thick black hair was matted and contained bits of crumbled dried leaves and shreds of grass. The front of his yellow shirt was heavily stained with dark circles of dried liquid and streaks of greasy-looking matter, and the left side had a sizeable tear under the sleeve. Thick, black hair poked through the edges of the ripped fabric.

Tabor's baggy jeans were stiff with mud and other unknown filth, appearing to have been worn for weeks on end without washing. A strong, foul sourness surrounded his unwashed body and quickly spread throughout the empty room. Chris felt nauseous as she breathed in the stinking smell, suddenly aware of the impossibility of maintaining normalcy in the next fifteen minutes.

"I don't mind tellin' y'all where I'm goin' after class," he replied loudly.

"Tabor, have you been out camping for awhile?" Chris asked, feeling she might be stepping into quicksand.

"Yeah," he said matter of factly. "I ain't been home fer a few days . . . been up at my place on the mountain. After you and me have our meetin' today, I'll be goin' back home then."

"Whenever we go camping or hiking out in the woods, I always think it's a good idea to take a shower and get cleaned up before going anyplace, don't you?"

"Reckon so. I never give it any mind," he answered. He paused and looked down at his jeans. "I reckon I'm dirty from bein' up there," he said. "Need to wash up when I go home."

Chris silently reveled in the small victory. He wasn't beyond understanding the nuance of suggestion. She had always believed he was more normal than people thought. She recalled a conversation she had heard between Mary Ella and Hal Southern at the departmental meeting. Hal had maintained that Tabor had to be within the normal range intellectually, or he wouldn't have passed the entrance exam required by the college. When Mary Ella questioned whether he had passed the exam, Hal confirmed that Dr. Cantrell himself had seen and validated Tabor's test. If Chris could get past Tabor's disarming facade, and help him change it enough so others could get past it, too, she believed he could succeed.

"Okay," she said in a friendly but firm voice, "you and I can meet today right after class, for fifteen minutes in my office.

That way, you can get home to your grandmother." Chris was unaware that Tabor knew nothing of his grandmother's injuries.

"Okay . . . but . . ."

"Excuse me, Ma'am, are you Miss Alford?" Buster stepped inside the door to allow room for the passing students who had begun to drift in.

"Yes, I am," Chris said, recognizing the same state police officer she had seen in Mattie's office last April.

"Hey, Tabor," Buster said. "How y'all doin'?"

"Okay," Tabor replied as a frown spread darkly across his face.

"Tabor, I just came from your grandma's house, and I need to take you home. I told her I'd come to find you for her."

"I'm here for my class," Tabor boomed, his voice a decibel louder than it had been a few seconds earlier. "I ain't done nothin'," he said angrily.

"No, you're not in any trouble. Your grandma just needs you right now. Come on. I'll give you a ride in the police car," he said.

"I don't wanna go in yer damn police car," Tabor shouted. "I told ya, I got a class now."

Students had gathered on the edge of an invisible line drawn around Chris and the two arguing men. A few individuals watched unemotionally, but most smirked and chuckled quietly and exchanged knowing looks, careful not to call attention to themselves.

"Tabor, let's step out in the hall. I need to tell you some things," Buster said, as he fought the urge to grab Tabor and wrestle him away.

"Okay, but I ain't goin' with ya. I got my class, and me and Miss Chris got a meetin' after the class," he said, looking at Chris for confirmation.

"We can meet on Monday, Tabor. Your grandmother needs you now." Chris felt the rush of relief that coursed through her body.

"I gotta talk to ya today," Tabor called as Buster gently shoved him ahead and out the door.

"Okay, everybody, take your seats. Let's get started . . . we have lots to do," Chris said, as she once again had to pull the class back from the edge of exuberant chaos. The students talked and laughed their way to empty chairs, buoyed by the unexpected entertainment that was becoming routine in Room 330 Comp I class. Chris quickly called the roll and returned the first graded papers before reviewing the procedure for assigning students to writing groups. Each name she called would be followed by the number of his or her group. The undercurrent of voices hinted at the anticipation she had hoped for.

The room was quiet as Chris called out names and numbers. She continued down the roster until she came to "Tabor Maclean, group three."

"The hell ya say!" a male voice said aloud from the back of the room. "Ya gotta' be kiddin' me. I'm in group three."

"Excuse me?" Chris said sharply. "That was a rude and uncalled for remark. I think an apology is in order." She stood looking at a tall, handsome boy who sat in the far corner of the room next to the windows, his face flushed pink with emotion.

"I'm sorry, Professor Alford, but I don't think I'm gonna learn anything from that kid, and he's sure as heck not going to learn anything from me."

"Peter, see me after class and we'll talk about it."

Chris quickly finished the list and assigned each group to a section of the classroom.

"Get together with your group and introduce yourselves . . . get to know each other. That's the easiest assignment you'll have for the whole semester."

The students drifted noisily toward their assigned places. They laughed and joked their way through the self-conscious introductions, but everyone participated and seemed to enter into the spirit of the exercise. The two girls and one boy who made up Group Three sat with their heads bent toward each other, talking more intensely than Chris expected would happen on the first time around. She knew their conversation wasn't about writing English papers. Half sitting on the front of the work table, she slowly scanned the room, looking for any who hung back, aware of those who were boisterous.

She had fifteen weeks to move them through the rigorous, demanding routine. In that time, she would come to know them in unexpected ways, and, if she was lucky, they would come to depend on her to lead them through the pit-strewn valley of discovery. What would have happened if Tabor hadn't been called away from class today? What was she going to say to Peter less than fifteen minutes from now? Once again, Tabor loomed large and clouded the overall picture. How could she help him and not short-change them? Or was it impossible. Chris realized that she had never been more uncertain or unsure of anything in her life.

Chapter 38

What had been a refreshing late summer breeze when Chris arrived on campus early Friday morning had grown by three o'clock to a stiff, gusty wind that scooped up puddles of dust from her patio deck and sent them upward in cloudy, gyrating whorls. She hadn't seen real rain in the mountains . . . maybe a shower or two and lots of soupy fog, but not a real thunderstorm or pounding rain. She sat with her back to her open office door, staring across the patio at the darkening charcoal sky and the towering purple and blue-black mountains beyond. As the rolling clouds and approaching layers of rain closed in, the mountain tops and craggy peaks disappeared, leaving only their distant forested shoulders as reminders of their great looming presence. Chris loved this view. She was coming to know the changing faces of the forested, granite giants as she was coming to know something intrinsic about the mountain people who moved in and out of her life in this strangely captivating part of the world. New York City had crossed her mind only a few times in the past several months, and she was no longer tormented by weekly graphic nightmares of her paralyzing loss of Jack and their baby son.

Chris swung her chair around, intending to pack her briefcase with plans and papers for the weekend ahead. Instead, she picked up the expertly carved image of the peaceful, sleeping cat that rested on the corner of her desktop and turned it slowly in her hands. She ran her fingers over its smooth, rounded back, and she felt its clearly defined folded legs and the graceful curve of its body-hugging tail. Now that she was familiar with the carver, she marveled even more at the delicate beauty and gentle presentation of the little piece of art. His creation was so unlike the persona he presented to the world. No part of it represented the Tabor that others saw, the Tabor that others turned away from and shunned and mocked. Somewhere deep inside of him, there must be a gentle-heartedness and kind of tranquil beauty that had allowed something so lovely to come from his big, clumsy hands. Was his world so closed, so painful, that no one would ever be able to enter and find who Tabor might have been? Chris didn't know the answer . . . but she guessed that he had been hiding for many years. Maybe he was a lost cause, and he would never be able to trust anyone. Then again, maybe . . .

"Chris, I was hoping I would find you were still here." James Cantrell stood outside Chris's open door.

"James . . . please come in. I was lost in some reverie or other," she laughed. "I didn't hear you come down the hall."

"Do you have a minute?" he asked. "I don't want to keep you on Friday afternoon."

"Oh, of course. I don't have any plans, other than to recover from the first week of class. Please, sit down."

"I seem to be the bearer of bad news," he said quietly. "I really wanted to talk to you before you went home for the weekend."

James pulled the green plaid chair closer to the front of her desk and sat down opposite Chris. He stared somberly out the glass doors behind her toward the view she had recently left.

I think the sky is going to open up any minute," he said pensively. "I think it'll be a real mountain gully washer when it

243

comes."

"That's a descriptive term," she said with a smile. "I haven't experienced a storm since I've been here. It hasn't really rained for four months. A "gully washer" gives me my first picture of what to expect."

He laughed softly. "One thing about us mountain folks is that we're expressive, if you can ever get us to talk to you."

Chris felt James's strong presence, the charisma she had noted on their first meeting and again recalled as they sat and talked in her office in the early summer. It was odd how he and Richard both exuded the same kind of magnetism that had made her uncomfortable last April. Each man was so different from the other, yet there was a mystical similarity between them.

"Chris, Buster Shewell came to see me earlier today. It seems Lucas Maclean was killed last night in a head-on collision over on Groundhog Mountain Road. He's Tabor's grandfather and Suelean's husband."

"Oh, James . . . how awful. How much more do those poor people have to endure?" Chris asked, feeling the sting of tears in her eyes. "Was that why the officer came to get Tabor out of class this morning to take him home?"

"Yes. Tabor didn't know about Lucas as of the time I talked to Buster, which would have been before your ten o'clock class. I think the plan was to wait until the boy was home with his grandmother before telling him. Mattie spent the night there last night, and she's still there." James paused for a deep breath. "I don't believe Suelean can be left alone, and she has no family other than Tabor. I'm not sure either one of them should be left alone, until Suelean is able to be up and around."

James was clearly distraught by the grim situation. He seemed exhausted by the back to back problems that were piling up on the luckless Macleans, problems that now had somehow become his.

"James, let me help in any way I can. I've been through this myself," Chris said as she unconsciously leaned toward him. "My husband was killed in a head-on collision. I know the kinds of thoughts and the nightmares Suelean and Tabor will probably face."

"Suelean, for sure," James replied. "I'm not so sure about Tabor. I don't think he and his grandfather really had a relationship. I've talked to the boy quite a lot over the years, long before he came to Jackson Clayton as a student. I don't think the old man paid much attention to him, maybe none at all." James was silent for a moment before he continued. "I do know he taught the kid to shoot a gun, because Suelean told me about it. I helped her get a hunting gun for Tabor for his birthday one year, and Lucas taught him to use it. I've heard Tabor's practically a sharp shooter, a lot better shot than the old guy was, so his grandma said."

"I don't understand this gun thing," Chris said. "Where I come from, guns are used for killing people. The first time I saw a pickup truck in Clayton Forge with a gun hanging in the back window on a gun rack, it scared me to death."

"It's the way of the mountains, Chris. You won't find people anywhere in this country who have more respect for wildlife than the folks who live right around here. But they're hunters. They kill the game and they eat what they kill. It goes way back to what my ancestors did, and probably yours, too, in the early days, what they did to stay alive and feed their families. It's almost like a celebration of our ancestry. The mountain blood runs deep, Chris, and it passes on so many of the old customs and the early ways, one generation to another."

Chris was surprised by the strength and conviction that she heard behind his words.

"Are you a hunter, James?"

"Yes, at least I used to be. I have six or eight guns, most of them up at Tuggles Gap. I guess a man's a hunter even if he stops shooting. It's in a person's head. I don't have the time now, and I get up to the homeplace in Tuggles Gap so seldom. That's where my family always hunted, where I've hunted. It was the only thing I did with my father, really, and it was the only thing I ever did that he approved of."

"I guess its good that Tabor has some skill that others around here can respect. He desperately needs respect, James. I've been sitting here thinking about our talk about him, and I'm sorry I brought all of it up."

"Don't be. You and Richard and I needed to get it out on the table. All three of us needed that. I'm still not comfortable with our decision, Chris, although I understand it and I support you in it."

"There's no chance that I'm going to shuttle Tabor into another class, James, not now. He needs us to give him a hand up, not a kick out the door. I get the impression that you've spent a good deal of time with Tabor, more than most people probably know."

"Yes, I have. My heart goes out to him and to Suelean. The first big issue they can't overcome is being here, in these mountains. They'd never make it anyplace else, but their opportunities for help are so limited here. If we can get Tabor through the technology course, I believe he can do one of the jobs over there in IT. I can make sure he has a job for his working years, and benefits even after I'm gone."

"You know, James, being poor is a big problem for the Macleans, also. It's a limiting factor in anyone's life. I know, because I grew up desperately poor."

"Yes, I'm aware of their poverty," he said thoughtfully, "but that can change."

"I'll do everything I can to get him through English," Chris said. "He has to do it himself, and I think he can. You have my word, James. I'll help him in every way available to me."

Chris looked at James and thought how much she liked this kind, compassionate man.

He sat quietly looking at her, his arms stretched out and his hands casually folded on her desk. "Chris, you're truly a gift to this school. For the first time in a long time, I feel as if I have someone I can count on, someone to really help me with my goals."

Chris was startled by the president's words, and felt a little awkward. She could feel the heat in her cheeks, and she knew she was blushing.

"That's very kind of you, James. I haven't been here long enough to really know what your goals are, but I sense that you care very deeply for the students, for this school, and for what you're able to provide for so many who would otherwise not be able to have an education. I admire that."

As they talked, rain began to dot the dry patio and to bounce off the surfaces of the glass wall and door. Chris switched on two lamps in her office, as the murky, overcast sky blackened the four o'clock afternoon into the dark of night. Thunder crashed off the distant mountains and jagged bolts of lightning announced a full-blown late summer storm, as the rain increased to slashing sheets that pounded the shingled roof and splattered the windows.

"I guess we're stuck for awhile," James said with a slight smile. "I can go sit in the botanical garden until it passes, if you have other plans."

"Please make yourself comfortable here," Chris replied. "Would you like a cup of tea . . . green tea?" she asked. "I can make tea, even in a storm."

"Sounds good," he said. "I'd like that."

Chris pulled a large bottle of spring water out of one cabinet, and from another she assembled everything else necessary for making two cups of tea.

"You have a regular tea house here," he laughed.

"What else do you have in all these cupboards?"

"No contraband," she laughed. "I don't smoke anything, and I don't drink on the job," she said. "I'm pretty dull, for a city girl."

"I don't think you're dull," James said, suddenly serious. "Quite the contrary. I find you're very easy to talk to . . . to be with."

"James . . . thank you." Chris decided not to continue what she had started to say. She was certain she had misread the meaning in his words.

"Here we are," she said as she handed him a steaming mug. "I have one of those little heating elements that makes this seem like magic."

"For me, it is magic," he said quietly. "I like green tea, and I haven't had a cup in more years than I can remember. It's Japanese, but I guess you know that. I first tried it when I was in Japan. My wife and I travelled there on our wedding trip, a two-week whirlwind trip for two mountain kids too young to appreciate it. I want to go back again and really take it all in."

"I've never been there," Chris replied. "But I've never really been anywhere outside of the continental USA. I'm thirty-nine years old, and I'm probably the only English teacher you or I know who hasn't been to England," she laughed. "I guess I'll get around to travelling when I retire."

"Don't wait until then," he said. "Enjoy life while you're young."

"Jack, my husband, and I had planned to go to France, but plans kept changing. He was an artist, and we often lived on my teaching income, so money was always an issue. He was really talented, but it takes awhile in that profession to become known."

"I've travelled a good bit," James said pensively, "but I've never done anything I felt was memorable. I think people make things memorable, not places."

"Yes, that's probably so," Chris replied.

"I've never been without money," he said. "I can't say I identify with money issues, but I do know that money hasn't brought me any happiness, at least not until I came here to the college. I would have given up all my money to have a family, . a father who loved and respected me, and a mother."

"I don't even know my father's name, or what he looked like," Chris replied. "And my mother . . . my mother might just as well have not been there. I lived with her until she died, but she never saw me."

"Maybe that's why you feel so strongly about your students, Chris. You've turned your own adversity into a gift."

"Thank you, James. I hope so. I know I want all of them, all of my students, to succeed."

"What have you seen of Virginia or West Virginia?" James asked.

"Clayton Forge and the towns and cities I passed through on my drive from New York."

"Have you been to Beckley, West Virginia?"

"No," she laughed. "I haven't even been to Beckley."

"There's a great French restaurant over there . . . Chez Maurice. Would you go over there with me some weekend for dinner? You could pretend you're in France." His eyes seemed to light up with his idea.

"Oh, James . . . thank you . . . it's nice of you . . . but . . ."

"Chris, it's okay . . . just two friends going to dinner . . . nothing else. We don't have to play our campus roles seven days a week. I don't live like that. I promise you it's okay."

Chris liked being with James, talking to him, momentarily forgetting the time and the rain, and everything else that was swirling and blowing confusingly around her. But he was her boss. No, Richard was her boss . . . and James was Richard's boss. She couldn't get out from under the discomfort of it, the need to keep it quiet, or pretend it didn't happen.

249

"I feel uncomfortable, James . . . it doesn't seem appropriate. I don't want to stir up rumors or resentment. I know how colleges are, how people are."

"Chris, I want you to go to Beckley with me because I like you. I like talking to you, laughing with you. We have things in common, and there's no reason in the world for us not to go. Two friends having dinner at a nice restaurant. That's all it is."

"I know, but . . ."

"Look, I'm the old codger here, the mountain hick who should be stuck in the old ways. You're the young city girl, with New York sophisticated lifestyles and living I couldn't even describe. What's inappropriate here? Would you go to dinner with Glen Cooper or Ron Dowd? I'll bet you would."

"I guess I would," she laughed. "But . . ."

"Then saying no to me is discrimination. Don't you like hillbillies?" he teased.

"You're about as far from being a hillbilly as I can imagine," she said.

"Chris, I won't push anymore. If you don't want to go, I understand."

James stood and looked out the window. "It looks like the rain is letting up a little. Maybe we should make a run for our cars."

"James . . . I'd like to go," Chris said.

He turned around and smiled at her. "I'm so glad. How about tomorrow night?" he asked. "It's forty-five minutes over to Beckley. I'll pick you up at six?"

"Okay. Thank you. I'll look forward to it.

Chris was conscious of their closeness as they walked silently through the dimly lit plants in the atrium to the outside doors.

"I'll see you tomorrow, Chris," James called as he

sprinted down the walk toward Bryant Hall.

Chris opened her umbrella and jogged to her car, as the wind stung her legs with blowing rain. Once she was in her car, she sat for a few minutes, mopping at her legs with a few wads of soaked Kleenex.

Had she accepted a date with James Cantrell, or were they really two friends going to a nice restaurant for dinner? She suspected the answer was "both."

James watched as the lights of Chris's Mazda came slowly around the college road and passed his parked car. She had said "yes." It was happening far sooner than he could have hoped it would. He would be cautious and careful, making sure that he didn't rush her.

He was confident that he hadn't made any mistakes this time, and this time he wouldn't lose the precious gift he had found.

Chapter 39

Tabor sat very still beside Mawmaw's bed, his dirty, rough hands folded as if in prayer.

He watched the faint wet line that started at the corner of her blue eye as it moved slowly across her bony cheek to nothingness on her pillow. He wasn't sure why she was so hurt and broken.

"When can y'all get up, Mawmaw?" he asked.

"Pretty soon, Son . . . jest a few more days . . . got to get my strength back."

"Did Pap hit ya and knock ya down?"

"No, Tabor. I done told ya that I fell down offen the back porch, jest after y'all went away mad. Remember when you and me had our fuss? Well, I fell jest after y'all left. No one was here when I fell." Her voice was so weak that he had to lean toward the bed to hear her.

"Was Pap dead then?" he asked simply.

"No. He was gone down to town in his truck. Buster said he wasn't in the crash till sometime in the night, round about ten or so."

Something inside of her wished that Tabor had cried or had seemed sorry when she told him about Pap. But he had been unmoved, as if she had been telling him about a distant neighbor he had met only a few times.

"Did he get cut up and everythin'?" Tabor asked.

"I don't know, Boy, but I don't wanna talk about it now. Y'all mustn't ask me about it for awhile." She struggled to hold back the anguish that threatened to explode inside of her.

"It makes y'all sad, don't it, Mawmaw?" he said, as quietly as he was able to speak.

"Yes, Tabor, it makes me sad. I'm gonna miss yer Pap so much."

He listened to her soft sobbing, and he wanted to make her feel better, to take away her sadness, but he didn't know how to do that. He knew how much he would miss his beautiful Chris if she died, and that was how Mawmaw felt about Pap. But Pap had not been good to her. He had hit her and cussed at her so many times, so often that Tabor could remember having lots of places he had found to hide when he was a little boy, to avoid hearing the meanness.

"Mawmaw, y'all told me one time, after we went to one a' them camp meetin's where the preacher man was yellin' fer us to go up front . . . ya told me that when we was saved, that we would float up to heaven when we was dead. Remember that, Mawmaw?"

"Yes, Tabor, I remember."

"Well, do ya reckon Pap has gone to heaven . . . floated up into the sky now?"

"Oh, Tabor, I don't expect Pap will ever leave the ground. He jest wasn't the type to want to be saved. He said he never wanted to leave the mountain, and I reckon he never did. He was born on the mountain, and he died on the mountain, too."

"Pap didn't like me much," Tabor said, looking down at his knees. "I liked him some, though, like when me and him went out shootin'. We liked each other then. But most a' the time, we jest couldn't get to likin' each other."

"He liked ya, Son. Pap jest had a hard time, knowin'

253

ya was Amber Jean's boy. He loved her so much . . . used ta call her his little blue eyed angel. Yer ma's up in heaven fer sure, Tabor. She's always up there watchin' over ya, and she loves ya, Tabor, jest like I do."

He wished he could see his ma's face and her hair. He imagined that she would look just like Chris, all smooth and pretty, with shiny hair the color of a slow burning fire. And she would talk pretty, too, nice words that showed she liked him, even loved him.

"I wisht I coulda seen my ma," he said.

"Oh, dear God, Tabor . . . oh, Boy . . . what are we gonna do? What's gonna happen to us now?" Mawmaw collapsed into deep, body-wracking sobs that brought Mattie and Kenny running from the next room.

"What happened, Tabor? Suelean . . . oh, Honey, you have to try not to cry so hard. You have to protect those poor broken ribs." Mattie pulled over the stool from the corner and sat close to Suelean's bed.

"Tabor, why don't we see if your grandma can get some sleep. She didn't sleep all night, and I know she's tired. Why don't you go and get yourself washed up, and get rid of some of that woods smell that's hanging on you. Seems like it might have been awhile since you cleaned yourself up real well. Do you want me to get you some supper?"

"Yes'um," he said loudly. "I ain't had nothin' for awhile. I'm empty."

"Kenny, maybe you can help find Tabor some clean clothes. There must be something clean around here, although I don't believe I've found it so far."

"Tabor, where do you keep your clothes?" Kenny asked, aware of the putrid smell that seemed to radiate from Tabor's body. "Maybe you can find some clean things there."

"Don't reckon I keep'em any place particular, jest where Mawmaw pus 'em after she takes 'em off the line out back."

"Okay, well we'll see what we can rustle up here. You go wash up. You folks have a shower here or a bathtub?"

"Don't have no shower. Got a bathtub, but don't have no water runnin' into it anymore. Pap never got it fixed. We jest use the hose and the washtub out back mostly. I kin do that . . . it ain't hard."

"Got any soap?" Kenny asked hopefully.

"Yeah, Mawmaw got some soap from down at Blount's. I'll get me some a' that."

Tabor began rummaging through assorted piles of clothing that were stacked in corners and on tables and chairs around the house. He pulled a pair of jeans from one and a tee shirt from another, continuing until he had a small pile in his hands.

"Got me some clothes," he called to Kenny. "Gonna go wash up now."

As he headed toward the screenless backdoor, Tabor stopped and returned to the stacks of clothing he had just gone through. He began to pull out other items and lay them aside, gathering a bundle that he dropped in the corner of the living room.

Kenny watched him place the chosen items together. "What are those for?" he asked.

"I gotta get back to town early tomorrow," Tabor replied. "I gotta have a meetin' with somebody at the college, and I need me some clothes fer Monday."

"Tomorrow's Saturday," Kenny said matter of factly. "I reckon you won't find anyone there on Saturday."

"She'll be there," Tabor boomed confidently. "If she ain't, I know where she lives, and I can go find her there."

"Who're you talking about, Tabor? One of your teachers? Kenny tried not to let his voice sound the alarm he was feeling.

"A friend a' mine," Tabor said loudly. "She knows I'll be

comin' 'round to see her."

Tabor knew that wasn't exactly the truth, but he also knew his beautiful lady would be glad to see him, just like she always was. Maybe they could sit on her porch and have a Coke, or maybe that kind of tea he saw her make in her office. He had never been in her pretty house, but he had sat outside of it a couple of times. It was kind of funny the way he had found where she lived. He'd been dumping the trash for Mawmaw one night when she was running late at the college, and some papers were scattered in front of the overloaded dumpster. Maybe the wind had lifted them right off the top, or maybe someone had dropped them when they were emptying their trash. One brown envelope had a big, black address on it, and he happened to see Chris's name. It had been easy after that. Tabor passed by River Road all the time. It was just one of the many paths he followed as he ranged up and down the mountain.

"Tabor, there's been a lot going on over at the college this first week of school. I think there may be some meetings with the president and the dean going on over there. I don't think it's a day any of the teachers will be around. Why don't you stay here and look after your grandma. She really needs you right now. You know, she's hurt pretty bad, and she's grieving for your grandpa. She needs you to be strong for her right now."

Kenny thought fast to put together a story Tabor might buy. He didn't know why this crazy guy was still a student over there. Who in the hell kept letting him back in the college? Kenny knew a lot about the problems Dr. Cantrell had dealt with last year, the lunatic Tabor on one hand and that schizo broad on the other. How Cantrell kept his patience and calm attitude he didn't know. Kenny decided if it had been him juggling those two psychos, he probably would have shot both of them or himself. But good old Cantrell just treated them both sweet as pie. Finally the woman got the message and high-tailed it out in the middle of the night, but the big, ugly kid was too dumb to see the light.

Kenny had always wondered where she went, that Allison woman. She was another highfalutin woman professor, all prim and proper, holding herself so much above everybody else because she had read a few books. He knew the minute he talked to her that he had more real smarts in his finger than she had in her stuck up head. It seems like her snooty ways didn't keep her out of old Cantrell's bed, though. Kenny had figured it all out a long time ago. Mr. President had his play things, too, and when he got tired of them, they were gone. Quick as a wink. Kenny wasn't quite sure whether he paid them off, or whether he threatened to turn them out as plain whores, but he knew how to get rid of them. Old James Cantrell paid him real well to turn his head the other way, and that wasn't hard to do. Kenny understood how it was. He had been pretty faithful to his own wife Bonnie, but that was different. He'd left North Carolina to marry her, and he still loved her like he had on the first day he saw her. Sure, he'd tried a few before her, but none had come close to being Bonnie. Cantrell was no different than any other man. He needed a woman, but he just hadn't found a keeper. Maybe he never would. So Kenny could keep his mouth shut while Cantrell looked around, and slept around.

"I gotta go tomorrow," Tabor said flatly. "Maybe I kin come back on Sunday."

"He doesn't give a rat's ass," Kenny thought bitterly.

"Tabor, I'm telling you, you need to look after your grandma. You have to be the man of the house now, at least until she gets well. She's a real sick woman. Stay around until Sunday . . . see how things are then."

"Maybe," Tabor said in his flat, annoyingly loud voice. "I ain't sayin' I will, though," he added as he clomped out the door toward the garden hose that snaked out of sight down the steep hill.

"Al? You out there?" Kenny called toward the barn where Al had been taking a break.

"Hey, over here," Al shouted back.

Kenny jogged across the rough, bare dirt of the backyard toward the dilapidated old bank barn. The huge grey stones of its foundation remained piled and fitted together as they had been when Suelean's grandfather had built the graying wooden structure. In its own way, it was grander than the farm house. Two rickety, louvered cupolas sat equidistant on the high, sharp roof beam, each topped with a hand forged black weather vane. There was a real window for each stall, although most of the glass was gone, and hand-carved black walnut posts held up the arch beam at each end of the cavernous two story structure. An old slatted wooden porch swing hung from the ceiling in the wagon shed on the side, and it was here that Kenny found Al, smoking his last Camel in the pack.

"Hey, Man, what's goin' on in there?" Al asked. "Is the crazy kid behavin' himself?"

"That's why I came out here, Al. That idiot tells me he's going down to the college first thing in the morning, on Saturday, for God's sake. Says he has a meeting with some teacher . . . a woman teacher, of course. I tried to get him to stay around here, but he says she's expecting him, says they're "friends." Ever heard that before?"

"Shit . . . here we go again. I ain't gonna go through that again, Kenny, not if Cantrell don't do somethin' about him. That kid's an idiot son-of-a-bitch, and I think he's dangerous. Who's this teacher "friend?""

"He didn't say, but he says he knows where she lives, and he'll go there if he can't find her at school. I think we need to tell Buster, and then Cantrell. That way the boss can't tell us not to call the police. It isn't right, Al. We can't just ignore it this time."

"Go get on the radio. Just tell Buster what you told me. He knows what's goin' on. He isn't gonna let Tabor pay any visits to any teachers. I can't believe Cantrell will, either, but after last year and all, I don't know. Who knows what he'll do."

"I'll go call them."

Kenny walked down the little hill toward his car. Halfway across the yard, he saw Tabor on the back side of the house, stark naked, washing himself from head to toe. His black, shaggy hair was covered comically in heavy white suds, as was the coarse, thick black hair that covered most of his giant-sized body. Kenny couldn't help but laugh at the strange sight. "Damn . . . he looks just like a big old grizzly bear taking a bath," Kenny muttered to himself.

He waited for the signal and then dialed the code numbers for Buster's patrol car.

"Shewell," came the static-mixed answer.

"Buster . . . Kenny Watts. I'm still up here at Macleans, and we've got a situation Al and I thought you should know about. Tabor says he's going to the college tomorrow for a meeting with one of his teachers . . . some woman. Then he says if she isn't there, he's going to go to her house, says he knows where she lives. I think somebody needs to keep an eye on this, don't you? At least let this woman know what's going on. Tabor says they're friends."

"Holy shit," Buster yelled. "It's only the first damned week of school, and he's already beginning his goddamned rampage. We gotta do something. Did you call Cantrell?"

"No. He was going to be my next call, after you."

"I'll call him, Kenny" Buster said, his voice tight with anger. "You work for him. I don't. He's gonna have to get off his butt this time. We're not gonna go through all that crap we did last year, not for one crazy kid. Thanks, Kenny I'll take care of it."

Kenny was relieved. He and Al could forget it. The

real law was in the picture now. As he hooked the phone to the dashboard, he saw Al standing a few feet from their car.

"I talked to Buster, and he's madder than hell . . . thanked us for calling and says he'll call Cantrell and take care of it. That was the right thing to do, Al. And now we don't need to play wishy washy with Cantrell. Buster will handle him."

"Got some food in here," Mattie called. "First come, first served."

"Guess she got right to that bag of meat and potatoes Cantrell sent up with us," Al said as the two men walked toward the kitchen door.

Tabor's plate was already piled high with fried steak, onions, and mashed potatoes when Kenny and Al came through the door. He sat hunched over the table with a fork in one hand and a big biscuit in the other, shoveling the food into his mouth in large dripping bites and wiping up the pools of gravy with the pieces of biscuit, before stuffing them into his full mouth.

"I made sure Suelean had plenty to eat, before I called anyone else," Mattie said with a roll of her eyes. "I have my plate over here. Help yourselves . . . quickly," she said, exaggerating the last word.

"Wow, Mattie, this smells and looks great," Al said as he heaped the steaming food onto the chipped white plate. "You're some cook. I never thought y'all did anything but type on a computer and answer the phone," he laughed teasingly.

"Well, I don't do this very often," Mattie said. "And I don't intend to do it again here. Dr. Cantrell is going to have to have some more food sent in to us, already prepared. I don't mind staying a night or two, as long as you guys stay here, but I don't want to become the cook, especially in this awful kitchen."

"Thanks for doing this, Mattie. I really appreciate all you've done, and I know Suelean does too. I don't know what she would have done without you . . . really."

260

Thanks, Kenny. Same to you two. That's what we do here, isn't it. Mountain folks help each other."

"Kin I have more steak?" Tabor boomed from the oilcloth covered table where he sat.

He wiped the back of his hairy arm across his mouth.

"Yes, there's more in the oven. Here, Tabor, you can use this for a napkin," Mattie said as she tossed a threadbare dishtowel on the table in front of him.

"I don't need no napkin," Tabor said loudly, as he pulled the black cast iron pot out of the old stove's oven and started piling more of the steak onto his plate.

Mattie rolled her eyes again and her upper lip curled downward in disgust as she looked at his greasy, food flecked beard.

"I cooked everything you two brought up," she said to Kenny and Al. "I had a feeling we'd eat it all, considering who was going to be eating."

The three men sat around the rectangular table, eating in silence. There wasn't anything Kenny or Al had to say to Tabor, and he didn't seem to notice they were there. When he was finished, Tabor took the two remaining biscuits from the stained metal pan and shoved them into the pockets of his jeans as he stood up.

"I'll sleep out yonder on the porch . . . got me a bedroll out there," he said as he started toward the door.

"Don't you think you should say goodnight to your grandma?" Mattie said, trying to hide her distaste for him. "I believe she'd like that."

"Okay," he said. "Night, Mawmaw," he shouted through the doorway that led from the kitchen to the little living room.

"Don't yell, Tabor," Mattie snapped at him. "Go on in there and tell her goodnight."

Tabor tromped loudly through the living room, and the three in the kitchen heard him bellow another "Night, Mawmaw." They couldn't hear her reply.

"I'm goin' on to bed now," he said as he trudged through the kitchen and let the door slam behind him.

"God he's a dumb ass," Al said in a low voice. "I can't hardly stand to be around him."

"Who can, except Suelean," Mattie whispered. "I thought I was going to throw up when I got a whiff of him earlier today. He smelled like a garbage dump. I'll swear, he scares me every time I hear that nasty voice of his."

The two men reviewed their plan to spell each other off through the night, so one of them would always be awake. There was no one to watch for tonight, since. Lucas wouldn't be coming around and they knew where Tabor was. Mattie settled down on the old sofa and drifted off before the men finished their last cigarette.

When Al went out to keep the first watch, Tabor was gone, and so was the little pile of clothes from the corner of the living room.

Chapter 40

Friday afternoon's flashing, rumbling thunderstorm that had shaken foundations and sent animals and people alike running for cover, had roared its way down the face of the mountain to nurture and restore the dry valleys below. The hot, parching wind that had blown for much of August was replaced by a cooler pine-laced breeze that smelled of fall. Tabor raised his head into the light wind and sniffed the earthy fragrance of his forest, the way a roaming black bear might do. As soon as he left Mawmaw's house on Friday evening, he went to check on his rifle in its hiding place in the middle of the giant dying oak. Earlier in the day on his way to the college, he had carefully wrapped the precious gun in its blanket cover and then a thick plastic bag before he had placed it in the deep hollow of the decaying old tree. Now he would retrieve it and carry it with him, if only for the night ahead.

Tabor's gun was the only thing in his life that he really understood. Unlike people, it was dependable and it was honest. He could always rely on the rifle's awesome and formidable power, a power that was transferred seamlessly to him when he summoned it. Tabor had spent endless hours working with the gun, getting to know its every nuance. He had learned that he had to be consistent if he wanted the very best from it, and he had to care for it faithfully if he expected it to take care of him. It was with this terrible instrument that Tabor had at last known success, and it was with the cold, unforgiving steel of this rifle that he had perceived the heady, addictive feeling of power . . . and of death.

The heavy rain had washed away wide swaths of surface earth along the sides of the road that wound down from the Macleans' farm, and it had left small, slippery rocks and pockets of gravel-studded baked clay that it had poured over but not penetrated. At times the walking was slow and hazardous, and the dying flashlight did a poor job of pointing out the danger. Tabor carried the small bundle of clothes tied and slung over his shoulder, just as an old vagabond, a tramp, might have done a hundred years before the boy was born. As he trudged along, he thought of his Mawmaw and of Pap. He had a strange feeling about Pap that made him uncomfortable, the kind of feeling a person gets when unsettling change comes into his life. In a way, Pap being dead was a relief to Tabor. He didn't have to dodge him anymore, physically or emotionally. Pap had changed his ways some as Tabor grew, wisely recognizing that if he hit the boy on the side of the head one more time or slapped his face so hard that the hand print stayed for a day, he just might find himself flattened by his towering grandson's awesome strength. But Pap never stopped the meanness, the shameful humiliation, the ugly belittling that convinced Tabor of his own worthlessness. He wasn't sad that Pap was gone, but he was confused as to who he was without the old man's input. And Mawmaw was sick . . . she couldn't even get out of the bed. Was she going to die, too? Was she going to go up to the heaven she talked about and leave him, like his ma had done? The panic of abandonment made him even more certain that he had to have his own special person, someone who wouldn't go away from him. He rejoiced in knowing that he had found his person, his someone . . . his beautiful Chris.

After picking up the rifle, Tabor continued another twenty minutes on the steep, winding path that led to his skillfully camouflaged mountain place. The storm's cascading water had made a spongy carpet of the dry, shriveled moss and leaves on the forest floor, slowing his climb and making the walk more treacherous. Several times, his heavy boot had slipped ahead of him, almost taking him down into the wetness. As Tabor cleared the last part of the path, he had to pull himself up by his hands and arms to climb over a small overhang, newly carved out by the waterfall created earlier by the sudden rush from above it. He was happy for the inconvenience, recognizing the steeper climb up as another barrier to anyone who might come too close to his hideaway.

The underground dugout had stayed amazingly dry, considering the quantity of water that had passed through the surrounding woodlands. Tabor lit Pap's old lantern and found only a few puddles here and there where water had run in the roof's air holes. The bedding in the corner was damp but not wet. He could sleep here where he felt some peace. No way in hell was he going to spend a night with Cantrell's watchdogs hanging around. They thought he was so stupid, that he didn't recognize they were there to watch him. Kenny and Al were so dumb they hadn't even had the sense to think he might take off before tomorrow.

He'd have himself a nice breakfast of biscuits and coffee in the morning. He still had some coffee in the last can he had taken from home. His rain barrel had plenty of water in it now, even enough to wash up before he went to see Chris. Tabor pulled the pile of ragged blankets and a lumpy, musty pillow from the corner and laid down to make his plans. He'd go to the college first. Maybe Kenny was right and Chris wouldn't be there. If so, he'd get himself a hot chocolate at the student union, and then he'd go to Chris's house. He'd taken ten dollars and some change from Mawmaw's jar when he went back to tell her goodnight, so he had some money. Good thing Miss Bossy Pants had told him to go back and tell Mawmaw goodnight, or he might not have remembered the money. When he got to Chris's house, maybe he'd lie in the bushes awhile before he knocked on the door. That way, he could see what was going on. Maybe she'd be down at Blount's buying food. That's what had happened the last time he went to her house. He'd had to wait a couple of hours before she came back and took the big brown bags from her car to the house. He hadn't paid her a visit that time, because things weren't the same as they were now. He hadn't been real sure that she liked him so much then, but now he knew.

Tabor fell off to sleep with no lingering thoughts of Pap or even Mawmaw. His brief dreams were a series of passing romantic scenes, pictures of him and Chris in all the passionate and happy episodes of life he had planned for them.

When he awoke, the sun was high over the treetops of the silvery pines, telling him that he had slept later than he had intended.

"That's okay," he muttered. "Chris prob'ly slept late, too."

After finishing off the smashed, soggy biscuits in a couple of gulping bites, Tabor dipped a cupful of cool rainwater from the barrel that was buried almost to its top in the earth beside his dugout. He carefully covered the plastic container with pine boughs before leaving the mountain each time, making it invisible to any trespasser. There hadn't been any water in it for several months, but now it was half full, and the animals would find it. He didn't mind sharing with the mountain creatures, but he had to find a way to prevent them from uncovering his secret. He would do that next time he was here, when he wasn't in such a hurry. He splashed some of the water onto his face and beard and ran his wet hands back through his tangle of thick hair. His clothes were still clean enough, so he'd save the others for Monday's class. Tabor shouldered his rifle and hurried back to the path that led closest to the campus. As he trotted off into the heavier parts of the forest, he felt light-hearted and excited inside. If he'd been able to whistle, he would have done so now, because he was whistling happy.

As he approached the clearing, he once again wrapped his rifle and deposited it into another of his many secure hiding places. This old pine wasn't as large as the oak, but it was closer to his destination. He wiggled the gun back and forth several times to get it firmly in place before stuffing the hole of the barren pine with soggy leaves and moss. He looked out toward the road and listened, but he heard only the silence.

Tabor walked and ran toward Cantrell Hall, arriving out of breath and panting, his red face dripping with sweat. His heart plummeted when he saw that Chris's car was not in the parking lot. Long ago he had learned the identity of the owners of each car parked in the faculty lots, thus preparing him for who might be waiting for him if he decided to go inside a building. Professor Cooper's car was the only one Tabor saw, and he sure didn't want to confront him again. Could Chris have parked her car by Bryant Hall? She had done it before. For an hour, Tabor walked around the campus, looking in parking lots, coming back to Cantrell Hall three times before he decided to wait in the laurel grove behind Chris's office patio. She was worth waiting for.

As soon as he had hunkered down into the thicket of bushes, Tabor saw Buster and another trooper hurrying toward Cantrell Hall. Where in the hell did they come from and what did they want? He hadn't done anything. He watched until they were out of sight on the other side of the building, his anger rising as he realized he couldn't leave his lookout until they were safely gone. What if they caused him to miss seeing Chris? What if they hung around for a long time, messing up his plans, ruining everything? Tabor suddenly wanted to get rid of them, to hurt them if he had to. Buster was always getting in his way, always sticking his big ugly nose into Tabor's business. Now it seemed like this fool was about to ruin Tabor's only chance to be happy. He clenched and unclenched his fists, wishing he had not left the rifle in the pine tree. A deep guttural sound rose involuntarily from his throat as he stared at the backside of the building, thinking they might have seen him as he had wandered around looking for Chris's car.

Within a few minutes, the two officers appeared again, this time having exited from one of Cantrell Hall's side doors. They walked briskly away from the building, back toward Bryant Hall. Tabor pivoted on his belly until he was turned toward the two men, and he saw them stop to talk to a third person they had met on the walk. Dr. Cantrell's familiar profile was easy to recognize, as he gestured widely toward the various buildings that surrounded them. After a short conversation, the three strolled together along the brick walk and went into Bryant Hall. What was he supposed to do now? If he came out and they saw him, he'd never get to see Chris. His legs were cramping from having to pull them up under him, and his back itched. A slight breeze ruffled the sharp, brittle leaves around him, poking their pointed ends into his arms, reminding him he couldn't stay there much longer.

Tabor's face was wet and his body ached to stretch out, but he didn't dare move, not until he knew he was safe from those nosy bastards. He pounded the damp ground with his fist and tears of frustration filled his eyes. He didn't know how long he could stand the smoldering resentment and the hatred that had been building in him for so long. This time might be the time he couldn't control any of it . . . if he lost Chris.

An hour after they followed Cantrell into the building, Buster and his uniformed buddy came out and got into their patrol car. Tabor watched as they drove slowly around the road that ran along the edges of the campus, each of the men looking intently out the open window on his side of the car. It was clear they were looking for someone, but Tabor had convinced himself it wasn't him, not this time. He had been with Buster only yesterday, and no trouble had come up between them since then. Still, Tabor hadn't wanted to rile them. They sometimes stopped a person when the notion took them, for no good reason. It had happened to him plenty of times. He wasn't particularly worried about old Cantrell, but he didn't want to set him off, either. Usually, Cantrell surprised him with how easy he was, but then, Tabor never knew when that would change. Best to stay out of his way.

Tabor looked around him before he wiggled out of the bushes and sprinted across the campus toward the big black gates. If he could get on the road, he would be safe. Although he didn't have a watch, he could tell it was late in the afternoon because of the way the blinding, orange August sun hung low in the sky. Mawmaw had never been able to find a watch at the thrift store that would fit him, but he had become real good at telling time by the look of the sun. For sure, it was time he got on over to Chris's house. He'd discovered that the best way to avoid coming down River Road, which ran in front of the houses, was to angle off into the woods behind. That's how he had been able to watch her come and go from the little screened porch, and he could also see into a couple of the windows of her house from there. The binoculars were up on the mountain, but he didn't really need them to see all he wanted to see. Images of her floated provocatively through his mind, causing him to quicken his pace until he was running.

When he got to the wooded area where he had kept his earlier vigils, Tabor was barely able to catch his breath. He fell to his knees behind a thick row of brown leafed rhododendron, gasping for oxygen as he craned his neck to see the edge of

Chris's driveway. Adrenalin coursed through him as he spotted the shiny side of her car. She was home . . . he had found her. He smiled as his breathing became more regular and he looked toward the porch and then to the windows.

Chris drifted past one of the un-shaded windows, the pale pinkness of her robe just visible from where Tabor sat. She was his pretty lady, so soft and gentle. The faint tingle of excitement crept through him, as he stretched forward, hoping to see her again. Was she going to bed so early? Perhaps she was just going to sit and watch the television he could see winking in the other window within his view. Then she was gone. He wouldn't knock on her door just yet. He wasn't quite ready. He could wait. What seemed like hours passed, and the late afternoon became early evening.

The tree frogs called to each other in their two-toned screaks as they competed melodically with the big, green cicadas that hung from the leafy branches above him. A few random lights had been lit in Chris's house, but Tabor hadn't seen her again. He fidgeted as he wondered what he should do. She hadn't gone to bed, because she had turned on lights. She had even turned on lights on the outside of her house and garage.

Before he could summon the courage to walk to her door, he saw the headlights of a car slow down on River Road and turn out of view into Chris's driveway. It was a car Tabor knew, a car he had seen. Surely it was one that was identical to the one he identified. Who was coming to see her? Maybe it was the lady he had met at the Fourth of July fair, Chris's friend. Maybe she was the one. How could he find out? Anxiety overcame him. He walked dangerously close to the sparsely wooded front of the little forest, so close that someone could have seen him in the full brightness of day. Could he manage to run around the end of the row of houses without being discovered? From there, he would be able to look across two narrow front yards to her driveway.

Tabor forgot all fear and caution in his blinding need to know who was with Chris. He lumbered across the narrow backyard of the last townhouse and peered around the front corner. He could see her driveway and the walk and part of the little front porch. He stood frozen behind the building that shielded him, teetering on the edge of panic. He had to see . . . he had to know.

"It's very peaceful here," he heard a man's voice say.

"Yes, I've come to like it," Chris replied.

Tabor watched Chris walk along the cement strip toward the car, followed closely by a man. He could only see the man's back. She was so very beautiful in her white dress that blew softly around her legs in the evening breeze. Her hair hung loosely around her lightly bronzed shoulders, moving gently with every step. How he loved her. Why was she with this strange man? Why wasn't she there when Tabor came to see her? He could barely stand the pain of his aching heart. He mustn't lose her . . . he wouldn't lose her.

The man closed the car door after Chris got in, and he turned briefly to gaze at the bright red glow of the sun as it began its descent behind the deep purple of the mountains beyond. Tabor stood mesmerized, horrified. It was Dr. Cantrell. Chris was going in the car with Dr. Cantrell. Tabor wanted to run to her, to tell her not to go. She mustn't go. He had to stop his beautiful lady, but his legs would not move. Fear had paralyzed him.

Chapter 41

"What's going on?" Richard asked as he strolled into James Cantrell's office. With his faded blue jeans and gray, loose tee shirt, he looked like one of the local farmers who had come to town for a sack of chicken feed.

James had called a few minutes earlier, a little after 8:30 a.m., and had asked Richard to come over to his office, which was unusual for a Saturday morning. Both men were usually on campus on Saturday morning, Richard more regularly than James, but they seldom got together for business. Sometimes they would head off at noon and get a sandwich and a beer at The Timber Ridge, which was a good thing. Each of them recognized the need for an easier relationship between them.

"Thanks for coming by, Richard," James said. "Buster Shewell and one of his deputies are on their way over. He called me early this morning. I think it's another tempest in a tea pot, but we have to listen to what they have to say. Want some coffee?"

"No, thanks. I had my two cups after my run this morning. Did he give you any idea as to what he wants to talk about?"

"Yes, a minimal explanation. It's another Tabor Maclean story, I think." James shook his head and frowned. "If I didn't know better, I'd think Buster had it in for Tabor."

272

Richard controlled his urge to say he agreed with Buster. "Well, I guess he's had a good bit of experience with Tabor. He probably has some pretty strong reasons for feeling the way he does. I'm interested to hear what he has to say."

"Now that the boy's lost his grandpa, I think we need to have some understanding of his situation, like we would for any other kid who has that kind of loss. Tabor has never known any other parents than his grandma and grandpa. As far as he's concerned, they *are* his parents. We need to try and understand that."

Richard rested his elbows on his knees and studied the blue and red pattern of the oriental carpet beneath his feet. He needed to avoid another angry confrontation with James over Tabor, particularly if they were going to find any kind of a solution to the growing problems surrounding this student. That's how they had to look at it. This guy was a student, and he needed to be treated like one. They shouldn't expect anything extra from him, but they shouldn't give him anything they wouldn't be willing to give another student. This was a four year college, for God's sake, not some institution for training the emotionally crippled.

"James, I think we need to try and be objective about Tabor. I need to ease up on my attitude and give him some benefit of the doubt, and maybe you need to tighten up on yours."

"Good mornin'," Buster said as he stopped at the door to the president's office. "I'm used to Mattie runnin' interference for me," he joked. "Don't want to butt in on your conversation."

"That's fine, Buster. We've been waiting for you," James said.

"This is JT Simpson, our newest deputy. Don't believe y'all have met," Buster said as he stepped aside to let JT move in front and shake hands with James and Richard.

"Good to meet you, JT . . . sit down," James gestured to three chairs that had been arranged in a semicircle on the front side of his desk. Richard already occupied one of them.

"Richard and I were just talking about Tabor. I believe you said your visit involved something about Tabor Maclean?"

"Yes, Sir," Buster said, as he laid his big brimmed hat on his lap. "Seems like Tabor's up to his old tricks, Dr. Cantrell. I took him up to his grandmaw's house yesterday mornin' . . . went to his class and got him. Mrs. Maclean had told us earlier that Tabor hadn't been home for a few days, so he didn't know anything about Lucas Maclean's death. We thought he was goin' to stay home for the weekend, go back to class on Monday. Instead, he hightailed it outta there last night, snuck out while Kenny and Al were in the house. Earlier in the evening, he had told Al somethin' that upset him and Kenny, and they called me. I told them I'd let you know about it," Buster said, attempting to control the resentment he felt over Cantrell's seeming inability to come to grips with the Tabor problem.

"What was that . . . that upset them?" James asked quietly.

"Tabor told Kenny he had an appointment with one of his teachers on Saturday mornin', one of his woman teachers." Buster paused to observe the reaction from the two college administrators, the one next to him and the one on the other side of the big desk.

"And?" James asked.

"Well, Kenny tried to talk him out of goin' to the college on Saturday, said none of the teachers would likely be here. Then Tabor said he knew where she lived, this woman teacher."

"Here we go again," Richard interrupted angrily. "I can see why that would upset them."

Buster felt buoyed by Richard's response. "Then he said

if he couldn't find her at school, he'd go to her house and talk to her there."

"Did he say who this woman teacher was?" James asked.

"No, but . . ."

"James, it's Chris. She's the only woman teacher Tabor has," Richard said impatiently. "Surely you don't think that's okay, James . . . surely you agree Buster has to find him and stop him." Richard's words were sharp and clipped as he looked intently at James.

"Look," James said firmly, "I agree that we don't want students visiting teachers at home, without an invitation, but so far, I haven't heard any threats or any kind of . . ."

"James, let's be honest. It's not as if this is something we've never heard before. This is last year and Allison all over again." Richard's face flushed as he gripped the arms of the chair.

"That's what I thought," Buster added quickly. "It seems like these are the same kinds of tricks he was pullin' last year with Miss Montgomery. I think we need to let him know he can't go over to his teachers' houses . . . period."

"Do we know that Professor Alford didn't have an appointment with him today?"

James knew his words would infuriate Richard, but he didn't care.

"James, what in the hell are you saying? Chris just came to you two days ago and told you . . ."

"Richard, let me remind you that the conversation with Professor Alford was confidential college business. We aren't free to discuss that here. I'm well aware of our conversation with her." James's eyes blazed as he spoke.

Richard ignored James and turned toward Buster and JT. "Officers, let me go on record here. I agree with you and Kenny and Al. I think you need to keep a close watch on Tabor Maclean. As Professor Alford's direct supervisor, I authorize you to prevent him from going to her home, now or any other time." Richard knew that he had just laid his own job on the line.

"You can't do that, Richard," James said as he leaned forward toward the three men who stared at him from the other side of the desk. "I don't authorize you to do anything until I've had a chance to look into this, until I've had a chance to talk to Miss Alford."

"Call her now," Richard said bitterly. "Pick up your phone and call her now."

"I plan to see her later today," James said, feeling the heat of outrage rising from his tight chest. "I will speak to her as soon as I'm able. I don't think Tabor Maclean poses any threat to anyone. I don't believe he ever has."

"Well, Dr. Cantrell, I don't believe I can agree with you," Buster said. "I think there were threats involved to Miss Montgomery last year, and I believe . . ."

"This is not last year, Gentlemen," James said sarcastically, "and we aren't talking about Miss Montgomery. In case you haven't noticed, she's been gone from here for over a year." His words were as contemptuous as he had intended them to be. "When one of you tells me what Tabor Maclean has said or done to Christine Alford that is threatening or even disrespectful, then you'll see me act quickly. At this point, you've said nothing that shows me he's done anything wrong. Are you going to condemn a college boy who has made an empty boast to a couple of mountain men he's known all his life? Come on, now. When you were a kid, didn't you ever brag about your manly actions, how many women you had running after you, how much moonshine you could drink on a Saturday night? Did anyone arrest you for rape or drunkenness because of your big words?" James smiled knowingly at Buster and JT. The three of them were mountain boys. They understood each other. Richard was the outsider.

Buster fidgeted uncomfortably in his chair. JT just stared at the college president.

"Well, I hear what y'all are sayin', Dr. Cantrell, but I don't think this stuff with Tabor is a college boy messin' around. I think he's not exactly right mentally, and I think he's posin' a danger to whoever this teacher is. I believe you said it was Miss Alford?."

"That's who it is . . . I'm sure of it," Richard added, his voice tight in his throat.

"On the other hand," Buster said after a moment's pause, "I can't go and arrest a man who hasn't threatened anybody, just because we think he might. I agree with that, Dr. Cantrell. But I can keep an eye on him without getting in his way, without taking away any of his rights."

"I don't know how you can keep an eye on someone who lives up the mountain and comes down here to school, and generally travels all over," James said. "It doesn't seem like something you fellas would have time to do, with all the real law enforcement problems facing you every day." James was clearly baiting the two officers, challenging them to defend a plan he didn't agree with.

"I guess we'll have to work that out," Buster said, staring steadily at James. "I don't want to waste valuable time, Sir, but I also don't want to neglect my responsibility." He stood up as he spoke his last words. "Thanks for your time, Dr. Cantrell, Dr. Shelton. Y'all keep things under control here on your campus, and we'll try to do the same on the mountain. Call us if you need us." Buster and JT walked out and left James and Richard in silence.

"Richard, I know we don't agree on the way to handle Tabor. Maybe we never will. But I don't appreciate your taking the position you did in front of those two troopers, telling them you were authorizing them to do something you knew I disagreed with. I can't accept that, Richard." James ground out the words slowly and deliberately.

"And I can't accept your refusal to offer protection and a safe work environment to one of my faculty employees, someone I'm responsible for. Your callous disregard for her safety is beyond my comprehension. I can't just sit and watch this whole mess blow up like it did last year with Allison, and that's where it's going, James, if we continue to sit on our hands."

"You know how I feel, Richard. I'm not going to repeat myself. I'll take personal responsibility for my actions, and you need to do the same for yours." James had gone far beyond being polite or accommodating to his number two in command.

"Tell me one thing, will you, something I can't understand. Why in the hell do you continue to support this deranged man. He's sick, James. You have to know he is, and yet you continue to protect him. Why? I'm baffled." Richard had stepped across all lines and knew he was clearly insubordinate in addressing his boss, the president of the college, in such an insulting tone.

James sat looking at him, not speaking. He had no answers he could verbalize, no rationale he could offer. Things had gone far beyond what he had ever imagined, far beyond what he had envisioned. Richard was proving to be another problem he would have to deal with.

"I'm not going to answer a question that stems from nothing more than your uncontrolled temper. What I think and why I act is none of your business, Richard, unless it directly affects you, and nothing about any of my decisions in the last twenty-four hours has been about you. Not in any way."

"You said you would speak to Chris. When are you going to do that?" Richard had lost all respect for James Cantrell and he was intentionally provoking him.

James hesitated before he said, "Chris and I will be seeing each other later today, and we'll be spending the evening

278

together. There'll be plenty of time to discuss this matter, although I know her well enough to know what her attitude will be."

He enjoyed telling Richard about his plans with Chris, letting him know that they had a personal relationship outside of the college. James had observed Richard on more than one occasion when Chris was around, the way he looked at her and made a play for her in a subtle way.

"I'm going to call her now, James, with or without your agreement. If Tabor is out there wandering around, she needs to know he's looking for her. That's what he said . . . if he couldn't find her here on campus, he would go to her house. You heard that the same as I did."

"You are not to call Chris, Richard. I'll handle this," he said sharply. "You're not in charge here. I am, and I'm telling you to back off. You're making some bad judgments, Richard."

Both men stood up at the same time, their eyes blazing. Neither extended a hand of apology or reconciliation, neither spoke a word. Richard turned and walked out the door.

Chapter 42

"That road over there to the left, that's the road that leads up to Tuggle's Gap, where I was born and spent the first eighteen years of my life," James said

"Is it a higher elevation than Clayton Forge?" Chris asked, as she looked out the broad windshield of the BMW at the sign that pointed toward Tuggle's Gap.

"Yes, it's a good bit higher, about 3,500 feet above sea level. Clayton Forge is about 2,900."

The shadowy, dense forest seemed to crowd the winding stretch of roadway that wound along chiseled ledges and narrowed as it passed between mammoth granite boulders. The sleek car hugged the twisting, climbing highway that had been laid where an ancient Indian path once led up the mountain. Small fir branches and moist patches of earth and gravel randomly marked the road, mute evidence that the heavy rain had passed through on its way to the valley. The fading day dimly lit the ribbon of highway, but Chris observed that deepest night had overtaken the interior of the woodlands. She liked the twilight peace and stillness of this time of day, although she knew the thick blackness of the mountain night would soon follow.

James glanced toward Chris, sensing that she was relaxing a little in this second thirty minutes of their ride.

Things had been awkward when he picked her up. He could tell she had serious reservations about the decision she had made to go with him. She had all but said so.

"I'm glad we're going to France for the evening, Chris. I'm certain you're going to like it," he said lightly. "Maurice is a fascinating guy and an outstanding chef. Do you like French food?"

"Love it," she said. "Even though this is my first trip to France, I did have a couple of favorite French restaurants in New York, small neighborhood bistros with unbelievably good cuisine." It felt good to joke with him, to play adult make-believe. She and Jack had done that, too.

"I've always felt Maurice could make it in a bigger city with more sophisticated tastes. But he wants to be here in the mountains. Beckley was his specific choice of a place to open his restaurant, and five years later, he hasn't looked back."

James breathed in the flowery sweetness of Chris's perfume. She made him feel so alive, awakened to new possibility and new life.

"Isn't it interesting the way some of us have come to the mountains from such different places," she mused. "Here I am a real New Yorker, and I'm learning quickly how much of an influence these towering peaks can have on one's life," she laughed.

"I left once," he said, "but I came back . . . not to home, but to the mountains I love. I don't know what it would be like to see the ranges for the first time, but I have a little understanding of what you're describing. Maurice tells me he left France when he was thirty. He'd been through the Cordon Bleu and had become a great chef in France, and here he is ten years later . . . in Beckley."

"Richard Shelton is another transplant," Chris said. "He came here from Florida. That has to be almost as much of a change as coming from New York."

"Yes, I suspect it is. I don't know if you know it, but Richard came here to get away from tragedy, much as you did. His wife was the victim of a horrible crime. Someone broke into their house when Richard was on a fishing trip, robbed them of a few hundred dollars, and killed her for trying to stop them. I don't know more, but I suspect the violence was more graphic than that. They never caught the murderer. I think Richard has found some peace here, just as I hope you have, Chris."

"What a terrible tragedy," she said softly. "Poor Richard. I didn't know any of that."

"He doesn't talk about it. Richard's a pretty closed guy."

Chris was curious about his description of Richard. Was he a closed guy?

"Yes, James, I'm finding some peace here. I've come a long way in the months I've lived in Clayton Forge."

"I'm glad. That's so good to hear." James hesitated and then continued. "Chris, Richard and I had another conversation with Officer Shewel this morning . . . about Tabor. I told them I would tell you about it."

She suddenly heard the steady humming of the finely tuned engine as the car pulled them up and down the steep grades. A chill ran through her as James touched on the high points of his morning encounter with the police officers and Richard.

"I don't think Tabor has done anything wrong, Chris, and I don't think you have anything to worry about. Tabor's a big talker. It's all he has . . . big talk. The boy isn't a person of action. I know him better than anyone else at the college knows him, for sure, and I'd be willing to stake my life on his timidity. He'll never do anything to harm you, Chris. He's just desperate for a friend, someone who shows him some respect. In your beautiful, gentle way, you've given him a sense of acceptance. To me, that's more than okay."

Chris was silent for a moment, taking in his comments.

"I'm somewhat confused, James. I want to help Tabor, truly want to help him, but there's a part of me that's afraid of him.   When I think of it rationally, I know I'm terribly influenced by what others have said about him, about last year and Allison Montgomery and all the speculation.   I'm also intimidated by his overwhelming physical size and appearance. I'm not proud of that, but it's a feeling I can't seem to overcome."

"I completely understand what you're saying, Chris, and I can empathize with your feelings. He's kind of a monster of a guy, I know . . . the way he looks, how he talks. That's one of the main reasons he's always on someone's hate list."

"I certainly don't hate him," she said quickly. "I don't even dislike him. It's just that I find him overpowering."

"Please don't get me wrong. I'm not saying I think it's okay for Tabor to come to your house. In no way do I condone that, unless you invite him. I just want to make sure we use "watchdog" measures that you agree with, that you need, rather than letting Buster and Richard make those decisions like vigilantes."

"I tend to agree with you. I don't think Tabor would come and bang on my door at my home. On the other hand, he is pretty determined. Even if he did come to the door, I don't believe he would want to hurt me."

"I know Buster is hanging around tonight looking for Tabor, watching him, so you can be sure Tabor isn't going to be around the campus or your house. Even if he wandered around, I don't believe he would ever have the courage to come to your home. He just doesn't have it in him. Believe me, I know. Now, let's try and set all this aside and get ourselves back on that plane to France, okay?"

James wanted to reach for her hand, to let her know that things were only going to get better for her from here on, but he knew he couldn't touch her. Not yet. Chris was breathtakingly beautiful tonight, with her shimmering amber hair and softly tanned skin. Her white, silken dress was woven with a subtle pattern of Chinese characters and seemed oriental in its modesty. Its mandarin collar fell into a vee that began at her throat, and stopped provocatively at the slight rounding of her breasts. A strand of jade beads rose and fell with her breath and complimented the astounding emerald blue of her eyes. When he had first seen her this evening, James had been overwhelmed, almost speechless.

"James, thank you for talking with me about Tabor. You've made me feel better. I'll keep working with him, and I believe I can improve some things for him. Any improvement would be a help, I know. Okay, we're back en route to France."

Chez Maurice was truly a remarkable little commune of culinary delight, a piece of rural West Virginia that excelled because it didn't fit. The little white brick building was charmingly lit with electric lanterns that flickered a welcome to guests. Inside, the small chestnut beamed and white stucco room seemed to have been moved piece by piece from Provence, and it was just large enough to accommodate eight cloth-covered square tables. Maurice was also a picture from a travel brochure, with his white starched coat and proper chef's pants that accompanied his high traditional hat.

"Bon jour, bon jour, Monsieur Cantrell. How are you . . . I have missed you . . . for so long," the short, stocky host said in his charming French accented English. "And this beautiful, beautiful lady . . . Monsieur Cantrell . . . thank you for bringing us such loveliness for this evening."

"I'd like you to meet my friend Christine, Maurice. I've told her good things about you, and I must tell you, she's from New York City."

"Mademoiselle, what a great pleasure it is to meet you. I am honored. I only hope my humble country café will be worthy of your fine taste," he said, as he took Chris's hand and kissed the back of it.

"It's nice to meet you, Maurice. What a lovely café you have," Chris said as she looked around the candlelit room. "I'm so happy to be here."

The next two and a half hours proved to be much more than James had prepared her for. Everything from aromatic sautéed shrimp appetizers to finely flavored beef bourguignon with a velvety wine flavored sauce were served to them by Maurice's friendly and pretty French wife. Chris sipped a glass of clear ruby colored Cabernet that she declared was the best she had ever tasted, and James happily told her it was his favorite. They laughed and joked as if they had known each other much longer than the four months they had worked together. When Chris took her last bite of satiny smooth mousse au chocolate, she told James that it had been, by far, the best dinner she had ever eaten . . . anywhere. He smiled broadly and told her quietly that it had been the best first date he had ever had in his life.

As they drove home through the deep darkness of the forested night, pale moonlight outlined the sharp peaks of the mountain ranges that rose formidably straight up out of the blackness. Chris's earlier discomfort slowly reappeared. How foolish was she? This tall, handsome white haired man next to her was the president of the college that had just employed her, at least twenty years her senior, and reputedly one of the wealthiest men in the state. Why was he interested in her? Was it her youth, perhaps, when compared to his age? She knew she wasn't bad looking, but surely he could have any woman he wanted, anywhere, considering all he materially could give her. Where was this relationship going? Where could it go?

"A penny for your thoughts," he said quietly. "Did I bore you to sleep?"

"Oh, James, of course not. I've had a perfectly lovely time. I can't thank you enough." Should she tell him she couldn't do this again? Wouldn't that sound as if she was assuming he would ask her another time?

"I've never had a better time, Chris . . . sincerely. Isn't it great to be able to laugh with someone?"

"Yes, laughing is such an important part of life. It's the part that makes the other parts livable, isn't it."

"For sure. I'm sorry it's almost over, for tonight," he said seriously.

"James, I hope you don't think I'm completely out of line. I don't know exactly how to say this . . ."

"Let me see if I can help," he interrupted her. "You don't think we should do this again . . . right? You feel awkward because you work for someone who works for me . . . right? And on top of everything else, I'm an old man. Am I anywhere close to right ?" he asked, in a semi-joking tone.

"Not really. I mean, maybe on part of it," she stumbled. "You're a wonderful person, James. Any woman would be foolish not to see that. And I certainly don't think you're an old man . . . that word hasn't entered my mind. But I'm painfully aware that I have to work with all the people who work for you, and that poses a big problem for me. You must see what I mean," she said, not feeling comfortable with her own words.

"I told you I don't worry about things like that, but I can understand what you mean . . . for you," he said. "Chris, I want to see you again . . . I have to see you again . . . unless you absolutely can't stand me. Chez Maurice is just the tip of the iceberg. There's so much here in these mountains and valleys that is not obvious, so much that makes it very special. I know about most of it. I know of its beauty, its magic, and I want to share it with you. At anytime, you can say, 'No thank you. I don't want to see or do anymore,' and I'll respect that. I promise you. But please give me a chance."

"I'm so confused," she said hesitantly. "You're very

persuasive, James, but something inside of me says it won't work, that there will be bigger problems than I can handle, at least for now."

"I have a suggestion, Chris, that might help you decide. What if neither of us tells anyone that we're spending some time together? What if both of us boldly deny it if we're asked? If no one knows, no one can make trouble. Up here, unless we go to Timber Ridge or Blount's store together, we won't run into anyone we know. I wouldn't tell you this if I didn't believe it would work for you. I don't care if the world knows, Chris, but total secrecy, and denial if asked, will take care of any problems for you."

Chris sat silently thinking of what he had said. There was something sinister about secrecy, something false about denying their relationship. What was she to do when colleagues told her things about "the boss" in confidence, and she pretended to agree with them? Wasn't James proposing that they live a lie?

"I don't think it's a good idea, James, to live a lie. I sound like Little Goody Two Shoes, but one lie leads to more lies, and then where does it all end?"

"Maybe it ends in something good, Chris. For example, people have been known to hide a relationship and only come forward after they've decided they want to spend the rest of their lives together."

"James, please don't say things like that. I have no intention of making plans for the rest of my life, certainly not right now. I've had a nice evening and I've enjoyed your company, but we are as you said it would be, two friends having dinner together. Please don't make it more than that." Chris knew she sounded harsh, but his comment was inappropriate and upsetting.

"I'm sorry, Chris. Please accept my apology. I certainly didn't mean I thought we would decide any such thing. I was just trying to come up with an answer to your question. I don't believe it would be a lie, Chris. It certainly wouldn't hurt anyone else, and it's worth it to me."

The drive home had gone quickly, most of it taken up by the unsettling discussion amidst Chris's growing anxiety. James pulled slowly into the driveway, and she unhooked her seatbelt before he stopped the car.

He opened his door, and Chris said quickly, "You don't need to get out, James. I have all the lights ablaze. Thanks so much for . . ."

"I'll see you safely in the door, Chris. It's just my mountain upbringing. I can't help it," he said with a big smile.

Chris couldn't help but laugh. She felt like a silly school girl, afraid to face that frightening first-date moment at the front door. They walked quietly side by side up the brick path, and he watched her put her key in the lock.

"Thanks so much for saying yes, Chris. I've had a beautiful evening with you. You have my word that I won't say a word about it to anyone, whether we ever go to another restaurant together or not." He stood quietly as she turned and faced him.

"I can't tell you how much I've enjoyed it, too. I really was able to have a good time, without letting other things creep in. Thank you, James. I'll see you Monday morning."

Chris pushed the door and turned as he walked down the path to his car. He stopped and looked back at her and she raised her hand and waved. She watched him drive slowly down the road toward Clayton Forge, and then she closed and bolted the door. Walking through the house lowering blinds and pulling drapes until no windows were open to the outside, she was aware of her aloneness, for the first time in many weeks. She ached for Jack, for his arms around her, for his love.

"Damn, JT. You know who that was that just brought Miss Alford home?" Buster said with a chuckle from the driver's seat of their patrol car. "That was old man Cantrell himself. Whadda ya' think of that?"

"Maybe they been to a school meetin' or maybe a school party of some kind," JT replied.

"I don't think so. No siree, the old man's got himself a young beauty again. It ain't the first time, my friend, it ain't the first time," Buster said with a lewd laugh. "Every man's entitled, JT, and he's entitled just like every other man." Buster broke into a real belly laugh.

JT couldn't see the humor in the situation, but he hadn't been on the job long enough to know much about any of the folks at the college. He knew practically everyone who lived on the mountain, but only a few at the school. They'd always been set apart by the locals. The two groups didn't seem to mix much.

"Well, I reckon we've sat here for four hours now, and old crazy Tabor seems to have taken himself in another direction. I figure we can go on patrol as soon as we see Miss Alford's lights go out. I can tell she's all locked up in there. Tabor isn't gonna be stupid enough to break into her house, and if she did call us, we could be here in less than five minutes."

"Y'all figure he might be hidin' in them woods over on the other side of that empty cow field?" JT asked, pointing across the fenced acreage that ran on the other side of River Road. "We been watching around here, but we never went over yonder."

"We can take a run over there, when we leave here, but I'm feelin' like he's probably sleepin' up on the mountain someplace by now. He goes up there campin' all the time. Seems the critters can stand him better than the folks down here can."

Fifteen minutes later, Chris turned out her reading light, and Buster started the car without turning on the headlights. He cruised slowly out of the woods where he had parked and illuminated the roadway just before pulling onto River Road.

As soon as Chris's house was dark and Buster's headlights went on, Tabor left the woods on the far side of the cattle field and lumbered across the grassy, manure filled stretch toward the row of houses. He could go back to his little lookout spot now, behind Chris's house. Somehow, he had miraculously avoided Buster. Fortunately, he was still squatting in Chris's neighbor's bushes watching his beautiful lady get into Dr. Cantrell's car when Buster had pulled his police car into the little woods, less than five feet from where Tabor had been lying not more than fifteen minutes earlier. Tabor had been too far away to see much when Cantrell had brought Chris home, but he had breathed better when he saw her go into her house and the big silver BMW had driven down the road.

Tabor had outsmarted them, all of them. But that didn't seem important to him now. He had to get Chris to go with him, somehow make her see that they could go and be together and everything would be okay. They could hide at his mountain place, and no one would find them. If she wouldn't listen, if she turned on him like Miss Allison had done, then it would be the same bad, awful stuff all over again, and he knew what he would have to do then.

Chapter 43

Chris ignored the flashing red of the telephone light until she had closed all her blinds and put on her pajamas and robe. It was almost midnight, and chances were she wasn't going to return a call until morning anyway. She unconsciously turned on David Letterman and then pushed the button to listen to the three recorded messages.

"Hi, Chris . . . Richard Shelton. It's about 6:30 p.m. Give me a call as soon as you can. I need to talk to you. I'll stay up tonight until I hear from you. Thanks."

The next two messages were a repeat of the first, each one an hour and a half later, and each with a greater sense of urgency than the one before it. Chris shivered, as she heard Richard's voice repeating itself, warning her of something before she could pick up the telephone and call him. Panic tore at her, as she listened for footsteps outside her door and imagined that she was being watched. A creak in the floor became a foot coming toward her; the familiar muffled rush of water into the pressurized storage tank suddenly sounded like someone brushing across the screen on her porch. She dropped the phone and ran to check the locked door to the little porch.

"I can't do this," she said aloud. "I can't take another round of helplessness and fear."

291

She fought the tears that welled up in her eyes, angry at herself for losing control. Her hand shook as she punched hard at the numbers on the ivory telephone.

"Chris . . . thank God," were the first words Richard spoke to her.

"Richard, what's the matter? What's happened?"

"Did James talk to you this evening about Tabor?"

She hesitated, irritated that Richard knew about her evening with James. "So much for promises," she thought bitterly.

"Yes, he told me Tabor had told some police officer that he had a meeting with me on campus this morning, and if I wasn't there, he would come to my home."

"Chris, I don't think you should stay there tonight. I know James is downplaying this whole damned thing, but I believe there is some real danger, with Tabor prowling around out there. Let me pick you up and take you over to the Starlight Motel in Clayton Forge."

"Richard, I'm ready for bed. James and I talked a good deal about Tabor, and I think I'll be okay. I really don't think he'll come here. Have you heard something new, something James didn't know?" she asked, aware that her heart was pounding wildly.

"I don't know what James told you, but I have every reason to believe that nothing good is going to come from any of this. My primary motivation is to keep you safe, Chris. Even if you're right, you need to be cautious until we know Tabor isn't up to something. Please consider going to the motel, just for the night. I'll pick you up and I'll take you back home tomorrow," he pleaded.

"I can't believe this is happening to me, Richard. It's like another awful nightmare." She hesitated, trying to grab hold. "I can't live like this, Richard. I don't have much left in the way of emotional defenses," she said tearfully, still fighting to stay whole.

"Chris, I'm really worried about your safety. When we can talk in person, there are some things I've decided I need to share with you. I'm sorry I haven't done it earlier."

"Richard, I'm not going to be stubbornly stupid. If you know some things I don't know and you feel this strongly about my safety, I'll go to the motel. I haven't seen Buster or anyone else around here since I got home just before midnight. I can be ready to leave in twenty minutes."

"Thank you . . . I'll be there. In the meantime, don't open your door for anyone until I get there."

Chris felt as if her blood had frozen, as if she couldn't move beyond the warm familiarity of her bedroom. She wanted to lie down, for just awhile, and to forget everything that was threatening to undermine and rip up the progress she had made. Maybe nothing could ever be the same after Jack, maybe this whole Jackson Clayton College thing was just a big, cruel mistake.

After pulling on a pair of jeans and a long sleeved kelly green tee shirt, she numbly put a few things in her red and green overnight bag and flipped off the muted television. She stepped into a pair of camel loafers, turned off the bedside lamp, and took her things into the darkened living room. The thought that Tabor might be just beyond her window or her door sent adrenalin rushing through her, even though she despised her reaction. He was truly a poor, unfortunate guy who had everyone against him, and now it seemed she was there, too. Why couldn't she be stronger, like she had been when she had lived with her drunken mother? No one had told her what to do then, no one had pushed and prodded her into decisions and relationships that didn't feel right. And now. . . .

She could see headlights through the drawn shades, and the moving light image as it crept eerily along the lightless wall.

Within seconds, Richard was at her door, knocking loudly and calling her name. "It's me, Chris. Everything's okay. You can open the door."

"Hi, Richard," she said as she opened the door into her unlit living room. "I just had an idea. Why don't I take my car, and you can follow me. Then I can come home in the morning and you won't have to come and get me."

"I don't think that's a good idea. I want to make sure everything is okay around here before you come back to your house. It's not a problem for me to pick you up in the morning."

"Okay, I'll do it your way . . . this time," she said quietly as she locked the door. "Thanks so much for your concern. I really am grateful, even though I don't sound like it."

They drove quietly down River Road toward Clayton Forge, passing the turn off toward the college.

"I stayed at the Starlight Motel the first ten days I was in town, until my furniture arrived," Chris said with a smile. "I vowed I'd never set foot in there again, but here I am. I can't wait to see Miss Personality again."

"You must mean old Caroline. She's a charmer, isn't she. I had the good fortune of staying at her place when I first came to town, too. It's a showplace," he chuckled.

"Her name is Caroline? She doesn't look like a Caroline," Chris laughed. "I expected her name to be Minnie or Daisy Mae. Isn't that terrible, making ugly judgments about people's names?"

"Be careful around here, Chris. Minnie and Daisy Mae live just down the road."

Just being with Richard had helped to calm Chris. She was surprised to hear herself laugh and make a joke, considering her state of mind fifteen minutes earlier. The pink neon sign of Clayton Forge's only motel flashed its erratic greeting as Richard's Jeep came over the hill and slowly pulled into the rutted parking lot.

"Here we are at the Ritz," he said as he opened his door and grabbed Chris's bag out of the back seat. "It may not be where you want to be, but I'm glad you're here. No one in his right mind would ever mess with Caroline. I know that."

"I believe it," Chris said. "You don't have to come in with me. I know she'll welcome me with open arms."

"I called her and reserved the room, to make sure she would wait up until we got here," he said. "I'll come in and pay my respects. She might treat you better if I do."

Chris liked the humor in his voice, the dry sense of humor she had noted before the Allison episode. He really wasn't a closed person, certainly not as James had described him.

"Hey, Miss Caroline, how are you?" Richard called as he strode confidently through the rickety metal screen door.

"Well, Professor. I ain't seen y'all in quite a spell . . . thought I might see ya this summer," she said seriously, looking over her glasses at Chris while she addressed Richard.

"Thanks for staying up until Professor Alford could get here. She has some problems at her house that she tried to get fixed, but couldn't get them done tonight. She was out of town earlier. That's when I called and made the reservation. Business been good?" he said, taking the conversation into something Caroline could talk about all evening.

"Not bad . . . not good . . . just fair," she said. "Who's gonna pay me?" she asked, staring at Chris.

"I'll pay, of course," Chris said quickly. "I'm the one who's staying in the room."

After the usual delay with the old credit card machine, Caroline handed Chris the key and said, "Room 3. You know the way and the rules."

As they walked out the door, Richard contained a laugh that had been rising up since Caroline began talking. "Don't forget the rules," he said. "No loud music and no visitors after eleven. Guess I'll just have to go on home." He laughed heartily at the absurdity of the evening.

Richard walked with Chris down the weed clogged path to the last room on the left. She opened the faded turquoise blue door and took the bag from him.

"Thank you for all your help," she said. "You've perked up my mood, in spite of whatever is lurking out there. I really appreciate it."

"How about breakfast at Timber Ridge in the morning? They have a decent Sunday breakfast."

Chris was surprised by his invitation. "Sure . . . thanks. What time shall I be ready to vacate Room 3?"

"Nine o'clock okay?"

"See you then," she said. "Hope you get a little sleep after all this."

"That's never a problem for me. See you in the morning."

Chris locked the door and switched on the overhead light. Nothing had changed since her last visit, except the color of the bathroom, which had changed from rosy pink to a shiny turquoise that matched the door and the trim of the Starlight Motel.

Tabor stood at the edge of the woods, staring across at Chris's dark house. His seething anger had turned to uncontrollable fury as he watched Dr. Shelton's car drive slowly along River Road and pull into Chris's driveway. Maybe he had been wrong, maybe she was going to be just like the others. First Dr. Cantrell, and then Dr. Shelton. His big hands clenched into deadly fists, as he sank to his knees and moaned soulfully into the lonely blackness of the night.

Chapter 44

Mattie's nerves were jangled and raw as she clattered around the greasy old kitchen looking for the coffee pot Suelean had said was "settin' on the stove." It might have been there on Thursday night when she and Al and Kenny had arrived to take up their charitable mission, but it had moved into unknown territory in the meantime. With her two watchdog companions banging around in the doorless, dirty cupboards, and that crazy Tabor rummaging his clumsy way through anything that smelled like food, Mattie was surprised she could find anything. For two days, she had made terrible coffee in a big aluminum sauce pan, and she was determined on Sunday morning to brew some genuine high octane. God only knew she needed it, and she suspected Al and Kenny did, too. Dr. Cantrell would just have to make new arrangements for looking after poor Suelean, because Mattie intended to go home before sunset. Pangs of guilt tormented her as she remembered Suelean's words from Saturday night, when Mattie had brushed the poor soul's thin gray hair and had gently washed her pale face and her spindly arms.

"I know most folks thought Lucas was a no-count, lazy drunk, Mattie, but I knowed him as a different kind a' man," Suelean said softly. "He wasn't nothing' like that afore our

Amber Jean died. That jest killed somethin' in him. He never came back to hisself after that."

Mattie had smiled and patted the old woman's hand, trying to think of something good to say about a man she despised almost as much as she despised his grandson.

"We women . . . we always stand by our man, don't we, Suelean? Sometimes my Joe can drive me plumb crazy, but the next minute he can do something that makes me see what a good man he is."

"That's what's wrong with Tabor," Suelean said, suddenly gripping Mattie's hand. "He ain't a bad boy at all. He's got a big heart, but Lucas jest couldn't take the boy on. He jest blamed him from the beginning, for us losin' Amber Jean. I reckon Tabor blames hisself, too, after all his Pap said to him. If it wasn't for that, Mattie, Tabor'd be a reg'lar boy like all them other young folks at the college. It's jest the way he looks at hisself that makes the difference."

Mattie was flustered as she got up to get the ragged gray towel that she had been using for Suelean's bathing. There was no response she could make to the grandmother's reasoning and explanation for her grandson. Clearly, love had blinded Suelean's ability to see who Tabor really was, an abnormal, frightening, freak of a man who masqueraded as an overgrown boy. Mattie didn't doubt for a minute that he could be a cold blooded, crazed killer, and she knew others shared her opinion.

"Well, family is important to us, I know," she said unconvincingly.

"I wisht I knowed where he was . . . my Tabor," Suelean murmured. "I reckon he'll come home sooner or later, when he gets hungry." Then she smiled weakly. "How that boy can eat. He'll come around when he wants his Mawmaw to cook him up some steak and potatoes."

Soon after, Suelean had fallen off to sleep, and Mattie had

gone back to the old couch in the bare living room. She had drifted off thinking that human love was a mysterious and miraculous thing. How the kind and gentle Suelean could love her monstrous, disgusting grandson proved the point.

"There it is," Mattie said aloud as she pulled the battered aluminum coffee pot out of an old box filled with plastic grocery bags. "The only way I'm going to be able to last through the day here without losing my mind is to brew up some good coffee. Praise God for small blessings."

"Hey, Mattie, how ya' doin'?" Al asked as the ripped screen door banged behind him.

"Glad to see you're makin' some coffee. I was getting' ready to run on down the mountain to the Exxon station to buy us all a big cup."

"Try to be a little quiet . . . Suelean's still asleep." Mattie knew she sounded bossy and distant, but she wasn't inclined to change her tone.

"Sure. Guess y'all are pretty worn out, too, what with lookin' after Suelean and cookin' for everybody. Don't blame you a bit. What do y'all think is gonna happen tonight?"

"We need to call Dr. Cantrell, Al. I have to get home to Joe tonight, and I have to go to work tomorrow. There's a lot to be done at the beginning of the school year, and I haven't even made a dent in the pile of work. Somebody else will have to come up here to look after Suelean."

"Yeah, I think you're right. Who knows when Tabor . . ."

Kenny burst through the door, talking as he came. "Tabor's coming up the driveway. I just caught a glimpse of him at the far end. Let's not alarm him, Al, but let's be ready for anything. I don't know what the hell might have gone on between him and Buster. It could be nothing, or it could be bad."

"I got my pistol," Al said, patting the side of his pants leg. "I'm tellin' ya, I think he's crazy . . . always have thought

299

so. Who knows what he'll do."

"Oh my God, what'll I do?" Mattie shrieked. "I'm scared to death of him. Should I go in with Suelean?" she said, her eyes widening in alarm. "What'll I do?"

"Try and calm down, Mattie. Al and I are both armed. We won't let him get in the house, at least not without making sure we have him subdued. Go on back and sit with Suelean."

"Should we go out and meet him?" Al asked, his hand resting on the holster on his leg.

"No, let him come on up. Let's see what he does. Just stay cool, Al. We don't want to shoot anyone unless we have to."

The two men stood back from the small kitchen window that opened onto the back porch, watching as the big lumbering figure made his way up the steep driveway. When Tabor reached the path to the house, he stopped and looked around him, as if he expected to see someone before he reached the house. Momentarily, he continued his way up to the back porch.

"Mawmaw," he called in his loud, flat voice. "Y'all still in bed?"

Tabor pulled open the door and was on his way into the kitchen when Kenny stepped out in front of him.

"Hey, Tabor," he said calmly. "We've been wondering when you were coming home."

"What y'all doin' here? Why y'all still here?" he asked. "Where's my Mawmaw?"

"Yer grandmaw's still in her bed. She isn't fit to be up, yet . . . someone needs to look after her still," Kenny said, watching Al out of the corner of his eye.

Al stood as if transfixed to the spot, staring at Tabor and touching his gun.

"Someone hurt her pretty bad, Tabor. Y'all know anything about that?" Al asked, his voice growing hoarse as he finished his sentence.

"When did somebody hurt her?" Tabor asked.

"Guess y'all know that. Ya saw her Friday, before ya took off outta here."

"She didn't say someone hurt her. She told me she fell offen the porch. She said Pap wasn't even here."

Tabor's eyes were almost invisible under the heavy thatch of hair that covered his head and forehead and curled tightly down his cheeks and around his face. Kenny couldn't see his expression, but he tended to think Tabor was sincere in his comments.

"Come on in, Tabor," Kenny said, stepping aside. "Let's just sit down here at the table and talk awhile," he said in a friendly voice. "You and Al and me, we'll just sit down and talk some."

"I ain't gonna stay," Tabor said matter-of-factly. "I jest come to get me some things to take back to my mountain place, some food and now I need me another shirt for school."

"I want you to sit for awhile, Tabor. It's early. You have plenty of time."

Kenny pulled out a couple of chairs and signaled Al to sit down in one of them.

"Here . . . you sit here next to Al. I'll sit across from you."

Tabor reluctantly sat down and folded his hands on the table. "What y'all wanna talk about? I gotta go in a minute."

"Where'd you go last night, Tabor?" Kenny tried to sound casual.

"None a yer business," Tabor said loudly. "I ain't gonna tell ya my business."

"Did you see Buster?" Kenny asked, ignoring Tabor's outburst.

"No, and I ain't talkin' to y'all no more. Y'all no real policemen . . . yer jest college guards. That don't mean I gotta tell ya anything at all."

"Just a minute, Boy. You don't go smart mouthin' Kenny," Al said sharply, half rising from his seat.

"I ain't smart mouthin' no one. I'm jest not tellin' y'all my business. Now get outta my way. I'm gonna go talk to my Mawmaw."

Tabor pushed the chair hard and it fell backward with a loud crack as it hit the old metal sink on its way down. Kenny heard a sharp cry from the direction of the living room, recognizing Mattie's terror stricken voice.

"Al and I are goin' with you, Tabor," Kenny said firmly as he stood and blocked the doorway between the kitchen and the living room. "Mattie," he called loudly. "Tabor's coming back with Al and me to see Suelean."

"Don't y'all get in my way," Tabor bellowed flatly. "This ain't yer house. This here's my house and my Mawmaw's house, not even my Pap's house no more." The lack of any modulation or expression in his voice made Tabor sound louder and more ominous as he and Kenny stood facing each other. "I could kill y'all, ya know," Tabor yelled.

"I expect you could," Kenny said, "but that would be a pretty dumb thing to do, wouldn't it . . . pretty dumb. Just calm yourself down. This is not the way to act with your grandmaw in the other room so weak and sick," he said firmly.

Tabor seemed to listen to Kenny, and he made no attempt to move through the door.

"Let me see my Mawmaw," he said in a more subdued tone.

"Okay. Just behave yourself, and we won't have any trouble." Kenny turned and slowly led the way to Suelean's bedroom.

Mattie sat cowering in the corner, her hands and body visibly shaking.

"What's wrong with her?" Tabor boomed. "Is she

sick, too?"

"Tabor . . . Boy, where y'all been?" Mawmaw asked, raising herself a few inches from the bed on her good elbow. "I been worried about you, Son." She laid back on the pillow and reached her hand toward him.

"I went up ta my mountain place, Mawmaw, and then around. Did someone hurt you?"

"No, I done told you I fell offen the porch while I was shellin' peas."

"Al says someone hurt y'all real bad. Did Pap hurt ya before he got killed?" Tabor spoke only to Mawmaw, ignoring the other three people in the dim room.

"Al's wrong," Mawmaw said softly, irritation apparent in her weak voice. "Al don't know nothin' except what I told him, and I didn't tell him that."

"I gotta get me some things and go back up the mountain," Tabor said.

"Boy, I need y'all to stay home with me tonight," Mawmaw said. "These here friends of ours has been helpin' out, and I thank them, but now you and me need to be here in our own place together. I need y'all right now, Son. I'm grievin' for yer Pap, and I need my own kin with me. Please, Tabor, do it for me."

Tabor stood looking down at the small figure of his grandmother, aware that she was not the same as she had been last week or the week before that. It made him feel afraid, to see her like this. He was silent, hardly moving. The other three in the room appeared to have been turned to stone, not even their breathing apparent.

"I gotta go ta my class on Monday, Mawmaw . . . y'all know that."

"Yeah, but that ain't till tomorrow mornin'. Y'all can stay the night with me," she said, her voice pleading but firm.

Tabor stared at her, seeing his Mawmaw in a way he

hadn't seen her before. He looked down at the floor for a few seconds, and then he said as quietly as he was able, "Okay, Mawmaw. I reckon I can stay the night, but only if Al and the other two leave. I ain't stayin' if they stays. I kin cook ya some supper, and I kin help ya, jest the same as them. You and me don't need them anymore."

"That's good, Son . . . thank ya. We kin manage, you and me." Mawmaw smiled.

"Suelean, I think Al and I should hang around outside and . . ." Kenny began.

"No. Me and Tabor'll be okay. He'll take care of me. Y'all get on home to yer own folks. Mattie, I bet Joe's fit to be tied . . . y'all bein' away two nights and all. I'm a lot better than when ya'll came. In a day or two, I'll be up and doin' again."

"Suelean . . . Honey . . . I don't think you should be up and around at all, not for another four or five days. Tabor can't tend to everything for you, certainly not when he goes off to school."

"Okay, then Al and Kenny can come back on Monday afternoon. That's time enough, and I reckon I'll be better by then."

"Y'all go on now," Tabor said. "Me and Mawmaw's gonna be okay. We don't need ya no more."

Mattie looked horrified, suddenly aware that she and Kenny and Al were leaving the helpless, injured Suelean with a hulking, deranged mad man, possibly a killer. How had this happened? Why didn't Kenny and Al do something?

"Suelean, Kenny and I need to stay around. Dr. Cantrell told us to do that. Those are his orders, and we have to do what he says."

"This is my place, Al, not Dr. Cantrell's. Y'all can tell him what I said. I ain't givin' ya a choice . . . this is my home. Now, y'all go and come on back midday tomorrow, when Tabor's at his class."

Kenny and Al stood silently listening to Suelean's soft words, knowing that they couldn't leave her alone with Tabor. Mattie had moved slowly toward the door, eager to leave the decisions to the two men.

"Okay, Suelean. If you put it that way, I guess we don't have a choice, do we. Tabor, you take good care of your grandmaw. Remember, she can't do anything for herself. She needs you to take care of her tonight."

"I will," Tabor said. "I reckon I know how to do that better'n y'all."

"Bye, Suelean. I'll come back in a day or so to see how you're doing," Mattie said, her voice shaky. "Take care of her, Tabor."

Tabor glared at Mattie, but he didn't answer.

Kenny, Al, and Mattie straggled through the kitchen and down the path to the driveway. As soon as they were out of sight of the house, Kenny pulled the other two aside behind a clump of wild rose bushes.

"Al, you take Mattie home. I'll stay hidden out here until you come back. You and I will stay outside tonight, just like the first night. If there's a problem, we'll be here for it. Stop at the Exxon and get us some coffee and a couple of sandwiches, something to get us through the night."

"I'm so relieved," Mattie said, touching her hand to her throat. "That Tabor isn't up to any good in there. I just know it."

"I'll get back as soon as I can," Kenny said, once again rubbing his hand over the hard, smooth side of his pistol. "Should I call Buster, let him know where we are?"

"Maybe it wouldn't hurt. He isn't going to come up here unless he has a reason, but it's a good idea to let him know we found Tabor."

"That dumb asshole better not try anything around Buster," Al said. "Buster'd jest as soon shoot him and get it over with . . . jest like me. There ain't gonna be any peace around here until someone puts a bullet in his crazy head."

"Rev the car some, so Tabor can hear it. Let him know we're leaving. When you come back, park down on the road, don't come up the driveway. See you when you get back."

Mattie and Al walked side by side through the dried mud and weeds to the police car. Al floored the gas pedal a few times, loudly racing the engine, before he drove down the rutted gravel driveway.

Kenny walked behind the row of wild rose bushes that ran along the far side of the Maclean's driveway until he came to a thick grove of mountain laurel. He sat down on the ground behind the tight knit of bushes, and then he laid back on the soft dried grass, listening for any sounds from the old farmhouse. Within minutes, Tabor banged out the back door and walked down the path to the driveway. He tramped noisily along the gravel ruts, passing close to the clump of wild rose bushes where Kenny, Al, and Mattie had stood talking minutes earlier. He stopped on the far side of the driveway, almost directly across from where Kenny sat holding his breath. Tabor reached into the dense gnarl of an overgrown quince bush and slowly removed an oblong black bag. He unzipped it and pulled out a long, cloth-wrapped bundle. Tabor carefully unwound the tattered blanket cover, slowly revealing the shiny steel barrel of his rifle.

Chapter 45

During his six years in Clayton Forge, Richard had come to feel that the legendary grandeur of the Blue Ridge Mountains became almost intimidating with its spectacular display that began in early autumn. Bright, crisp mornings of temperatures in the sixties were followed by dry, breezy afternoons full of the fragrance of the last cutting of hay from the feathery, waving meadows that were tucked into the gaps and valleys. Mountain pines turned from iridescent silver to a hazy, pale yellow as they shed their long needles in late August, creating an aromatic carpet that covered roadways as well as the forest floor. The purplish blue haze that hovered around the towering peaks during the hotter months seemed to have been sucked up by the steep granite walls as the weather cooled, coloring the ranges themselves the astonishing hues that had named this part of the Appalachian Mountains. Richard never tired of the breathtaking vistas that awaited him each morning as he ran along a mountain ledge or scrambled up a ragged cliff. Sometimes, he felt as if he was breathing in the view, making it an integral part of himself, of his being.

As he drove toward Clayton Forge, the bronze Jeep Cherokee hummed around the curves and steadied itself on the climbs, silently releasing the pungent scent from the layer of needles that covered the sun-warmed highway. Richard couldn't help but think that all the natural beauty and apparent peace of this vast mountain world was only superficial, a representation of life's possibilities, not its reality. The past year at Jackson Clayton College had been one hell of a roller coaster ride, and he saw no sign that it was going to change anytime soon. With each passing month, the mysteries seemed to have grown murkier, and the characters more puzzling. As the academic semester moved into its second week, he realized that he had reached a point that caused him to doubt his ability to continue on at the college. He could no longer ignore Cantrell's shadowy, incomprehensible attitude toward Allison, and his bewildering protection of a volatile, mentally ill misfit, who clearly threatened the safety of faculty and students alike. Richard had wrestled with the dilemma a year ago, when Allison left without explanation, but his anxiety and frustration had continued to grow as the problems repeated themselves. Now, he was on his way to pick up one of his teachers from a safe haven, and he was going to throw her back into the middle of a dangerous, worsening mess. Even the law was pussyfooting around, claiming no threats had been made, no harm had been done. Richard's stomach churned and his chest was tight. He could leave with thirty days notice, wash his hands of the whole unsavory situation. But what about Chris? Who would help her or save her?

The flickering Starlight Motel sign was still lit at 8:45 a.m. "Maybe Caroline never turns it off," he thought. "Guess it's easier that way." Richard parked the car and walked toward the office.

"Richard, I'm up and ready to go," Chris called just before he reached the motel's office door.

"Hey, how'd you sleep?" he called back as he strolled to meet her on the walkway that connected the identical turquoise trimmed units.

"Not well, but what could I expect, considering the circumstances of my late night check in. I can catch up tonight."

"I'm convinced you did the right thing, Chris. I'll tell you why over breakfast."

"I'm not sorry I slept away from home last night, but I can think of many places I'd rather stay," she said as they walked to his car.

"Come on, we can go, since you paid Caroline last night." Richard turned to Chris with a faint smile. "Of course, unless you want to go in and tell her goodbye."

"That's okay, I'll catch her next time," she replied with a laugh. "What a beautiful day! It really feels like autumn, not the temperature, but just that fall feeling. The mountains are spectacular . . . look at that color."

"When I first came here, I read a lot about the Blue Ridge Mountains because I was so intrigued by their blue and purple color. We certainly have nothing like that in Florida," he said. "Scientists say that the pine trees are responsible for the color. They give off a chemical called *isoprene,* and when it mixes with the atmosphere, it creates that blue haze and blue color we see from a distance."

"Interesting . . . I guess up close, there's no blue."

"That's right. Are you hungry? I'm starving." he said as he opened the car door for Chris.

"Breakfast sounds great. I haven't been to the Timber Ridge since our notorious departmental meeting."

"I heard you guys were a pretty rowdy bunch that night. We need to be careful of our reputation at the Timber Ridge, you know. If they throw us out, we don't have any other place to go," he laughed. "Seriously, the English Department is made up of a great group of people. I'm not supposed to play favorites, but it's my favorite, probably because I was an English teacher type before I became a dean."

As they drove the short distance to the restaurant, Chris

thought of several questions that had been swirling around in her mind overnight, but she decided not to ask Richard. She didn't want to risk another communication drought.

"Here we are. Prepare yourself. This is everyone's Sunday morning breakfast spot, from the folks at the Baptist church who come after their service, to the good old boys who have been out hunting or drinking all night."

Chris was relieved when she walked into the country cafe and didn't see anyone she knew.

"Hey, Bud, how's it going?" Richard called to a large, balding man wearing a coat and a tie, who sat in a corner booth with a gray haired woman in a bright pink cotton dress.

"Fine, Professor. How y'all doin'?"

"Can't complain on a day like this." Richard waved his hand as he and Chris sat down in the second booth on the wall. "That's our mailman," he said. "Nice guy. Every now and then I find a little religious pamphlet in my mailbox . . . no stamp, no address. I think Bud uses his job to try and save the heathens who populate his delivery route. I've actually read some of the material he's left . . . not to say I'm ready to join his church."

Richard and Chris sat quietly as they looked at the stained, plastic-covered menus. They ordered from the teenaged waitress and both leaned back on the red plastic covered cushions that made up the fifties décor.

"I'm really sorry, Chris, that this school year has had such a bad start for you. I can't tell you how sorry I am."

"It's not your fault, Richard. It's not really anyone's fault, just circumstances. I suppose personalities play a part, too, but no one's to blame for what's going on. Think about it. Tabor is randomly selected to be in my class . . . he likes me too much . . . his grandmother gets hurt . . . and his grandfather gets killed. All of this in the period of seven days." Chris shook her head and smiled at Richard when she finished. "Don't worry, I'm pretty resilient. I've had some pretty tough training, and

I'm a survivor."

"I'm sure of it," he said, folding his arms on the table and leaning toward her. "This college is so fortunate to have hired you. I just hope we can keep you."

"I have no plans to leave," she laughed. "If I disappear overnight, call the police. I won't have planned it," she laughed. "That's a bad joke, but I'm as permanent as I was when you hired me."

"Chris, you know what I think about Tabor. I don't think the guy can help himself, but I do think he has the capability of hurting someone, even killing them. He has a sick obsession with pretty, red-haired women. We both know that, and I think he has focused on you. I can't think of a softer or kinder way to say it. It's frightening and threatening, and I believe it's absolutely real."

Chris stared at Richard, as she tried to think of what to say. Her thoughts were fragmented, as she considered his bold, direct warning. It was about her. She was the "someone" Richard referred to, the someone that Tabor could hurt . . . or kill. She tried to speak, but words wouldn't come.

"I'm sorry, Chris, but I have to make you understand the seriousness of this. James has fed you false information, and he's allowed you to believe that you can change Tabor through kindness and personal attention. That's wrong thinking, Chris. Dangerously wrong. The more attention you give him, the more he'll need. When you withdraw, and you will have to withdraw, he'll turn his sick love into sick hate, and you'll become his victim. He'll see you as the person who lied to him, fooled him, and then you won't have any choice but to run."

"Richard . . . I don't . . . I can't . . ." Chris blinked rapidly as she fought to contain the tears that flooded her eyes. "I don't know what to do. Maybe I should go, before it all gets out of hand."

"No, that will only push this onto the next person. I want you to help me convince James that Tabor has to be dismissed from this school. We can call it a transfer . . . make it sound better. We need to enlist his grandmother's help and get him into the school in Martinsville, the residential technical training school. It's a good place, Chris, a school for people with average mental ability, but who have serious emotional problems. I believe strongly that it would give Tabor the best chance, maybe the only chance, he has of learning how to fit into a society that up until now has rejected him. Now that his grandfather is gone, it might be a little easier. I know James would pay for it if he believed it was right for this student, this kid. He's paid for so many in the past . . . it's what he does. I have to give him that."

"I don't think I can convince James of this, Richard, particularly now, since he and I have agreed on what we can do together to help Tabor."

Chris rubbed her forehead as she closed her eyes. Last night she had told James she agreed with him and would help him with Tabor. This morning she was shrinking in fear, as she thought of how she could avoid ever seeing Tabor again. She wanted to scream and run out of the restaurant, get into her car and drive back to New York.

"Chris, I know you were with James last night. He told me he would talk to you because you were going to be together. It's none of my business . . . I mean that. I'm only your academic supervisor, but I'm going to tell you a few more things, some of them disturbing. If you don't want to hear it, tell me to be quiet, and I'll shut up."

"I can't bury my head in the sand, Richard. Go ahead . . . tell me."

"First of all, I need to tell you that I knew Allison well, and I'm very aware of happenings in her life during the year before she disappeared. I wanted to help her when Tabor started making her life miserable, and I spent a good deal of time with her, talking with her about it. Unfortunately, she read more into our relationship than was there, which was awkward for both of us, but she was never more than a friend to me, one of my faculty who was in trouble. I know James believes she and I were involved with each other beyond the professional level, but it's not true. For the last few months Allison was at the college, something changed, and she pulled back. She wasn't available to talk, and she didn't even answer my messages. We never exchanged more than a few words after that."

As Chris listened to Richard's revelations about Allison, she recalled a comment from James on Saturday night that "Richard had a close personal relationship with Allison that he continues to deny."

Richard sat quietly, staring at the table top between them. "Chris, you need to be very, very careful . . . with James. I think he knows more about Allison's leaving, or disappearance, than he has told anyone around here. He and Allison had become closer the last few months or so before she left. It was strange. Tabor was hounding her, really stalking her, to the point that she would literally disappear from the campus for days on end. Then, when I would talk to James about it, he would tell me he'd talked to her or he'd seen her, and that she was just fine. He'd tell me she was "working" with Tabor and things were going well, and she just had a flu bug. He'd say we should just post a notice for her classes, that she was sick. Now, when we talk about Allison, James acts as if he hardly knew her, as if none of that happened. You heard him, Chris."

"What do you think that means?" Chris felt cold and nauseous.

"I don't know, but there's more. I was in Bryant Hall one night about a year ago, and I heard voices coming from

313

Cantrell's office. It was pretty late, at least eight or nine o'clock, and I could hear that Allison was in his office. I shouldn't have, but I listened outside the door. He was telling her he wanted her to "go with him again," and she was crying and telling him she couldn't and not to say anything else. The way they were interacting clearly told me that their relationship was more than college president and faculty member. There was a familiarity, at least on his part, although she was too upset for me to tell much. The next day, a Friday, Allison was out of school, and James was 'away' as Mattie put it."

Chris remembered Glen's chilling story of what he had overheard in Bryant Hall, the night Allison had disappeared from campus.

The waitress had brought the food and poured the coffee ten minutes earlier, but all of it remained untouched by either of them.

Richard continued. "All the time Allison was having trouble with Tabor, with his overbearing attention and his hanging around, James did the same thing that he's doing now. He told her not to be afraid, said he knew Tabor, and he knew she could help him. And I know she tried.

"Do you believe Tabor had something to do with Allison's leaving or . . . ." Chris seemed barely able to say her last three words, "with her disappearance?"

Richard looked intently at Chris for a few seconds before he answered her. "Yes, Chris, I do."

"But I thought you just said you believed James knew something, or was involved in whatever happened to Allison. If you think Tabor is somehow responsible, how does that fit in with any questions you have about James's behavior regarding Allison?"

"I think James may know more about her situation than he's telling us. Maybe he has some misguided idea that he needs to protect someone . . . like Tabor. I don't know, Chris. I just feel strongly that something bad happened, and there are ominous signs that it could happen again."

"Tell me what you think I should do," Chris said quietly.

"After your classes on Monday, I want you to go with me to talk to James. I want you to be honest with him, and I'll do the same. We'll tell him everything. I'll have all the information for the school in Martinsville to present to him. We'll emphasize his benevolence, Chris, which is real, and we'll tell him how he can really help Tabor by getting him into that school. I'll set up a time with James for tomorrow's meeting. Let's give it one more try, Chris. With Tabor out of the way, we can move on to the next aspect of this, which is the part Cantrell played in Allison's disappearance."

His words confused and somehow disturbed her. She did not want to be part of a witch hunt. "I'm not sure, Richard, that this is what I should be doing. I'm a new teacher here, and I really don't know anything about Allison . . . maybe . . ."

"Please trust me, Chris. I've lived with this growing concern for a year now, and suddenly I see the nightmare forming again. You and I have to try to do something. I'll call Buster and ask him or JT to sit outside your house tonight, and every night until this whole ugly situation is cleaned up. I'll make sure you're safe, believe me."

She remembered James telling her something similar . . . together they could do this, she should call on him anytime she needed help, she could trust him. And now Richard, almost the same words, applied for a different reason.

Chris sat numbly staring and not seeing, her hands icy, her heart pounding. She didn't know what any of this meant, what James had told her, what Richard had said. Panic wrapped itself around her as she realized she didn't know the truth about any of it, and, most of all, she didn't know who she could believe or trust.

Chapter 46

"Chris, you sound to me like you have a death wish! Honest to God, you aren't making rational decisions."

"You're an alarmist, Rachael," Chris had replied angrily. "I've managed to get this far in life without being afraid of my shadow. Maybe extreme caution works for you, but it's never been a part of me. I need to do this my way."

"Fine, Chris. I've only tried to talk some sense into you because I care about you. So be it. Let me know how it turns out." Rachael had hung up the phone with a cursory "goodbye," not waiting to hear Chris's similar irate response.

It was after a long, drawn-out conversation with Rachael on Sunday evening that Chris had done a complete review of her five months in Clayton Forge, and it was then that she had made the firm decision to rely on herself and her own judgment. Her friend had loudly expressed shock and disbelief when Chris had said she "wanted to give Tabor a chance before condemning him."

"How many chances does he get, before you get it?" Rachael had yelled. "You need to get out of there right away, tonight. You're being stubborn and totally unrealistic. This monster is real, Chris. Your very life is at stake!"

It was at that moment in Rachael's dramatic monologue that Chris had determined that she was going to begin the second week of classes without interference from anyone else, including Richard, James, or Rachael. She was fed up with all the intrigue and the paralyzing anxiety that had consumed her first week, and she was focused on taking control. She would meet with Tabor, as she had told him she would when he left with Buster on Friday, but it would be on her terms. The meeting Richard was arranging with James could be helpful, but she was not at all sure what her position would be after she heard what the president and the dean had to say, when facing each other. She couldn't promise either of them anything.

No matter what the others said, Chris couldn't believe that any of the people involved in her life intended to hurt her in any way. Each had his own agenda, his own personal remembrance of the past and view of the present, maybe even unrealistic hope for the future. That didn't mean she had to agree with it or cave in or give in to it. Poor Tabor had little worth remembering, as far as she could tell, and here she was, listening to every tale that came her way and on the verge of taking away an opportunity he would never have again. If she was going to agree to anything that so completely affected another person's life, like sending him off to a residential school, it was only going to be after she had given it careful thought and had come to her own independent conclusion. As best she could, she was going to look at everything that James and Richard had told her as opinion and speculation. The few facts she had been able to sift out, she would hang on to. In the meantime, she was going to meet and teach her classes, the job that she came here to do.

The early morning sun cast a mellow, rosy hue on Cantrell Hall, softly lighting the bright beds of deep red and golden yellow chrysanthemums that curved gracefully along each side of the entrance. Chris balanced her briefcase and book bag against her body as she pulled open the door and stepped into the coolness of the arboretum. The perfumed fragrance of the tropical flowers mixed subtly with the faint woodsy musk of the rich soil and trees, reminding her of the extraordinary beauty that surrounded her each day. At eight on Monday morning, the atrium and halls were deserted, the building almost empty. Chris liked this time on campus best of all, finding the quiet and solitude conducive to personal reflection and preparation for the day ahead. Even the lights in the hallways seemed softer, more welcoming than they were later in the day, as if the noise and the hustle and bustle magnified their brightness.

She stepped resolutely into the hall that led to her office, annoyed by the tension she suddenly felt in her body. "Get over it," she mumbled through clenched teeth as she looked straight ahead. She reached her office door and fished in her pocket for the key. As she opened the door and flicked on the light, she pushed her book bag into the room with her foot.

Chris looked around the pleasant, well-decorated space that had brought her so much pleasure this summer. More than anything, she wanted to feel that way again. She pulled up the blinds into a tight slice of white at the top of the glass wall and looked at the mountains outlined softly against the bright blue of the sky. The view was a kaleidoscope, changing as she watched, the sun and clouds alternately casting bursts of brilliance onto sharp peaks that moments later became dark with moving shadows. Her breathing quieted, confirming her belief that she was in charge, and that everything would ultimately fall into place as she wanted it to. The office door stood halfway open, and she decided she would close it this morning, not to keep anyone out, but to get some work done. Chris sat down at her desk and opened her notebook to the plans for today. "Presentation of the basic plan for an essay, hints for getting started, and . . ."

A sharp knock jolted her, causing her to stand up quickly and start toward the door to the hall. When the loud rapping came again, she realized it was behind her, at the door to her patio. Chris whirled around and saw Tabor looming on the other side of the expanse of glass, his bearded face pressed against the big door panel.

"Let me in, Miss Chris," he rumbled, his loud, flat voice only slightly muffled by the wall that separated them. "I come fer my meetin' with y'all."

Chris's eyes darted to the little banjo clock. Eight thirty. They had an hour and a half before class.

"Tabor, I'm doing some work now. Let's meet at 11:30, after class. That's a better time." Her hands felt clammy and she felt cold all over.

"I need to talk to ya now. Open the door and let me in." He put his big hands up to the glass, making a frame for his face, as he attempted to see inside.

"Tabor, I can't let you in that door. If you want to come in, you'll have to come to my office door inside the building." Her breath came in gasps as she heard Rachael saying, "Your very life is at stake."

"I want to come in this door," he roared. "Let me in this door."

Chris stepped into the middle of the room and faced him directly. "You heard me, Tabor. If you want to meet with me, we can do it now, but you have to come in the proper way, through my office door. I don't let students in this door."

Tabor raised his big fist as if he was going to hit the window, but he stopped in mid space.

"Okay, I'm goin' 'round there." He picked up a large, rectangular bag that had been lying beside him, and he disappeared through the opening in the patio wall.

Chris quickly pressed the button beside Glen's name. "Glen Cooper," he said after the first ring.

"Glen, it's Chris. Will you be in your office for awhile?"

"Until ten," he replied.

319

"If I call you again, please come to my office, even if I don't say anything. I have a student meeting, and I just want someone to know. I don't anticipate any problem."

"I can come right now," he said, his voice suddenly alert.

"No, I need to do this without anyone around. Thanks."

"Okay. You sure you're okay, Chris?" Glen asked.

"Fine. I'll be fine. I'll call you when the meeting's over."

Chris hung up the phone and opened her office door, pushing it back to the wall and lowering the little metal doorstop with her toe. As Tabor's heavy boots hammered unevenly against the floor tiles in the hall, Chris quickly pushed a large chair into place on the far side of her desk. She waited, staring at the door.

"Why couldn't I come in the other door?" he boomed as he seemed to lunge into the middle of the room, no more than five feet from where she stood behind her desk.

"Because I don't let any students come in that door, Tabor. This is the door everyone needs to come to. There's a chair for you. Sit down over there," she said calmly, directing him back a few feet.

Tabor hesitated, looking first at the chair and then back at her. He moved slowly to the spot she was pointing to, still holding the bag when he sat down.

"You can put your bag on the floor right beside you," Chris said with a forced smile.

He carefully laid the large bag close to his feet.

"I'm sorry about your grandfather, Tabor. I didn't know about it until Officer Shewel came to get you last Friday. I'm really sorry."

"Yeah," he said flatly. "It don't make much difference fer me, 'cause me and him didn't like each other much."

"I understand you want to ask me about your work and get some help with it." Chris struggled to remember that he was just another student, like all the rest.

"Well, I want to talk to y'all," he said. "Afore we talk about the work. Some other stuff. That's what I want to talk about."

Chris was aware that Tabor's foul smell had considerably improved since last Friday, and his faded yellow shirt was somewhat cleaner. His beard and hair were still a hopeless tangle and snarl that enclosed him above his chest, but it appeared to be free of the debris that it routinely seemed to hold.

"What is it you want to talk about, Tabor? We have about twenty minutes for our meeting this morning, because I have to complete my work before class at ten. We'll need to stop at nine. Maybe it would be better for you if we worked on the assignments now, and you could talk to me later about the other things." Chris concentrated on being specific and direct.

"No," he boomed. "This other is important. Y'all need to watch out fer yerself," he said suddenly. "I can take care of you better." He suddenly seemed agitated as he rocked slightly in his chair and rubbed his big hands together. Noise gurgled from his throat, but he seemed unable to form the words to continue.

"Tabor, I know how to take care of myself. You and I need to talk about getting you through English composition class this year, so you can go on to some of the Internet Technology courses you want to take. Dr. Cantrell has told me .that . . . "

"No," he thundered, "he ain't a good man. Y'all can't be with him." Tabor lurched out of the chair and was suddenly standing next to Chris's desk. He stood looking down at her, flexing and unflexing his oversized, rough hands into tight fists. "Y'all need to stay away from him . . . y'all need somebody better . . ." He began to rock side to side, from one foot to the other, his enormous body wracked with emotion he couldn't express.

"Tabor, Dr. Cantrell is my friend, and he's your friend, too. He says very nice things about you."

"No . . . not a friend . . . he don't like me . . . y'all can't let him . . . can't be yer friend . . . he's bad . . . and I ain't gonna let him . . ." Tabor's jarring, flat voice came out of him in staccato bursts, and then trailed off into a low, throaty moan.

"Tabor, I don't want to talk about Dr. Cantrell anymore. If we aren't going to talk about your work for English class, then you need to leave. When you want to talk about the work, you let me know." Chris had stood up and was talking to Tabor from behind her desk. She glanced at her telephone.

Tabor stared at her and then awkwardly backed up to the doorway. He reached down and picked up the long bag on the floor, never taking his eyes from Chris.

"Y'all ain't gonna be any different than Miss Allison," he boomed angrily. "Y'all gonna be sorry." He quieted for a moment and then he said, "I wanna show ya' my mountain place . . . it's nice . . . and nobody knows where it's at."

"Tabor, that's nice of you to want to show me something special. But you and I need to work on your English class, on your papers. That's what my job is, Tabor, to help you with your class work, and I really want to help you." Chris's hands were shaking, and she held onto the edge of the desk so Tabor wouldn't notice. She fought to keep her words steady.

"I know I ain't supposed to tell y'all this. I'll get in trouble . . . but somebody's gonna die, Miss Chris. Dr. Cantrell and Dr. Shelton told me I couldn't tell nobody that again . . . or else. But I gotta tell ya' . . . cause I know it."

Tabor was gone before Chris could find her voice. She stood motionless, staring at the empty doorway, trying to find meaning in his terrifying, menacing words.

Chapter 47

James glanced in his rearview mirror at the distant church steeple and roof tops of the sleeping town of Clayton Forge. Ahead of him, the early dawn's light crept slowly over the highest peaks of the Blue Ridge, seeming to squeeze its brightness between the sharp angles of adjacent mountains into the gray valleys below. His night had been short, and he yawned before taking another drink of the tepid coffee he had poured an hour earlier, just before he left his home next to the college campus. The evening with Chris had been much better than he could have hoped for, and it left him confident that his future plans were beginning to fall into place. He pondered her reluctance to commit to any repeat in the future, which he had expected. Allison had been the same. The comparison stopped there, however. Chris was much more self-confident than Allison, which strangely meant she would be easier to convince than Allison had been. That's what he believed. The other factor that clearly aided his case was Chris's strong, happy marriage. She was far lonelier than Allison had been, because she had lost real love. From what Allison had told him, she appeared to have had only one short, bad marriage and a series of unfulfilling one or two month relationships. The loss of a true soul mate made Chris all the more susceptible to another who might come into her life. James recognized that he had human nature working for him, too . . . men and women always tried to recreate what had been good in their lives.

This trip to Tuggles Gap was one he undertook with some sense of accomplishment. His mission was to complete a final check, to make sure the lake was in good shape and his goal had been achieved with the raising of the water level. However, it would also give him a chance to begin plans for next year. That was his timetable, one more year. James thought about the problems he might find at the lake, and he momentarily became anxious. How long must he wait before he could be certain that everything was permanently settled? Sharon Edwards had prepared the necessary papers for the final step over a year ago. She had brought them and gone over them with him when she came up for his Christmas party. Then the whole thing had gone haywire, over night, when Allison suddenly lost her mind. He had been a fool to ever think she would fit in, but now he had it back on track again. He realized how glad he was that she was gone.

James shuddered at his stupidity when he remembered his inane comment to Chris about people keeping a relationship a secret until they decided to spend the rest of their lives together. He didn't have the sense of a dumb schoolboy when it came to beautiful women. Hopefully she would come to see it as a silly comparison made on the spur of the moment, not as a threat to her independence.   He felt a hot surge of embarrassment mixed with anger as he hated himself for being so empty-headed. His father was probably smiling in hell over that one.

The two hour drive passed quickly, as James occupied himself with taking stock of the present and rejoicing in the future. The past was dimming, and over the next twenty-four hours, he would bury it forever. As he neared the estate gates, he reminded himself that he had only this day and part of tomorrow to accomplish everything on his list. Today, he would go to the lake by himself. Then if he needed help, he could call Lester. He'd figure out what to tell him if it came to that. Tomorrow, plans for redoing the house would be discussed with the Abernathys, before he drove back to Clayton Forge in the afternoon.

The velvety green grass was pristine in the early morning, with the sparkle of dew sprinkled across the meticulously mowed lawns. Lester and his boys did a good job, and James rewarded them handsomely. The Abernathys were getting up in years, and he knew he'd be faced with replacing them someday. The thought oddly brought him some pleasure, because he realized he wouldn't have to make that decision alone.

As James drove into the driveway at 8:00 a.m. on Sunday morning, Lester and one of his helpers were trimming the old boxwood bushes that lined one side of the property. James watched as the old man dropped his shears and started across the lawn, intent on meeting him as he got out of the car.

"Hey, James," he called. "Y'all made good time I guess. Got here earlier than you expected."

"How are you, Lester? Yes, I think I was the only car on Caleb Mountain Road. Everyone must have been sleeping in on Sunday morning. How are things going up here?"

"Can't complain. Found us a good bunch of workers for the fall. Guess the problem with the mines, everybody closin' down, has put a lot of folks out a' work. Several of these boys is miners, at least they used to be."

"Glad I don't have to worry about that anymore," James replied. "If Cantrell Mines closes, that's the business of the folks who bought it. They have the blockbusters of mines, several mountains of them, if they only knew how to run them. How's Audrey?"

"Good. Her arthritis gets her sometimes as the weather

cools, but that don't keep her from naggin' at me. Still keeps me hoppin'," he said with humor in his voice. "I reckon that's my cross to bear."

"Could be worse, Lester," James laughed. "I'm going to change my clothes and go for a hike today, spend some hours trekking around the property. I haven't done it for a long while. It'll be the last time until next spring. Before we know it, the snow will be flying."

"Want me to come along?" Lester asked.

"No, I'll just take my time. I'll have Audrey make me a lunch, and I'll enjoy some of my favorite spots." He hesitated and then asked, "You been down to the lake recently?"

"No, not since we checked the water level a couple a' months ago. When we raised the gate on the dam last year, like ya'll wanted us to, me and Jake watched it every day, and once it got up to the mark on the pole you left for us, we didn't change it. The lake is a couple a' foot deeper now, and holdin' steady. Ya'll goin' over there today?" Jake stood shading his eyes from the intensity of the morning sun.

"Maybe . . . I haven't decided," James said casually. "I'll let you get back to your cutting. See you later." James walked toward the house, looking around at the perfection that pleased him so much.

"Hey, Audrey, what good things do I smell in that kitchen?" he called as he walked into the front hall.

"James, welcome home," she said with a wide smile. "I quick set some cinnamon rolls when Lester told me you was comin' . . . I know how you like 'em."

"Like them . . . they make me plumb crazy!" he raved as he gave her a hug. "Can you throw together a sandwich and some fruit for me? I'm going off on a nice hike today. Maybe put in a couple of bottles of water. My pack is in the front closet. Just stuff it all in there. I'll go change my clothes. Thanks, Audrey."

She hurried happily toward the kitchen, glad to be doing something for the boss she adored.

James pulled on a pair of jeans and a long sleeved, waffle-weave gray tee shirt. It would be hot by midday, but he didn't want to get mixed up in poison oak that infested the property or risk a sunburn. He pulled a small tool kit from a hall closet and checked it for strong clippers, a hatchet, and a sharp hunting knife, just in case he had to hack his way through the forest.

"Thanks for the grub, Audrey. I should be back by early evening, but don't worry if I'm not. Why don't we eat supper about seven. That work for you?" he asked, knowing what her answer would be. "See you then."

James headed for the trail that entered the woods on the backside of the abandoned barnyard, behind the oldest of the two barns. It was really an old logging road his father had cut in, and the path that led directly to the lake. He loved exploring the hundreds of acres that made up the estate property, or climbing the mountains that he owned, but today he had to remain focused on the task at hand. Wild rose bushes and heavy, thorny brambles unceasingly tried to reclaim the wide grassy roadway as their own, but Lester kept it clear, as James had instructed. Except during the snowy winter months, a vehicle . . . farm wagon, pickup truck, or car . . . could easily navigate the two miles through the forest, from the trail's beginning to its end.

After walking and cutting away a few insistent brambles for the best part of two hours, James came onto the rolling, grassy meadow that had been clear cut by his father early in his marriage to James's mother. She had loved wildflowers, and Mr. Cantrell had opened up several acres and planted them heavily with seeds. The soft blue bells and dainty white daisies still welcomed spring and summer to the bright green meadow, and fall brought the blackeyed Susans that peppered the flaxen grass. James knew that the bright golden flowers with the whimsical black and white faces had been his mother's favorites. He hadn't known his mother for very long, but he always remembered her meadow and the happy times they had there.

Just beyond the rolling, rock-strewn grass was a glassy, dark lake, created when his father had dammed a tributary of the Dan River and flooded a small canyon. Because of its formation, the lake was very deep, the edge of its shoreline falling off steeply into the black abyss of the rocky canyon. No one had ever measured the depth of its waters, and his father had named it Bottomless Lake. James had never seen the lake when it wasn't inky and mysterious, even when the sun was bright on the meadow and the trees. Just as the meadow always reminded him of his mother, the black, formidable lake brought cold remembrances of his distant, ill-tempered father.

James tramped through the yellowing, flaxen grass and the bobbing blackeyed Susans to the edge of the frigid, opaque water. The remnants of an old boat dock were barely visible below the surface, having been submerged by the raising of the dam gate that James had ordered a year ago. He sat down on a flat bolder that had been his seat for six decades, since before his mother had died. He remembered the row boat that she had allowed him to paddle around the lake, while the two of them laughed at their fat stomachs made by the puffy life vests she insisted they wear. He and Elaine also had rowed around the lake a few times, when they were first married and still having fun. They never wore the bothersome, old fashioned life vests. Even though his wife couldn't swim, James had earned medals and honors for his skill on the college swim team. He had always told her he could easily get both of them to shore if necessary.

He looked across the smooth expanse of motionless water to the far side of the small lake. It appeared that no one had been over there for years, even though the rough logging path ran all around the shoreline to the hand-built dam. James relaxed as he realized that the remote body of water was his alone, no one else had even passed this way. He unwrapped the thick ham salad sandwich Audrey had made for him and enjoyed the quiet of the peaceful day. Later, James walked around the lake, stopping longest on the shore opposite his rock seat, probing the water with a big tree limb he had cut and tromping and stamping the ground closest to the water's edge. He bent over and knelt down, seeming to stare intently into the deep dark water. He then continued briskly over the walkway on the old dam and around the remaining shoreline. He gathered the remnants of his lunch into the worn pack, and wandered back across the meadow, turning once for a last look at the dark, brooding waters. James was at last satisfied that the troubled times were behind him, and the future was clear and bright. Maybe he would bring Chris here someday, and then again, maybe he never would. It could be that he himself would never come back to the lake again.

That night, James slept well, in the pale yellow room, his mother's room. Tomorrow, before he left, he would go over plans with Audrey and Lester for redecorating the big master bedroom down the hall. The old, high-backed oak bed where his father had slept and died would be hauled away, along with the oppressive dark chests and tables his father had bought in England when he refurbished the house. All would be replaced by beautiful flowery fabrics in soft colors and French country furniture. Over the next months, the house would be reborn, as it was readied for the new occupant and the happiness she would bring to it.

Chapter 48

"Hey, Tabor, I think there are some girls in there who want to sit by ya'," the tall, good-looking blond boy said with mock sincerity. "No kiddin', Man, they're hot for you."

Two other boys hung a few feet behind him, suppressing laughs.

"Y'all leave me alone," Tabor said loudly.

"Come on, Man, I ain't joshin' ya'. These babes were just talkin' about you last week when you weren't here. I'm tellin' ya', they're knock outs, and they want you."

"I ain't listenin' to y'all," he boomed angrily. "Yer jest makin' fun a' me. Leave me alone."

Tabor picked up the big rectangular gym bag he had set on the floor outside the locked classroom and started to unzip it. Just as he was reaching inside, it fell heavily to the floor.

"Hey, ya' dropped your lunch," the blond heckler called. The other two boys broke into loud, raucous laughs. "That must be some ham sandwich ya' have in there."

Tabor picked up the half open bag and lumbered off down the hall toward the door.

"Guess he's goin' home mad," the ringleader said. "He doesn't know what he's missin'."

Chris turned the corner and walked down the hall to the classroom, aware of the students who had already gathered in the bright hall, and more aware that Tabor wasn't one of them.

"Hi, everyone," she said as she approached. "Ready for a new week?"

"Yes, Ma'am. Hope you are," someone joked.

The class settled down quickly as Chris called roll, gave assignments, and answered questions. The students moved into their groups when she gave directions, and, as she had hoped, they jumped right into sharing their essays and talking about ways to improve them. The fifty minutes flew by, and everyone seemed surprised when she said it was almost time to leave.

As they were packing up, one student said, "I wish we had more than a fifty minute class to do this. There's a lot to talk about and not enough time."

Chris smiled broadly as she watched them shuffle out of the classroom, only vaguely aware that every day wouldn't bring the same kind of result.

Her mood changed as she thought of the one absence in the class. Why had Tabor decided not to come? Her feelings see-sawed from relief to regret, alarm to disappointment. She knew she had to do something about his deeply disturbing warning . . . or was it a threat? Chris wanted to believe he was warning her in some misguided, irrational way, but the possibility that "someone's gonna die" could be at his hands was an overwhelming thought, one that she couldn't keep to herself. She knew it would be enough to push Richard over the edge, and he would call the police. It would be downhill for Tabor from then on, because Buster Shewell had been ready to bury Tabor long ago. James? What would James say about this? Maybe she needed to find out.

Chris took her books back to her office and shoved them inside the door, locking it behind her. She walked resolutely toward Bryant Hall, determined that decisions of some kind had to be made. If James was going to "help" with Tabor, then he had to get involved right away. Richard hadn't called her

331

about the meeting time today, so she would get it first hand from him or James. She was ready for their meeting.

"Hi, Mattie," she said as she walked into the reception room.

"Hello, Chris. How are you? I haven't seen you for a few days. How are your classes going?"

"Fine, thanks. I have a nice group in each class,at least so far." Chris didn't feel like small talk. "Is Dr. Shelton in?"

"No. He was here, but he left mid morning. I'm not sure whether he'll be back today or not."

"What about Dr. Cantrell . . . is he in?"

"No, he's out today. He might be back by four or five, but I'm not counting on it."

Richard could have been courteous enough to call her when he found out they weren't going to meet, particularly after his big show of alarm Saturday night. Chris knew her irritation was unreasonable and she tried not to let it show. "Dr. Shelton had suggested the three of us might have a meeting today after my classes. I guess he didn't realize that Dr. Cantrell would be out."

"Well, he was here when Dr. Cantrell told me he would be away today. I'm sure Dr. Shelton heard him when he said it. You know how it is, though. Those two have so much to do that I wonder how they can keep anything straight. Dr. Shelton probably just forgot. Should I have him call you when he comes back?"

"Yes, please do. Thanks, Mattie." Chris hesitated before she asked, "How did everything work out at the Maclean's over the weekend? I knew you were going to go up and help Mrs. Maclean."

"It was a mess, Chris. I shouldn't say it, but that's about the worst house I've ever been in. That poor soul has the world on her shoulders, I'll tell you, what with Lucas getting himself killed when he was driving drunk, and that grandson of hers. I guess you know about him, though, don't you."

"The whole situation is such a tragedy, her accident and the loss of her husband . . . and Tabor's loss of his grandfather."

"Grandfather. That's a joke. That man never even talked to that boy. That's probably half of what's wrong with him. Tabor I mean. A boy needs a man's attention when he's growing up. Although Tabor is just plain crazy, as far as I'm concerned."

"He's in one of my classes, and I feel he really wants to learn. I've decided I'd like to help him if I can." Chris felt slightly guilty for her manipulation, but she decided she would forge ahead and see where it went. It was obvious that Mattie felt it was okay to tell Chris the inside story, and enjoyed doing it.

"That's what Allison Montgomery thought, too . . . that she could help him. He drove her straight out the door. She was kind of a nervous little thing, anyway, and he just hounded her right into a breakdown. Dr. Shelton wanted to throw Tabor out of the school, but it didn't happen."

"Did Tabor threaten her, or did he just hang around her all the time?"

"Oh, he threatened her, alright. He told her she was going to get killed if she didn't watch out. I know that for a fact. Dr. Shelton and Dr. Cantrell both had a fit when they heard that."

Chris acted shocked and then asked, "Did Tabor actually tell Allison he was going to kill her?"

"No. He was real clever. He's a whole lot smarter than he wants people to think. He told her "someone is going to die," and, of course, she knew that someone was her and he was the one making the threat."

"Maybe he was trying to warn her," Chris said.

"Warn her about what . . . or who? He's the only real

nut case around here. We have some bad boys, but no crazy ones like him."

"Maybe it wasn't one of the students who he was talking about." Chris felt numb, but she pushed a little more.

"Well, maybe someone like his drunken grandpa . . . might be someone like that. Or maybe one of the workers around the grounds, but I don't know of any trouble with them. Who else could he be warning about? No, he was threatening her. That's clear."

"I'm just surprised that they let him stay after that," Chris said.

"Well, don't quote me, but Dr. Cantrell insisted. He said he would be responsible for Tabor, said he wanted the poor kid to have a chance to get through school. He has such a good heart, Chris, too good sometimes," Mattie said with a little shake of her head.

"Did Allison and Dr. Shelton agree to that?"

"Well, Dr. Shelton about went crazy. I just left the office while the two of them went at each other . . . Dr. Shelton and Dr. Cantrell. I shouldn't be talking about this, but I know you won't say anything."

"You can be certain I won't say anything," Chris said, knowing Mattie was right.

"And Allison . . . she was such a wreck by that time, I even heard her crying a couple of times in Dr. Cantrell's office, but I didn't let on that I heard anything. I was kind of surprised she stayed on as long as she did."

"That is hard to understand, isn't it, if she was so unhappy," Chris said with an affirming nod. "I guess we never really know what's in someone else's mind."

"That's for sure," Mattie said. "It's nice chatting with you, Chris. I don't get much of a chance to talk to the teachers. When they come in here, they're most often looking for Dr. Cantrell or Dr. Sheldon, not me."

"It's been nice talking to you, too, Mattie. It was so kind of you to go and help poor Mrs. Maclean. I know she's so grateful."

"She's a fine woman, Chris. So was her sweet daughter Amber Jean. That girl was cut from the same cloth as her mother. It's hard to believe that ugly drunk was her father, and harder to believe that freak Tabor is her son. She was so small and really beautiful, a soft, kind of fragile beauty. She worked around here as hard as her mama did, and she was like a ray of sunshine, always smiling and singing. All of us tried to help them out whenever we could, without insulting them. We'd give them pretty things sometimes, thank you gifts, we'd call them. Dr. Cantrell is such a kind and generous man. I know he helped them both an awful lot, and he never took any credit for it. He just kept it all to himself. That little Amber Jean thought the world of him, you could tell. I think she looked up to him like a father figure, you know, with that no good father she had at home. Dr. Cantrell's such a generous soul, Chris, kind and big-hearted. He really is."

"Yes, I think he is, Mattie. I know he's been very nice to me. Well, I guess I'd better go back and grade a few papers before my next class. Take care." Chris hurried out the door, not sure whether she felt better or worse for having heard Mattie's information.

When she got back to her office, she made a cup of tea and took it out onto the patio. The autumn sun was warm, and the leaves on the bushes and trees had taken on a hint of color. She was looking forward to the change in seasons here in the mountains. Maybe Rachael could come and spend Thanksgiving with her, since neither one of them had any family. Perhaps she should suggest that they take a trip together over Christmas break, go someplace warm and drink Margueritas on a white sandy beach. She couldn't bear to think of Christmas without Jack, even though she had lived through the first two. The first one she had spent in the hospital, weeks after the accident, with Rachael sitting beside her bed, and the second in Rachael's gaily decorated townhouse in Blacksburg. Chris felt guilty and sad about the ugly argument she and her best friend had on Sunday night. She'd call her when she got home this evening and apologize, get things settled down.

As Chris gazed across the lawn at the sun speckled mountains, she thought she saw movement and a flash of yellow in the thick grove of laurel that grew twenty-five or thirty-yards beyond her patio. She leaned forward and focused on the grove, thinking she might see an animal looking for a winter den. Again, she saw something move deep within the thicket, close to the ground. Another ten minutes passed, and she saw nothing else. Whatever it was had either seen her or had run from the other side of the grove. Chris carried her cup inside and gathered her books and papers for her next class.

Tabor lay stark still in the middle of the snarl of sharp-leaved bushes, afraid that Chris might have seen him. He had scooped out a nest for himself a few weeks ago, early one Saturday evening when the campus was deserted. It was the only way he could stand to lie among the pointed, razor- edged leaves. Earlier this week, he had brought the binoculars down from his mountain dugout, since he would be spending most of his time on the campus. He then discovered that when he focused them from this new observation spot, he could bring Chris closer to him than he had ever imagined possible. He could see her body in detail, how the silky shirts fell over her breasts and the way her loose pants hugged her long slender legs and slid between them when she first stood up on the little porch behind her office.

He had come here today and he had waited for her when he had to get away from that son-of-a-bitch in his English class who wouldn't leave him alone. Tabor had his gun with him in his big, long gym bag, and he had been too close to using it to hang around for any more of the stupid kid's crap. Tabor knew he would be thrown out of school if anyone knew he had the gun. Even Dr. Cantrell had told him that. But he thought maybe he'd have to protect his beautiful lady, and he might not have time to go and get it from the tree where he usually left it. The gun was in his big gym bag, carefully wrapped in the old blanket and a ragged towel he had used in his hideout, and he knew it was well camouflaged. But he also knew he couldn't help himself if that bastard son-of-a-bitch kept picking at him. He'd have to shoot him, right there outside Miss Chris's class. Then he knew there wasn't any chance that she'd like him better. She wouldn't like him at all if he did that and ended up in prison.

She was gone now, but he had to wait. He couldn't leave until late in the day, maybe close to dark when no one would see him. A time or two he had gone onto Chris's little porch outside her office when it was all dark and everyone had gone home, and he had sat in her chair. Tabor had imagined that she had come and sat on his lap, putting her smooth, pretty arms around his neck, and he had held her close to him. Maybe that would happen someday, if Dr. Cantrell and Dr. Shelton were gone. Maybe then she would see he was the good one.

Chapter 49

"Chris, may I talk to you for a minute?" Richard asked as he stood outside her open office door.

"Of course . . . come in." She closed the folder of papers she had been grading and pushed her chair back slightly from her desk. "Please, sit down. I'm happy to take a break from narrative essays."

"I want to apologize for not calling you before I left this morning . . . about the meeting. I intended to call from my car as soon as I was on the road because you were in class when I left. I never remember that we live in the mountains and signals are hard to come by. My phone was dead for most of the day."

"It's fine. I had a lot of work to do anyway," she said casually.

"I didn't know James was going to be out today. Mattie says he told her and me at the same time, but I don't remember. I just wanted to come over and tell you I'm sorry. The whole thing was a mistake on my part. Can you come over to my office tomorrow morning about nine?"

"Sure. That's good for me. I don't have a class on Tuesdays until eleven. Will James be back?"

"He's already back. He pulled into the parking lot just as I did, about five-thirty. I mentioned the three of us getting together tomorrow, and nine o'clock was his suggestion. Richard hesitated before he continued. "Everything been okay around here today?"

Chris knew he meant, "Was Tabor around?"

"It was okay. I can tell you about it in the morning, when the three of us get together. I think that's the best idea." She was suddenly on edge, uncertain of what she should say or do.

"Did you see Tabor today?" Richard asked directly, leaning forward in the chair he had pulled around to the side of her desk.

"Yes, I talked to him here. Richard, I'd like to tell you and James about the conversation at the same time. Tomorrow morning will . . ."

"I'll call James now. He's here and we can talk now. We can't let this thing keep festering, Chris. "

Before Chris could say anything, Richard had reached for her telephone and punched in James Cantrell's number.

"James, I'm over here in Chris Alford's office. She saw Tabor today, and we can't wait until tomorrow morning to talk about it. Do you want to come over here or shall we come there?" He wasn't going to give him a choice, not this time.

"Richard, I got up at dawn this morning. I was up at Tuggles Gap, and . . ." James began.

I'm tired, too. I understand, but this can't wait, James. Where do you want to meet us?"

"Come on over here," James replied wearily, "if you don't mind. I'll make a pot of coffee."

"We'll see you in ten minutes."

"Richard, I haven't even told you what happened today. I don't think . . ." Chris began.

"Chris, with all due respect to you and James, I'm not prepared to let this drag on any longer. I also want to tell you and James about my day and what I did regarding Tabor

339

Maclean. I want us to make some decisions tonight. We have
to. I don't even have to hear what happened when you were
with Tabor today. I already know from experience that it
couldn't have been good."

Richard stood up and walked over to Chris's patio door,
which she had not unlocked since coming back from her
afternoon classes. She could tell he was upset, maybe
anticipating another major battle with James. Mattie had filled
in some of the blanks for her, giving her a better understanding
of just how long this conflict had been going on between the
two top administrators in the college. Had it always been about
Tabor, or were there other factors involved that were unknown
to her?

"Chris, I'll wait while you finish up whatever you need
to do before we go. When the meeting's over, I think it's best if
you don't come back over here." Richard had turned around
and Chris could see that his jaw was rigid as he talked, his eyes
intense as he looked at her.

"Okay, that's fine. I'll take the rest of this work home.
You don't have to wait. I can come over . . ."

"I'll wait," he said firmly. "I'm not able to do it any other
way."

They were silent as Chris put her books and papers into
her bag and cleaned off the desk, and they were silent as they
walked in the early evening quiet to Bryant Hall. Just before he
opened the door, Richard stopped and turned to face her.

"I hope you understand my attitude, Chris. I don't mean
to be a son-of-a-bitch, excuse my language. But you need to
know that we're in a dangerous situation, as we speak. Tabor is
not your everyday unruly kid or disruptive teenager. I'm
convinced that somewhere inside of him is a cold blooded killer.
I'm not an alarmist, .but I am a realist, and I'm not going to play
psychological roulette anymore."

"Richard, I respect what you know, and I'm scared. But

I'm totally at a loss as to know what we should do, without some kind of proof that we're dealing with a killer. My other problem is that I feel as if, somehow, I'm responsible for what's happening."

"That's not right, Chris, not right at all. Come on, let's go meet with James."

The administration building looked deserted, the rooms darkened behind glass paneled doors and the light-sensitive exit signs beginning to glow red. Chris always felt office buildings and department stores after closing hours were unsettling, unnatural and eerie in their emptiness. What had seemed to be the peace of solitude and a quiet time of healing for her this summer, as she wandered around the unoccupied buildings and deserted campus, had now become a chilling awareness of being alone and isolated. Circumstances had changed, and so had she.

"Hi, Chris . . . Richard . . . come in." James was subdued but friendly as he motioned for them to sit down. Three leather easy chairs had been casually grouped around a low glass-topped cedar table in the library corner of his spacious office. A stainless carafe of coffee and three white pottery mugs imprinted with the Jackson Clayton College logo sat in the middle of the round, beveled glass.

"I hope you understand the need to meet this evening, James. Chris would have waited until tomorrow, but I didn't feel that was an option."

"I guess I'll understand after I hear what you have to say," he replied curtly. "Chris, why don't you tell me what happened with Tabor today."

Chris had not lost her resolve to make sure some action would result from a meeting between the three of them. "James and Richard, before I talk about my conversation with Tabor today, I need to say something that I had planned to say this morning if we had been able to meet. I feel that we have to make some decisions about Tabor, and once we make them, we have to work together to implement them. The school year has just begun, and I'm totally confused as to how to handle this student . . . and I'm getting mixed signals from you. I'm not going to be able to go on like this and do the job you hired me to do."

"I told Chris that I hoped we could meet this morning. I didn't know that you were going to be out today, James," Richard added.

"James, I spent Saturday night at the Starlight Motel, because Tabor was out roaming around, and Richard was concerned for my safety. I left my home willingly, because I was afraid, too. Officer Shewell and his deputy were out looking for Tabor, trying to find him, because of what we're afraid he will do. I'm not willing to go through that again."

Chris wasn't sure she would leave this meeting with a job. James or Richard might fire her for her attitude, or she might quit, but she was going to be honest in her assessment of her limits.

James wrinkled his forehead and looked first at Richard and then at Chris. "You went to the Starlight Motel late Saturday night," he asked incredulously, "to get away from Tabor . . . who hadn't done anything?" He turned to Richard, his eyes narrowing. "What in God's name were you thinking, Richard? Why didn't someone call me if there was an emergency?" He was clearly angered by what Chris had told him.

"Because you aren't dealing with this problem in a realistic way," Richard fired back. "For reasons only you know, you won't believe that Tabor is stalking and pursuing Chris, just like he did Allison. I'm not going to waste my time or yours rehashing what we just talked about last Thursday. I'm here to make sure we don't leave until we've made some choices and decisions that will protect Chris and all the rest of the people who work for you. Chris, go ahead and tell us what happened today."

Chris reviewed her encounter with Tabor outside her patio door and briefly described his initial behavior in her office. "Then he became infuriated when I mentioned that you, James, wanted him to take the IT courses that would prepare him for a job. For the next minute or so he ranted, saying, 'He ain't a good man . . . you can't be with him . . . he don't like me . . . he's not my friend or your friend . . . he's bad . . . you need to stay away from him.'" Chris paused, as her heart pounded and her face flushed. "Then he said, 'You aren't any different than Miss Allison. You're going to be sorry."

James sat stone still in his chair, his face a pale mask. He was stunned by Chris's words and what they revealed about Tabor. He had always thought Tabor liked him, after all he had done for the boy. Why would he say James was "bad . . . not good . . . not a friend?"

"The last part is the worst part," Chris said quietly. "He said, 'Somebody's going to die, Miss Chris. Dr. Cantrell and Dr. Shelton told me I couldn't ever say that again, but I have to tell you because I know it.'"

"My God," Richard said, emotion clouding his voice. "James, does this prove to you that we've got a maniac on our hands? We need to call the police right now. They need to find him and lock him up . . . before 'somebody dies.'"

"Chris, I'm so sorry you've had to endure this," James said. "I promise you we'll deal with this in a way that will ensure your safety and peace of mind. What a nightmare. Let's think this through for a minute before we call the police.

James had to think on two levels, the one he had just addressed with Chris and Richard, and the one that had turned his blood to ice. Had Tabor seen anything that would lead him to call James a 'bad man . . . not a friend . . . not good'? What did he know about 'Miss Allison' and all that had happened last year?

"James, we need to call Buster now. We can talk after he has been alerted." Richard was insistent, unbending.

"Goddamn it, Richard, hold on. Listen for a minute." James was struggling to control himself.

Chris was surprised by the uncharacteristic outburst from the calm and dignified college president, and Richard momentarily backed off.

"Let's see if we can make any sense out of Tabor's words," James said. "Could he be thinking that someone else might be a threat to Chris? Could he know something about people Allison knew that we don't know?" James skated on thin ice, as he tried to align himself with the two of them and clear himself of responsibility for Tabor's accusations and condemnation. Like Chris and Richard, he had no idea why this crazy kid had said what he said.

"I don't know, James. Do you suppose Tabor knows something that we don't know?

"It's possible, the way he hangs around here and appears at all hours of the day and night. Maybe Buster should ask him after Buster picks him up."

"Maybe we should ask him," Chris said quietly, "instead of Buster doing it. Why don't the three of us talk to him, together, before anyone calls the police?"

"That wouldn't work," James said instantaneously. "He's so often unable to speak his thoughts; I think it would only tend to confuse him and make it worse. I don't believe we could learn anything."

"Then if talking to him isn't a good idea, we need to call the police. I'll do it," Richard said, as he reached for a telephone on the small table next to him.

"No . . . wait. I have a better idea, one that might work. I'll talk to Tabor alone. He and I go way back to when he was a little boy, when Suelean used to bring him to work with her. I used to play with the little fellow, even took him out for ice cream or a hamburger a few times. I can talk to him and learn more than we would if all three of us ganged up on him. Chris, what do you think?" James smiled at her as he turned his chair slightly in her direction.

"I'd like to hear what he has to say before we call the police on him. Richard, I know how you feel, and I understand it, but I don't feel Tabor was threatening me today. I think he was warning me of some unknown, indescribable danger he has in his mind. I honestly don't think it's reality, but it's his reality. Maybe James could find that out by drawing on their relationship from way back."

"If you and Tabor are such old buddies, how do you account for all the things he said to Chris about you?" Richard asked.

"I can't imagine why Tabor would say that. Maybe he's acting out the anger he feels toward his grandfather . . . Lucas and I are about the same age. That could be it, a general hatred for anyone who reminds him of Lucas."

"That could be," Chris agreed. "From what I've heard, it seems you're much kinder to him than his grandfather ever was, but he may be unable to see that right now."

"I've tried to help him along. He's just one more poor mountain boy who deserves better than he's received." James ignored Richard and spoke directly to Chris.

"James, when will you talk to Tabor?" Chris asked.

"How about as soon as we can get him over here, with Buster and his deputy in the next room, and me in my office right over there?" Richard cut in, pointing toward the door. "I'm not going to leave here without a concrete, safe plan in place that we all agree on, or a police officer escorting Tabor Maclean to lockup for making threats. The latter is my choice, but I'll compromise, if the plan is a good one." Richard had ceased to care if James fired him or praised him.

"What kind of plan are you talking about, Richard? It doesn't sound as if you have compromise in mind. What if I do agree to talk to him? What then?" James asked indignantly.

"Then we proceed with a plan I looked into today, one we can all agree on and one that would be in Tabor's best interests. At a conference a few weeks ago, I met the president of the Bluestone Mountain School, which is a residential training facility for people like Tabor. He invited me to come over and see the school, and he suggested this week. I drove to Martinsville today, and I toured the facility and talked to some of the personnel. I have literature in my car, which I had planned to share with you. I won't take the time to tell you about it now, but it's the one positive in this whole ugly scenario. It would be a real chance for Tabor, maybe his only chance." Richard's tone had softened as he spoke.

"So you want to ship him off, one way or another, either to a school that won't let him leave once he gets there, or to a prison. What kind of compromise is that?

"James, maybe the school is worth considering," Chris said. "I don't know if talking to him is going to lessen the problems he has, and the ones it creates for us."

"We can take him out of your class, Chris. We'll get someone in the English Department to tutor him one on one. We haven't tried that." James seemed to be pleading with her.

"How in the hell does that keep him from showing up at Chris's door? That's not even logical, James. He's stalking her, pursuing her like he pursued Allison, and you and I know where that will end. I won't allow that to happen," Richard shouted. "Fire me . . . I don't give a damn . . . but I'll fight you all the way on this."

"Maybe I should leave," Chris said before James could respond to Richard's outburst.

"No, Chris, stay. This is your student and you're as much involved as either one of us are," Richard replied.

"No, I mean maybe I should leave the college . . . and my job here. Maybe if Tabor was in a man's class, and I wasn't here, he'd be able to get through his courses."

"No, Chris, that's not a solution," James said emphatically. "Please, don't even think that. We'll find another way. Richard and I can find a way through this. Chris, you're too important to us . . . to the students . . . to everyone."

"You know how I feel about that, Chris." Richard said, remembering their earlier conversation. "So, what's it going to be, James? How are we going to work this out?"

"Call Buster. See if he can find Tabor and bring him over here. I'll talk to him and see what he says. We'll do it your way, Richard. You and Chris and Buster can sit in your office, and I'll talk to Tabor in mine. We'll all make a decision after I spend some time with him." James seemed almost too tired to speak, as he slumped in his chair and voiced agreement in a flat, toneless pattern.

Chapter 50

"We've done just about all the lookin' we can do. I've had four deputies and myself out there, and no one even spotted him," Buster said as he stood in the reception room that connected the president's and the dean's offices. "I went on up to his house first of all, thinkin' he might be up there with his grandmaw. But Suelean said she hadn't seen him since last Friday. Miss Borden was up there stayin' with her until she's able to be up and around, and Miss Borden said she hadn't seen him either."

"When you find him, can you pick him up and take him to the jail?" Richard asked, knowing the answer but hopeful he might be wrong.

"No, Sir, since Miss Alford doesn't want to sign a complaint sayin' that he threatened her. Without that, we have no reason to arrest him and take him in. He hasn't hurt anyone, that we know of. I agree with you, Dr. Shelton, he's a crime waiting to happen, but that's not a reason under the law. I wish I could, but I can't." Buster was clearly on Richard's side when it came to Tabor.

"He didn't threaten me," Chris said calmly. "I've told all of you that from the beginning."

"Yes, M'am. If you didn't feel threatened and he didn't

use the language, then it's not a threat under the law."

James watched quietly as Richard and Buster discussed finding Tabor. He had no stomach for what they were doing, feeling the same as he had when he was a boy watching a pack of snarling dogs chase a fox to ground. James wasn't sure how long he could protect Tabor, once they found him. And they would find him, because the poor kid didn't even know they were looking for him. He had no reason to run.

"Guess we'll be on our way," Buster said. "Any of you need us tonight, just give a holler. We'll be around in full force."

"Thanks, Buster," James said. "I hope you don't hear from any of us."

"Appreciate your help," Richard added.

"I think I'm going to go home," Chris said. "It's been a marathon school day, and it's only Monday."

"I'll walk with you to your car," James said as Chris picked up her bag. "I parked over there this afternoon because I had to carry something into Cantrell Hall."

"Thanks. I'll see you tomorrow, Richard," Chris said as she walked toward the door with James. "Let's all hope for a quieter day."

"I'm all for that. You sure you'll be okay this evening?" Richard asked.

"I'll be fine. Thanks for your concern, though."

James held the door and walked out behind Chris. Richard watched as they strolled down the brick walk toward Cantrell Hall. He wanted to run after her, tell her to stay here where he could be sure she was safe. Once again, he was observing it all from a distance, a watcher, almost a voyeur. Something wasn't right. Tabor was loose, and nothing Richard could do would change that danger. But there was something else. He had that gut level feeling that he wasn't seeing the forest, because he was too busy looking at each of the trees.

Maybe he would call Chris tonight, just to make sure she was home. What kind of a ridiculous idea was that? She would quickly tire of his overbearing concern, and if he wasn't careful, he would be as troublesome as Tabor.

As Chris and James neared the walk that led to the parking lot, James said, "I bought a new piece of art on my way back from Tuggle's Gap, another wood sculpture. It's a representation of two ragged backwoods children, a boy and a girl, sitting on a rock with their dog between them. I put the pedestal for it in Cantrell Hall when I got back today. The piece is by the same artist who created the mother and child sculpture that stands at the end of your hall, Earl Wilcox, an old fellow over in Baileytown."

"Richard mentioned him when I first came to work here. I love that sculpture of the mother and child. I look at it every day, James. I'm in awe of it."

"Earl wasn't quite finished rubbing the new one down, so I told him I'd pick it up later in the week. He has a fascinating studio about an hour up the mountain from here. Would you like to ride up there with me and see his other work? I thought I'd go Wednesday or Thursday afternoon . . . maybe leave here about three."

"Thanks, James, that's kind of you, but I have so much grading to do. I'm afraid I won't be able to." This time she had to be firm. Art was her weakness. Even her love, her Jack, had been an artist. But it wouldn't be okay for her to go, as much as she would like to see the studio and the artist's work.

"What if I promise to have you home by supper time? That leaves your evening free to grade your papers. We could make the trip up and down in three hours . . . probably less, if you don't look at all the magnificent sculpture he has," he said with a smile. "I'd really like it if you'd go. I think it would be a good break from a difficult week . . . for both of us."

"James, you're a great salesman, but I don't think it's a

350

good idea right now." Maybe after things quieted down, she'd go with him, or maybe she and Rachael could go.

"Why is it a bad idea? No one will even know we're gone. I promise. Mattie won't have a clue. She sees me run in and out all the time. When someone attends as many meetings and art openings as I do, no one pays a bit of attention."

They had been standing at the intersection of the two walkways, which seemed silly, since they were both going to the parking lot. "Why don't we walk over to our cars before it gets dark," Chris laughed.

James looked at her seriously. "Chris, my car isn't over here. I did bring the pedestal over, but I took my car back to the other parking lot. I just wanted to spend a little time with you, and I didn't want you to walk to your car alone. I know I'm acting like an old fool, but it's just the way it is. Please forgive me. I won't push you to go to Baileytown. I understand how you feel. Come on, I'll walk to your car with you."

"I'm flattered, James, and I'd like to see the studio and the art," she said as they walked slowly to her car. "It's just as I tried to explain to you on Saturday evening. I don't think it's appropriate."

"If you want to see the studio, go with me. Forget the appropriateness. I promise you no one will know, and you'll be bowled over by Earl's work. Take your car home on Wednesday afternoon, and I'll pick you up at three." He smiled at her and said, "You'd make me very happy if you said 'yes.'"

"James, this has to be on the same basis as dinner was, a couple of friends going to see an art studio. Please understand that this is what it is to me. I don't mean to be blunt, but that's what you need to understand."

"I understand," he said happily. "I understand completely. See you tomorrow."

Chris started her car and watched him disappear into Cantrell Hall. He was a very attractive man, no doubt about it.

He was handsome, tall and rangy, and charismatic, but she would have felt much happier if Richard had been the one who was introducing her to the artist.

Tuesday and Wednesday were good productive days in all of Chris's classes, and, once again, she found herself excited about the possibilities for the semester. She was implementing new programs and revamping old ones, and the students were soaking it up. Absenteeism was almost zero, with only one seat empty during the two days. Tabor missed class again on Wednesday. No one had seen him on campus since he left Chris's class on Monday. She kept expecting to see him sitting outside her office door or waiting for her before class, but he didn't appear.

Chris was perplexed and relieved at the same time. Would he come back? If not, where was he? And what would she do if he did? At night, she closed all her blinds as soon as she got home, and she didn't open them again until she was ready to leave for class. When she was in her office, she left the patio door locked, and she felt uneasy when her office door stood open.

As she drove home on Wednesday afternoon, Chris revisited the uncomfortable feelings she had struggled with before going with James to Chez Maurice. Part of her was excited about going to an artist's studio, particularly this one. Yet, she believed she was doing the wrong thing to go with him, because he was the college president, and because she didn't want to encourage him into believing their relationship would be anything beyond what it was now. She had no thoughts of a physical or romantic relationship with him. She actually found the idea to be slightly humorous. It had nothing to do with his age, but it had everything to do with the way she perceived him. James was kind, compassionate, and very wealthy, all desirable qualities for a mate, but he was not soul-mate material. He was sexually a non-entity to her, a fatherly kind of intellectual. Chris smiled, somewhat embarrassed to think she was examining James Cantrell in such earthy, finite detail. She couldn't imagine that her feelings would ever change. And just what or whom would she consider to be soul-mate material? Her cheeks flushed as "Richard" flashed into her mind. Unfortunately, he looked at her as another teacher on his staff, nothing more.

James was waiting in the driveway when Chris arrived home at two forty-five. He called to her as she got out of the car, "Sorry to be early . . . take your time."

"I'll just put my things in the house . . . be right out," she said as she passed his car.

James was standing beside the open passenger door on his BMW when Chris came out.

"It's a beautiful day for a drive," he said as she got into the car. "I know you're going to be happy you came along."

"I'm happy anytime I can be involved with art galleries and artist's studios," she replied. "I'm looking forward to seeing this one."

When they were about fifteen minutes outside of Clayton Forge, James turned left onto the road he had pointed out to Chris last Saturday, the one that led up the mountain to his family estate at Tuggles Gap.

"Someday I'd like to show you my old homeplace up on Caleb Mountain at Tuggles Gap. It's another couple of hours on this road beyond Baileytown. I think you'd like it up there."

"How long have you had the property?" Chris asked.

"My grandfather built it around 1915, and my father and I were both born there. I don't have a deep attachment to the house, but I love the land that surrounds it. It's really something."

"I can't imagine what it must be like to have that kind of family security," Chris said thoughtfully. "I mean, a house and everything in it that passes from generation to generation. It must be wonderful. My family background is so sketchy, completely opposite that. I realize now that I was lucky to have a roof over my head when I was growing up."

"My mother died when I was seven, so I grew up in a pretty austere household. My father was a tyrant and he had a hard time keeping servants, so I had a new nanny every few months during most of my growing up years. We may have had the house and grounds, but we didn't really have much feeling of family. I've always longed for that, but I never found it," he said wistfully. "It seems I was always looking for it, that sense of family."

"I can understand that," Chris said. "I never even knew who my father was. I guess I could find out now, but it isn't important anymore."

"I'm in the process of changing the whole house up at Tuggles Gap, getting rid of all the austere Victorian darkness and redecorating everything. I'm in over my head, though, when it comes to choosing fabrics and colors and all that. I'm good with the gardens and plants, but I'm hopeless on the inside of the house. He hesitated for a moment, and then he said, "Are you any good at that sort of thing, with colors and decorating?"

"I'm not a decorator," she laughed. "I have a good friend who's a whiz at it. Her apartments and houses always look like pictures out of magazines."

"I'll bet you can do it, too," he said. "Your office looks wonderful. I can imagine your house does, too."

Chris didn't want the conversation to go any further. "Just a plain, simple house," she said unemotionally. "The trees are brighter up here, the higher we go. Obviously the season is ahead of our lower elevation."

"Yes," James replied, aware of her maneuvering to safer ground. "I always enjoy seeing the difference between the two areas, at any season."

They spent the rest of the drive talking artists and mountain crafts, a topic they could comfortably share. "There's Earl's barn and studio," James said, pointing ahead to a beautifully restored bank barn, built close to a rushing stream.

"It's beautiful," Chris said, overcome by the rugged, natural beauty of the setting.

Earl Wilcox's studio and gallery was a sculpture in itself, a contemporary showplace of polished wood and carved stone set into the large, angular barn. Stunning wooden sculptures of local mountain people were tastefully lighted and displayed throughout, giving the space an aura of holiness, a place of reverence and respect for a people who were far more than the label that had been attached to them, far more than the perception of Appalachia.

Earl was a stooped, wrinkled mountain man, more than sixty and less than ninety. It was hard to tell his age without knowing the kind of life he had survived. He cheerfully showed Chris all he had created that remained in his studio, and stood with her as she paged through the book that catalogued much of what he had sculpted in earlier times. James stayed in the background, glowing with happiness as he watched Chris's interaction with Earl and his work. The sculpture James had purchased was not quite dry, needing another day or two to absorb the special oils and wax Earl had applied. As they were leaving, James agreed to come back on the weekend to pick it up. Earl had smiled broadly and said, "Bring your pretty lady with you."

"I'll try," James said, looking sideways at Chris. "I'd like to."

Chris was overjoyed with the experience in Earl's studio, and she realized that she had not been in a gallery or at an art show since Jack had died. It was as if she had recovered something of herself that had been lost, something she had feared would never be reclaimed.

"James, thank you so much. That was one of the most wonderful experiences I've had since I came to Clayton Forge. I became totally absorbed in Earl's mesmerizing art. I was really lost in the magnificence of it."

"I enjoyed watching you," James said quietly. "I was totally absorbed, too."

The drive home was quiet and comfortable. Chris remembered so many other galleries and so many openings, when Jack was the artist and she was his proud wife. He had always told her she was a part of what he did and what he created, because she was a part of him. Jack had asked Chris to marry him five weeks after they had met. He said he had fallen in love with her the first time they had talked to each other. "I knew," he had said. "I just knew. But," he had jokingly told their friends, "it took me three weeks to convince her to be more than my friend."

Chris could feel him, right at that moment, as if he was sitting next to her, and she could see the twinkle in his eyes as he teased her.

"Are you still dreaming art?" James asked.

"As a matter of fact, I am," Chris replied. "Art is such a part of my life . . . and me."

"I'm the same," he said. "When I discovered art, it was as if I had finally discovered life itself."

"I know what you mean," Chris said, amazed at their similarity. "My husband was an artist, a really fine painter."

"That doesn't surprise me at all. Artists are sensitive people. I would expect you to be with someone sensitive."

Chris was surprised when she saw James had pulled into her driveway. "I've had a wonderful time, James. Thank you for the opportunity and the experience," she said as she opened the door.

"That's all we can hope for in life, isn't it, opportunity

and experience to come our way. The rest is up to us." James looked at her intently, aching to reach out and hold her.

"Those papers are waiting," she said. "See you tomorrow. Thanks so much again."

Chris walked toward the door, feeling his eyes on her. She was unnerved and intrigued by this man James Cantrell, this man she feared was falling in love with her.

Chapter 51

Tabor lay on his back in the damp darkness of his mountain sanctuary. He hadn't bothered to light Pap's old lantern, since there was nothing he wanted to see at night anyway. He'd cleaned and oiled his gun today, and it was all ready. Nothing else to do.

He was too upset to even eat the remaining slices of ham or the soggy bread he had managed to grab from Mawmaw's kitchen while she and that Borden lady snored in the next room. He'd seen the patrol car while he was lying out in the barn waiting for the cover of the night, but lucky for him, Buster didn't go anyplace but into the house and out again. Finally, those two snoops from the college had gone home, so all he had to do was keep nosy Borden from seeing him when he sneaked into the house.

Maybe his beautiful lady had missed him, since he had been out for two classes. But maybe not. He felt all raw inside, kind of like a deep down hurting that never went away. It didn't seem like she was going to be like he had thought she was, the way she had been when he first met her, although he couldn't bear to think he had been wrong. It was that damned Cantrell again, turning her against him and wanting to take up with her himself. He knew that's what it was, just like last time. Except now, he was ready for him. This time he wasn't going to lose her, no matter what that son-of-a-bitch did.

Today, he'd watched as Chris sat out on her porch behind her office, but then she left, and she never came back. All the bad feelings had come back up inside of him then, as he thought about her and where she might have gone, and who she might have been with, and that he might have lost her. And then he imagined the rounding of her breasts and her long, smooth legs, and he wanted to touch her and do things with her, but he couldn't, and he knew it was just because of who he was. In the heat of the autumn afternoon, Tabor began pulling angrily at his ugly, greasy hair and clawing at his pale, dirty body, and then he picked up his knife, as he had done before. Thick, guttural moans rose from deep inside him, as he slashed viciously at his own flesh. He didn't remember any more after he sank into the bottomless pit of self-hate. When he woke up, he was bleeding, and this time he had cut himself much worse than ever before. He had wrapped the stained towel and a ragged strip of the dirty blanket around the wounds and made pads to stop the red oozing, but his body hurt like his heart did, and his head pounded.

Maybe he wouldn't ever see his Mawmaw again after he went to the college tomorrow. He knew his Mawmaw would miss him if he didn't come home again. But he had made up his mind this time, and he wouldn't back down. Tabor reached out his arm in the dark and felt the smooth cold of his rifle. He pulled the gun to him and rested its length against his leg, and he fell asleep, happy for the comfort of it.

When Tabor awoke on Thursday morning, the sun was just beginning to rise over the rim of the mountain, not yet lighting the narrow doorway to his underground refuge. Miss Chris would be at the college today, and he would be there watching after her. She would come back to her office in the late afternoon, like she always did, and he would go and talk to her then, after most of the students had left, and the parking lot was mostly empty. This time he would tell her the truth, all of it, and she would see what a big mistake she was making. It meant he would have to talk to Buster, and Buster might blame him, but he would do it for her. He had thought about it for a long time and he had made up his mind. He carefully wrapped the rifle in the blanket and put it in the bottom of the long gym bag, stuffing a towel and some clothes in on top of it, along with the food he had left. He laid the binoculars on top. Tabor knew he had to go early, before anyone came to the college and just after the guard left at six. Then he could go to his place in the thick laurel grove outside her office. He had a piece of heavy black plastic in his bag to cover everything so no one could see him as he lay in the thick, dark snarl of bushes.

Tabor moved easily through the green thickness of the forest, as if he had been born to it like the other creatures who surrounded him. When he came close to the college road, he skirted it, staying to the edge of the sparse woods in the still lingering shadows of night. He watched Kenny light a cigarette and get in his car, and he watched as the lights bobbed slowly along the wide drive and turned onto the road to Clayton Forge. Tabor lumbered past the darkened buildings and across the damp grass to the thick stand of laurel. He quickly pushed the bag between the outlying bushes and into the dense inner growth, before falling to his knees and crawling and slithering in behind it. The dugout nest had partially filled with spiny, razor tipped leaves, shed by the thick branching bushes. He scooped them aside and settled into his space. He pulled the black plastic from the bag and then carefully removed his rifle, setting the precious gun close to him under the black covering. Tabor chewed on a piece of ham and wiped his greasy hands on his blood-stained shirt. His body still ached, but he had seen no more blood this morning.

The sun continued in its path upward, and the campus slowly came alive, as students and teachers moved along the bright brick paths. Tabor knew he had a long day ahead of him, and he was resigned to it. This is where he needed to be, and he was clear in what he had to do.

Chris opened her office door and dropped her blue and green canvas bag next to her desk. She walked to the window and looked out at the sunlit, cloudless sky and the majesty of the deep blue mountains that outlined her view. This morning she had stopped to look at the mother and child that stood in repose at the end of the hall, feeling as if she knew them better since yesterday. She had been deeply moved by Earl Wilcox's interpretation of Appalachia, sensing that she had a new, enlightened understanding today. She thought about Tabor and his grandmother. They were Earl Wilcox's people, the very ones he wanted the world to know. Chris was troubled by her underlying fear of Tabor, hopeful that she would somehow come to know him as he really was, not as she and others saw him.

Tabor watched her through his binoculars as she stood gazing out over the laurel grove to the mountains beyond. She liked the mountains as he did. He could tell that. Maybe he could someday talk to her about the mountains, tell her of the things he knew because they were a part of him. He looked at Chris's long, silky auburn hair as it hung loosely at her shoulders, and he longed to touch its smoothness and smell the flowery fragrance he knew would be there. She was his beautiful lady, the only one he had really, really loved. She closed her eyes as she tilted her face toward the sun that shone through the glass, and he could see the satiny skin of her graceful neck.

Chris made a cup of tea and took it out onto her patio, feeling the warmth of the September morning as it penetrated her light sweater. Peace seemed to infuse her, as she took pleasure in the moment. The reverie would be short, for she had research to do in the library this morning, before her class at eleven.

The day slid by, with soft breezes blowing through open windows and doors into classrooms that would soon be closed to the chill of a mountain winter. Chris felt a sense of euphoria, almost spring fever in autumn. Perhaps James had been right. The time in Baileytown had been a much needed break after a difficult week. As Chris gave her last assignment for the day, she marveled at how quickly and smoothly the classes had progressed. It was as if everyone was feeling the joy of the changing seasons, basking in this time of new beginnings.

Chris walked leisurely back to her office, leaving the door open behind her as she stepped into her comfortable space. She unlocked and pulled back the door in her glass wall, breathing in the gusty cross breeze as it moved through the room. As she sat contemplating the work ahead of her, she saw Buster Shewell's patrol car cruise slowly along the road that ran around the campus. Was he still looking for Tabor, or had they given that up after the Monday face-off in the administrative office? The sharp ring of the telephone jolted Chris out of her dreaminess.

"Chris Alford," she answered.

"Chris, it's James. How do you feel after your afternoon with Earl?"

"Actually, I've spent some time contemplating the mother and child, and I feel as if I know them better after yesterday. Thank you, again," she said. "It was wonderful."

"I'm so glad to hear that," he said, happiness evident in his deep voice. "I was wondering if you have some time this afternoon to get together, to talk about Tabor and a few other things that I'd like us to put behind us."

"Yes, whenever it's convenient for you and Richard," she replied, surprised that another meeting was called so soon.

"Well, I hadn't planned to ask Richard to join us. I'd like to discuss this with you, before we involve anyone else."

"Oh, well, yes. When would you like to meet?" Chris was puzzled as to why James wanted to talk to her before involving Richard. Perhaps the rift between them was wider than she had realized.

"Why don't I come over to your office about five o'clock. Do you mind staying a little later this evening? I have some other people I have to see between now and then, another meeting that was scheduled earlier."

"That's fine. I have nothing planned," she said. "If you find you're finished before five, just come on over. I have a stack of papers that will keep me busy until then."

"Thanks, Chris. I'll see you in awhile."

Chris felt strangely uneasy, almost secretive, to be meeting with James without Richard's knowing it. She had learned long ago, in her earliest jobs, that you should never bypass your boss, and that's what she was doing. But how could she refuse to meet with the president when he requested it? Wasn't that equally risky, maybe more so? She remembered yesterday, and some of the things James had said. She had to be diplomatic, no matter what he said, but she would also stop anything that became uncomfortable, if the meeting went beyond a business agenda.

"Chris . . . what's up?" Glen said as he stuck his head in the door. "Everything going all right for you?" He, too, meant "Has Tabor been around?"

"Fine, Glen . . . thanks. Are you surviving the second week?" she laughed.

"Barely. It's hard to accept that I need to teach the multiplication tables to my students before we can move on to Algebra I. Want to go get a cup of coffee or, excuse me, tea?" he asked. "The Student Union's open until six this evening."

"Thanks, I would, except I have an impromptu meeting at five or a little before. I need to be here in case he calls earlier." She really wished she could get out of her office, away from the pressure it had suddenly taken on.

"Richard's keeping you hopping, huh. You gotta watch the boss . . . he'll do that. Okay. I'll see you later," he said as he ducked out before she could reply. She hadn't had a chance to tell him the meeting wasn't with their boss, which magnified her discomfort.

Tabor had seen the math teacher come into her office, and he watched them closely. He just seemed to be laughing with her, which was okay. Tabor hated Glen Cooper because Glen had thrown him out of Cantrell Hall last year when he had tried to talk to Miss Allison. He wasn't going to let anyone stop him this time. Another hour or so, and it would be safe to go to Chris's door.

Richard walked into the Student Union and started to put money into the Coke machine when Glen called to him.

"Hey, Richard, don't drink that stuff. Get a cup of coffee with me. I'll even buy."

"Hi, Glen, how's it going? Okay. I need something to keep me awake. The caffeine is all the same, coffee or coke."

They sat down with the steaming Styrofoam cups and chatted about the comings and goings in the math department before Glen asked, "What's going on with the crazy kid, Tabor? Is he still around here?"

"Unfortunately, yes, but not because I think he should be. Actually, he hasn't been in class since last Friday, so maybe he finally gave up. I hope to God he has. It's been a nightmare," Richard said bitterly. "I've about had it."

"I know Chris has had a belly full of him," Glen said. "Is he leaving her alone now?"

"Not as of last Monday."

"I just stopped by her office, and she seemed fine. I think she's waiting for you. Maybe that's why she seemed so happy," Glen joked.

"I'm afraid she's not waiting for me," Richard laughed. "She doesn't have much to say to me."

"No, I meant the meeting you two have this afternoon. She said she couldn't come for coffee, waiting for your call."

"We don't have any meeting," Richard said with a puzzled look. "She couldn't have said it was me . . . must be with someone else in the English Department."

"Guess so," Glen agreed. "How are things with Cantrell? I don't see much of him, but I guess that's a good thing."

"You can be damned sure of that. He's getting on my nerves. Honestly, he's a mystery to me, but then he always has been. I'm just tired of his waffling on this Tabor Maclean thing. He just won't give up on that kid."

"I found that, too, when Tabor was in my math class last year. Cantrell did everything possible to get me to tutor him, do a one on one class, even offered to pay me extra, but it wasn't worth it to me. That kid's too much of a pain in the ass.

"Maybe we should become forest rangers," Richard laughed. "Animals and trees are pretty easy to get along with. I have to get back before Mattie leaves today," he said as he got up from the table. "See you around, Glen."

Richard felt the tension in his neck and temples as he walked back to Bryant Hall. Who was Chris meeting with? Was it Ron Dowd or Ben Evart . . . or was it James Cantrell? His face felt hot as he hurried into the building. He walked over and knocked on the door to James's office.

"Dr. Cantrell has gone for the day," Mattie said. "He said he wouldn't be back until midday tomorrow."

"Do you know where he went?" Richard asked.

"No, he didn't say. I think he might have gone home, or maybe he had a meeting that I didn't have on my calendar. That's possible," she said with a little laugh. "You two do that to me, you know. By the way, did Buster find you?" she asked. "He was looking for you about fifteen minutes ago."

"No. Do you know what he wanted?"

"Not really. He said he was going to be around this evening. He did say he would come back to talk to you."

"Okay. I'm going to be here for awhile," Richard said, still preoccupied.

"Speak of the devil," Mattie laughed. "Here he is."

Buster and JT ambled into the office, stopping in front of Richard.

"Do you have a couple a' minutes?" Buster asked.

"Sure . . . come on in." Richard closed the door as the two officers stood in the middle of his office. "Here, sit down."

"That's okay," Buster said. "I won't take much of your time. We think Tabor's out runnin' around again. The fella' that drives the bread truck, who delivers here to the cafeteria, called us about six thirty this mornin'. He said he was unloadin' at the doors behind the union a little after six, and he saw some guy that seemed to be hidin' behind the trees and sneakin' along the edge of the campus, said he thought maybe the guy was goin' to break into somethin' at the college since he had a big bag with him. That's why he called us. Then I asked him if he saw any weapons, and he said 'no.' But then he told me the bag was big enough to carry a rifle. He described our buddy Tabor to a tee when I asked for a description. I reckon he's up to no good. Me and JT are gonna stay around here until later tonight, make sure everybody's gone before we leave. In the meantime, maybe we can catch him with a gun on the campus. That'd sure get him locked up and thrown out of school."

"I'm glad you'll be around . . . thanks. I'm going to be here till later myself. Let me know if you find anything."

Richard sat down at his desk and leaned his forehead against his upraised hands. How in the hell had the situation come back to this? He remembered another night a year ago, just like this one . . . police on campus . . . everyone afraid. But

Tabor had stayed on at the college. Even after Allison was gone, Tabor remained. Somehow, it had to end.

Chapter 52

Both doors to Chris's office were still open when James arrived a little after five. He was dressed casually in khaki pants and a dark blue polo shirt, and he had a small brief case that he set inside the door.

"I hope this is okay, keeping you after hours," he said apologetically.

"Yes, of course it is. It's not as if I have someone at home waiting for me," she replied with a smile.

"I decided I needed to talk to you, and I didn't want to do it in the middle of a crowded day. It shouldn't take more than three hours," he laughed.

"However long it takes, please sit down where you'll be comfortable." Chris said, still sitting behind her desk.

"Do you mind if we pull these two easy chairs over toward the patio door? We can talk and enjoy the breeze, since it's such a nice evening," James asked tentatively.

"Sure, that's fine. Those chairs are a lot more comfortable than these straight back types," she said as each of them pushed a plaid upholstered chair across the floor.

"Let me grab a notebook," Chris said as she pulled one from off her desk. "Would you like something to write on?"

"No, I'll just get my briefcase from over here by the door," he said, setting it on the floor next to his chair.

"I'm glad we're going to talk about Tabor. I'm so troubled by him," Chris said. "Not by him, really, but about him. He's such a sad soul, James. I just feel there's so much more to him that we probably will never see."

"Chris, I've sensed from the beginning that you have such genuinely good intentions to help Tabor, and I believe you can do so much for him, if you have the chance. That's one of the reasons I wanted to talk to you, like this." James hesitated and then asked, "Do you think we could have a cup of your famous green tea, while I get my thoughts together?"

"Of course. It sounds good to me, too." Chris moved to the cabinet and began the preparation James had watched the first time he was in her office. He sat staring at her as she moved through the minor steps of brewing the tea, aware of her grace and beauty.

Tabor lay shaking in the middle of the thick darkness of the laurels, his hands clutching the gun that lay in front of him. Cantrell was with her, close to her, and Tabor was frozen in fear. Dr. Cantrell was going to try to make her his, and she didn't know. Only Tabor knew what could happen, what this man might do to his beautiful lady. He had seen it before. Tears ran down into the heaviness of his beard, and low sobs escaped from his dry, aching throat. He watched in horror as Chris carried the cups to the little table she had set between them, handing one to Cantrell and smiling at him.

"Thank you, Chris. This is just what I need. It's like a magic potion," he said, smiling at her.

"I have some things to share with you about Tabor, things I haven't told another living soul. I know it's right for you to know, because I believe you're the one who will ultimately help him become what I know he can be. It will also explain a few things to you."

Chris leaned back into her chair, waiting expectantly for the psychological profile or the confidential medical information that would help her understand the problematic young man who had created such havoc, seemingly for so many.

"Tabor is my son, Chris," he said quietly, "my only son, my own blood. He's a Cantrell." James's eyes took on a haunted look, as he spoke softly. "Amber Jean was so beautiful, and so good," he continued. "I was lonely, and a foolish man facing forty alone. Being alone is a terrible thing, Chris . . . you know that, too. She loved me, and I made her life happy, if only for a short time. I would have taken care of her after the baby came, but I never had the chance."

Chris sat in stunned silence, unable to speak. Why was James telling her this sorrowful secret that he had kept for so many years?

"James . . . I don't know what to say. It must be so hard for you . . . with everything . . ."

He interrupted her, as if he hadn't heard her words. "I haven't been a father to him. I was never able to reveal myself to him . . . just like my own father," he said flatly. "But I can't blame myself . . . I'll make it up to him . . . with your help . . . I've been waiting . . . I knew it could happen someday."

"I'll work with Tabor, of course, but I don't see . . ."

"Please don't say anything, yet. There's so much, Chris, and I want to tell you everything. The Cantrell money and all that goes with it must go to another Cantrell, someone who can take care of it, protect what that money has brought forth to so many. If I have two children, they will share equally, and the wealth goes on through the lines of inheritance. Tabor is the only Cantrell left after me, Chris, and he can't do what has to be done to preserve the legacy. Tabor needs a sibling, someone to look after the money and help him, someone who can have children and perpetuate the good."

"Are there no cousins or relatives who might . . ."

"No," he said firmly. "There is no one. Tabor is the last, Chris. Please understand, if Tabor dies, the entire estate will go to charities my father chose, nothing to do with education or art, or anything to do with helping our mountain people. After I die, the good will stop with Tabor. My father made provisions in his will that prevent me from making my own bequests. That's how much he despised me. But my child, my son or daughter, once again will have the power of control over the estate. I'm sixty-one years old, Chris, and time is running out."

"James, surely there is some way . . ."

"There is no way," he said emphatically. "Only my child, and the legal guardian of that child in case of my death before his majority, has the power of control over the Cantrell wealth. I have papers waiting to be signed, Chris, by me and the mother of my child . . . my second child."

"I'm without words . . . I don't know what . . ."

"I want you to marry me, Chris. I love you, and I know you could learn to love me. I could give you everything, more than you could ever dream possible, and you could give me a child." He looked imploringly at her, his eyes bright with anticipation.

"James . . . stop! Please don't say such things . . . we hardly know each other. I don't want to marry anyone . . . please . . . don't tell me anything else." Chris was shaking, shocked by what he was saying and fighting back tears.

James stood and moved next to her chair. He knelt down beside her and said, "Please don't cry, Chris. It's not a sad time. I can make your life so good . . . we can go to my home in the mountains . . . we will raise our child . . ."

"I don't need you to make my life good, James!" she shouted. "I don't want to go anywhere with you. This is insane . . . please leave . . . get out of my office. I'll leave the college right away . . . I don't want to be here anymore."

Chris was sobbing, trying to control herself. For the first

time, she noticed that James had closed her office door when he had moved his brief case. He now moved behind her and closed the door to her patio. No one could hear her. It was after six o'clock, and she knew they were alone in the building.

"Sit down, Chris," James said sternly, his face suddenly rigid and pale. "Don't tell me to leave. This is my building, my school. You're being irrational and foolish. Stop it, and listen carefully to me." His voice had taken on a harsh, commanding tone.

He stopped speaking and reached for her hands, trying to hold them in both of his.

"Please don't, James . . . please don't touch me." Chris tried to pull away, but he held her tightly.

"You will listen to me, Chris. I told you I love you. Do you understand? I want to take care of you and be your husband. I want to give you anything you want and take you to places you have only dreamed of. Our children . . ."

"There aren't going to be any children, James. I don't love you . . . I never could . . . now get out of my way," she screamed as she struggled to get out of the chair.

James pushed her hard, knocking her back, his eyes a blaze of anger. "God damn you," he rasped, his voice husky with rage. "I didn't expect this of you, Chris," he said, pressing her back into the chair with one hand and picking up his briefcase with the other. "You're no better than the others. God damn you for what you're doing to me," he said in a frightening whisper, hovering over her. "No one treats me with such disrespect." His voice suddenly was calm, almost peaceful, as he said to her, "You'll get to see the lake after all, Chris. I really didn't think I would take you there, but now I know. You'll go to the lake with Allison . . . and the beautiful Elaine."

Chris was paralyzed by the horror, unable to scream. "Please don't hurt me, James . . . I'll go away and . . ."

Her plea was interrupted by a sharp crack, followed by another that shattered the glass wall, scattering shards across the desk and onto the furniture. James put his hand to his chest, his eyes wide with shock as he fell to the floor, a wet stain quickly spreading over his dark shirt and running in red rivulets onto the pale carpet.

Chris pulled herself out of the blood spattered chair and backed toward the door. As she reached for the telephone, she saw a large, dark figure move unevenly away from the laurel grove and break into a lumbering, uneven run toward the forested foothills. Two more shots rang out, and the huge moving shape crumpled slowly to the ground. Chris ran out on her patio, screaming hysterically, as two men ran across the lawn toward her, followed by a third a distance behind them.

"It's okay, Miss Alford . . . I got him . . . Tabor's dead!" Buster shouted, as he and JT ran up to her. "Are you okay? He didn't hurt you, did he?"

"What happened?" Richard shouted, breathless from his run across the lawn. "I heard shots . . . I knew they came from this direction. Chris, are you all right. Oh my God are you hurt?" Richard said as he saw James's blood splattered on her face and the front of her blouse. He reached out and pulled her into his arms, holding her close and rocking her back and forth as she cried.

"Tabor's dead," Buster said. "I got him as he was tryin' to run away."

"Buster shot him, Chris . . . he's gone. You don't have to worry about Tabor anymore," Richard said soothingly.

"No," she screamed, pushing Richard away. "No . . . , please . . . no . . . he saved my life . . . oh, God, no . . . he can't be dead," she cried.

"He got Dr. Cantrell . . . shot him twice in the chest. I'm afraid he's dead," JT said as he came out of Chris's office and back onto the patio. "There's a hunting knife and duck tape in there, too. Looks like it fell out of something onto the floor. Maybe Tabor was in here first, before he shot from outside."

"Tabor saved my life," Chris sobbed, as Richard gently sat her down in a chair. "James was going to kill me . . . it's his knife. He was out of his mind, Richard . . . James was out of his mind." She covered her face with her hands as she cried hysterically.

"My God, Chris . . . James? None of us had any idea about James. We always thought it was Tabor we had to fear." Richard knelt in front of her, holding her hands. "Chris . . . it's okay . . . it's all over now. You've been through so much."

"Tabor died for me, Richard. He had to know he couldn't get away." Chris looked across the field where the police flooded the still body with light. "He was running toward the mountain, toward his special place. He had told me about it. He was trying to go there."

They both stared at the bright light that was but a speck against the dark, brooding peaks behind it.

"Richard . . . James killed Allison . . . and he told me Tabor was his son. Tabor killed the father he never knew."

"Dear God," he said incredulously. "I guess that's why James always protected him and gave him another chance. From the little he told me, I suspect that's more than James's father did for him."

"I should have helped Tabor more . . . I should have done what I started out to do. He reached out to me . . . and I pushed him away."

"You can't blame yourself, Chris. So much has changed tonight, much more than we could ever comprehend. We have to accept that, and we'll just take it a day at a time . . . as the healing begins."

"We'll need to talk to you tomorrow, Miss Alford. Seems pretty clear what happened. Y'all can go home now and get some rest. Are y'all sure you don't need a doctor?" Buster said quietly as he stood looking down at Chris.

"I'm okay," she said. "I'll be all right."

Chris realized that she had been clutching something in her hand, something she had picked up from the shattered glass on her desk. She looked down at the tiny sleeping cat that curled in her palm, and she remembered the day Tabor had given it to her.

Richard looked at the beautiful little carving that sat in her open hand. "What's that?" he asked as she held it out to him.

"Tabor made it, and he gave it to me. It was a special gift from him, and now he has given me another." Tears of gratitude and relief flooded her eyes.

"Let me take you home now, Chris."

Richard held her close to him as they walked slowly down the wide brick path bordered by the immaculate green lawn, past the expertly planted beds of vivid, bright chrysanthemums and the specimen maples that were beginning to turn soft shades of yellow and red.

Made in the USA
Lexington, KY
11 October 2012